American Genius, A Comedy

Also by Lynne Tillman

Novels

Haunted Houses (1987)

Motion Sickness (1991)

Cast in Doubt (1992)

No Lease on Life (1998)

Stories

Absence Makes the Heart (1990)

The Madame Realism Complex (1992)

This Is Not It (2002)

Nonfiction

The Velvet Years: Warhol's Factory 1965-1967, photographs by Stephen Shore (1994)

The Broad Picture: Essays (1997)

Bookstore: The Life and Times of Jeannette Watson and Books & Co. (1999)

American Genius, A Comedy

Lynne Tillman

soft skull press
brooklyn, ny · 2006

American Genius, A Comedy

ISBN: 1-933368-44-6
ISBN-13: 978-1-933368-44-3

Soft Skull Press
55 Washington St, Suite 804
Brooklyn, NY 11201
www.softskull.com

literaryventuresfund

investing in literature
one book at a time

providing a foundation
for writers around the globe

www.literaryventuresfund.org

Distributed by Publishers Group West
www.pgw.com

Cover Art by Robert Gober
Cover Design by David Janik
Interior Design by David Janik and Anne Horowitz

All quotations on pages 224-231 are from *Franz Kafka: Letters to Felice*, eds. Erich Heller and Jurgen Born, translated by James Stern and Elisabeth Duckworth, New York: Schocken Books, 1973.

Excerpts from *American Genius, A Comedy* appeared in: *Gregg Bordowitz: Drive*; *BOMB*; *The Literary Review*; *The Mississippi Review*; *Blindspot: Tribute to Kim Zorn Caputo*; and *John Baldessari: Food for Thought.*

Library of Congress Cataloging-in-Publication Data

Tillman, Lynne.
American genius : a comedy / by Lynne Tillman.
p. cm.
ISBN 1-933368-44-6 (alk. paper)
I. Title.

PS3570.I42A84 2006
812'.54--dc22

2006004047

Printed in Canada

For Joe Wood

1965–1999

Unforgettable

Life is unfair. Some people are sick, and others are well.
—President John F. Kennedy, 1962

Woe to him whose beliefs play fast and loose with the order which realities follow in his experience; they will lead him nowhere or else make false connexions.
—William James

The food here is bad, but every day there is something I can eat and even like, and there's a bathtub, which I don't have at home. I can have a bath here every day before dinner, which is at 7:30 p.m. and usually unsatisfying. But I can't wait for dinner because it's the official end to my day, and there will be other people around with whom I can talk and who may distract me. I'm often distracted from the things I must do, which I feel compelled or expected to accomplish. But here I hope to discover what might help me or what I need to know, or what I don't need to know, for instance, about the other residents in the community.

Sometimes I have a chance to have a bath before dinner. I eagerly undress and fill the old-fashioned, footed bathtub with very hot water, pour bath oil under the faucet, three capfuls which is supposed to invigorate your body, moisturize your skin and soothe your mind, and though this never happens, my mind is never soothed, I still liberally pour in bath oil that claims to soothe the mind and help the skin. My skin is dry during the winter and also during the summer, it is dry the year long, I have very sensitive skin, which is what the Polish woman at home who gives me a facial every two months tells me, repeating each time I have a facial, Your skin is very sensitive, probably because we don't have much else to talk about. We don't have much in common, but I hear stories about her life and know she was once married, and that she now goes on dates with men and on trips and outings with girlfriends.

One day while I was having a facial in the salon, a dignified word for the cramped, dingy space, the doorbell rang and she answered it. She is the only one working there, except on weekends, when the owner, an attractive woman who takes good care of herself and has two children and a husband, works, too. The woman who gives me facials doesn't have a husband and children but would like to. She is also attractive and takes good care of herself, and works five days a week. At the door was the man she was just telling me about, who was pursuing her and asking her for dates, which she declined, putting him off evasively. He entered the cramped space.

When the Polish woman, known professionally as a cosmetician and beautician, had finished cleaning my pores and moisturizing my sensitive skin, he was still there, waiting, crudely handsome and glowering, sitting on an ugly plastic-covered chair near the table with out-of-date beauty magazines. I glanced at him, someone I knew slightly, but didn't remember how, which is often the case, many faces are unbearably familiar and indistinct, so it was embarrassing, because he was waiting for her, and I shouldn't have seen him in this setting, when she didn't want to date him or maybe ever get married or perhaps couldn't, because she took care of her mother, or she's too picky or because she doesn't really like men. Probably I should have warned her that he was not a good man, it was easy to see, because why else would he surprise her, coming unannounced and perhaps unwanted to her place of work, where she was supposed to be safe from such incidents, but I didn't, because people, women especially, like to hear they have sensitive skin or that they are sensitive. It supposedly distinguishes them from animals who are not sensitive in the way that human beings apply the word. An animal's skin is usually not sensitive, though I have a friend whose cat has sensitive skin; it often has sores at its mouth and is allergic to many kinds of food, and my cat, the one I put to sleep because it stalked me, had dry skin and dandruff. Animals and some men are predatory, though female cats make better hunters. People are strange about their animals. I like animals, especially cats and dogs, birds, too, and I am often disturbed about the fate of animals, though I eat meat, fish, and fowl, and don't appreciate the audible disdain or silent criticism of a few self-righteous vegetarians who sometimes sit at my dinner table here. Two dogs nearly killed one of the kittens our family cat gave birth to, nearly tore it in two, but my mother rescued it and carried it to the vet, where it was sewn up and lived. My mother loved our family cat, then she gave it away after it decapitated and ate my bird, and neither of us, her two children, was able to forget the terrible fate of our cat, certainly not I, even now that my mother's brain is damaged. No one brings it up, not anymore, though when my mother talks about the family cat now and how much she loved her, how special the cat was, I avert my eyes, I look down, I have to, because otherwise I might shout, You killed the cat.

Before I arrived here, a tarot cardreader, whose predictions I would ordinarily dismiss, since I believe only the past can be read, though it is also unknowable, but who struck me as unusually astute, predicted that I would meet an obstacle or person who would forever change my life. My cards were powerful, he said, which I heard with incredulity, though, as he spoke, it occurred to me that it didn't matter what I believed of his philosophy, since the notion had already taken hold, one that might come to my aid, a placebo, or one I wanted to accept, since belief is important, everything, and also nothing much, an attachment like a skein of froth. About the prediction, I told no one, and my life did change, but not in the way the cardreader foresaw.

My parents gave away my dog, because they said they couldn't take care of her, but I didn't believe them. I should have saved my dog, who was devoted and good, and never hurt anyone, except maybe a plumber. When I left home at eighteen, thrown out by my parents, which had consequences for the future I didn't consider then, a plumber came to the apartment where I stayed for a time with friends to fix the toilet, when only I was there, and because my dog was nervous and scared, protecting me in a strange, new place, she bit the plumber on his calf. He couldn't be reassured she wasn't rabid. The next day a policeman came to the door and served a summons, legally compelling me to bring my dog to the ASPCA, to a division called BITES, where my dog had to be examined, the smallest dog in an ugly office, obviously not rabid, terrified of the bigger, growling dogs near her, and it was after that I gave my dog back to my parents, because I couldn't take care of her. She couldn't live in an apartment, having been raised in a house with a lawn in a neighborhood where she was able every morning to go for walks around town with her best friend, Pepe, a standard black poodle, one of the two dogs who had mauled and nearly killed the kitten, but that was long ago and forgiven because the kitten lived and Pepe was such a good friend to our dog, even though he once bit her on the genitals and she had to go to the dog and cat hospital.

When Pepe came to take her for a walk around town the next morning and she wasn't there, he refused to leave the house until my mother opened the door and let him search for her, and only then, after he'd gone upstairs and downstairs and into the basement, only then, when he didn't find her, did Pepe go home. I gave my dog to my parents for safekeeping, until I could take care of her, because in the winter, when there's snow on the ground, my dog couldn't go for a walk on a leash since the City salts the sidewalks with minerals that hurt dogs' paws, and walking, she whimpered and yelped, and I had to carry her to a place where she could be set down to piss and shit, and after she did, I would have to carry her again. I gave her to my parents, then my parents gave her away, had her killed, though they insisted someone adopted her, after they lied about her age—she was eight, but looked younger, my father contended—so she was adopted under false pretenses, and neither of us children ever believed the story, that she had been adopted, that she had not been killed, but there was nothing to do, it was too late, she was gone.

I'd been asleep, absorbed in myself, not thinking about the animal I professed to love, while I convinced myself theirs was an empty threat, because it was inconceivable that my parents would give her away, then my dog was gone. I know a woman who defended her dogs from criticism even when they attacked a stray cat, which could have been torn apart and killed, and also didn't express any concern for the cat or believe that her dogs should be controlled; instead, the dogs' owner talked about another cat who had successfully defended itself against her occasionally vicious dogs, and, from a safe place, hit them with its paw. Cats can defend themselves was her spurious point, but a domestic animal shouldn't have to know how to defend itself against predatory dogs. People defend the bad actions of their animals, themselves, or their children rather than face the unsavory conclusion that there is something wrong with the animal, their children, themselves, with the world, and their job is to acknowledge it, even to rid the world of it, certainly not to pretend that it isn't there, that everything is all right, that they and their animals are good, because they didn't mean it, and can't help themselves. Instead they do nothing, accepting the brutality of animals, themselves, other people, and the world, since they believe it has nothing to do with them, they want to think it has nothing to do with them. A slap in the face is not a slap in the face when it comes from them, because they didn't mean it, because they had sad childhoods, their parents gave away their dogs and cats, their parents gave them away and didn't love them.

I love my animals. People love their animals, the way they love their own farts and everything else attached to them that is close to them yet not them. Because they are not their animals or their farts, they love them. Eskimos have a saying, Every man loves the smell of his own farts, which most people wouldn't admit. I know a man who was kicked out of a fast-food restaurant because he farted. I was once in a restaurant when an obese boy farted, the smell was overpowering, and a friend and I had to move to a different part of the restaurant, but the boy appeared satisfied, because he loved the smell of his fart. Everyone loves their own farts, which could get them kicked out of restaurants or humiliated in public settings, where people try to act not like animals but sensitively, if it serves their purposes, but no one is sensitive enough about other people. They are sensitive about themselves, their animals, their feelings and beliefs, and other people can go to hell with their dogs, their farts, and their feelings.

At breakfast, I noticed the expressions on two women's faces, women in their late-twenties who looked unhappy, something had not gone well for them, was not going well for them in that moment or in their dreams or in last night's telephone call, but I didn't say anything to them, though I believed I should show concern. I walked past them and ordered two fried eggs over medium—which I like, though when I was a child I would have gagged on—before the kitchen closed, otherwise I wouldn't have eaten until lunch. Lunches are rarely good, they are often the worst meal of the day, and sometimes there is very little anyone can eat, but I didn't want to be hungry later, waiting for dinner, alone, thinking about the dog I hadn't saved, who loved carrots, seeing her guileless face before me, her tail wagging happily, as she ran up the driveway which had an oil slick on it, a leak from my father's gray Buick, of which he was proud, the dog unaware that one day she would be given away by the people who loved her. I've never had another dog. I've had cats, and one especially I cherished, in Amsterdam, all of whose kittens but one died in a week from an infestation of fleas, which occurred frequently during Amsterdam summers, but of which I'd had no experience and no one spoke, never warning me of the inevitable and severe consequences for newborn kittens, for whose deaths I take responsibility. They lay in a drawer in my desk as their lifeblood was drained away, sucked by fleas, whose own life may be valuable to some, but I now have a young cat, technically a kitten, rescued from the streets by animal lovers, who resembles the sole survivor of that doomed litter. My young cat had distemper but he survived, because a veterinarian believed it was worth dosing him with strong, expensive antibiotics, while warning me soberly that the kitten had only a 50/50 chance of survival, but when I visited my cat during the four-day ordeal in which his life hung in the balance, I was chastised by the veterinarian's receptionist, because, upon hearing my kitten cry, I ran to the room from which the cries emerged, a room no bigger than a closet, and messy, and the receptionist became angry, suspecting that I might steal her bag and coat, which were also in the room with my lonely, sick cat. Though the vet saved my cat's life, I have never returned.

My cat plays, purrs, bites, and goes for people's hands. He is a little wild and may become vicious when he's older, or he may calm down, but I don't want to have to put him to sleep, to kill him, if he turns vicious and attacks someone. When I am no longer here, eating breakfast with other people whose complexions and facial expressions signal a distress I don't want to deal with, wondering how much I should get involved with them and their problems, I won't have people come to my apartment and meet my young cat. I don't like their coming, anyway, I don't like people seeing or saying things about what I have around me, on my walls or on my shelves; it is no business of theirs how I live or what I put on a table or my desk, a wooden board with a plate of half-inch-thick glass over it, a reasonable desk in an unexceptional apartment, in which I live with a young cat, and for some years with a man, but not now, and the cat may or may not become vicious, which is a problem for the future.

Everything is a problem in some way, I can't think of anything that's not a problem from the past for the future, and I often worry, frowning to myself, unaware that I'm frowning, my lips turning down involuntarily, which I've been told to stop doing since I was a child, because it creates the impression that I'm sullen and also etches fine lines around my mouth, but I can't. My father worried about the future, which presumably he could imagine, but I can't, just as I can't imagine lines like tributaries running from the river of my mouth the way they do from my mother's, who was angry, who'd abandoned her girlish hopes of marrying a violinist named Sidney, and who often speaks of him now that my father is dead, wondering where Sidney is, and also wondering where my father is, if he is outside, waiting for her in the car that he loved. She might have seen the future in us, if we'd been someone else's children. By the time I knew my brother, he was thirteen and I was two, so he and my parents were the future that lived with and preceded me, it lay before me and also excluded me, so I didn't consider it, not when I was a small child, since it was already in their lives. I didn't mature fantasizing its arrival, and even knowing that I won't be here to witness another future and be dedicated to it, or of it, that I exist as one version of the future I hadn't fantasized, I'm only vaguely intrigued by its promise. The tenacity of the past makes me melancholy, though people like to say the past was a simpler time, but there is no simpler time, there are only simple people, and even they are not simple, but so exhaustively undermined as to be plain. Memory can be consumptive, a sickness, whose effects are wily and subversive, worthy of flight or fight, and tenacious unwritten histories leave tremulous marks on bodies in action, at rest, but not their final rest, and under siege. My body is encased in sensitive, dry skin. Skin is an organ, and the body's largest one, protecting the body under coats of many colors. The story of Joseph is one of two Bible stories I remember, because it was about fabric and colors, both of which my father mentioned, since he was in the textile business, and it was also about rivalry, which my parents never mentioned, though I wasn't aware of reticence then.

My mother has beautiful skin, which she protected regularly but not slavishly. Human beings need to be protected, to enjoy being protected, especially when they are young, because they have a long period of dependency, and for some it is interminable. The past that can't be recovered or changed has already shaped and damaged the present, and how I arrange a chair, where I set it, in what relation to my reasonable desk, or what kind of couch I have that also won't protect me won't tell people what they need to know about me, to protect them from me, though people spend endless amounts of time thinking about their furniture and what it says about them, and how they will appear to themselves and others. No one need come to my apartment to see how I've arranged the furniture, to learn about my problems from the way I've placed objects, to learn what damage I've done and might do in the future, in which they will also live, unless someone murders them, they kill themselves, or they die of natural causes before their supposed time.

My father enjoyed himself, especially when he was playing cards with his friends, or dancing and swimming, and he was also charming, when he didn't glower, like the man who waited for the woman who gives me facials. I need a facial. I've been away from home for a long time, and my skin is very dry, but I don't put cream on it at night. I can't bring myself to apply cream at night, when no one would see me, though it would be good to do in my bedroom where it's very quiet, where not a sound can be heard except the heat rising in the pipes or the toilet flushing. But I'm the one who makes noise, who flushes the toilet most often, going to the bathroom in the middle of the night, because I can't sleep, I'm afraid to dream, to surrender, and I have to piss frequently, which is a sign of age in a woman, and maybe a man, but I know less about men. My father never told me if he had to piss frequently as he grew older, though I watched him piss when I was four years old, fascinated by the stream of hot yellow-white urine that shot from his penis. But when years later, I told a friend about his urinating in front of me, she contended, her lips tight with horror, that I'd been abused, a word like "environment" whose use is pervasive and compromises my individuality of which I have less and less choice. My father had generously allowed his curious daughter the opportunity to see how a man pisses, when she wanted to know, because she was curious, I am still curious, and interested in the world and in penises, especially her father's; and when another person would instantly think that a girl had been abused by seeing her father's penis as he pissed, though that is what she wanted to see, I thought to myself, but did not say, the time we live in is a problem. My fearful father was not afraid of my seeing his penis, but he stopped letting me when I was a little older, which was too bad, because I never had the chance to ask him how frequently he had to piss when he grew older, or before he died, since asking other men wouldn't be the same, because it was my father I wondered about, though I could've asked my brother, who disappeared from my life, who may be living on the streets of Cincinnati or Mexico City, but it wouldn't be the same.

My mother is very old, incontinent, and she doesn't remember that she had my dog and cat killed, though she often mentions the story she wrote about the family cat she loved but later had killed. It is laden with lovingly embroidered details about the antics of our remarkable cat, though she doesn't remember what I was like as a child, even before she had brain damage, except to say that I was fast at everything, that I rushed. I'm still rushing, because there's a lot to accomplish before death, which defeats accomplishment, and my mother often wants to know what I'm doing and why I'm away, not with her, though when I'm with her, she doesn't talk to me but watches television, with ardent attention. She doesn't know me, I don't know her, and each time she asks why I'm leaving or where I'm going, I tell her, but then she forgets. I tell her again and again, and then she says she misses and loves me, which she never said when I was young and she wasn't incontinent.

There is an assortment of tables in the dining room of the main or big house where I have breakfast, along with the others, if they are able to wake up, without effort or by having set their alarm clock, as I have, for breakfast, often the best or only edible meal of the day. Many arrive bedraggled by sleep, talkative, or muted, and some arrive hungry, even starving, with a zest for the day ahead that overwhelms, stymies, or exhausts me, and everyone usually can find something they like to eat, if they are on time and the kitchen is still open. Sometimes there is a table for vegetarians, if their number is great and the head cook has become aggrieved by the volume or multitude of demands, including that of commingling us. But it is only at dinner that the vegetarians, when their number has swelled, are seated separately; smokers and nonsmokers had been regularly segregated, but now the smoker is simply banished, forced to smoke out of doors in the cold or heat or in a lobby that is perpetually foul-smelling so that the smokers also don't want to be in it. There are many more kinds of separations that are not as significant as those of religion, race, ethnicity, class, and these newer, odder discriminations may subtly cover more profound insensitivities, like flounces on a bad design. In all there are nine tables, unless there is a problem, and our number varies, while rumors circulate like the residents.

Residents such as myself float from one to another, avoiding specific individuals, choosing a chair at the last minute, but others take the same position, table, and chair each meal, and if that seat is snagged by another, a new resident or a mischievous older resident, there are consequences. Some residents don't appear at breakfast, for instance,

Gardner, or the Count, who is obsessed with time and antique timepieces; he never appears, as he sleeps during the day and wakes only for dinner, which serves as his breakfast. When I, nearly late this morning, rushed past the two young women into the kitchen, I didn't fail to notice that they were ensconced by themselves at a distant table near a window; that the young, clever, married man was at a table alone, reading the newspaper, which was his habit, because he doesn't want to speak to anyone during the first meal of his day, and no one dared speak to him, and that the rest of the group was settled around a third table and in various stages of eating. Everyone could have eggs for breakfast. But some wouldn't, since they refuse to eat what could become alive, an egg might become a chicken, but they could also, on different mornings, have a choice of oatmeal, fresh and canned fruit salad, dry cereal, pancakes, French toast, crepes, or whole wheat, rye and white toast with marmalade or grape jelly. There was coffee, with and without caffeine, tea, herbal and black, water, and orange juice, and, depending upon who was in charge of the kitchen, sometimes it was freshly squeezed juice, which was a treat residents appreciated, took for granted or didn't seem to notice, like the young married man, whose morning face was hidden behind a newspaper, and who, though often grumpy, liked all of the meals, adored his wife and his mother, and his occupation and obsession, ornithology. He writes prolifically about birds native to South and North America, and, while here, hopes to compile a comprehensive glossary of the local birds, particularly avid to discover rare ones, as he did in Mexico when he spotted the hard-to-see Pauraque, whose feathers and coloring match the ground to disguise it. His cheerful appetite sets him apart from many of the others, while his grumpiness, which may come from missing his home, since he receives many telephone calls from his wife and makes many to his mother, also distinguishes him. I'm not sure what I miss, I often think I miss nothing, that there is nothing to miss, and yet I'm aware that I do, since I am often missing to myself.

My parents sent me to a sleepaway summer camp when I was six. I didn't understand where I was, I had no idea what I was doing there, like my dog, who didn't understand why she was suddenly unable to walk the city's streets without her paws hurting. I couldn't understand why I was thrust into a gray bunk, constructed of wood, somewhere in the country, sitting on a cot covered by a rough wool blanket, which tortured my sensitive skin, with seven other little girls I didn't know, who were not my brother, who, like him, didn't pay much attention to me when I was that age or any other. He disappeared when I was eight. I didn't know these strange little girls, I didn't know what strangers were, and the little girls in my gray bunk were not sensitive to me. But strangers have potential. I didn't know the two women who were our counselors, I didn't know what a counselor was, and, melancholy, I sat on the bed, observing this unfamiliar place, and miserably awaited letters from my mother who never wrote, because, she told me later, I didn't write her.

I don't remember the food at camp, but I remember walking to the cafeteria every day, passing the infirmary whose name was frightening, where I was told a girl of eight was being kept because she was very, very sick and wasn't allowed medicine by her parents, who were Christian Scientists. She might die without the medicine her parents refused her. All summer long, every day for eight weeks, we seven little girls walked in a straggling line past the infirmary to the cafeteria to eat our meals. I was the youngest, no one else was turning six at the end of that summer, so I was five, the youngest child in camp, where another little girl was very ill and might die because her parents did not believe in medicine, though it might cure her. I disdain religion, which some sensitive people believe can heal and redeem them, but I have no faith, though I was born into one, which I abandoned, although people can't abandon and be entirely through with anything into which they were born.

I didn't write my mother when I was away, because I didn't know what away was, I had only recently learned to print, and I didn't know I was supposed to write her since she was supposed to be with me. I also wasn't supposed to be in a gray bunk with small strangers and larger ones, counselors, who asked me to do incomprehensible things, like steal the pin from the other team in Color War. I didn't understand what Color War was, I had no idea what it was, and even though my older cousin was also in the same camp, but we were not in the same bunk, she never spoke to me about it, no one explained it. I didn't know Color War wasn't real, just as I didn't know that I wouldn't have to live in a gray bunk for the rest of my life, sent there by my parents who believed I should be there, the way the sick girl's parents believed she shouldn't take medicine and die instead.

I was afraid of dying and had many fears, like my father, but he never appeared afraid. He and my mother visited me once during the eight weeks, a visit I hardly remember, but there were photographs of the event in one of several shopping bags kept in a closet in the house where I grew up and which I loved but that was sold by my parents against my youthful protests. The photographs were meant to be pasted neatly into albums; for all those years, my parents said they should be pasted into albums, but they weren't and still aren't, though my father is long dead and my mother is old. My parents arrived at the camp with my father's brother, my favorite uncle, and his wife, whom he divorced shortly afterward, to visit their daughter, my older cousin, who was supposed to be looking after me, but whom I rarely saw. Ever since her father died, I have not seen her; I never saw her again after my favorite uncle's funeral. My uncle's psychiatrist told him that the chest pains he complained of in the last week of his life were neurotic symptoms. Later, her family accused my father of not handing over all the money my uncle had in the business, owned by the two brothers. There was no other money in their textile business, none that was my uncle's, who liked to gamble, knew gangsters and fast women, and who had spent all of his own money, as well as money that was not his, since my father, incapable of denying his adored, neurotic younger brother anything, had lent him money from the business. My favorite uncle's family, only weeks after he was buried, turned against my father and treated him like a thief, but some years later, when my father was in Penn Station, his dead brother's son spotted him walking to the train, went over and offered an apology, which would never have been given if they hadn't been in Penn Station, by chance, at the same time near the same track. Penn Station may have been in the process of being destroyed then, to clear way for an ugly building that will also be temporary, and, unlike the previous building, it has nothing of beauty, grandeur, history, or maybe hope, and while the significant station, with its history, was obliterated and lost, my father and his nephew were likely oblivious to its demise, especially in that instance, when something of grave and appalling dimensions transpired between them. My father was being apologized to by his nephew, the son of his beloved brother, for something he had never done but of which he had been accused and that had caused him great distress, even despair, in the months and years following his brother's death. Without this accidental meeting, there would have been no letter or telephone call, no genuine consideration of my father who loved his brother and who was blameless in this situation, but not in all others. His brother's family, like most, believed they were right, sensitive, and caring, because of their religion and skin, and their need to feed, clothe, shelter and protect themselves.

Textiles is an ancient craft and one of the earliest manufacturing industries, and, in America, in the 19th century and later, many of the mills were situated in the North, in New England, especially Connecticut and Massachusetts, notably the city of Lowell. Cotton was shipped from the South to Lowell and other Northern cities, but in the mid-to-late 20th century the mills began to disappear, many small manufacturers disappeared, and textiles again came from the East, where they had originally come from and where now labor was much cheaper. My father often drove his gray Buick far away or traveled by train to the mills to speak to other men, other owners, about the material he and his brother designed, whose threads they selected, whose weight they decided, which would be transported to their office by truck, many bolts, all smelling of dyes and other natural and unnatural substances. My father loved his brother.

At breakfast, like the young married man, I would prefer not to talk, to ignore people, sit quietly, and eat my fried eggs, which are sometimes prepared over easy when I asked for medium, but I don't say anything. I would like to be still, or just quiet, and chew the eggs without a sound, because I dislike many sounds associated with eating, and sop up the too-runny part of the yolk with dark, dry wheat toast. Then I would prefer to sip my coffee and look out of the generous window and contemplate a spacious field where deer might be grazing. Seeing deer is always a happy surprise, though they usually run away, especially when you approach them, but if they feel safe and are in the distance, they might continue to eat grass or stand dumbly, with dark brown eyes, limpid and soulful as pathetic fallacies. Sometimes they leap across the field and over paths into the woods, their bushy white tails quickly disappearing into foliage, and the deer are always a welcome surprise. I have also, in that same field or near it, spied a mole, entirely unexpectedly, it was pointed out by another resident, who stood still and motioned me over to her, to witness this exceptionally rare sight. A mole has a tiny, well-articulated face, a longish snout, thick fur, like mink, that covers its small body, and it's not supposed to be walking on paths, but was lost or confused by an unseasonably mild winter, until finally it found its way back to its hole, though sometimes it scuttled around in circles. The hole was covered by earth, bits of wire, and a piece of thick, black denim, and I wondered where the moles had found it. Denim is often close to an American's skin, and once I wore it, but these days, unless pressed and unable to think of anything else, I don't, because it's heavy, and only the oldest jeans are soft and wearable, and I no longer have the pair I wore for years, which finally felt good. Many people around the world wear denim jeans, maybe because they're durable and also because they constitute a uniform, a classic, which has stood the test of time, though one day it may fail that. Denim is a stout, serviceable, twilled fabric made from coarse singles yarns. The standard denim is made with indigo blue dyed warp yarn and gray filling yarn, and denim is the most important fabric of the work clothing group, extensively used for overalls, coats, caps, but sports denim, also called faded denim, is lighter weight, made also in pastels and white and colored stripings, used for leisure wear, which is how most people wear it, though its association with work remains, since supposedly Americans play and work hard and have marketed this idea to the world. There is also upholstery and furniture denim.

I join the conversation at breakfast, especially when it's entertaining, distracting, provocative, or annoying, and, afterwards, I might feel soiled and wish for night, the end of any long day, when nothing is expected from me and I expect nothing and can lie in bed, on top of or under the sheets, surrounded by books and magazines, and ugly brown furniture, which I didn't choose, but which has become a sort of friend, or at least harmless, though I'm aware that some people couldn't tolerate this furniture and would request or demand another room or buy themselves other furniture, rather than adjust to its design and atmosphere, since an adjustment to these objects might impugn or indict them to themselves or in the eyes of others. The man who has a sodden smell, whose source I don't want to identify, especially when eating breakfast, though I believe it's vodka, and whose skin has large pores, usually wears jeans and a T-shirt, whatever the weather, though this morning his T-shirt is wordless, the way I wish he were. Gesticulating and scowling, he demands attention every morning and begins conversations from which I leave the breakfast room sullied, smelling sour to myself the way he does to me, and longing for night, that near future, which is one I can easily imagine.

When there are no sounds in the house where I sleep, except for the toilet flushing and the heat rising in the old pipes, I know I should apply cream to my face, but I usually don't, even though the Polish woman will admonish me when I return to the cramped, dingy salon and will be disappointed in me because I have not listened to her. But I'm stubborn, my mother is stubborn, many people are, no one likes to apologize, no one likes to listen, no one wants to be wrong, yet everyone is and has been, but few people will admit they are wrong and will rarely admit their errors or their farts, in public or in private. People need to be protected from others, who may hurt them, as I need to be protected, but I don't listen to everyone, though I'm a good listener, and I'm curious, though curiosity killed the cat, my mother would say, but she had the cat killed. I listen to others more than most people, sometimes at my peril, though I hope to learn something, but often I don't or what I learn is of no consequence, though it might be to the person who spoke, yet many people tell the same stories again and again, which represent them best or are in some way significant and come to define them, but if they didn't repeat them, they wouldn't in any way define them, or matter, or be of any discernible consequence, since often it is what is not said that is of consequence. I try not to repeat myself, I attempt to be cognizant, not retell stories, I refrain often, but sometimes, when I'm bored by others' stories, I tell an old one, or if I feel I must enter the conversation, rather than withdraw from it or betray my impatience or brusqueness, my lack of concern for others, I trot out a tried but not necessarily true tale, sometimes just to entertain myself, and I don't care which it is. Many people think they are good listeners, many more than who actually listen, since someone has to be doing the talking, and most people will say they're good listeners before they'll say they're good talkers, though most aren't good talkers or listeners, but persons who tell stories that fill time, and many explain how they were hurt by others, because they are sensitive, but never admit they hurt others. People tell stories, often indignantly and without discrimination, including others' secrets, sometimes in minute detail, and then, later, when they have finished their orations, they admit, occasionally cross or with astonishment, that they don't understand why they went on like that. When it happens in my presence, even before those precise words are spoken, I see the formulation of the sentence and nearly say it too, but resist, guarding my tongue where words are dry and glued to the mucous membrane lining of my mouth, otherwise it would appear that I was mimicking or in some way trivializing their discovery. In this instance, as in others, I was merely being quiet, paying attention in an undivided manner, looking into their eyes, never wavering in my belief that she or he could tell me something I'd never heard before; because when a person really tells the story, the one he or she must tell, even to a stranger, and usually I am a stranger, then no matter what that story is, it is generally interesting if not illuminating or unique, though its manner of expression could be unique, and the story in some way special or different; for it must have been lived differently to have been articulated unusually or inventively, or that is my hope. On many occasions the story is dull and flat, and, like reading a bad book, since listening is similar to reading, you want to stop listening, especially if it is about a career failure or for that matter success or a monotonous love life, or the monotonous lack of a love life, or a deficient one, when the speaker is obsessed by a particular man or woman and needs to recite every pain or insult that person has inflicted, so then I, and many others, become bored, almost outraged at the wanton disregard of themselves, the speaker's dinner companions. One night at dinner, a woman whom I had just met talked incessantly about a man she loved who had mistreated her repeatedly, and though I had just that night met her, a recent arrival who fortunately became another, quick departee, she consumed all of the dinner-table time, at which I usually hope to be drawn away from myself in an arresting manner, with ideas that quicken the mind or provide solace because they spring from mindful solitaries. Instead, she regaled me with episodes of unrelenting romantic agonies and expected instant counsel, which, to be polite, since for all I knew she might also turn out to be interested in someone other than herself, I reluctantly gave, until I couldn't, and reaching my limit, I rose from the table, after she thanked me for listening, and said, too evenly, I suppose you needed to talk. Then the stranger closed her mouth tightly, even murderously, and glared at me with the ferocity of my mad cat who had stalked and attacked me, and I was sorry not to have left the table sooner and wished I hadn't said a word, since it's often better not to say anything. The stranger metamorphosed into an insignificant enemy, when moments before she'd been revealing the most intimate parts of her life to me, also a stranger, but one she needed to listen to her. I wondered at her sanity. I wondered about the man she loved, whose every sentence to do with her she could recite, with his inflections, and whose every touch still scalded her like a hot stove, those were her words, and into whose hands she was only too happy to offer her febrile body, but he might have been the victim of her murderous glances, too, often enough that he needed to escape her as much as I did my deranged cat. I was also insensitive to her.

Other people's stories can mollify and soothe, like a few capfuls of bath oil in a hot tub are supposed to do, and how-to and grammar books, along with biographies of philosophers and criminals, generally bring relief and a sense of safety—safety is a reasonable amount of risk—since a philosopher's life includes contemplation and a criminal's is at least not my own. These books facilitate sleep or delay sleeplessness, with its onslaught of nameless hurts, when I listen to steam belch through the pipes and other noises that don't occur during the day. When I'm in the other room assigned to me that is not for sleeping but has a cot on which I never rest, because for rest I can return to the bedroom, which I'd rather do, I can look at the photographs of friends on a wall. I tacked them on a white wall, careful not to pierce their images, including ones of me and my mother, who can't live too much longer, because no one lives forever, and several of my dead father, and friends, dead and alive, and also scenes I relish or postcards that have recently been sent to me. My collection is growing. Often I think about my dead friends and wonder why people who complain about the unfairness of life want to live forever anyway, since most do want to live forever. Many people complain about how hard life is, but no one wants to die, or very few people want to die. My uncle died before his time, my father never recovered from his brother's death, or his son's furious flight, some of my friends died before their time, and I may not recover, because there are some things you don't recover from. The past can't be recovered or changed.

Billy never told me his real name, I never knew it, just the one he gave himself, and I didn't push him, I thought there was time, and his reticence or shyness about his given name, which named his past, was a curiosity but didn't bother me, since I thought one day he'd tell me. Melvin was his given name, a stranger beat and murdered him, and was never caught, which is not unusual. A stranger to whom my existence is nothing, and who would not listen to me, could end my life, and I wonder if, when the two young women are my age and start to piss frequently, they will remember me and the sound of the toilet flushing in the middle of the night, which must wake them. But one told me it doesn't, that she can sleep through anything, even my machinations, I thought, and I might remember her for that, something I don't exactly believe, or I might remember both of them because they slept in rooms near mine, crept into and out of their bedrooms, one had short hair cropped to her head, the other long, curly hair she brushed from her face like flies, and they didn't make much noise or play their radio late at night, the way I did during this certain, momentous period of my life, when I was sequestered with strangers in a place not unlike the one where I was sent to summer camp when I was too young to know that I wouldn't always be there. The two take fewer baths than I do, they prefer showers, I also like showers, but want the slowness of a bath, and though I never stay in a bath long, the idea of slowness draws me to it, and the wonder of near-total immersion, which I'm advised relaxes the body, as well as the mind, along with the salubrious oils liberally poured into it that also could help my mood and moisturize my skin, restoring the precise oils that a good, hot bath depletes. But I must take care, my heart is a problem, there is often a pressure or a weight on it, a tightness that has no discernible organic cause, my internist tells me, still I'm careful about immersing myself in extremely hot water and let cold water run, to reduce the temperature. Maybe their skin is less dry than mine, not only because they are younger but also because they take showers. Still, bathing is salubrious, a luxurious waste of water, though it is plentiful here, so I don't have to worry about it now.

I won't always be here, and if I consider that, and regularly remind myself that I only have to be in a particular situation for an hour or two, whether I'm unhappy or not, I can manage it. An hour is a short unit of time, unless you are being tortured or are in some other terrible situation, like starving in a refugee camp. I can imagine myself in almost any situation for an hour, except awaiting execution, being slowly suffocated, being chased and hunted down like a fox, or being tortured, and if I am able or allowed to leave or even escape a situation, since almost anything can be managed for an hour, I'm reassured. I've been cold and miserable; I've been lost; deceived; I've been bored silly; drunk; my underpants have been wet from nervous agitation; the skin on my inner thighs has chafed to a fiery red from rubbing against wool; I've been robbed; fainted from shock; and I've been alarmed beyond words or stricken with fear hearing bitter words flare between friends in freakish eruptions of hatred in bizarre locations, since most sites are not right for confrontation, and when I have no right to speak and no involvement, except self-protection, I have become itchy, my skin a plane of heat, as if a match had been struck against it and my entire body set ablaze. But I was able to withstand it, only because I knew it would end. I have, since cast from home like the carrier of a deadly virus, been the object of virulent words and some violent acts. It is when you're a child and dependent and have no sense of time and don't know that things will end—your parents will die, you don't have to stay in school, the kids you hate won't always live near you—that it is sometimes impossible not to cling to old things and places, because what might come and who could be there and take their place could be worse.

The two young women often looked disconsolate, the way they did this morning, and as usual I didn't want to become involved in and acquainted with their deepest fears, familial or romantic problems, and so I avoided them, walking directly into the kitchen to order two eggs over medium from a woman who has worked in the kitchen most of her life and whom time, in whatever dimension it dwells, has not treated well. Her thin skin was wrinkled, having lost its elasticity, and she had probably never had a facial, certainly not with any regularity nor does she apply rich moisturizers to her desert-like skin. I couldn't help but notice also how everyone who ordered breakfast spoke to her beseechingly, their voices pitched higher, the women almost squeaking in deference, the men suddenly sopranos, all awaiting a sign that she was aware of their presence and, more, that she liked them and would feed them munificently, but the head cook, who has been here many years, was often moody, tired, or overwhelmed by her outside life, about which none of us was privy, and avoided their eyes and gestural entreaties for easy affection, sympathy, or love. I wrote down my order and, instead of begging for notice, kept my head low and eyes fixed on a notepad upon which I scrawled 2 Fried Eggs Over Medium in block letters, but with gusto, after finishing, said: Thank you. The cook reminded me of the Polish woman, because she served people, as the Polish woman served me, for a price, one I could pay, though the cook couldn't or wouldn't have a facial, never having cared much about her skin, never wanting to spend the money, or never having been told she was sensitive and so was her skin. The Polish woman might be insensitive, I've sometimes considered.

After I sat down to wait for my eggs, while the dining room clamored with more near-latecomers, I avoided the eyes of the others at our table, which was near the toaster and convenient, but the man in his T-shirt who always began conversations that annoyed me assaulted us with his longing. He said he couldn't eat his eggs and poked their yolks with disgust, which bothered Violet, a mysterious woman, whose light brown skin suggested biraciality, or a mulatto, as she preferred to call herself, who averted her eyes to ignore his agitations, but whose lips twitched, as she refrained from eating her meal. Violet, I soon named her Contesa, paused when she brought the yellow eggs to her mouth and her mottled gray eyes, which could have been laughing, metamorphosed into titanium, but he went on, the demanding man. He hadn't slept because his dream—which he annotated with his arms whirling like a miniature windmill, while he also alluded to Don Quixote, simultaneously, to underscore his relationship to his mother and mother country—had disturbed him, and none of this mattered to me, yet I listened. He rubbed his beard and forehead repeatedly, so his oily skin shone even when weak sunlight hit it. I had learned, in another breakfast discourse, that he'd had impetigo as a child, which left no trace, except the type that is invisible and most immutable, but maybe his early surroundings were unclean, his mother inattentive when he was an infant, perhaps he lay in his own urine for hours, dependent on others for the care he never received and now seeks in strangers. Yet he tells us his mother doted on him, that she did everything for him, that he was spoiled, which he proclaims proudly, as Violet, or Contesa, smiles, nearly laughing, I think, but this is conjecture. Impetigo is not unusual. It is a staph infection that occurs most often in childhood, when its prognosis is best, since it's worse in adulthood and usually occurs in hot humid climates or during the summer. His mother may have adored him, as he insists daily, and still he caught a staph infection. Impetigo occurs most frequently on the exposed parts of the body, the face, hands, neck, and extremities. There's impetigo of the scalp, too. The lesions rupture and a thin, straw-colored seropurulent discharge appears. That exudate dries to form loosely stratified crusts that accumulate layer upon layer until they are thick and friable. The crusts can be easily removed, though, and what's left is a smooth, red, moist surface that soon collects new discharge or exudate, and this spreads to other parts of the body, through fingers, and by towels, or household utensils. But, in the history of the disease, it is an extremely superficial inflammation. The demanding man had been born in a hot climate, though he no longer lives there, but instead resides in a cold, midwestern city, about which, though he's well dressed and fed, boasting a burgher's belly, and claims to lead the good life, he voices voluminous complaints: its climate, especially, bothers him, raw cold shoots through him like a spear, as he puts it, and also he is so far from his mother. His dependence is interminable, his complaints unassuageable, and I have known many such people.

My mother doesn't refer to herself as sensitive. She has beautiful skin that is still unlined and smooth, to which, during the majority of her life, she applied nothing but cold cream, though regularly, and to which medicinal creams must now be applied daily, because her skin has become more dry and sensitive with age, but she can no longer apply it herself. Her hands, once capable, tremble and sometimes shake. The cold cream jar was milk glass, large, with a wide mouth and black metal top, and sat on a shelf in my parents' bathroom, smelling of sweet dreams that might fragrantly coat not only skin but the whole body of existence. I often watched my mother apply the cream and rub it rapidly and efficiently onto her face and neck, which she appeared to do without any significant pleasure, as if in the act of replenishing her skin she was also denying it, but I can't remember if, afterward, she washed her hands, rubbed the cream onto them thoroughly, or wiped the cream off her hands onto a soft cloth or towel. Her only sister, and the oldest in her family, there were four brothers younger than her, had skin as slippery as butter, like my father's cottons and silks, smoother and softer even than my mother's supple skin. Her sister used ordinary Jergen's Lotion, my mother explained, that was her secret. Still, if I apply cream now, when I didn't for years and years, in the vise of a perverse vanity, it's because of the Polish woman and her concerned, attentive expression when she tenderly pats and caresses my face. It is this picture of her and the thought of her future admonishments, when she clucks her tongue slightly, a sound I dislike and associate with eating habits I also dislike, that arouses me and makes me uncomfortable enough to close my book, get off the bed, walk to the dark wood dresser, a piece of furniture I would never have bought, but which is appropriate for this old-fashioned room, open a large jar of moisturizer and rub the expensive cream upward on my cheeks, careful not to rub it under my eyes where the skin is more delicate and might become damaged by vigorous motion. I've never understood why. Still, I'm cautious, having been warned of the possible damage many times before, and when I became aware that skin could be damaged by use, as I did at the age of ten and a friend's mother strenuously warned us not to laugh too much or too freely, because lines would form around our mouths, I heard her words with worry, since I loved my friend's mother better than my own. She was pretty and young, unlike my mother who had waited years to marry, whose prospects with my father had always bordered on failure, but who finally claimed victory or success with a man she would then find undemonstrative. My friend was her mother's first child, born when she was just twenty-one, while I came late, when my mother was forty, and the second child, or baby, and certainly the last she brought into the world.

I rub any excess cream onto my hands and then onto a towel, chiding myself that I shouldn't use the towel, but instead wash the cream off my hands, but that would mean trespassing through the halls, treading on old floorboards to the bathroom and running the water through the old pipes that make noise, even at the faucets, merely turning them, no matter how studied my effort, and waking the two women near me on the floor. Across the floor, at the opposite end, there are two more people, a man and a woman, who sleep separately, but who also may not, and whom I never see in the house, and I don't believe I wake them. I carefully wipe off most of the cream onto a towel, which I'm not required to launder, since I'm not responsible for washing my sheets and towels while I'm here, but I also rub off the cream carefully, because I don't want to ruin the pages of the books I'm reading and because I dislike the feeling of grease on my face and body. The cream might prevent my skin from breathing, and I could feel suffocated, but I try to do what I'm told is good for me, though often it is contradictory.

I don't want to think about the two young women or the Polish woman, whom I hardly know, but who has made as strong an impression upon me as people I know better and see more. The Polish woman plays a part in my life, unimportant to anyone but me, one of many unacknowledged relationships of which I never speak, since the relationship between the person who gives you a facial and yourself is assumed to be insignificant and would not become an account I would offer people, even close friends, who have busy lives. Everyone has a busy life, and generally I don't want to make others listen to me. People don't usually want to listen, and often only wait for their opportunity to speak, generally about themselves, and most don't know how to listen, especially about matters that to them are insignificant and about which they will silently protest, Why did he or she mention something of no interest to me. To me, the importance of the Polish woman is clear. No one else applies cream to my face or tells me how sensitive my skin is, no one else regularly admonishes me and appears to worry about my skin, and, when I am with the Polish woman, I experience feelings that are remarkably different from feelings I have with anyone else. I feel entirely relaxed and comforted, and have thoughts I don't often have elsewhere, like thinking that she, a Polish woman, is there to serve me, though she is unhappy, and her unhappiness has to be masked in order to serve me properly. She tends to my skin and me, a woman of Jewish origin, a faith in which I have no faith and feel no spiritual kinship, but into which I was born, and tells me how sensitive my skin is, when not many years ago Polish people, possibly her parents or grandparents, might have made skin like mine into lampshades, and it is the only time I ever have that particular, almost wry thought, which occurs fleetingly in the cramped, dingy salon.

I entertain that abhorrent and impermissible idea wholly for myself, amusing myself with its horror, as she goes about her work. She cares for my skin, having different thoughts from those required by the job she is doing, her hands performing routine actions which leave her mind free, and she may not want anyone, especially her clients, to know what she is thinking, maybe about the glowering man waiting outside this small room for her, wanting to date and fuck her, or she may be reliving carnal scenes in which she dominates the strong man, sits astride him, her well-tended skin glistening with sweat, or she may be concocting a plan for her future, since people often desire a future different from their present, which may be painful or lackluster. It's better not to complain in many situations, servants know this, and everyone is sometimes a servant, even the very wealthy can become servants, insecure in love and fearful of rejection. Louis-Ferdinand Céline said that ten percent of galley slaves were volunteers, because people want masters, since existence is painful, though no one wants to die, or very few want to die, and it's often better not to say anything at all. I don't remember mentioning my dread and anxiety of the gray camp and bunk to my counselors, though I might have after lunch, when I tried but couldn't nap on the rough brown woolen blanket, which irritated my skin, desperately waiting for the amnesia of sleep, sorrowfully longing for mail from my mother who didn't write, because she expected letters from me first. I had learned to write but had no familiarity with the protocols of correspondence and didn't answer her initial letter, and I didn't think about it, or I can't remember what I thought, since I didn't know what to think, and didn't know the dangers of unawareness. But when I was asked to steal the bowling pin of the enemy team on the last day of Color War by the head counselor of the team to which I was assigned and which, like my family, religion, and sex I didn't choose, having heard that anyone who is captured in enemy territory will be thrown into jail, I dropped to the ground and wailed, No, please, I don't want to go to jail, please don't make me, please. The head counselor suddenly, and only then, comprehended my chronic, active distress and said, to quiet me, that she'd ask my cousin, the one I haven't seen since my favorite uncle died, to do it. Soon my cousin sneaked across enemy territory, risking capture and jail, and succeeded, making her the hero and me the coward. But her cowardly, brutal older brother didn't go into the textile business, as mine didn't, and I didn't, though I often wish I had, because I would like to be around fabrics, examine patterns, and study threads rather than be around many other things, in an endeavor at which my uncle and father were successes, then they weren't, and which compounded my father's sense of innate failure and made it nearly perfect. I can remember my uncle trying to cheer him up, urging him to accompany him on vacations, to lose himself far away from the bolts of beautiful fabrics of their own design that increasingly lay unsold on the deep shelves in their stockroom. The stockboy, Junior, whose skin was a deep brown, who was muscular and short, shorter than my father—my father often rested his arm around Junior's shoulders—had taken the bolts off the truck, unpacked and set them on the long, deep shelves in the stockroom, and when potential customers visited, when business was good, a phrase I heard often, a few words belying their heft—business is good—Junior stalwartly carried the bolts to the showroom, and my father would sometimes slap him on the back and joke with him, but I don't know where Junior went after the business failed. I remember him, indistinctly and distinctly, especially that he was called a stockboy, had an impressively compact body, a round, brown face, a seemingly cheerful demeanor, and wore colorful shirts, maybe of my father's material, when he was not wearing a T-shirt, denim jeans, or some other uniform for manual labor. I wondered what he thought of my father, his boss, when I was young, but I never asked, and then he disappeared, so I suspected my father and uncle of giving him away, like our cat and dog, but instead my father said, We had to let Junior go, because business is bad.

In Tutankhamen's tomb, there was a linen shirt, which is now housed in the Victoria and Albert Museum in London, where I lived briefly during a period when I was also among strangers, though some of them became friends, lovers, or enemies, but I don't know what happened to most of them. I had no cat in London, but in Amsterdam, where I stayed longer, I found a stray, and then found homes for her and her sole surviving kitten when I left for the place I call home. The earliest textiles had pictures of animals on them; there are images of animals being tamed on Byzantine silks of the 6th or 7th century, and they are not sentimental, though today animals on clothes would be considered sentimental, any animal on a shirt, cup or postcard is in some way sentimental, though everyone loves their animals and their farts. If I were to tell the story of my dog, how she was adopted from a shelter when she was pregnant, how my father disliked her—my mother demanded we keep her anyway—how he came to love her, because of a special feat she performed, how we found homes for every one of her puppies, if my story included the dog's many exceptional acts, or a description of her tail twirling in gleeful circles as she ran toward me on the grass, it might seem a sentimental story. But I feel worse about the fate of my dog than about anything else in my life over which I had some control, however puny, since most of the significant things in life can't be controlled, and about them I had no choice, though in retelling them, I could also be accused of sentimentality, and I expect such accusations. Still, I never wear clothes that have pictures of animals on them.

Altobasseo was a special, luxurious velvet, made by the Genoese, who also developed a way of crimping the threads of the pile, and used gold thread, too. Velvet has varying heights of pile and touching it is pleasurable, though I haven't worn it with much pleasure since I was a child, when a black velvet dress and jacket, with white lace trim at the neck and sleeves, felt urgent to buy and wear. I was aware, then, that the design of the dress was old-fashioned, but I wanted it anyway, since it might announce to my circumscribed world that I wasn't of it but another one, which others couldn't inhabit or touch. Since then, I have kept small pieces of cloth cut from cotton T-shirts and other favorite clothes I wore as a child that shredded from wear and tear and nearly fell off me, evidencing the demise of their function, but which I never wanted to stop wearing or throw away. Similarly, I regretted losing a tan, when I didn't worry about the damage the sun could do, cancer, aging, or have much concern about my skin, except for the many heat rashes and irritations that flared from being clothed in rough wool sweaters or leggings during the winter. The redness and the stickiness caused by one moist inner thigh clinging to its twin was awful, and I don't now know why this torture, which is how I experienced it, continued day after cold day, and why I was unable to convince my mother of my discomfort, when its effect, the unsightly rashes, should have been apparent to her naked eye.

When I awaken, I anticipate, often with foreboding, the others at breakfast, like the demanding man, in front of whom I might say the wrong thing, declaim vociferously, and for no reason expose a passion I don't necessarily feel but which is born in opposition to the presence or even the undeniable fact of the existence of someone like the demanding man, who calls forth in me adamant, unwanted feelings, or I might also let out a malodorous fart. If something slid off my tongue or from my body that shouldn't have, which I felt I had to say or about which it appeared I had no choice, especially when I have just awakened—I once heard that the French don't prosecute people who commit crimes of passion twenty minutes after waking—I would be embarrassed, so I malinger in bed, listening to the radio, which can be turned on and off. I often turn it on and off, simply because shutting off those voices, disposing of the news and others' incessant opinions, is pleasant. On occasion, I have missed breakfast, malingering maliciously, turning on and off the radio many times, but breakfast is regularly the best meal of the day, and if I remain in bed, if I haven't merely overslept, I ruminate anxiously about how I will pass the time until lunch and whether I will become hungry and regret my decision. Time passes, quickly or slowly, but always independently of me, while I turn over and over in bed, caught in my sheets, my pillow a triumph of regrets, as I fret about avoiding people, missing breakfast, and the consequent long, hungry aftermath until lunch. I may also be checked up on. But I like breakfast best and can also feel touched by the inevitable presence of other people who, like me, have traversed a night of deep sleep, wakefulness, ecstatic or conflicted dreams.

I may be the cause of waking some of them, but no one says anything, to me, at least, though lately I learned, to my piquant chagrin, that a man who was here briefly, whose face I can't remember, whom I never again thought about and who in a sense didn't exist for me, took exception to my telling him that his early morning showers woke me, which surprised me, since I was, then, entirely unaware that my complaining, with a dull annoyance, probably, that his showering at 6:30 a.m. in the bathroom next to which I slept, the old pipes rattling like thunder, was the cause of his abrupt departure.

Sometimes in the morning the cook is in a talkative mood, and her smile and her moderately stained teeth both disquiet and cheer me, so I might stay a while in her kitchen, its odors reminiscent of other times, many of which were probably unhappy, but whose smells are still redolent, the ordinary aromas saturate remote or vivid events bittersweetly. I wait for her to describe her life, but she is usually circumspect, having worked many years for other people, and probably she knows it's often better not to say anything, especially statements that admit to or betray dissatisfaction, that risk exposing her to censure, ridicule, or disrepute, especially comments that reek of bitterness, like a fart, though some might anyway nurse their foulness and be profligate with their bitter complaints. But an enemy's bitterness is never foul, an enemy's complaints are revelatory. Inadvertently, I've marched into enemy territory, unprotected on a street, encountering persons I hate who hate me, but I fought the instinct to run into a doorway or collapse onto the sidewalk, to pretend I was faint or about to vomit, and kept walking, as if I were fearless, which I'm not. Once, I strode past two treacherous dissemblers and waved, pretending there wasn't a great, mysterious enmity—enduring hatred runs like water, elusive in its origins, as Chekhov shows, more mysterious than its opposite, since in love we love ourselves, while a hater's chiasmatic relationship to the despised one and to herself or himself is not precisely self-hatred and more difficult to plumb. Between the dissemblers and myself, there grew a steep, eternal divide, which has a kind of magnificence, specifically, its venerability, and which, if we could have, if it were appropriate, if we lived in a different place among different people, we might fight about, physically, or go to war to settle, though it wouldn't ever be settled. Sometimes there is nothing to do other than resist or fight, but some people are locked inside their own wreckage and can't do either. Sometimes an individual must fight or flee, if able and not already irrevocably ruined or paralyzed by a past that can't be recovered, because there is no other possibility to survive than to fight, in some way, for what's needed or wanted, though some people would never fight or don't ever feel personally threatened, but when they do, when an ominous threat occurs, they might take up arms in some sense. And in some, these fears or emotions might be considered skin deep, for which they could find treatment. But skin lets us know that a surface often isn't superficial. Dermatologic diseases recognize no national or hemispheric boundaries, doctors confront a global dermatology, since an exotic disease might appear in the Congo and Los Angeles. There are resurgences, of syphilis, for one, and a peculiar diagnostic sign of unilateral congenital syphilis—called Higoumenakis' sign, discovered by its eponymous Greek doctor—is a raised or protruding collarbone. Serologic tests for syphilis can reveal an individual's immunologic condition, but not whether he or she is currently infected. Other conditions that indicate congenital syphilis are the saddle nose and

Hutchinson's teeth, or peg-shaped upper incisors that are centrally notched. These teeth never occur outside of congenital syphilis. It was a Dr. Hutchinson who also noted opacities of the cornea and eighth nerve deafness that, together with the teeth, form the diagnostic Hutchinson triad. Less dramatic skin eruptions can become violently infected—around a cuticle, say, but there is no stigma attached to it, unless it goes untreated. A bad tooth, untreated, its infection appearing first as an inflamed gum, might descend farther under the gum into the jaw and ultimately infect the brain and cause death. Many people died of tooth decay before the 20th century particularly and still do. Skin is not what it appears to an untrained eye, and for this I appreciate my dermatologist who carries within him, after much training and research, an ability to read texts I can't. Skin is a parchment for the body. He can spot something inimical to me when I can't and what appears benign may also be harmless for a time, but then a small spot on the cheek can grow into a murderous melanoma.

The intransigent enemy is often a friend who wordlessly turns, embroidering insult upon insult and calumny upon calumny within himself or herself, while the other is unaware of these rank occurrences, and so the former, though still-present friend, an incipient enemy, acts against the unknowing one, cannily, all the while pretending to friendship but causing damage and havoc, and only in retrospect, which is dumb wisdom, does the friend realize the existence of an enemy, whose enmity lasts a lifetime but which has come about slowly and stealthily in the darkly benign nights of supposed friendship. I have had several episodes in which I wandered, without presence of mind, into enemy territory, imagining I was among friends, and sometimes it was I who may have provoked or caused the rift, without knowing I did, and sometimes whoever I am or was was not the cause of the hatred, since its origin belonged within the friend, to whom I, the other, am nothing more than a suitable object. One such friend, someone I liked but didn't know long, to whom I was indifferent for a period of time, unaware of her growing anguish in a time of my own trouble, disappeared, not only from my view but from others', and when I searched for her, but could not locate her, but then finally did, she would have nothing to do with me. I expect I am an enemy of hers now, while she will always be someone I like whom I may have hurt inadvertently, and those are the saddest enemies to have. Although, since I didn't know her well, she may be a shallow, thick-skinned, insensitive character, an opportunist or someone so damaged as to be incapable of love and compassion. The saddest enemy is her kind, and I don't want to dwell on it, so I never mention her, because for one thing she was never vital to my life, and also it's usually better not to say anything, especially about subjects plagued by illegibility.

When I first arrived here, in a voluntary manner but wearily, as I had little hope, a woman inquired in the main hall, right upon meeting me, at what hour did I regularly awaken, and I felt alarm. I didn't understand why she needed to know, of what moment my rising was to her, but she explained she was only curious. I wasn't curious about when she awakened, though I have curiosity about many things, so I thought, quickly, my stomach slightly upset, as I have a nervous stomach, since the stomach is a second heart I was told by a Greek therapeutic cosmetician, there might be a problem. She might be a potential enemy to my sleep or even to my being, though this seemed farfetched, but it would be a miracle to arrive somewhere and find no problem or obstacle. It would have been a miracle if the girl in the camp infirmary, who was not allowed medicine to cure her, because of her parents' religion, grew up and lived a blissful life. When I was nearly six, walking past the infirmary on the way to the cafeteria, I wanted to visit her, to go to her bedside and comfort her, or at least see her, though I was afraid I might become sick and die as soon as I entered the infirmary. I feared also that I might encounter her religious parents who were depriving her of medicine, maybe even killing her. She might have survived the summer, and, if she did, people could say it was a miracle, God's work, and be thankful, though by now she might know how close she came to dying and blame her parents for endangering her welfare, and have nothing to do with the stern people who gave her life and then played dice with it. Or, she might believe in miracles and love her parents and the religion into which was born about which she had no choice, no one has a choice about the most crucial things in life, though maybe she doesn't object to her fate.

I didn't have a choice about many things, but I disdain all forms of religion, and I have always been allowed medicine. I suffered many sore throats when I was a child, so the family doctor visited often, with his black bag, the kind of bag I haven't seen in ages that now becomes a happy image from a bad or an unhappy time and childhood, but at that time I didn't want to see the bag or the doctor and didn't want shots of penicillin, a wonder drug then. I remember appreciating its magic before he injected me, that soon I would be well because it was a wonder drug, and, while my mother looked on with her discerning, critical eye, I took the shot, the doctor promising once he was using a new kind of needle, a rubber needle, which would be painless, he said, and which I believed, because I trusted the doctor, and afterward, having felt the needle's sharp point penetrate my sensitive skin, though it's less sensitive on the ass than on the face, I was disillusioned. I spent many weeks in bed every winter, drawing, reading, listening to the radio, watching TV, or sleeping, while my infected tonsils ached and my schoolmates played. But I never thought of myself as sick, my parents were never sick, and they didn't think of themselves as sick, though today, because of greater sensitivity, many people consider themselves sick, at risk, or threatened.

As I entered the dining room on my first morning in this institution, when time seemed elastic, a ripple of interest from the others, as well as a rustle of discontent, directed at an unknown, intrusive object, which was my person, broke like waves at my feet. But the ocean, even in winter, was warmer, certainly neutral, and though its waves also alarmed me, so wild yet regular and implacable in their movement to the shore and then back to the sea, I wasn't entirely discomforted, since I was told the ocean's movement was natural and it was clear it had nothing to do with me. It was a place and world I couldn't know whose momentum would always be indifferent to my own, but whose majestic forces could swallow me easily. Still, the waves and ocean caused a profound contentment, probably because my father was beside me, happy in this setting, when often he wasn't happy, because business was bad, or he was anguished, suffering a distress whose origin he himself didn't know, couldn't subdue, and that didn't abate.

Around and before me, in this setting, a dining room, were human waves of inchoate, indeterminate feeling and emotion, which I wasn't supposed to respond to, and to which I didn't, since I understood my place as a newcomer, an animal who might be a threat, and knew it would not be in my interest to arouse undue suspicion. It was the end of breakfast. I was immediately shown into the kitchen to meet the cook, and assistant cook, I believe, and her helpers, college and high school age students, who greeted newcomers pleasantly but awkwardly, and who were themselves somewhat glum or circumspect, though everyone who works here is expected to behave judiciously and be friendly to visitors and residents. One night, when it was very late and no one else was around, when I was restless, reading the town's newspaper, unconsciously looking for something, one of the helpers, a girl of seventeen, advanced with several of her friends into the main room. They squealed with delight at their transgression. The incursion was prohibited to her and her friends, but it was she who did it arrogantly, with a certain disdain for me, when she spied me. She guffawed triumphantly, and stared at me, daring me to object, but I closed my book and turned down my lips, to indicate my displeasure as well as the fact that she was in danger, endangering me, also, since my peace of mind could be altered, when I'm supposed to be calm here, and shortly afterward, they left the dark brown wood room. Later, there was an awkwardness when she was in the kitchen and I entered, it was a slight obstacle that ruffled my composure, since she and I were expected to know our places and respect them, but I never spoke of her infraction.

First, the assistant cook wanted to know what I could and absolutely wouldn't eat, and, as I wrote this down on a blue-lined index card, I was conscious of impinging on her time. Then the head cook, who immediately knew what was occurring, as it had again and again with every new resident, she had been the head cook for years, walked into her kitchen, and I saw that her pale forehead creased, her blue eyes receded under eggshell-hooded eyelids, and her head angled toward the low ceiling, which hung over all of our heads. Fearing her boredom or weariness in this repetitious event, I wrote quickly that I ate everything in moderation, except octopus and Jell-O, that I liked greens, fruit, cottage cheese, cheeses, generally, though I wanted to avoid fats and some carbohydrates, ate fish and beef, chicken, didn't like fried foods, and when the assistant cook handed the head cook my list, she read it and nodded but didn't look at me. Instead, the head cook warned, her back turned to me as she fastened her gaze upon tomatoes meant presumably for slicing or chopping, that if I were late for breakfast, I wouldn't be served, though there would be dry cereals out on a table for a while after the breakfast hour had officially ended, which pleased me, though I don't often eat dry cereal, yet I felt, in a pinch, I could.

But the second or assistant cook was sometimes on duty in the morning, and she wouldn't deny a latecomer a hot breakfast, so it was a better beginning to the day when she was in the kitchen, but on the days she wasn't, it transpired, since she had a frail constitution, though she had a solid build, she might be home with flu, backache, or migraine headaches. At forty, she was a sick woman, it was said by several of the community, when she hadn't appeared yet again, disappointing all the latecomers, of which I was one, because she was a kind woman; she too often lay in bed feverish, her stomach upset or with a headache's sick drumming, and it was easy to imagine that there were other problems causing her body's maladies. The stomach is a second heart, I now believe, but of the first heart, she never talked, and, about hers, no one else did, either.

I don't remember my parents sick, lying in bed, though I do remember my mother's screams one night, even though I was shut away in my bedroom, because they tore into the fabric of my young night, one I didn't know wouldn't last forever. A glass bottle had exploded and its shards had badly gored my mother's calf. The doctor came to the house, but I didn't see his bag then, or him, but I heard my mother's agonized cries, as he removed the pieces and slivers of glass from her leg and stitched her up, without, my brother told me, later, on a rare instance of contact, anesthetic, and, even so, I never thought of her as sensitive, but she, like everyone, has scars, especially on that calf.

Today there are no serious latecomers, and all of us are served breakfast, while in the corner, the two young women whisper, their mouths opening and closing greedily, hushed words falling from them or morsels of food, as they keep their heads close together, intent on spilling and absorbing great secrets, which interest no others, except a tall balding man, who sat at my table and who had recently shown up. He seemed to be sensitive, at least to the propinquity of the demanding man who flailed his arms, because the relative newcomer inched farther from him, even going so far as to move his plate down the table, toward mine. He may have sensed the other man's pain or felt his own, or have felt no pain at all. People can feel a lot of pain and not be sensitive, in the way the word is used, which doesn't include the experience of animals. Many people have sensitive skin and skin problems, and people who are very kind to animals can be entirely insensitive, concerned mostly with their own pain, not others' pain. Some might think I was insensitive because I didn't want to talk with the two women, who listen to music, play chess, read with conviction, are vegetarians, and who never impose themselves upon me, but seem to be preparing to tell me about their lives, which is what people want to do. One of the two has a history of psoriasis, and today it has flared on the backs of her thin hands, and, if her elbows were bare, the inflamed, encrusted flesh, angry and purple, might be visible, too. She is wan, skinny, and never exhibits anger, but always seems malleable, or breakable, too fragile, like a good wineglass, and holds her tidy body erect, drawing her head up, to peer deftly at the world. But she stares, sometimes vacantly, though this is not necessarily anger, and I have caught her watching me, but then she shifts her eyes downward or smiles sweetly. She especially stares at the tall balding man.

She was one of the first people I came upon, noting her presence, slight as it was, but I didn't really take her in when I arrived, though what was indistinct then has gained in definition with time. Now I remember her in the big room—which is as familiar to me as my family's living room that I rarely went into because of its formality, along with the fear that I might damage it—and, because I've seen her every day after, I can claim to remember what she looked like then, though I didn't really see her, similar to how a line-up works, inadequately. If I were to have noticed people in a line-up before, anywhere, but not in the act of committing the crime of which they are accused, rightly or wrongly, those people could appear to be the perpetrators when they were only people seen before in a different context. Everything here seems familiar today that was, not long ago, uncannily strange and even foreboding, because it was a new place, and everyone who resides with me, in this place, is no longer a complete stranger but an incomplete one. Stranger crime is unusual. Leslie Van Houten assisted in the murder of a stranger, which is unusual, since people usually murder people they know, and at the time, 1969, it was still more unusual that a woman helped to murder another woman, though Mrs. Rosemary LaBianca was already dead by Tex Watson's hands when Leslie Van Houten stabbed her in the lower back nineteen times. It was never in doubt that she participated in the crime, and she never was in a line-up, but what was in doubt, and still is, is why she did it and what exactly she did do, if she committed a murder or had been only a violent follower or merely a fiend, who stuck the knife in, many times, after Mrs. LaBianca was dead.

When I was escorted into the big house, into its spacious, dark wood lounge, or main room, I was immediately conscious of an anxious wanting, after I inadvertently noticed the two young women, lounging on couches opposite each other, to whom I was introduced, but whose names I quickly forgot, and a few men, whose names I also forgot, while being handed the keys to my rooms. I adamantly wanted a comfortable chair, an appropriate table, and a good light to read by, I read a lot, I can happily read all day and night, when I should be doing other things, but most important, I explained to those in charge, who stood by impassively while I orated my demands, ones they were familiar with, I needed a good chair, it concerned me most. In a way, it alone concerned me. Nothing mattered but a chair, to whose acquisition I gave all my attention and energy, speaking of its necessity with an urgent eloquence that surprised me and those in temporary charge of my comfort and well-being, which was another reason I scarcely noticed the other residents.

I take exception to ugly, badly made or poorly designed chairs, uncomfortable chairs, and I have an interest in well-made, well-designed chairs, marveling at their efficiency and beauty, though when I was a child, I didn't. In the family den of the comfortable house I loved that was sold over my protests, there was an Eames table and chairs, around and on which we sometimes ate, though I was unaware of the kind of furniture it was or what it meant, or that its possession meant anything, but I liked the set, blond and modern, even though some of the chairs' backs loosened and fell off later, the black rubber splitting from the blond wood, and, when the house was sold, the set was, also. I often think of those chairs and that table, but especially the chairs, since anything can be significant later in the present or future that wasn't in the past. The chairs were different from the sober brown velvet club chairs and pale gold brocade couch in the living room, where I rarely went, though it was comfortable, but the couch needed to be plumped, and if I sat down, especially to hear the sighs of the stuffed cushions collapsing under my young body, I would have to plump them up again. The other chairs and couches in the den were made of wood, like the Eames chairs, covered in hard foam rubber that didn't show traces of bodies pressed upon them, not mine, fundamentally, and that furniture appealed more, since it was durable and as remote and invulnerable to my childish roughhousing as the Swedes who designed it, who lived far away from the place and people into which I was born and about which I had no choice.

More time goes into designing chairs than any other kind of furniture, a chair is more like a car than a bed, and many read sitting on chairs whose shape most closely resembles a human body, its base or bottom is especially for the bottom or buttocks and its back the spine, imitating the human back, but people also like to read on beds, the way I do. The Eameses, Charles and Ray, designed the chairs in our den in the early 1940s when they, like my father and his brother, either sought new materials or new ways to use material, in the case of the Eameses, molded plywood, but in the case of my father and uncle, who couldn't use natural fibers, as cotton was needed for war, they experimented with modern techniques to innovate synthetic fibers. Invention flourishes in war, for the war effort, and there's always change and reversals of fortune, progress in industry, and even society, which requires more progress to correct, since wars have consequences about which few have a choice, almost no one, and fewer make decisions. But design is chiefly about choice, design is satisfying. Few people want to fight, and fewer want to make designs, but some wars and designs are universally reputed to be better than others, though opinions shift, since what is most definite about the contemporary is that it is primarily temporary.

The history of chairs records human sensitivity, or consciousness, since chairs, over time, have become ever more closely molded to the body, to fit its growing dominance, though it was long after the Enlightenment, especially after the 19th century, that chairs were really designed for comfort and style. Long ago, chairs, while made for people, had rigid backs, their seats were unpadded, and people adjusted to the chair, its design and exigencies, or people didn't expect to be comfortable or comfort was once different, and always relative, or maybe people didn't sit long, since many worked in the fields, ate miserable dinners in squalid huts or hovels, though kings and queens probably were seated for hours on hard, ornate chairs, wearing clothes, which today might be called costumes, that were heavy and also uncomfortable. For a long time people mustn't have complained too much about stiff clothes or rigid backed chairs, since it wasn't until 1297 that chairs were even mentioned in a poem, "up I chaere he sate adoun, al vp be see sonde," and at that time the word "chair" changed from a three syllable pronunciation to two, and then finally there was, in English, the one syllable word.

I wanted a sensible chair, since I don't like too much ornamentation, but I can like some, though what kind is changing, which is why I remember the Eames chairs, as they were sleek, bare of decoration, and they should have been more comfortable than they were, though they were not uncomfortable, especially for short people, like children, or medium-sized people like my parents. My mother is shrinking, though she doesn't have osteoporosis, and I must be shrinking, too, though I don't feel it and don't want to be measured, since there are some things I don't want to know. But other things I really want to know, such as, what is going on in the mind of the cryptic, balding man when he notices the psoriasis on the hands of the young woman, who clearly is affected just by his touch, but does he want to touch her. Some things are easy to learn, since if you are interested in why people do or think what they do, which may be foolhardy, impulsive, self-defeating, or unworthy, people will usually answer your questions and tell their stories, if your interest isn't merely self-serving or salacious, since mostly everyone likes to talk about themselves and would usually rather speak than listen. Most people will divulge more than you want to know. People often want to recite the tragic events that have deformed their lives, offering up their pasts as a series of tableaus of deceptions, or unspeakable insults, since people blame others endlessly, and these assaults and imprecations clutter, like a dog's defecations on the street, their lives and stories. What is said is often unremarkable, though sometimes horrible, but it's still easy to feel the tiresomeness of another's life, as well as your own, since interest in other people is also an interest in yourself, because human beings are interested in themselves and in ways of survival. All stories are somehow survival stories, with bad or good fortunes.

Some tragic cases relate their stories with verve, though their accounts are no less sad than others' boring recitations, but they are compellingly told, and often these people draw others to them, no matter what story they tell. There are terrible stories set, especially, in hospitals and jails, and I realize it is inevitable that one day, for one illness or another before I die, a hospital will claim me, but I've never done time in jail, and I don't want to, ever. According to Contesa, whose occupation was social work and who initiated and ran the Center for Urban Peasantry, which endeared her to me further, but whose preoccupation is Franz Kafka, his writing, his loves, particularly Felice Bauer, Jean Genet, whom, it turned out, Gardner—the Count—had met in Paris, claimed he didn't care about Kafka's writing, because it was infused with the terror of going to jail, a middle-class person's fear of public shame and humiliation, and because he, Genet, had been to jail and didn't fear it, Kafka's writing didn't interest him at all. I thought, at first, since cleverness resides in glossy surfaces over which even thoughtful characters glide like skaters, that Genet's was a reasonable, even apt observation, but with more attention I decided that Genet's imaginative powers were as limited by his having been to jail, which allowed him assumptions about Kafka, as Kafka's fear of it, so if I'm not interested in people who have gone to jail, I'm not interested in Genet's writing.

Some of the acts I've committed have been illegal. When I was five, I stole candy inadvertently from the candy store several blocks from my house, on a main road, in the suburb where I grew up, because its sign said, Take One, and later I stole lipstick from the town five and dime, and then shoplifted clothes from department stores, packing a skirt into the voluminous shoulder of a ratty fur coat, and purchased small amounts of cocaine, all relatively mild infractions of the law. Other people, who have scant education, less economic or skin privilege, might have been arrested, convicted, and sent upstate for the same relatively harmless but illegal acts, and other people have records against them that are public, so that anyone can find out what these people have done wrong, and while I have no record of crimes against property or person, nothing that would show up on police blotters or computers, nothing that I am aware of, or that might hurt me, though I am not aware of everything that might hurt me, I have committed illegal acts that have gone undetected, but I know what I have done, and I know what was wrong and illegal. Legally, I am sane.

Contesa asserts that, without desiring it and unacknowledged to Kafka or maybe in unconscious enjoyment of his cruel but limited power, he tested Felice Bauer, as he did himself—she was twice his fiancée—and dangled her from a rope of ambivalence until the possibility for a marriage he thought he should have, because she was the woman he should have loved but couldn't, snapped, but then, Contesa also contends, he wasn't equipped for a middle-class life, not capable of it, or of marriage, since he wasn't inclined to its petty rigors, and he wasn't physically well. I wondered if Contesa were talking about the Count, or herself, since, as she put it, she'd fled for her life from her upper-middle-class Negro family of doctors and lawyers, in Mount Vernon, New York, one of whose ancestors had received his freedom early, making his fortune farming in New Hampshire, because the black bourgeoisie was as boring as the white, and, after being forced to debut in a cotillion, she sailed to Paris, where she met the Count and where, she said, we Negroes were appreciated, Josephine Baker, le hot jazz, it was a philonegro thing, she declared, amused by her neologism. She'd sooner take that over its American version, negrophobia. She added, with irony, that Kafka dangled Felice from his elegant hands, and why wouldn't he, she was free to object and leave him, and the Count and she nodded, barely concealing their mutual satisfaction, and I didn't contest her, though I believe that about most things we usually don't have a choice, yet in love there seems to be some liberty, but that may be a very necessary illusion.

Like Kafka, the Count and Contesa, if the analogy is sensible, many of the residents here are not equipped for life as it is commonly regulated but they struggle on, the disconsolate woman who has psoriasis and is anorectic, a female radio announcer and musician with chronic fatigue syndrome, the young married man, who pretends nothing afflicts him, the sodden, demanding man who consumes a fifth of vodka every night and is an irritant to my skin, like scratchy fabric, and others. Each has a story and a sphere of complaints, with some hope of improvement, each soldiers on, which is how my father would put it, they keep going, right or wrong in their thinking, my father said many people had wrong thinking, and books of philosophy lay resolutely on his bedside night table, but then he'd shake his head, since wrongness, his own especially, was sad to contemplate. I blush furiously when I have done something wrong and been discovered, or might have been observed in the act of doing wrong, exposing me to threat, derision, or disgust. Drinking wine flushes my skin, I pinken like a schoolgirl, some people's necks engorge with blood when they drink alcohol, a common, easily obtainable psychoactive drug; but I have not turned red, when alone, because of a thought I have had that might be incorrect or indecent, lying on the bed, reading, although that may not be the case since I can't see myself. Before others, I have colored, flushed, reddened, just as people darker than myself, so-called black people, those whose epidermis and dermis contain more melanin than that of Caucasians or Asians, have burnished with embarrassment, their cheeks have turned, in my presence, a bluish-purple, their skin intensifying in color, the way a bright red rose turns purple when it dries, or when shocked or embarrassed, their skin has lost color, become pale or ashen, graying subtly from fright or shock. I have also blanched, just before I fainted, color draining from my cheeks, I've been told. My skin has a yellow cast. When a colorist analyzes it, in order that she, usually, might sell me products to keep it moist and free of wrinkles, whose presence connotes worry and age, though once or twice a man has sold me lipstick, enthusiastically, and also tinted moisturizer at a store dedicated to cosmetics that are for sensitive skin and people and uses only organic materials, she or he tells me that my complexion has a yellowish tone, or sometimes olive, which isn't apparent except when I have walked about without sun block, which would dishearten my dermatologist, or because I haven't slept well, but often I do, often I sleep too long.

Without a record, which enforces the reality that I haven't done anything very wrong, which is incorrect, I can appear blameless. Sensitive people need to feel blameless. To me, it's worse to have performed harsh acts than minor illegal ones, and it is for those I feel guilty, not infractions of the law that are nowhere indicated or recorded but the improprieties and everyday cruelties of which I am the agent. These ruffle any contentment or peace I might seek or even deserve, though no one deserves anything, good or bad. Leslie Van Houten's acts were illegal, violent, vicious, colloquially heartless, incomprehensible, except that she followed a charismatic leader, people need leaders and are easily led, or enjoy being led, people want leaders, political and spiritual ones, like a Charlie Manson, the way she did, though she was less committed to him than the other girls who were convicted with her. People enjoy devotion to a cause, which makes life seem worthwhile, and for her devotion to Manson's cause, to helter skelter, to the manufacture of a race war that, Manson declared, would proclaim the dark-skinned race victorious, Leslie was imprisoned in California in a women's facility, where she might remain all her life, or until she is very old and will not, upon leaving that institution, have much life ahead of her, or even much of a life to lead, since having been jailed for the great majority of her years, she knows hardly any other life than it, except for the six months that she was on parole in 1977. Leslie might never be forgiven, except by a few, nuns and priests, for instance, who are hell-bent on forgiveness, but not for baby killers, as they prefer to call doctors who perform abortions, and maybe even by the victim's family. She stabbed Mrs. Rosemary LaBianca maybe nineteen of the forty-one times she was stabbed, though Leslie believes she stabbed Mrs. LaBianca only after she died. The coroners can tell which wounds come after death, because the skin doesn't pinken as much, since, after death, less or no blood rushes to the wound. The LaBianca family might forgive her someday, but having been a member of Charles Manson's family, into which Leslie wasn't born, about which membership she had a choice, it is unlikely most people who still remember those events will forgive her, though 1969 is many years ago. When she was nineteen, she wrote her parents that she would be let out of prison in seven years. Leslie Van Houten will most likely never be completely or generally forgiven or even released from jail, or let out only when she is very old, and every day she must suffer the consequences of vicious acts she committed when she was nineteen.

I'm guilty of infractions of the law as well as bad or misguided acts, but I don't want people to know I am guilty, of what infractions of the law, or in what way I may have hurt others, since what I do with my secrets, my past, or what I apply to my skin or where I place my desk in my apartment or what couch or chair I have or what kind of cat sleeps on my bed is no one's business. Most people wouldn't want to listen, most people want to talk, everyone's busy, though my young cat is not busy, he's never busy in the way that people vacuously insist they are busy. My cat likes to sleep on my favorite chair, he sleeps a lot of the time, probably he is bored, and he digs his claws into it, ruining the chair I'm partial to, because he is a little wild, not affectionate and may never be, but if no one enters my apartment, I won't have to worry about his becoming vicious, badly clawing a friend, who might view my cat and me in a chilling light and then exhort me to have my cat killed. In order not to lose the friend, to appease the friend, I might have to kill my beautiful, slightly wild cat, but I won't want to, and I will begrudge the friend this act, because I love my cat, probably more than the friend who'd ask me to have him killed, and while I would like my young cat to sit on my lap as I read the books whose pages I worry about dirtying with face cream and other grease, like chocolate, which I occasionally eat when I read, because it helps me sleep, when finally I decide it is time to fall asleep, I can accept for the time being that he is still a young cat who is not ready to be affectionate or to stop clawing the chair, which I bought to sit on and read, but do not. I love my cat so much I want another, one who would lie contentedly on my lap when I sit in my favorite chair or lie on the bed, reading, though I know it's better for the disposition of the spine to sit in a chair with lower back support when reading.

When the demanding man concluded the recitation of his dream, in which he reported coming under attack from a few characters who might now be at the table, he stared haughtily and aggressively at the relative newcomer—the tall balding man—who responded to the obvious insult. Provoked, he threw down his napkin and rose quickly from the table. At this moment the tall balding man's stature was nearly magnificent, though generally he slumped. Across the room, the disconsolate woman whose psoriasis had again flared, but fortunately not on her face, also rose. Oddly, she was in her pajamas, and they had small blue flowers on them, a cotton flannel, and, now standing, her inappropriate costume was apprehended by all. The two signaled a message that none of us was supposed to receive, but by their secretiveness its romantic content was revealed, and the other disconsolate woman, who was lactose intolerant and had asthma, glanced at her half-eaten scrambled eggs, probably not to acknowledge the palpable intrigue of which we were all informed and that thrust itself upon her, too, in the cozy dining room, where we residents were now drawn into a burgeoning affair. They were involved, a term which carries little of the resonance of love affair or the attenuated drama implied in a relationship, so it's a word used too easily, though involvements don't register neutrally to those involved, even when most will be temporary and insignificant, but even so I shy away here from involvements with others, though the tarot card reader told me that against my will I'd be taken into one—of which kind he couldn't prophesize—and from which I might not easily be disengaged.

Intrigue at breakfast is a diversion, and I brightened at this unexpected occurrence, whose effect relegated my own adventures and misalliances, to a temporary amnesia. "How we need the comedy of other people," I heard Contesa, whose dark glasses sat on top of her head, say to herself, or maybe to the demanding man, who anyway heaved a fat sigh, as if everything that he'd been prey to or a captive of had escaped. It was his dream. He was aggrieved, since the older woman should have been, but wasn't, tending scrupulously to him as she sometimes did, the way his mother did, who hovered over him, he often asserted, doing everything for him, everything, and then he'd throw his arms out to take in the big world around him. Now, once more the demanding man realized he had lost a potential love partner, this one spirited off by a tall balding, slump-shouldered man, who, the demanding one must have acknowledged, in a flash of terrible knowledge, he now hated resolutely. But he was helpless, affixed to his chair like a crab on its back, a burden to anyone nearby, because his growing despair was sharp and bitter, he could probably taste it, though I hated to imagine his tongue coated with bitterness over the brown slime of nicotine and sour vodka. Contesa leaned over to me and quoted Langston Hughes, who wrote in a letter to Carl Van Vechten of "the weariness of the world moving always in the same circle." Here people talk about being in or out of certain circles.

Tension rifled the dining room, while the long-legged male kitchen helper collected our dirty plates, as the demanding man realized his surroundings, rudely shaken awake, when he saw what occurred when the tall man had risen; also that Contesa was again ignoring his many silent entreaties for counsel and sympathy, and that across the room a moderately attractive woman was being courted and responding to another man, and that she was already involved with the other, when he hadn't even guessed at their mutual interest, but he was always loved by his mother. His oily skin darkened, further stained by the stress of feeling, acutely, the poignant aggravation of being unchosen, his jacketed eyes became crevasses for seeing. He was blind, not literally sightless, as an actual sightless man here once exhorted was the correct language, his guide dog by his side, his bravado a daily comfort and whip to me, but like him the demanding man never saw what was in front of him, as his sense of himself demanded another picture or scene, one in alignment with the elevated treatment and position his mother had given him the right to expect, so the demanding man reminded me not only of the sightless man with the seeing-eye dog he treated better than a lover, but another who was faraway, out of sight for years, dead to me though not literally dead, with whom I had sat, on other occasions, and to whose stories I was attuned as to a radio whose frequency I alone heard. He had been severely nearsighted, with a tendency to squint even when it wasn't sunny, an effect or affectation that painted his face with the gravity and concentration it otherwise lacked, since he was perennially, genetically boyish, even with gray skin that erupted in rosy florets and brown, puffy circles under his jet-black eyes. He needed to be regarded as serious, he taught 19th century European history, and he wanted to have been born at an earlier time—the Enlightenment—because he believed he knew how people thought and felt then, a mistaken notion much loved by people who can't stomach their present and whose fantasies of the past won't indict them, never make them accountable, or guilty. He was phlegmatic, relatively thick-skinned but he bruised easily, since he suffered from a blood deficiency, and often there were purple welts on his legs and arms, which, though I knew he was susceptible to bruising, shocked me, since violence appeared to have been done to his body. In some ways he longed to be physically hurt or in pain, since he never felt alive, a feeling I understood when I listened to him. Other things, like his sly treacheries and useless manipulations, I didn't perceive. The demanding man lacks perceptiveness, for he expects and wants our attention, but paradoxically, fearing he won't get it, he installs his computer on the breakfast table, in front of his plate, partially obscuring his face as he sends and receives messages or watches news on it. All the while he is waiting and hoping for attention from us, who, seeing him behind his computer, are even less likely to show it; but still he waits for the moment when he might narrate the events of his beleaguered life.

I hope, after breakfast, to leave the dining room quickly, even invisibly, regularly planning my getaway, deliberating when is the right time, though the right time for me isn't for another resident, and sometimes I have become invisible, on occasions when it appeared risky to be present, for a number of reasons, not only because of the arrival of police, although that has occurred, the police have arrived and I have vanished, brushing past them as if I were a spirit, but I don't yet have a criminal record. I leave fast especially if there is peace and contentment, when nothing aberrant has happened, believing superstitiously that malingering might provoke the furies, or I leave fast if the conversation has upset or altered my mood, affected my humor, especially in a direction I didn't want it changed, though I anticipate alteration around people, which is why I malinger in bed, switching on and off the radio, not sanguine about being subjected to what is uncontrollable, which may be the reason some claim the table's attention and don't allow others to speak, since any control might protect them. If in a discussion about history or politics, the residents parrot TV and radio commentators, or an argument ensues that is older than its speakers and as intransigent, I'm disheartened or discouraged, and all at the table might leave it disgruntled, whether they ate cereal, eggs, or blueberry pancakes. If a newcomer who, just the night before, told a beguiling tale that entranced me, but then the stranger proclaims a dim conviction at breakfast, what he or she said previously is revamped by this dimness and I lose interest. If I have recently enjoyed a stranger's tales, because the narration was vivid, delivered with an awareness of its listeners, though the stranger may have told the story many times before, I can prefer that person's company to that of longstanding friends, since I am curious about how people live and why, and, in some respects, I'm a xenophile, but in order for my love of a stranger to sustain itself, strangeness must be sustained, and the foreign body mustn't reveal too much. I want the stranger to remain untouched, which contradicts my other desire to know more than I should, yet some things I never want to know, fearing disillusionment, while a friend, someone I have known for a long time or who knows me, may be excused or rather understood for the same opinion. This is unfair, but that doesn't matter, because to achieve fairness requires work, equanimity requires effort, a position comes from a sense of place, and if you lose yours, you also can't maintain a position and continue to believe in it, you can't be fair. I don't want to exert myself, especially in the mornings, which is usually why I don't want to go to breakfast, except that I'm hungry. More and more, I want the freedom to be arbitrary.

After a discussion in which righteousness of every stripe has been broadcast, during which, against my better judgment, I might voice my own, I might dejectedly return to my bedroom, whose bed has already been made by a housekeeper, who has also placed my nightgown on the pillow, folded just so, fluffed the three pillows to their fullest, screwed on the tops of plastic bottles, and stacked the books and drawing pads

I threw by the side of my bed into a neat pile, and then, entering the room, which is now without some of my traces, I immediately lie on the neatened bed, with hospital corners that invariably and nauseatingly remind me of camp, the gray bunk, and the six other little faceless girls. Again my head is a mob of arguments, a clutter of loose phrases and ill-conceived ideas, so then my skin starts to burn, and I know that the small veins on my nose and chin have become irritated by the exchanges to which I was subjected and engaged in, to my regret. On some mornings, the residents' table talk ropes me insidiously to my plain wooden chair, simply because I hope that something might happen that affects, in a positive direction, the course of the conversation so that I won't leave it disgruntled, but this rarely happens, since the longer I stay the worse it is, and then I flee, feeling worse than I might have had I not hoped for something better. Hope is necessary, but it is the cause of many dilemmas, and sometimes my day is ruined, its promise assassinated, and then I wish I were in any other place, or alone, or with any other persons, especially the Polish woman, who is an efficacious stranger, whose deft strokes on my forehead might remove more than dead skin, though I know that isn't likely. My organs won't be healed of a mysterious ailment that thrives undetected, but the alleviation of worry, the elimination of dead skin from the body, has a placebo effect, the truth of which can disconcert some. Placebos often help as much as medicines, and to some it begs credulity that the mind can affect the course of an illness or cure the body of physical suffering, but it can, since the mind is part of the body, or the mind is also the body, and mental illness is also physical illness and vice versa. The actions the Polish woman performs on my face, or the massages she gives me, calm me, her indifferent strokes placate me, and sometimes I imagine her powerful hands and arms kneading away the impurities that threaten to overwhelm my system, and in its anonymity having a facial restores me to myself and contradictorily encourages a sense of dissolution into a larger humanity, since all have faces that could be steamed and cleaned, if they had the desire, inclination, or money, though even if they could afford it, some might not want a facial, thinking it wasteful and without redeeming value. I could defend a facial's worth, were I forced, and if I were tortured, I would tell everything I knew.

What I'll never know is significant, but some of the people who could have given me answers are gone, and some who are here, to whom I speak or listen regularly, wouldn't know, since what I want to know might not have definite answers, or I might not have the way or wherewithal, even the words, to form the necessary and appropriate questions. I'm a recorder and collector, a listmaker, I studied history, philosophy, literature, and have taught American history, but dissuaded from the academic life after receiving a Ph.D., or unsuited for its piquant rigors, even though well equipped to be an historian, since I could hear or read something and remember it, I subsequently trained as an object-maker and designer, while haphazardly pursuing odd jobs. I also wait, in the sense that a young man here, when asked what he did, responded, "I'm a waiter," and, when asked, "But where do you work?" the young man said, "I'm just waiting." I am waiting, not just for a letter or telephone call, but for that which has so far escaped me or might come unexpectedly, I can easily wait for mail to arrive, especially here, and waiting for it, even with the advent of cyber deliveries, can be a meaningful part of my day, as can waiting itself.

Sometime ago, months and months I believe, though time is unimportant here, and seemingly grows more insignificant every day, when I hadn't been expecting anything specific, but had the gnawing sense that something must happen to me soon, and should, even an accident, because otherwise life would be the same, and I seek change or create a situation that might effect it, a postcard arrived. It was typed on an old-fashioned typewriter and induced a blurry recognition, similar to confusion between a memory and a story about the past. Its signature looked scrambled or scribbled, even scratched, and I'd seen the handwriting before, I thought, or knew the hand, but also in this guise or context didn't know how I knew it or from where or when. On the front, there was a jumbo jet plane flying in a blue sky and on its back the sender had typed: "Out of here, going here and there. But where? Where are you? Miss you." Then the scratchy signature. The stamp was franked in Omaha. I was pleased it had arrived and spent an hour, more or less, on it. I don't wear a watch, which bothers some of the residents here, who are concerned with time as I am, though less concerned than people in more ordinary or less-privileged situations, who suffer from the stress of regular schedules, but I was trying to figure out what the jet plane postcard portended. The beginning of worry sounded inside me during that hour, and my skin crawled, but then I worked to subdue myself by various methods, including a mug of herbal tea and slow, deep breathing. Some people's skin crawls incessantly, they suffer from vermiculations, or the sensation of skin crawling, and there are also various neuralgias, or nerve irritations, in which the skin burns and is accompanied by inflammation, which is painful, since often it is inflammation, when white blood cells flood an area of the body, that causes distress and pain; peripheral neuritis is the sensation of damage to a peripheral limb, one that is gone, like an amputated leg, which still produces sensation, but it is in a way a feeling of loss, since the body, or the mind's body, remembers what is no longer there. But soon I looked out at the field, where there were no deer but some small birds, and decided not to think further or badly about the postcard, not to imagine the worst, to assure myself it was harmless and probably nothing, since nothing had occurred, and it was probably meaningless. It might be an omen, which would be a kind of vanity, but better that than futility or meaninglessness, since at the least the postcard addressed to me meant someone was thinking of me in a curious, unusual manner, someone I wasn't thinking of before, but would now, and so I was joined to him, or maybe her, and enmeshed in his travels, though he was distant and anonymous to me, but the intimacy was intriguing, it was intimate, it came close to me, when so little does or is intimate, yet everyone here talks about intimacy, which finally disgusts me, and I must go to bed. The postcard incited my imagination and had brought surprise to my routine and habit of mind, for which I was grateful, since I like surprise and abjure routine.

I like to believe I enjoy surprises, that I'm someone to whom an eruption of the unusual should be usual, or who branches out to advance the implausible. I might fly a jet, become a man, walk backward without a care, threaten like a stalker, speak my mind freely at all times, swim the Atlantic on a greasy back, be silent for months like a Carthusian, have absolute faith, research the first humans and how they knew food from poison and learn their early, even fatal mistakes. The first people, Bushmen, ate raw food that must have carried inedible matter as well as microbes, but then there was the discovery of fire, and cooked meat and maybe grasses, but I might find out when bread made its first appearance and how; I once read a book about pizza, flat bread with cheese is ancient in origin. It is difficult to comprehend a world without the discoveries that are commonplace, but I'd like to. More, I'd like especially to research failure, the dustbin of human effort, upon which our world is also based. Sometimes images and sensational ideas come to me in torrents, but they may actually be worthless or insubstantial, or answers arrive to questions, or some thoughts arrive with remarkable clarity, but they may not be what I need, or they may be parts of wholes and not capable of conclusion, like a scientific experiment just before it's completed. A friend had a stroke, and he could barely form words, his brain a frustration to him when it was ordinarily a boon, giving him ease in speaking effortlessly and precisely, but he was now without words, and felt deficient, so his skin erupted in a red sea. He pointed to a wastepaper basket of basic design but ugly material, wanting me to toss trash into it, and said, with great effort, "Throw it into the waiting for forgetfulness." His ability to read was never affected, and language returned to him, but his naming a wastepaper basket "waiting for forgetfulness" was, with his recovery, lost to him. He has lived in the same house for years, not far from where I first ate Indian food, which I instantly liked, whose spices and smells were new to me then, as was the man I first ate it with, whom I fell in love with for a short time, but Indian food is no longer new, though I still appreciate its tastes and smells, and that friend's house is also near the beauty salon where I first had my legs waxed. The salon's chairs mocked 18th century French design, and its walls were flecked with gold, to invoke that other, supposedly golden era, one of abundance and elegance for a relatively few people, while its beauticians, in street clothes of varying, inconsistent style, provided ordinary care and treatment, haircuts and dye-jobs, as well as leg, arm, and lip waxes, sometimes roughly given, on the worn scarlet silk chairs, and a client such as myself, uncomfortable in this discordant atmosphere, could not relax.

If the colors of the room were blue and green rather than gold and scarlet, I might have relaxed. They are soothing colors, but reds and yellows are exciting, it says in *How to Sleep and Rest Better*, a 1937 manual in the community's small library, whose blue cover attests to its psychologist author's belief that readers can free themselves from the day's worries, with soothing colors, in order to succumb to a blissful unconsciousness. It is important, the manual claims, to calm down in the evening, to prepare for sleep as you would for any other activity, to slow down thinking, forget serious or exciting things, to make the mind blank. The moron, the author says, does not have to make his mind a blank before going to bed since it is blank day and night. Mental patients are given hot baths and hydrotherapy to calm them, but the manual says people should have sufficient control to calm down at will, they should be superior to their environment, but anyway color schemes should be carefully administered, the author says. To relax the body for sleep, the poor sleeper must develop a different mental attitude, to regard sleep as a peaceful sanctuary, when a person sets aside all worries, resentments, and fears, and learns to relax, but a person must be relaxed about learning itself, otherwise the body will become a taut, keyed-up machine. There is something called "progressive relaxation" in which with each successive minute the sleeper relaxes more. Truly beautiful women, the author says, know the secrets of relaxation and beauty naps. I am waiting for forgetfulness.

For years, I shaved my legs, then decided to have them waxed, and now there is barely any hair on them. The woman who first ripped hair from my legs was born in Mexico, and appeared, when I met her, healthy and without problems, while she served me in a spacious salon, where I, along with other women, was catered to adequately and sometimes courteously or lavishly. Every two months I visited the salon, until one day the Mexican woman, whose skin was several shades darker than my own and oily, asked me if I would come instead to her apartment, so she could keep the entire fee, and where, I discovered, she lived with her husband, her son, and her father. Her daughter had left home, and there was enmity between them. Her husband, who'd hurt his back doing factory labor, was usually at home, staring out of the window, a wide, leather belt around his waist and lower back for support. I rarely saw her son, since when I was having my legs waxed, she set me on his bed in his bedroom. But I have my legs waxed now by the Polish woman, who has degrees and certificates in several of the cosmetic arts displayed prominently on the semi-transparent plastic wall of the small room in which she also waxes legs, for which a license is required, and I can't remember all the reasons why I didn't want, after a while, to return to the apartment of the other and first leg waxer, to whom I thought I should have been loyal but wasn't.

The Polish woman has almost no hair on her body, or hardly any that's visible, except for light blond fuzz above her upper lip, so fair as to be negligible, though she might wax her lip and legs weekly, but now little grows back, which is what happens when hair's waxed from the body repeatedly and diligently, it dies, except the most stubborn kind, which on my body is at the outer sides of my ankles, where cold probably most affects or touches it. But it is at my throat and neck that I feel cold most, and I have never had hair there, and the neck is also, next to the nipples, a place that, when kissed, licked, sucked, or, in most ways, touched, arouses me most quickly, and none of these parts, so quick to arousal, have hair on them. I don't remember my nipples ever feeling cold. Hair is of little functional value to people, but hair does alter appearance, its amount, its curl, its thickness, its fineness, and hair products for men and women multiply dizzyingly on drugstore shelves. Male-pattern baldness, though, is especially curious, since it's common to some extent to all men, even those who live in extremely cold climates, where it would seem necessary for protection. But human hair must be primarily for sexual attraction, and only second to indicate illness, since hair loss in men and loss and hirsutism in women are controlled by the steroid sex hormones; an abnormal appearance may also be a symptom of diseases produced by vitamin deficiencies—protein starvation, inadequate iron, or reactions to cytotoxic drugs, for instance, those used in chemotherapy. The Polish woman probably waxes her underarms, which sickens me, since waxing in tender areas, like the upper, inner thigh near the pubis, is painful, but the underarm must be worse, yet the Polish woman does it, as do many other women whose bodies I've noticed at the beach, where men and women, driven by hormones, desire, and social mores, cluster and expose themselves to the dangerous rays of the sun and to each other; women also, in changing rooms in stores, undress, and the exposed underarm, though hairless, is somewhat darker in hue than the rest of the skin of the body, as if indelibly stained or dyed.

The woman who first waxed my legs had much more hair on her body than the Polish woman, though she also waxed often, but still the pores on her arms and legs, even her upper lip, were bigger and from them short black hairs, stubble, sprang vigorously from her oily, olive flesh. Regular shaving incites a hair follicle in its determination to thrive, so because I started the practice before I should have, the way my friends did, and I might need to wear stockings, tougher hair raised itself immediately through the pores of my sensitive skin, making my legs rough to the touch and irritants to each other. Soon rashes colored the areas around the short hairs, livid pink circles, and also some of the hairs turned inward, with small bubbles of flesh forming over them, in which the hair continued to grow and which, like a pimple, had to be squeezed, to release the fugitive hair follicle. Folliculitis is the inflammation of the hair follicle, and, as a girl, I enjoyed the outbreak of one or two. Hair is sometimes used to make art objects, woven into cloth, or braided into bracelets, and in 19th century America it was common to keep locks of hair of loved ones, dead and alive, when women also wore hair lockets that hung from a velvet ribbon about the neck. I found some hairs from my dead father's comb, but I don't remember where I put them, they were very few, not an ample, coiled lock that might have represented him, but only a sample of his DNA, predictive threads, the body's oracle.

It's easy to imagine the pain of having your underarms waxed, but I can't imagine and never want to, because it would be very much worse, being a captive, hooded and locked in a hot or cold room, since suffocation is terrible, and asthmatics must understand the experience of being hooded without wearing a hood, or people with chronic eczema, who are imprisoned in their skins, condemned to scratching their itchy flesh until it bleeds, requiring some to be strapped down and disenabled from clawing the disturbed flesh off their bodies. Photographs of hooded prisoners cause me to gag; I immediately experience a loss of oxygen and inhibition of movement in horrible empathy, which is another reason I don't read the newspaper, the way the young married man does, at breakfast, but wait until a more appropriate time, not accompanied by food, just as when I read *Naked Lunch*, whose characters inhabited airless hovels and sought veins into which they could inject themselves, their blood squirting onto walls or dirty sheets. William Burroughs must have been transfixed by injecting himself, by the act of fixing itself, by the blood of his own body and others, so I needed to be selective about the novel's place in my day. Burroughs loved cats and Colette, too, she was one of his favorite writers, and to her the cat was a talisman and companion, but I don't imagine Colette or Burroughs wore images of animals on their shirts or coats, though they might have been tempted to buy a souvenir of an adorable cat, as I have been but didn't, aware that it portends a slide into a vat of sentimentality. Colette was photographed with her cat and her dog, she loved cats and dogs but not her daughter, and she didn't go to her mother's funeral, though she wrote about her mother, Sido, as if she would have thrown herself onto her coffin during the funeral and buried herself, too. Burroughs was afraid to die, like my father but not my mother. Some say it's simpler to love cats or dogs than mothers, or it can be more rewarding.

My young cat came from a vacant lot in a city and may not have known his mother long or at all, but at four months old he was rescued by animal-lovers, who devote much of their lives to abandoned animals, whom human beings sometimes have kept for a time and then left on streets or in parks, because they no longer want them, the way their parents may not have wanted them, but couldn't as easily throw them out onto the cold street, and then they say, after they've abandoned the pet, I couldn't keep the dog anymore, it squealed at night, pissed on the floor, or the cat clawed my furniture, and in the dark of night, they leave helpless, domesticated creatures under a car or near a park and flee to the safety of their complacent homes. It's not surprising that my cat fears the touch of human beings, since he may have been abandoned by one, or because, early in his life, at two weeks or three, he wasn't petted by one, in addition to his mother's absence, and he spent his first four months alone, scavenging for food and warmth. When I went to the animal shelter, located in a pet store, to select the cat who might be right for me, I had in mind a gentle, smart cat, about four months old, who was alert and relaxed with people. Immediately I saw my cat, the one who would become mine that very day, and I put him on my lap, where he sat calmly, and, I decided, he likes people and he's gentle, then to test his intelligence and alertness, I carried him to a nearby fishtank, where he avidly stared at the brightly colored fish swimming back and forth in the large tank, and, I thought, he's alert, then signed the adoption papers, promising never to have him declawed and that I'd return him to this shelter rather than ever abandon him. One of the cat people or rescuers escorted us to my home, so that she could see for herself I wasn't running a laboratory that experimented on cats or didn't have many badly treated cats trapped in foul-smelling cages. Once home, my smart, gentle cat saw a litter box, which was empty of litter, and immediately pissed in it, confirming his intelligence. Three days later he could barely lift his head, and the vet diagnosed distemper, saying, he might not make it, he has a fifty-fifty chance, but he survived.

The Polish woman is hearty, her lungs thrum inside her body, her ample breasts quiver as she waxes my legs, and she has told me that she loves being outdoors, in densely shaded forests or hiking on mountains, but I don't know if it's because she fears caves and places where she might not get enough air, as I do, or if the simple pleasure of walking up a mountain or through a forest, where small animals might be hiding or larger ones, so there is always some danger and consequently excitement, though I don't imagine she's a thrillseeker, or the challenge of scaling the side of a mountain, calls to her and makes her feel vital. People want to know they are alive. Hair is dead cells or skin, like nails, there at birth, usually, though some infants arrive in the world with very little of it, and there is barely any hair on my legs now, so it takes the Polish woman no time to rip off what's grown in, like the persistent and small cluster at my outer ankles, and when I am hairless, I sometimes remember that people mourn even the loss of what was once annoying or uncontrollable to them about or on their bodies. Women mourn the loss of painful menstruations, which made their bodies ache, imprisoned them in their bedrooms, lying on their sides holding their knees to their bellies in the fetal position for days until the pain had passed, and men mourn a loss of potency, when potency led them to insert their penises into almost any orifice, vagina or rectum, available, and sometimes produced unwanted pregnancies or hemorrhoids, yeast infections in women and STDs, and other infections and diseases in men. Being waxed is almost painless now, except when I have a bikini wax in the summer, when I might wear a bathing suit, but usually don't, and then, even though there isn't much hair growing from the mons Veneris onto the inner thigh, it hurts, and the Polish woman's hands are closer to my genitals than any friend, except a lover, who may or may not be a friend, ever is, but this intimacy in the small cramped space is never remarked upon.

At dinner one night, the youngest resident, Lois, an enthusiast, who'd had several drinks, though some of us never do, she always did, her face never flushing, explained the Brazilian wax method, in which the hair at the crack of the buttocks is removed, and she'd heard about a woman in Brazil who, while she underwent this procedure, as the hair was ripped from the split between her buttocks, lay on her stomach and moaned loudly, became wet, her skin hot, then returned for the treatment frequently, experiencing arousal and climaxing each time, until the beautician refused to service her. The youngest resident who talked about the Brazilian wax method, whose reason for being here is a secret, an American born of Latin American parents, was bright with a ready laugh, and often related stories I listened to with pleasure, especially her sexual adventures, of which she had an explosive store, since, except for the tall balding man, who, I learned, was an electronic composer, who scores for computer, and, for money, worked as a programmer, and the woman with psoriasis, no one seemed to be having sex with anyone else but themselves. Nobody but the youngest female resident, Lois, I called her Spike, whose hair was long and brilliantly red, mentioned masturbation. It was, like a fart, something much adored by the person doing it in private, who was embarrassed to admit liking it, since, as a sex manual and dictionary from 1958 defines it, masturbation is "sex-abuse, the manipulation of the sexual organs until sexual satisfaction is experienced. At one time considered the cause of innumerable diseases, such as: consumption, idiocy, insanity, cancer, locomotor ataxia. Now regarded merely as a bad practice, because it is apt to become habitual, in which case it can become very injurious, whereas occasional indulgence is not. Many of the evil effects are due not to the indulgence in masturbation itself, but to the fear that it will have evil results. Also called Autoeroticism and Ipsation. In European literature this practice is wrongly referred to as Onanism," whose correct meaning, according to the manual, "is coitus interruptus and nothing else." About this difference the manual is adamant. 1958 is not long ago, it is recent history. Contesa, gentle-faced, but attentive as a cat hunting prey, its tail quivering, said once, after a swallow of red wine, "For some it's masturbate and wait, masturbate and wait." Most at the table laughed or smiled, especially J and JJ, former actors, women who have lived together for years, and like to rehearse past scenes, I'm told, naked, and also their informal male sidekick, a square-jawed Midwesterner, whose quiet, downbeat style doesn't dampen the rumor that he did something very awful once, unspeakable even, which necessitates his guilt-ridden silence. He is a lyricist, whatever else he is or was, and rarely bothers me, though his sycophancy can be cloying, but I once heard him say, "I don't feel secure right now, I'm just going to keep my eyes open, mind my Ps and Qs," so his dependency made sense and again he never bothers me. But the demanding man flinched with annoyance, his skin darkened and reddened, and all who paid attention recognized him as what a quaint Englishman once called a secret masturbator.

Residents can borrow books such as the sleep and sex manuals from the library, which has four rooms on as many floors, each furnished with dark wood furniture, several benches that are functional and unattractive as well as institutional, uncomfortable chairs, because the decor is meant to encourage seriousness, studiousness, or contemplation, though in one room there is a piano and two lutes; in the others, reference books like the sex manual, outdated, in the future to be replaced by newer ones whose information and definitions, which are just explanations and interpretations, will also turn outdated, and these ponderously line the shelves of the four rooms. I'm drawn to manuals and reference books, which sate my ravenous curiosity and often lead me away from what I should be doing, the way some others are, so with these residents I may trade citations at dinner, and I prefer to read these books like stories whose repetitive tellings shape the world. To be distracted from worry and hurt, or entertained, when I'm alone and the peace and blight of night eliminates what I like as well as what I don't like seeing during the day, I read in bed, keeping the pages of books free of stains, especially the old, borrowed ones, but some marks come anyway with time, like foxing, small brown stains, and wormholes, which are caused by worms, actual bookworms, that subsist on paper. Some damage appears almost miraculously, though I don't believe in miracles. I have known people who do, spiritual people, people who believe in God, along with their own and other peoples' goodness, and who depress me, like the Polish woman who gives me facials. She is religious and goes to church on Sundays with her girlfriends, or mother, possessing guilty secrets, sinful thoughts, about the glowering man who waited impatiently for her when I was there, hearing his restless movements just outside the dingy room in which I was being tended carefully, though I don't know what was on her mind as she steamed my pores. She will never tell me what is on her mind, and I don't want to know, since I don't want to listen to her when I am being attended to and cared for like a baby, just as I wouldn't tell her what I was thinking, observing an unwritten code that allows us to be at ease with each other in a regular, but intimate situation in her cramped place of work.

Each time I visit it, I wonder if her life will have changed significantly, and if she will ever be happy, because she never seems happy, though she has a lovely smile. She usually appears to be sullen, or even sad, or just reticent or expressionless, though she might simply be stupid and dull, the way I think one of the two young women is, dull, mostly, though days ago, I watched her lusterless eyes quicken, sparkle, when the tall balding man spoke to her, yet I didn't guess at their involvement then, just her desire, which had arced from her like a rainbow. He had arrived some weeks ago, the tall balding man, virile, though his posture was poor, and his comments were usually cryptic, I discovered and liked, and he stooped over still more to talk with her. My father stressed posture, and this man sagged, his head hung, he was slackjaw, and yet the young woman responded gaily, ignorant of how the world bore down on him, though demonstrably it burdened his lanky frame, since he couldn't keep himself upright. It is hard for me to look at people with terrible posture, since my father, who held to a high standard for Homo Erectus, impressed its importance on me and held his frame up, defying his depressions, and I can't much contemplate or converse long with a person whose shoulders slouch severely, whose skeleton is skewed, or whose head juts far forward, since misshapen and rounded shoulders look full of pain, which is unspoken, and could indicate rough, early treatment, insufficient care, or inadequate childhood exercise. Bad posture can also indicate an inner disturbance so fundamental it forms the basis of the skeleton, the curved and twisted bones declaring a person's initial and formative inability to meet the world, instead withdrawing from it, bending under the burden, and some retreat into their carapace, one they might want later to shed. The skin registers the inner world on the exterior, as the world external to it marks it as well. There is also the deleterious effect of badly designed chairs on a young, growing body.

I want to take apart an Eames chair, especially this morning, I believe I dreamed of it, I have taken apart other chairs, though none as beloved or significant, for about these chairs there is no disagreement, and I have split apart boxes, mattresses, TVs, and a corroded car that sat in a field, but I don't have an Eames chair here, just its memory as well as photographs of it and its designers, the Eameses, husband and wife. It's satisfying not to make things, to undo them, the way experiences can't be, since undoing is an activity like doing, or I think it is, and thinking is an activity like riding a horse without a horse, and it's especially pleasing to engage with and analyze the undone object, since after destroying something inert I can see its construction, even its larger design in my life. When I took apart a square box, I thought of the satisfaction I had learning geometry, the simplicity that resided in planes and angles, as well as of the geometric character of a family of four, how from each corner a mother, father, daughter, son must relate, each in and with a corner, and that any balance was necessarily of two and two, which was why my parents must have wanted another child, for balance, but they delayed too long, so when I arrived I unbalanced my brother's corner, he had lived in a triangle, which has its own balance, and then he fell from his pinnacle or place, never to forgive me or them. Taking apart a TV, I thought about impulses and connections, its delicately colored wires like nerve endings, and when the guts of the TV were scattered on my floor, life itself seemed disconnected. Invention is a human necessity, and lasting value has nothing to do with it, since everything is temporary. For a while now, I have found it hard to make things, when once I wanted to fabricate what I hadn't seen before—before trying that, though, I had to overcome a phobia to three-dimensional objects—and once I did, I could easily build them, but then I also overcame my need to build what wasn't there and wanted only to unbuild what was. Now I rarely want to do even this, except in thinking, where I test spatial relations and imagine space bounded and unbounded, and happily move non-things about in unreal places.

When I was first here, no chair gave me what I wanted, and I tried many, though ostensibly I just wanted a chair that could support my frame, so that I could forget about it, as I ruminated, awash in thoughts I wished I weren't having, or in some that I wanted to have, roaming into places where a chair and its design had no function, since I also wanted a chair to do more than it was designed for. The chair designer Harry Bertoia said, "The urge for good design is the same as the urge to go on living. The assumption is that somewhere, hidden, is a better way of doing things," and that's sensible, or in my life it is, because I'm looking for a chair that fits me and in which I can feel at home, since homeyness is easier to locate in things than in people, or even in animals, but I like cats, dogs, and chairs almost equally, though I have more control over chairs, which are inanimate, but any cat or dog is in some way pleasing, while most chairs aren't.

When he was first here, the tall balding man gave his attention to the Count as well as to the disconsolate or sad-eyed young woman, divining in her some pleasing quality or grace no one else did, except the other disconsolate woman. Early on I observed an acute scene between them, the man of no consequence to me or the woman, when he held her skinny, psoriatic hand to his face, brushed her palm against his sunken cheek, and then uttered some words I couldn't hear, but their thin-lipped exchange held some fascination. Thin lips are scant protection, a mere lining to the crater in the face, that worthy hole, but my lips are full, suggesting a lushness I don't believe I deliver, just as big breasts incriminate the female body with lusty abundance and comfort. My mother told me to be happy if my breasts were small—and I'm rather flat on the chest, full in the face, tall for a woman, lean everywhere, something like an aging boy—because when I was old, like these women, my breasts wouldn't drop to my waist. I was four when I gazed rapt at a cluster of old women, their pendulous breasts touching their waists, while my mother and I sat on a bench in a Turkish bath near the ocean I loved in a beach club I also loved for a time.

It would be a miracle if, in two or three months, the Polish woman changed demonstrably, because people don't often change, and, if they do, it's in small ways, unless they've undergone a trauma, watched an accident when they were old enough to remember but not comprehend; no one will ever entirely comprehend specific events or irrational acts that forever remain outside human comprehension, though human beings committed them, or witnessed their father murder their mother or their sister or brother die, unable to help, in a fall, or saw a house burn infernally to the ground, hearing terrible screams inside. My father told me that men never change, that women should never expect to change men, though they do, and that my mother was angry because she could never change him, or that is what I surmised, because he didn't say that was why my mother was angry; he said, Never expect to change a man, don't be the omnipotent female, your mother always tried to change me, but she couldn't. I wouldn't think that was entirely true, anyway, that was why she was angry, I don't know all the reasons why my mother was angry: her older sister was prettier; she was a middle child, forgotten; her father was in the Austrian army and he kept his treasures in a small box and she never saw them; she didn't ever have a birthday party as a child; and her husband, my father, was a vain, lively, sometimes cold man, whom everyone liked better than her. But she is not angry now. My mother is old, her brain is damaged from a condition whose cause is unknown for which she has had seven operations, or procedures, and though she is remarkably strong, resilient, capable of falling and not breaking a bone, her mind and body slowly deteriorate. She takes a variety of medicines, to which she has never been opposed, though like many people her age and younger, she is distrustful of pills, but unlike many, she favors doctors, especially if they are men with whom she can flirt. She should've been a medical doctor, it might have brought her the contentment that my father couldn't; she diagnoses herself and others freely and well, noticing symptoms early and astutely, calling them by their medical names, never flummoxed by the onset of a physical problem and ever practical about it, interested clinically, and calm, when about most other things she is not.

The disconsolate young woman, often listless and withdrawn, fearful of exposure, hiding more than her anorexia, a flamboyant symptom, is careful and circumspect, but she and the tall balding man have been flirting ever since he arrived. The staff discourages such behavior but it is not forbidden, while the staff may not become romantically engaged or fornicate with residents, though it's happened once or twice I'm told. The tall man, a formidable systems analyst, is a striking if severe figure, and his baldness is only male pattern baldness, often he wears a baseball cap to cover it; but on some days he takes it off and displays his scalp. It is not Alopecia areata, which, in the male, shows itself in the late twenties or early thirties, and is characterized by a rapid, complete loss of hair, first in patches, usually on the scalp, the bearded area, then the eyebrows and eyelashes, and, rarely, the other hairy areas of the body. With some, there is a total loss of scalp hair, which is called Alopecia totalis. When it's lost over the whole body, it's Alopecia universalis. It was first described twenty centuries ago by Celsus, but its cause is still unknown, though emotional stress is most frequently mentioned. But even impacted wisdom teeth might have an effect. My dermatologist explained that it could have been incurred first by trichotillomania, a psychiatric disorder which shows itself mostly in children, when the parent might notice sizable, persistently bald patches on the scalp, or in the female adolescent, when she plucks her hair, strand by strand, and that could incite Alopecia, but generally it's not the case. The appearance of the neurosis, trichotillomania and also trichokyptomania, in which hairs are broken off instead of torn out, has increased since the advent of TV, he said, about which interpretation I wanted to ask more, but he's a busy man. There is usually a characteristic mother-daughter relationship disturbance, with various borderline psychoses, and many sufferers require psychiatric help. But the tall man's is only male pattern baldness, and few residents have noticed the two, except Contesa and myself, though neither of us expected a serious involvement, which was, in a sense, manifested this morning, but we'd observed that the two watched each other for signs of interest and flirted harmlessly, which is often how brief libidinal investments are characterized. The young woman may believe she can change, even transform, him, so that his poor shoulders straighten and that she might rest her head on them, or that she will lift his spirits in other ways, compel him to shed his carapace and grow a new one. I see them mostly at a distance, though sometimes I have moved nearer, to hear what they say. He fences, a parry and thrust dialogist, while she picks words slowly, as she does food, pushing most aside, hoping to hit upon the best one, to please her sense of truth or her companion's sensibility.

—The worst thing is it's not over yet—we're not safe, the disconsolate woman says haltingly.

—Safety's everyone's Maginot Line, the tall balding man teases.

—What's the marginal line? she asks.

The disconsolate woman tenses, reddens.

—Mag-i-not. Maginot Line. In World War I, the French expected the German army couldn't attack across its border. Couldn't penetrate it, but they did. Voilà.

—There's no safety then, she says.

—Here?

Here, strangers are thrust together, intimately, eating two meals together, whose intake betrays them, and, as I eavesdrop on their conversations at breakfast, still drowsy and inside a dream, like one about Saint Bartholomew, of whom I knew nothing, preaching inside a Gothic church, until I looked up his name, which turned out to be my father's in Hebrew, I am wary that my day might get off to a bad start and proceed badly, so I try to be careful about what I swallow and absorb. Living with unfamiliar persons who will never be more than relative strangers, whom I awaken at night by going to the bathroom and flushing the toilet, since I usually get up twice in the night, I can have fitful dreams. I have dreamed of tiny mice, who, though adorable, are nuisances and must be destroyed, I have watched them die slowly and in agony on glue traps, which I chose rather than traps that beheaded them, because I thought it more humane, but when I watched the mouse squirm with pain, I realized it wasn't, or, if Contesa has again spoken of Kafka and Felice and showed me their pictures not long before I go to bed, I dream about them, who are strangers to me, as is Contesa, relatively. She believes she knows Kafka, especially through his letters to Felice, though she can't know Felice that way, her letters to Kafka aren't extant, but still it is by her faith in their intellectual and spiritual connection that they invade my unconscious world. Felice's pleasant, homely face was oily and dry in patches, even scaly, and around her nostrils an irritated aureole of pimples the size of pinpricks. She broke out in welts, red hives on her back and thighs, just as she was about to meet Kafka, who looked like the tall balding man, but was wearing a frayed black business suit. Felice, like the disconsolate woman, but much stouter, stood at the door to the café discreetly rubbing her thigh. Suddenly she was terribly skinny, suddenly, and her digestion was poor, so there was a terrible smell coming from her mouth, like the breath of the demanding man, she wasn't a vegetarian like Kafka, and horrified she ran away and fell down. She tore the skin on her leg, and the ragged wound bled furiously, so in my dream I became dizzy and nauseated. Her skin inadequately protected her, it now flaked like snow on her cheeks, as dry as mine. But skin is the agent of the body that protects its other organs, by covering them, and by being an information station that allows the other organs, my doctor explained patiently, to adjust to changes in the outer environment. My condition, dermatographia or dermatographism, skin writing, is not life-threatening, but because of it my skin tingles, pulses, and itches, and if I were to stroke my arm with a fingernail, white lines would surface and be visible for at least fifteen minutes, as my skin releases histamines, which produce swelling, and this occurs in about ten percent of the population, but the swelling is not a hive, since in dermatographia only raised lines surface, which resemble writing on the skin. My dermatologist says friends could leave messages on my back, but they'd fade quickly. The skin is a barrier against dehydration; it can lower body temperature by the increased evaporation of sweat; it synthesizes keratin, a flexible, durable, and resistant protein. Keratin is available in some shampoos, but it is likely not helpful, since my dermatologist has often remarked that expensive skin products do little or nothing, that people, women especially but also men, are fooled regularly, though now there is surgery to correct the aging body that produces quick, sometimes disastrous results. If even the skin fails, then much worse can be expected to follow. The skin reveals and encloses, too, its failings are revelatory, failure is more revelatory than success. Contesa believes that Kafka despaired and reveled in writing's failures, its fundamental inadequacy to the experience of life, that he was stern with himself but failure for him was expected, since it was true and exigent. In my dream of a severe Berlin winter, even the skin around Felice's fingernails cracked and bled. I believe Contesa is writing something, but she doesn't talk about it, and here silence and circumspection are honored, when in the outside world, they usually aren't, since people want to find out what may help or harm them.

Months ago, when the second or assistant cook arrived, she was in the kitchen and around the dining room first at breakfast, then at dinner, when she had met the standards set by the head cook, and, instantly, she reminded me of Leslie Van Houten, because her hands were unsightly, she was a nailbiter, and though she was clean and scrubbed, a reluctance or remorse in her stained her solid body and made it unsightly, and, though armored, or because, she had an almost palpable vulnerability. I couldn't imagine her life outside these walls. I liked but nearly pitied her, though pity's a disgraceful emotion, for, though younger than the head cook, she waded in a shallow trough of regret where she was stuck, exposed and raw, and couldn't crawl out, like the animals trapped in the swamp less than six feet under my family's lawn. During the winter, when the ground was frozen, when the wind whipped my face and seemed to penetrate places it shouldn't have, my father drove me to the ocean, whose waves were dark without the sun to lighten their mood. Without sun to warm the sand, I didn't run barefoot or stroll at the edge of the ocean, the border to the safety of my world. I thought then my father didn't love my mother, but that she loved him and dressed well for his approval, except when she stayed at home doing housework, which she hated, but she always dressed in good materials, silk, cashmere, fine wools; I can't remember if the fabrics were usually his. She applied the same brand of real red lipstick to her lips for years from a golden tube kept in the bathroom of the house I loved but which was sold against my protests, along with other precious objects, like the Eames chairs and table, or thrown out, like my childhood relics, mercilessly, or she carried it in her pocketbook when she and my father went out to dinner or the theater and opera, where my father might fall asleep. My mother's devotion to one lipstick brand and color, like my father's to his gray Buick, signaled a consistency or even a character to them, I thought when I was young, and even though I often hated both of them, especially my mother, I admired their capacity for devotion. But it wasn't the case, I realized, for to other things, more important ones, my parents weren't devoted, like our cat and my dog.

Our family cat, who was the uxorious companion my father wasn't, who followed my mother when she shopped or visited neighbors, walking by her side like a dog, also regularly followed my mother into the bathroom and watched her apply her red lipstick. The cat once stayed behind after my mother, who had neglected to close the lipstick tube, left it on the sink, and later the cat emerged, her lips and mouth as red as my mother's, and it was this cat my mother and father abandoned to a shelter, to be killed, and it may have been then my brother abandoned us, I'm not sure, since coincidence plays a role in memory, contorts it or condenses events, mostly in the rememberer's favor, as memory has the subject's limits, and we forget much more than we remember, with little or no control over it, though its insistence at having happened can determine our fates, that is, how we speak about the past and consequently live in the present, but he did run away around then, I'm pretty sure, for which my father condemned him, since my brother might have saved the business. Now, when my mother talks in her sleep, and I sometimes stand at the foot of her bed, with her devoted cat whom she rarely pets beside her, she addresses her dead husband and tells him, "I have a cat, and you should see how adorable she is, she plays with me, and puts her paw on my face and then I stroke hers like silk."

Silk was discovered in the 13th century. Silkworms feed on mulberry bushes, seeds of which were smuggled in the socks of Buddhist monks who carried them to the West. The soft wool of the angora goat made a fabric called camlet, and it was imported into England from the Near East; earlier, in the first century BC the Chinese brought textiles to the Mediterranean by camel caravans. Bruges had 40,000 looms in the 13th century, and in the 15th century, Italians tried to limit silk wearing to the upper classes, but they couldn't. It was once believed that the love of finery caused women to become prostitutes. In the Renaissance, the center of silk production was Lucca, Venice was famous for ribbons, Naples decorative trimming, and when I enter a warehouse of fabrics, textures and colors undulate, like a harem of dancing men and women, and material sensation runs riot. I breathe in a variety of pungent smells that blend into the aromas which wafted in my father and uncle's office, its stockroom, especially, where the stockboy, Junior, worked. When I'm around textiles, I sometimes wonder if he is still alive and what he's doing, the way I do the black women who worked in our house, and the son of Harriet with whom I roller skated. Harriet took care of me, and later Cassie cleaned the house for my mother. Cassie worked for my mother for ten years, she was a squat, cocoa-colored woman with sharp black eyes, whose son died of a heroin overdose, though I didn't know that when I was ten, when I was given my dog for Christmas. I knew nothing about her life, except what there was of it in our house, since she was very quiet, though I was rude to her sometimes, but she never spoke to me or even glanced at me. She appeared neat and solemn, and my mother picked her up at the bus station and returned her there at the finish of her workday.

The assistant cook was at breakfast this morning. On some days she will cook eggs after breakfast is officially over, and then the latecomer feels inordinately grateful. On some days even her forbearance is limited, and she averts her eyes from the pleading face of the latecomer and says, I'm sorry, you're late, and returns to her kitchen duties, wiping a countertop or closing a jar, an insignificant activity that further humiliates the latecomer. But that is that, there is no talking to her, no cajoling will affect her resolve to shut down the kitchen and go home. I don't know what happens in her home, and sometimes when she keeps the kitchen open, I think she is being kind or delaying her return there, because of a problem at home, since everywhere there are problems, though we are not supposed to think of the staff's problems, only of our own, which here we can or might ignore or resolve, but whether anyone can change enough to uncover a solution not previously in evidence is questionable. Some of the staff were once residents, and recognize our challenges and difficulties with more sympathy or even empathy than others might, having once experienced them themselves; but for the same reason, they can also be indignant and less patient. Breakfast can be a hopeful time, except when the head cook is on duty, since she never allows latecomers into her kitchen, and sometimes even takes away the bread outside the kitchen proper that could be made into toast, abating someone's hunger, and unlike the other, younger cook, she never relents. But since there is something for everyone, breakfast can still mostly be a time for optimism, which is regularly in short supply at the other meals. The other two meals are more complicated, coming when they do in the day, for one thing, and the cook, to achieve the feat of pleasing a highly diverse set of palates and food prohibitions, must prepare many more different kinds of meals, but few residents are ever fully satisfied. Sometimes no one is satisfied, and almost never are all satisfied. There are omnivores, carnivores, dairy eaters, nondairy or lactose-intolerant eaters, fish and egg but no red-meat eaters, vegans, raw-food eaters, lifelong vegetarians, some of whom feel sick at the sight of red meat and others who don't, and everyone claims to be sensitive. Hitler was a vegetarian who loved animals, but the head cook who cooks regularly and never has facials who has been here many years is not.

The head cook labors, unfulfilled, pleasing fewer and fewer people, and it is rumored she may quit, or retire, and as she has given so many of her years to this place, her purported leavetaking, or desertion, as some residents have insisted, has upset many of the residents or fellows who are here all year and even some, like myself, who are frequent guests, because though the food is sometimes terrible, the cook's fate has implications for us all, and change is often worse. So when I enter the kitchen, I try to be calm, to modulate or moderate my ceaseless demands, because while I'm also often dissatisfied, I'm not sure it has anything to do with the food the cook prepares, to accommodate so many people, though I also have complaints and wants that go unfulfilled. Food is easy to complain about, and everyone thinks, or most believe, they have the right to complain about it, but not about money and sex, and these topics at breakfast or dinner might provoke strong adverse comment, so usually they're avoided, while response to what has been served on big, china platters is ordinarily whispered out of the cook's hearing, though some believe she hears everything, and this is why she is leaving. On occasion the forbidden topics arise, and, like farts, they leave a rank odor in the cozy dining room.

On another morning, two months before, though time is shapeless here, the gentlefaced woman, Violet, whom I secretly named Contesa, sat alone, her eyes hidden, as was her habit, by dark glasses, which she wore because, she once explained impatiently, her aging eyes were ultra-sensitive to light, perhaps it was night-blindness during the day, she kidded. She was tucked into a corner reading a tome, whose pages she'd turned back and whose many underlinings were evident even from the place I sat near the two disconsolate women and another female resident whose face and figure I can no longer remember. Somehow I recall her as a fugitive, though from what I can't remember. Contesa arose and arrived at our table, amused and vexed, as she had just read of an incident that restored to her, in detail, an event which she'd forgotten for years. Her uncle had taken her and her older sister to the country, where they had stayed in a hotel which allowed colored people—perhaps her mother, she said, was in labor again—and where the sheets on the bed she shared with her older sister were heavily starched. The movement and subsequent rubbing of the top sheet against the sensitive nipples of her prepubescent, budding breasts excited her to her first climax. While Contesa spoke, her eyes darted from side to side, returning mentally to that time, it appeared, so she didn't observe the others at the table to whom this information might have been unwanted, since a discussion of sex, in any form, or any intimacy might never be appropriate or might cause embarrassment. But hers was not a case of anomia, the nonrecognition of objects by any of the five senses, or anoia, idiocy, that might have given license to Violet, or Contesa, but rather, I thought, it was her greater age and the common, divergent femaleness we shared, and then, as part of her off-color wisdom, as she put it, she offered us a page from Ars Amandia and strolled languidly—she liked exaggeration—to her chair, where she again entered her book without concern for her most recent effect upon us. I wondered if it was by Kafka or about Felice, though that seemed unlikely. The disconsolate woman who was not psoriatic had other complaints, she was lactose intolerant, suffered from frequent attacks of tendinitis in her left arm, asthma, and she explained that Ars Amandia was the Art of Love or of sex, and Lois, or Spike, who had read the old book, listed some methods from it to excite your partner, while I noted, silently, that Contesa was in fact wearing a starched blouse, and it could have been the sensation of the stiff linen, along with what she read, conjuring an image or even a single resonant word, matched to the feeling on her skin, which brought to the surface of consciousness the long-forgotten erotic memory. Aloud, I repeated some terms from the outdated sex manual I'd discovered in our library, to return and restore Contesa's disclosure to the texture and pattern of our daily activity and also to shift the discussion to safer topics. Apanthropia was the morbid love of solitude and an aversion to human society, while a plutomaniac was one who thought he was rich. I had known one, I said, which wasn't exactly true. Somehow all of this conversation, but especially Contesa's memory, disturbed me, since the surprising return of this sensual memory indicated the magnitude of the burial of mostly everything one has experienced, and why I held some memories, and not others, why they asserted their dominance and became my history, piqued my disquietude. Soon I left the cheerful breakfast room, to return to my bedroom for a rest.

It never occurred to me to think of my mother as sensitive, even after hearing her pain-filled screams, when I could only imagine the bloody scene, just as I imagined a mother whose animal-like cries and moans echoed in the neighborhood where I lived, when she found her three-year-old daughter dead in bed from walking pneumonia, and afterward I didn't want to be a nurse or doctor, though I admired our family doctor's hard, black bag and read stories about nurses, especially. I learned to doctor from my mother who would have been a good one but with a poor bedside manner, since she believed truth should be served unadorned and cold, like our food here often is at lunch. Since the time I heard her screams, I have been afraid of blood, the observation of it, and any wound, and have fainted at witnessing it or from a vivid picture of it. Watching operations in movies, like the one in *Bullitt*, which was not sensational, but scrupulously filmed, observing the details of a celluloid operation, I fainted in my seat. When I was thirteen, a friend asked me to accompany her to her doctor's office, where, unknown to me, her blood was going to be drawn. It was a hot summer's day in the place I grew up, not far from the ocean, where our house sat on land that once was swamp, as the water is very close to the surface, lying just beneath the sandy earth, so I reflected on water often when I was a child, how it flowed magically beneath our feet, the house I loved, moving and unseen. Though I was pulled out to sea once, nearly drowned in an undertow, and swallowed gallons of salty water on another occasion, when wave upon wave knocked my eight-year-old body down and dragged it under, not letting me breathe, I loved the waves, the ocean, and, in the summer, going to the beach.

In the summer, on mysterious, sultry nights, mosquitoes viciously attacked my family and other families—I was not then concerned with other families, except that I compared mine negatively to them—though we had screens on all the windows of our comfortable house, which I loved more than anything except our cat, the ocean, later my dog, who was my present for Christmas, when I was ten. I had begged for one, our cat having been killed by my parents, after my ice-blue parakeet was decapitated by the cat, and my father had refused me a Shetland pony that could have lived in our garage, I had implored. No one, or very few, had air conditioners then. At night I'd lie in bed and listen to insistent electric fans, insects hovering close to light bulbs, the thrum of the electric night, and, outside, high above, to the sound of powerful engines, jets flying low, readying to land or to fly far away. Sometimes on those long, hot nights, I could smell the ocean. My father loved the ocean, my mother feared it, and I loved summer, the ocean, and the beach.

It was during one oppressive summer, at the end of August, and I was home from camp, when fans were ineffective because only hot air was stirred, that the sight of blood caused me to faint for the first time, outside a doctor's office in my hometown, where many people of the same religion lived. I grew up among clannish people, who have nothing to do with my life now, and in the doctor's office, I stood next to an anxious friend, whose face and name I don't remember, when he drew blood from her, which I didn't watch, and then her doctor directed me to hold the vial of her drawn blood. His nurse was not around, or he did not have a nurse, and I didn't say anything, since it's often better not to say anything. I did what I was told. The doctor handed me the vial of her hot, dark-red blood, even the tube was hot, like the heat of the day, and I began immediately and for the first time in my life to feel faint. The word occurred to me, though I didn't know how I knew what it was I was experiencing, or what I was going to do, and I rushed out of the doctor's office, abandoning my friend, whose name and face I don't remember, who is no longer in my life, as most of those people are not, and, once outside, under a determined, blazing sun, dropped onto the doctor's neatly mown lawn and fainted.

My father had no stomach for the sight of blood, either, but I didn't know this, along with many other things about him when, as a small child, I saw his penis as he urinated or when he took me to Thanksgiving parades. I remember the parades better than his penis, but I remember both vaguely, and I couldn't describe his penis at all, maybe because he held it in his hands when he urinated, and I can't detail the parades, which we attended for some years, though I can't say how many, since I retain only sensations about both, along with an image or two. He is standing at the toilet, I am standing to his side, his left side, and the parades are crowded, noisy, colorful, there's movement everywhere, it's cold and I'm bustling with life, my father smiles, excited, his face is flushed with pleasure and red from the cold day. He had a full face like mine now, and, like a child, he loved parades and carnivals.

When my mother, in anger, pushed her arm through a glass storm door, which led to our patio with its smoky gray and blue slate tiles, cutting her arm badly, there was blood everywhere. My father, who was a good driver and proud of it, though he wasn't proud of much, certainly not his two children, was unable to drive her to the hospital, since he was faint. I didn't see my mother push her arm through the glass door, fighting and furious with my father, who became dizzy, but even so he accompanied her to the hospital. Her arm swathed in towels, or in a tourniquet of some sort, but bleeding profusely, she drove herself and him, he almost fainted beside her, to the emergency room. When a Christian Scientist bleeds, bandages must be allowed, and if the girl in the infirmary had cut her arm badly, white gauze strips would have been bound around her little arm, to stanch the flow, but since those who believe in divine intervention and miracles like the Red Sea's parting do not allow medicine, they could reject bandages. They might rely on prayer to make the blood clot quickly, though why anyone would is another mystery, and the little girl could have bled to death, which might have been a better fate than having been forced to linger in an infirmary sickbed all summer, unable to play under the sun, but eventually to die, in any case.

Sometime ago I found it especially hard to leave the breakfast room, since I was caught in an unfolding drama or a scene which suggested its possibility, when the demanding man's recitation of his dream provoked interpretations, which he sought as if he were starving, though he'd eaten plenty, and also the young married man seemed especially upset reading the paper, all of which didn't augur well for my peace of mind. He slapped the newspaper's pages open and then, turning to another page, shook his head and looked around, priming himself for the telephone, positioning his body so that his ear was directed toward the old, wooden booths, and he kept glancing toward the hallway that led to them, since his wife or mother might call soon, since they must miss him, the way he was missing them. He told me at dinner one night, where he liked company and ate with his usual gusto, no matter what he was served, but without the newspaper in front of him, that human beings create all of their own problems and that the universe itself was perfect and beautiful; and just as breakfast reached its end, everyone finished, those of us who hadn't yet fled watched the newcomers arrive, two men, who were accompanied by one of the staff, the most effervescent of a generally sedate crew. The new, white man, Henry, was a melange of pigment, with light acne around his nose, stubble on his chin and above his lips, and a rash, which turned out to be sycosis, a chronic inflammation of the hair follicles, especially of the beard and scalp, and he was thin and short, while the other new resident, Arthur, was black, several shades darker, but his skin, in places, was mottled, especially on his cheeks, and he was taller but rounder, with a slash of red like a ribbon at his throat from, I believed, a recent shave, and just as when I arrived, many heads involuntarily looked up and then, voluntarily, down, mine did, too, much as I didn't want to but was helpless against the effect of new stimuli, as if I had a nervous system like a leaf and was exhibiting a tropism. I heard them say each other's names familiarly; maybe, I thought, they'd arrived as a couple, sometimes that was permitted, with some goal established between them. The whiter one, Henry, has thinning blond-gray hair, the darker one, Arthur, a full head of longish, loose and braided black hair, and both trod on the floor in a lively, determined manner. Later, they explained they were partners in every aspect of their lives, they had no secrets from each other, which discomforted me in my skin, but they must keep secrets from others, and they finished each others' sentences, so at first and in some ways it was hard to separate them, even though they were physically quite different. They had met in dental school, where they trained to be orthodontists, after Arthur had quit studying physics in order to be in a less abstract world. Their project, if they had one, was maintained in secrecy, Arthur had frail lungs, Henry acid reflux disease and an ulcer, and they never wanted to talk about their work, since they came for a break. Both had a penchant for poetry, Arthur especially, he might have been writing some, but I forced them to talk about teeth once, by telling them that orthodontists were teeth designers and sculptors of the mouth, but I didn't admit that if I were a dentist, oral surgeon, or orthodontist, which I couldn't be, because of the spilling of blood, I'd be tempted to take out teeth and not put them back in, to set teeth crooked, but in a beautiful way, and then remove my handiwork and start all over again.

The demanding man groaned and slapped at a buzzing fly that had settled on the table, but didn't hit it, and everyone else was silent as the two new men, partners, walked into the kitchen, to tell the cook what they would and wouldn't eat. I wondered in a mild way whether these people would be boons or obstacles in my life, but then the tall balding man slapped the table hard and killed a large, bluebonnet fly, and Contesa muttered, "Beautiful specimen." To what she referred I wasn't positive, since either the fly or the new men might have been in her sightline. When the men disappeared into the cook's theater, I knew they would instantly establish a good or bad rapport, which would likely worsen or ameliorate during their time here, with the cook and the kitchen staff, since certain attitudes shift before they settle and harden. "Beautiful specimen," Contesa repeated, as we all rose from the table. The phone rang, clamoring, finally, for the young married man who raced to it, while Contesa scooped the dead blue and black fly off the table. The newcomers might have precipitated the drama, for the tall balding man sputtered and then uncharacteristically pushed or shoved the demanding man, who was lingering around balefully, and one of the staff saw the incident, scurried over to them, and guided them, presumably, to the director's office. None of us said a word, Contesa's gray eyes found mine, but the disconsolate anorectic clutched her friend's arm and shuddered. Another fly buzzed around me, and I slapped it harder than I meant, killing it. The disconsolate women frowned at me, and I left the dining room soon after, without being introduced to the two men, whose partnership I envied and disliked.

During the summer, at camp or at home, mosquitoes buzzed close around me, and I had extreme, allergic reactions to their bites, fat, pink welts budding on my legs and arms, and later I required antihistamines whenever bitten, but back then calamine lotion regularly dotted my body, its hot pink a humorous retort to my tanned legs, chest, back, and arms. I tanned under the sun for hours when I was young, listening to the ocean or rock and roll on a portable radio set close to my ear, but mostly I listened to the waves as they tossed themselves thoughtlessly against the sand, landing and lapping patiently and repetitively, then retreating, and I had a feeling of contented exhaustion, so complete and good that I knew it wouldn't last, that the best things don't last, and that I should try to preserve a moment which would, like a wave, retreat, but unlike a wave, maybe never come back. I associate this happy exhaustion only with going to the beach, lying on the sand after swimming in the ocean, whose waves sometimes dragged me under, compelling me to acknowledge forces much bigger than myself, whose will I couldn't shake or dent, of walking under a hot sun on the wet sand, leaving footprints whose impressions faded quickly, and letting the ocean nip at my toes and ankles, when standing at the edge of the ocean and the world I knew. The waves crept higher and higher, almost to my tanned knees, depositing a salty residue on my skin, and I thought I never wanted to be anywhere else but at the foot of the ocean and wished I could advance and recede like a wave.

There was always a pink mark on the back of one leg, a birthmark that my father called a cherry, which seemed to please him, either the word "cherry" or the fact that I had one or something else which was unimportant or which has gone with him to his ocean grave off the coast of Maine where his shards were tossed over the side of a sleek, white yacht, by his wife, his daughter, his wife's sister, his only living friend, who was also on his way out, as my mother noted, but not his prodigal son, as my father had regularly referred to him, nearly with pleasure, as if citing the Bible condoned his son's absence or made it palatable, because it was traditional and historical. He told me the cherry birthmark would be a way to identify me always, though it puzzled me why I would need to be identified, and I imagined terrible fates for myself, when it would become necessary to flip my limp body over and find the cherry, so as to be able to record, with certainty, that I was who I was. But in the years since, I often forget I have a cherry on the very top and back of my upper thigh and usually can't remember which leg it is on, but I do know that it could be used to distinguish me from others in time of war, or if I suddenly fell down in the street, unconscious, and did not know anymore who I was. I have never told a doctor about it, or friends, and it may be scarcely noticeable, since, as I've grown, it must have grown smaller, comparatively, and it might even have completely disappeared, which would be sad, as if much more had also vanished, and that's true, it has, so I don't want to look for the cherry, since with its diminution or demise, my father, along with everything else from the past, is deader.

The cherry isn't part of my medical records, since our family doctor, whose visits when I had sore throats were never welcome, but who was a good man, with a face I vaguely recall, especially because of his black, bristly moustache, and whose ministrations I remember better, since once he tricked me with the pain-free rubber needle and could have noted my reaction in his file on me, along with my sore throats, childhood inoculations, allergic response to mosquito bites, sensitive skin, must be dead for a long time. His files must be lost or were discarded after his death, and unless I pointedly remark, Please note the cherry birthmark on the back of my upper thigh, and record that in my file, no one will know about it, it wouldn't identify me. My mother wouldn't remember it, she is not who she was, though she knows her name, often is lucid, and realizes, sadly, that she is incapacitated, but as her memory falters, she knows less of herself and others. One day when she was exceptionally present, she asked rhetorically: If I can't remember, who am I? It's not an uncommon idea, but a poignant observation, the kind I hadn't ever heard her make, she was, throughout my childhood, usually blunt and even brutal in her expressions. Some years before her illness or condition presented itself undeniably, before she and I knew her brain was under pressure from an abundance of trapped fluid, we walked past a store in front of which a man, the apparent owner, stood, when my mother uncharacteristically commented, "I think I know that man. He looks helpless. He's waiting for customers." But even then, as I took note of her unique, jarring comment, I didn't understand it might have indicated or been a harbinger of her own incipient helplessness.

It was my father who first made me conscious of the cherry on the back of my upper thigh. My father paid attention to color, because he had an eye and was in the textile business, and, once, when the Polish woman was gently rubbing my face, in preparation for the steaming my skin needed, the probing of my oil-clogged pores, when she squeezed out any impurities she found, I told her about my father's business. I don't imagine she was truly interested, but I felt that her interest, if it was interest, maybe involvement, in skin, was akin to my father's in fabrics. He had looked, I explained to her, through a special magnifying instrument to measure the warp and weft of every fabric he designed and had manufactured, he weighed individual, single threads with another simple machine, and early on I knew that even a thread, which appeared to be unimportant and without substance, had weight.

In a fabric warehouse, rolls of fabric, which are worlds in a world, beg to be touched. Satin, moire, voile, faille. Jacquard, cotton, silk, brocade. Opaque, transparent, or semi-transparent lengths of cloth. Possibilities array themselves in colors, patterns, warps and wefts, weights and textures, while description doesn't account for what my fingers realize, which is uncategorizable. With a flourish, the polished salesman pulls out a bolt I have indicated, carries it on his shoulder or in his arms, like a body, and then pulling and stretching the fabric across a long wooden table, which usually has scissors and threads over it, it's always messy in a fabric warehouse, the salesperson spreads a length of material across it, so that its details may be seen and appreciated, and any mistake in the weave might be caught, and then he, rarely she, grabs a tape measure and cuts the material. It is an event, the gestures and cutting of the material, a high, almost noble, moment in the warehouse, when, I have noticed, other salespeople will stop what they are doing to watch, attentively, a fellow salesman unfurl the bolt, wield the stubby scissors and cut the cloth. The salesman also always pulls out a little more material, making a display of this, too, in a ritual or tradition that all of them follow and which is habitually mentioned to a client, or else you would feel cheated, everyone wants and expects a little bit more than the yards paid for. I could easily stay with these mute bolts of cloth for hours and hours, but I never do, because I'm busy, rushing, so I stay as long as I permit myself, gently fingering the cloth, careful not to stain or otherwise damage the material, and occasionally buying some yards for friends who sew; I don't, but my mother did, and often I merely want to have in my possession the redolent fabric, which appeals to a cosmopolitan primitive.

The span between breakfast and lunch is inconstant, unnervingly patternless, random. Theoretically, mathematically, randomness is impossible to produce, though on the ground there are traffic patterns, which come close to it, they are unpredictable because of error and accidents, but in most other things, especially numbers, there arrives a discernible pattern or logic. Generally, there is always less time between breakfast and lunch than between lunch and dinner. No one will go hungry, every resident knows that food will be supplied here, that lunch will ultimately arrive at our various doorsteps or we can visit the kitchen, but we don't know precisely when lunch might be ready, because each day something occurs that may change the schedule of the male kitchen helper, rumored to be a college dropout or recently expelled, who usually brings it to each of us on bicycle. When that happens, as it does each day, almost without fail, so he is part of my day and habit, I have to decide whether to say hello to him, which might alter my and his late morning rhythms. He pretends that he doesn't see us residents, so he won't startle or annoy anyone, but I always see him, unless I'm tending the fire or in the bathroom, where I worry that the curtain won't block me from view, and he might see me seated in an awkward, all too human pose. I tell myself it doesn't matter if he does, but I also know that this view could become the one he'll remember best, especially if it's silly or sad, and he could report my behavior to the cook or assistant cook, financial officer, to the janitor or groundskeeper, or, if it's especially peculiar, he might inform the director of the community, who could be called upon to speak with me privately and even caution me or put me on probation, which has happened but not yet to me. The staff talks about us the way we residents talk about them. The boy is handsome, especially on his bicycle, his long, strong legs, similar to other legs I've known, move automatically, and they distract me, since I particularly like long, strong legs, and recall those of a Dutchman, who, on a certain summer's night, wore white satin trousers. We took pills that turned us to rubber, I awoke surrounded by others having sex or making love on the floor, wanted to go home, he followed and kept coming round, I lost interest, bored even with his legs, which in retrospect aren't boring, and I wonder if they are as strong as they were then, if he cares for his body and exercises daily. It's easy to be distracted, especially if you relish the past, dislike it, or wonder at its other, unchosen possibilities and also if you collect things, including mementoes, and deduce or speculate about the multitude of outcomes. Since I have good hand/eye coordination and reflexes, a slow pulse, and can run fast, I could've become a long distance runner, but I didn't, which I regret abstractly, I played tennis but didn't relax my studies at the age of ten to practice eight hours a day, to train for the circuit, though training my body and thinking only of a backhand, forehand, when to approach the net and other techniques, might be the life I should have led rather than the one I do, and it still appeals to me. I am often sedentary, except I work standing up or squatting, and go for energetic walks and solitary night swims. I played chess, rode a dirt bike, liked multiplying and adding sums, memorized encyclopedia and dictionary listings, to keep my brain agile, was adept at setting my friends' hair in curlers and tweezing their eyebrows, and I also enjoyed squeezing the pimples on the back of one boyfriend; I liked to draw, jump rope, dance, perform acrobatics, but heights made me dizzy, so jumping over horses in gym didn't make sense as an activity. Instead I preferred to walk backward, do somersaults, act like a horse or dog or cat, even a vegetable, in dance class, read philosophy, American history, especially, and stories, and could diagnose medical problems, which, like my mother, I often accomplish with an accuracy some call intuition, though I don't believe in intuition. But unlike her, I faint at the sight of blood gushing from a gash, so I couldn't have been a doctor, and lose interest in reading some medical research material, though I'm attracted to the study of skin and genetics, especially as a model for the humanities and social sciences, since some aspect of your fate is carried in code from another's body to yours, though the body's not a stable foundation, as it reflects human ideas about it. It is, in a sense, both transparent and opaque, since, with study, like my dermatologist, you could read its signals, though a brain scan, an MRI, may be read differently by neurologists, whose knowledge is imperfect, or the object of their knowledge remains defiant, the sum greater than its parts, the parts in need of and subject to interpretation. Genetics proposes that people aren't merely the sum of their parts, which somehow reassures me, we're bits and pieces, and parts of bodies no longer have to be the bodies' own parts, heads might be grafted, and there could one day be full-body transplants. Human beings lie in shreds of DNA in laboratories, studies for the future, designs for better-performing bodies, like car models in Californian and Japanese labs.

I like the kitchen helper's legs and his clear skin. He has good color. I have a strong sense of design and color, as my father did, but when I was young, I didn't want to go into his business, though by the time he sold it, over my protests, like the house I loved, I contemplated joining him and my uncle, since looking at weaves and warps and studying color combinations satisfies me in ways other activities don't. I like history, but it is slow. I am fast and quickly lose interest in things, and some people, and this dismays me, but I start and stop many reasonable pursuits. If I travel, I often take in where I am quickly and want to be somewhere else, though I'm aware that once in another place, I will feel similarly, so being where I am now, which I have come to not for the first time, isn't for the sake of novelty, but rather for a less novel form of discovery or a pursuit of knowledge that requires my foreswearing certain adventures that might take me far from myself, but I find it almost impossible to quit my mental meanderings, though I've arrived with a goal and want to make headway, like a person sailing in life toward a destination, hoping for accomplishment. I haven't a passion for one thing only. I vacillate and gain or lose enthusiasm, and like a Don Juan might in love, I'm lost to the singular pursuit, disappointed that nothing is compelling enough, that I lose interest, or always want something else or more to sustain it. But mostly I lose my way to it because I'm easily distracted, the way another resident did. He stayed a short time, as he was permanently adrift, since nothing fully animated him or gave him reason to live, and he said he would have wanted to have been a philosopher, since it was a calling, he told me, higher than any other except the priesthood, if he'd had the concentration or the energy. But instead he learned and mastered carpentry and became a devoted member of his church choir. He also muttered once that he was beginning to enjoy the luxury of impotence, something I'd never heard a man claim before or since, and, when he did, he gazed into the distance over my head. I thought I understood his melancholy, since it could have been like my own, though not about that type of impotence, but he also seemed foolish gazing into the distance, assuming a pose that might indicate a depth he didn't actually possess. It was an attempt, though, to signify the pursuit or impossibility of headway. But, then, I'm also aware that I may encounter a person who could change my life or an idea that could undo others I hold dear, which was reinforced by the card reader, and I want to believe his prophesy, and I do think that, while destinies are not carved in stone, I have a fate, that which has already been written, not alone by me but by forces bigger than myself, like an ocean's mindless waves, since I believe that about the most important things in life human beings don't have much choice. I am making do, unmaking too, being as watchful and free as I can with what I've been born into.

I have certain choices after breakfast and before lunch; for example, I could go back to bed, or, if energetic, I might tackle a pressing problem and find its solution, though my optimism dissipates as hours go by when I don't generally find a solution or answer to questions I pose myself, ones that challenge or haunt me. Then a minute elongates and seems greater than it is, during which I might accomplish nothing, time plodding on a barren highway, or time contracting, when, for instance, I haven't noticed anything except what's in front of me, a pair of scissors or a book, so I haven't felt aware of being alive, sad or happy, and big hours become tiny minutes, and I don't know, in the most prosaic sense, where time has gone. No one knows where time's gone, and it may be that there's no time, only the peculiar, winsome present, in which I seem to be alive, though I can also feel dead, like a diseased tree in the forest outside my picture window, which I watch as a season mutates infinitesimally, except when there is a sudden frost and buds die or a great wind chases all the leaves off a tree. But the dying tree I'm watching now hasn't changed like that. I've watched several seasons change here, and no one ever knows where time has gone, but to me it's in the faces of the people on the wall of my room who are gone, whose expressions never change, and because of that no time exists. I've heard that truth is the daughter of time, and on the slowest days, when I can hear the clock tick, and my heart, my second stomach, beat nervously, and nothing I've eaten satisfies me, and I don't know what to do with myself, I can fantasize I'm time's daughter, or believe I'm the Count's, but not my father's or my mother's, because when I was a child and nothing pleased me, when I didn't know what to do with myself, I blamed them for the lack of steady excitement, when I also didn't recognize temporariness or finality.

Leslie Van Houten's parents divorced, and neither of them could have predicted her choosing Manson's family over their amicably separated one, but she did, when she was nineteen, she came under his spell, though not as completely as some of the other girls, and she has been in jail for a long time, and will be kept there much longer, though she's become a model prisoner, teaches other prisoners, has received a college degree, works on the prison newspaper, and could care for herself on the outside. At Leslie Van Houten's 1991 parole hearing, her eighth, she wore a black and white checked cotton dress, a bold print, with a wide, white collar, and white trim on its short sleeves, a dress like a house, too large for her, so that though she was tall and big boned, she was dwarfed by the dress, an unfashionable one that might create the impression she was an administrator in a small midwestern company. Leslie answered the three parole commissioners' questions in defense of her suitability to leave prison after twenty-two years. She clarified, as she had before, that she'd wiped off their fingerprints to look busy, so that she wouldn't be asked to mutilate Mr. and Mrs. LaBianca, as Charlie wanted them to do, as Tex might have required of her, Tex might have asked her to do more, also, she said, and, when they were leaving, they took cheese and chocolate milk from the refrigerator. She believed in Charlie, did what he asked, and before they left the car to break into an anonymous middle-class suburban house, owned by the unsuspecting LaBiancas, he ordered them "to all do something." It was like war, Leslie said. To her, then, Manson was Jesus Christ, and sometimes she read him passages from the Bible, but now when she reads the Bible, with her minister, she must push away that pernicious memory, to forgive herself for her terrible acts, which, after three years in prison, she began to recognize and for which she developed a strong sense of responsibility, but which, it appears, was absent before then, and for which she must now seek and allow herself some sort of peace, even forgiveness.

The right to pursue happiness sends me and other Americans, even here where we are meant to resist outside temptation, on a hunt for it. If I'm not hungry, I might seek other forms of happiness, or pleasure, which is part of my American birthright, though the most misconceived of them or the most difficult to realize; I can pursue several means and ways to be happy, if I am able to forget what makes me habitually sad. The woman who hates me or may not hate me, since she abandoned all of her friends, must believe she has embarked upon a truly new life, but I wonder how she narrates its many divorces, more than just from her first and second husbands, by whom she had several children, since she has excised the past as if she were an immigrant and it the old country, with a language she no longer speaks. She was an expert horsewoman. Does she still ride? My own scale is teased by such questions, which I can't restrain, and then, overtaken by cloudy intangibles, I might walk to my bedroom and go to sleep after breakfast, feeling smaller. Without looking at it, I easily forget my appearance, and my body can feel gigantic, but also not sturdy enough, or when I feel small, my scale reduced by puny conjecture, I could be a mole, my skin pulling and drawing, prickly, demanding that I shed it and everything else, too, to begin again in a common but unique American fantasy of life as an entirely different person with a virgin's body, whose hymen, a membrane of thin skin protecting an essential orifice that, once penetrated, effects a change whose connotations defy it a single definition, and is also just another frontier. Frederick Jackson Turner theorized that "waves" of human movement westward defined the character of the American nation, an idea mostly disputed if not discredited now, but which held sway for a time, though when teaching it, I focused mostly on a single aspect: "In this advance, the frontier is the outer edge of the wave, the meeting point between savagery and civilization." I told my high school seniors, after I'd banished myself from college teaching, that our American civilization can be treated as a series of periods of its individual colonists or members overcoming their own savagery, and because of this the American character retains a roughness and crudeness unlike the European or other civilizations. The students didn't like my interpretation of the Frontier Thesis, and felt indicted by it, but I included myself, I told them, and didn't mind being compared with so-called savages or animals, which we were, too, and insisted on a nation's theoretical similarity to a fetus's development, in which ontogeny recapitulates phylogeny, except, in the case of the American political and social body, the fetus is born over or born again, and the infant introduced into a new context, but without advancement, repeats it all. Not long after Turner published his paper, which he delivered first as a lecture in the 1893 World's Fair, the

Viennese architect and designer Adolf Loos, in his essay "Crime and Ornament," used a similar ontological argument: "In the womb the human embryo goes through all phases of development the animal kingdom has passed through." Loos compared ornamentation with criminality and degeneracy: "The evolution of culture is synonymous with the removal of ornamentation from objects of everyday use." The relationship between Turner and Loos marked a moment when thinking about American history and international art and design collided, at least theoretically, at the beginning of the 20th century, often called the American Century, and is the subject of another of my partially written essays, "Backward Movements in the Modern." "We," Loos wrote, "have the art that superseded ornament." And, "those who go about in velvet jackets today are not artists, but clowns or housepainters." I like velvet. Hubris and vanity hold hands with so-called progress, as well as with advances, innovation, and invention, so Loos's words haunt me, as do Turner's, because a mistake or failed idea can also detonate the imagination, since it may explode a period's codes or unconscious habits and actions better than its successes, and much erupts from the erroneous. In Vienna, a city I visited with a friend whose accidental death I still can't accept, often I stare at him in photographs, but also, more often, I don't let myself and, instead, walk to the main house, fancying he will be waiting like a letter, though I know he won't, just one of the disconsolate women, who vacillates as I do and doesn't get done what she should, or the woman with Chronic Fatigue Syndrome, who will be reclining on a couch reading or sleeping, my dead friend and I took an architectural tour. Walking about in the old, stately city, with its terrible, grand history, we hung on the words of our impassioned guide, while snow fell, the city's first snowstorm in years, which coated us and it in white, my friend, whose mother's ancestors had been slaves in Mississippi, pointed to the blizzarded sky and whispered impishly into my ear, "I think it's telling us something." The gentlemanly guide tutored us on Vienna's place in architecture, art, and design, which reached its apex during the time Freud also lived there, at the start of the 20th century, and much of what the guide taught—dates and names—I've forgotten, though I remember we took him for pastries and coffee in a capacious coffeehouse where he sipped from a white cup, and my friend tipped him generously. Our guide accepted the money modestly, but most of what my dead friend said to me during those days is lost.

There is nothing more satisfying than sleeping whenever or wherever you want, in a bedroom that is yours alone, removing your clothes, throwing off the weight of the world and sliding under the inviting clean covers of a bed that is also yours alone, to fall into a blissful, ignorant sleep, to wallow in unconsciousness, when nothing else exists, when nothing disturbs your peace, except dreams, when you are left to yourself, since no one expects anything of you when you are sleeping. A bed whose mattress is firm, whose laundered all-cotton pillowcases smell of flowers, whose good cotton sheets have been washed with detergents that don't irritate the skin, comes close to heaven on earth, and nothing is better than to sleep in this circumstance and forget everything and everyone, without trying to forget or knowing you are forgetting.

During her parole hearing, Leslie Van Houten defended herself and her lawyer also defended her, arguing that twenty-two years in prison was enough time for her crime, that the California matrix, which defines sentencing guidelines or parameters, was served by her having been punished for those twenty-two years, that she was a model prisoner, that she was attending to her drinking and drug problems, and was drug-free since 1983. The psychologist's report agreed she was no longer a threat to society, she presented no threat to anything or anyone, and should be given every consideration for parole. But the prosecutor, the same one who prosecuted her and the Manson family twenty-two years before, argued Leslie Van Houten should never get out of jail, that her crimes were horrible, that society doesn't want her out, that she can do good in prison for the rest of her life. Something inside her, he argued, will always cause her to fall off the wagon.

Trouble for the day could include the male kitchen helper whose sly winks and glances remind me of other sly glances, especially at the beach in the summer, when I was a teenager and dreaded going to the pool in my tank suit, my budlike breasts shaping the material to my body in ways that might provoke notice; though once I'd loved the ocean and the beach, suddenly, between the years of twelve and thirteen, these loves were compromised by other so-called natural phenomena, also greater than myself. I tugged at the straps of my navy blue suit, making sure it covered my small bottom, but the cherry on the back of my leg was visible to everyone, especially the little boys I'd gone to grade school with who had suddenly shot up a foot, whose pudgy bodies were now lean, whose rib cages protruded, whose faces were decorated with red spots, whose company was once easy to be in but now wasn't. They could see me exposed. The ocean was far from the pool, when once it was close, and to get there I'd choose circuitous routes to maintain invisibility. The kitchen helper is like the boys I went to school with, and I can easily be the same age as he in my mind, where much of the past resides, resistant and patchy, and this analogy could produce trouble; still, if I've forgotten something I need for lunch, like mustard or olive oil, if I want to make lunch last, prolonging its conclusion with an excursion, I must go to the kitchen. But I might meet some of the other residents, who, like myself, always want something.

Possession is nine-tenths of the law, what's contained in houses or worn on bodies, what people claim as theirs, what they fight for in court often are possessions. A lust for ownership is telling, some seem incapable of denying themselves, though it's regularly insisted that the only thing we possess is our bodies, a weird consumable to me who often feels not in it, but also we are expected, in death, to leave our bodies, and exhorted that the body doesn't matter, only the soul or spirit. On her stolid body, Leslie's bold print dress dated or outdated her, since fashion bends time, style is a timekeeper, and many people dress stylishly, to feel present or vital, though in a year or less what was new is old, and they are older too, and in photographs only five years old, everyone looks out of time, like the changed styles they wear, since fashion is a futile method to remain vital or timeless, but even futility demands change, there are new styles of it, also, but submission to some method is necessary, along with creepy death. Still, I don't like to change my outer gear, though I do, not to appear mad, out of time, like Richard II, but when I like something, I don't want to have to renounce it arbitrarily unless I'm weary of it, so often I buy many copies of a style or design I like and am indignant when, for instance, the shoes I prefer are taken off the market to make way for a similar, inferior model, because of fashion and commerce. One pair, Italian heeled sandals with straps that crossed over the arch, showed my foot off better than any pair I have ever had since, and no one makes them anymore. I hope to buy something that might become a classic, a simple design, like the Eames chairs or tennis shoe, so I won't have to change, especially into an inferior model, most people can't change, but styles represent change and also propagate the illusion of change, they distract from mortality, especially most feverishly in changing rooms, where women and girls say, Does this look good? and while textiles are as old as the need for shelter, they are somewhat freer of the taint of style, even though textiles have changed radically over time and because of it. But there are still four basic materials and synthetics, to which I am irrationally attached.

In India, the delicate thread for the famed Dacca muslin was produced by revolving needle-thin pieces of bamboo in a coconut shell. I'd like to have a coconut shell machine, keep it on a table to regard with wonder, and one day take it apart bit by bit. When architects designed all aspects of a house, including its couches, chairs and tables, wallpaper and rugs, Frank Lloyd Wright regularly used natural fibers for his interiors, taffeta, mohair, goat's hair satin, he and other likeminded architects in the early 20th century favored handcrafted fabrics. But his chairs were straight-backed, heavy, and rigid, he didn't cherish comfort or consider supporting the lower back, but not long after in Europe Marcel Breuer and Gerrit Rietveld did, and Le Corbusier and the Eameses more than any of them. Curtains and drapes go in and out of style, venetian blinds and shades, fabric hanging on walls is art or craft, and any long-held attachment to a style marks its advocate as a zealot. So it's said that it's important to change with the times, whose effects are thrust upon people, anyway, when, for instance, they can't buy a pair of shoes they loved that has gone out of style in a year, so about this perpetual motion toward change I'm dubious, since how do you know when it's time to stop, I usually don't know when to stop, I'm merely projected into the future.

Irrationality incites futures that are unknown but in some sense already spoken, though reason is trotted out, like a winning racehorse, to predict the unknown for our admiration. But it's the wild stallion, the uncapturable horse, I cherish, it can't help itself. I understand coming under a spell, because I have with men and women, and I might again, and if people tell their messy truths, the way the daughter of time must—I wonder what the son of time must tell, if not the truth, if like the Count he merely keeps its instruments or guards and hoards it—or if he is profligate like my brother and wastes it, the way he wastes himself, the way my mother said he does, somewhere in Cincinnati, they might say that, at a certain period in their lives, they couldn't help themselves, they were captives to someone else, they didn't know who they were anymore, or why. On occasion, when nothing else occurs to me, and it is quiet, as it is this late morning, while I await lunch and nothing stirs in the room but myself, I might ask: Is there a principle worth dying for? Would you intercede in a fight that wasn't yours? Do you think people get more or less what they deserve? Can you tell a difficult truth? Where does your most persistent hope lie? Do you expect your life to stay as it is? Do you rely on surprise to make you happy? Are you disappointed? Do you keep it to yourself? Do you have many secrets? Has something happened that you'd never tell anyone? Have you ever done something too horrible to mention? How many times?

The woman who's no longer my friend may dislike me, and I can't know for sure the reasons for her alienation, I can only guess at them. I like some friends less and less, when their bad or good habits stop being charming. I once left a man and didn't have a reason, then I fell under the spell of another, but I can't gather up in a basket the waxings and wanings of my affections, toward men and women, people have come and gone, I come and go, but if I could count up everyone in my life, I might be better prepared to leave it, knowing its erratic sums and scores, though my theory is disputable. I dispute it regularly, as when, for instance, I take an object apart and look at its innards scattered on the floor without sense, or when I labor to achieve nonsense. Lately I've been remembering the first time I had sex, an incomplete, unsatisfactory act, he was years older and confused, as confused by me as I was by doing it, as I would have said then, and I recall the night but not him vividly. I rejected him soon after, without any subtlety or concern for him, as bad as the sex was. Any passion is better than none, I remind myself.

Lunch is eaten alone in the room that isn't for sleeping, and like breakfast and dinner, there is a rotation of menus, so that every two weeks the kitchen helpers might place tunafish, cheese, or egg salad sandwiches, for the vegetarians who eat fish and who are not lactose intolerant, in the bags, or a spinach pie, there is a variety of salads, carrots, celery, beets, tomatoes, romaine lettuces, hummus and other dips for the raw food, steak or roast beef sandwiches for the meat-eaters, and many kinds of soup, creamy mushroom, beef and barley, chicken, vegetable, and all of these may be in your lunch bag depending upon preferences and dietary needs, and there is dessert, freshly baked cookies or cakes, though the vegetarians complain that their desserts are less luscious than the meat-eaters', but there is fruit for everyone, and, especially when it is in season, fruit is delicious. Some invite others to join them. I never do, because lunch would resemble breakfast, with a similar cast of characters, and it could further damage my day, since the presence of others is capable of disrupting whatever headway I aspire to make. Occasionally, I want the Count to join me, his stories and mystery don't seem diversionary, there are rumors spread about his eccentric and illustrious past, about his wife, who might have been murdered or is a hermit, about his belief that human history's two best inventions are time and reason, but he is asleep at noon, at rest in timeless dreams. So I keep the lunch hour to myself, open for whatever occurs to me, and to eat it when and how I want. Each time lunch arrives, I decide I won't look inside the brown paper bag in which it's brought, to sustain interest in its contents, even enrich the mystery and future pleasure it might contain, to maintain a lively desire, desire is life, for the meal that is usually the poorest of the day.

Today I heard the boy on the bicycle when often I don't, and instead of greeting the long-legged kitchen helper, I remained in my compromised chair and pretended not to notice how he placed the bag on the steps to my door, which was partly open, because I like fresh air or fear suffocation. Instantly, as he rode away, I regretted my decision, since he has beautiful eyes, long legs, and a sly smile, but if I engaged his smile, if I looked into his eyes, I might face an unruly element in my future. Lunch today was poor. It included an egg salad sandwich. I like eggs and don't subscribe to the contested dictum that eggs are harmful, the way many do, but I'd had eggs for breakfast, as did many of the others; there was also a sickeningly sweet apple juice and a thin tomato soup with spaghetti, cold, though it was in a thermos, soups always are, so it was surprising, but maybe the top of the thermos hadn't been screwed on tightly enough, yet when it is, I often can't open it. I like soup. Everyone could eat the tomato soup, unless the person was macrobiotic, disavowing the tomato for being too yin, one of a group designated as deadly nightshade, or someone was allergic to tomatoes or disliked tomato soup or felt, as I have felt, that it tasted like blood. I have, on occasion, alone and in company, choked on the clotted juice, though curiously, I can enjoy the taste of tomato soup, with cream or without, overcoming my initial visceral disgust to it, and even to the clotted juice, by substituting the mental idea that it tastes good or by repeating the phrase "it tastes good" to myself silently over and over. The tomato soup was suitable for almost all of the diets offered: low fat, dairy-free and vegetarian, dairy-free and meat eating, fish-eating vegetarian, non-red meat but not vegetarian and not dairy-free, anti-candida, and other plans. The head cook tries to find tasty, winning recipes or ways to use leftovers from dinner that all of us can eat, but in working to please or accommodate the residents all of her years here she has mostly been unsuccessful, especially as their requests for different diets has increased and residents' sensitivities to the world around them—the air they breathe, the objects they touch, the materials on the floor or on the walls—and their resistances to the many products human beings have invented to ease the stress of life have grown exponentially. During the time I have been in residence, which will extend into the future I have scant curiosity about, though I know it will be, in some ways, dissimilar from today and could be charged with potent events I would never have predicted, but which in some ways I hope for, because excitement can't be predicted, the cook has become uneasier, more frustrated by or unwilling to cater to the residents' demands, since they have blossomed in variety, vociferousness, and even self-righteousness, and she, like the Polish woman, wearies, exasperated. A flash of movement charges through her rail-thin body or a crease streaks across her startlingly pale forehead, deepening the line already engraved there, and she might quickly move to the sink or cross to the stove, where a pot is always nestled and steam always rises, to avoid a resident's need of her compassion.

The Polish woman sometimes winces when the telephone rings, which, because she is alone in the salon, she has to answer, forcing her to abandon me, lying under a soft pink or blue blanket with cream on my face, and this affects her schedule, since there may be another customer waiting, though only once was it the lusting man, but I continue to expect him, or even hope he'll return, because the prospect is exciting, especially his presence, dark and brooding, and her response to him, whether she will allow him to have her or not, or continue to keep him waiting until it's the right time for her, since she may lust for him, or maybe she takes greater satisfaction in attenuating her rejection of him. She might be delaying, even playing with him, and I could be resting on the couch inside the walls of the salon at the moment she finally tells him. But then what would happen. Sometimes the Polish woman expels a breath fraught with resentment, addressing some of what she omits in our routine conversations, but I don't think she would refer to herself as sensitive, the way my mother wouldn't.

I might throw the tomato soup into the toilet, since, with no one here to see it, I could easily do that, though I have qualms about doing it, even alone, when no one would see me. I dislike any self-enforced prohibition, but even an unimportant act might have consequences impossible to foresee, or problems I couldn't predict, since there are always problems, and some are surprises. People have become more sensitive over the years. Obesity, allergies, and food aversions have spread like wild flowers do in spring and summer over Virginia's countryside, which has the greatest number and variety in the U.S., belying the countryside's otherwise homogeneous genetic human population, though there are always differences among people. The environment, a word I find somewhat objectionable because it's bland but whose use is endemic and impossible to ignore or avoid, has become more poisonous, or toxic, and there are new viruses and diseases dotting the human field, while old ones disappear, and allergies and sensitivities may be the onset of still unknown, more virulent plagues, as this is the time Stephen Jay Gould named "the age of bacteria," when "maximal bacterial simplicity" dominates man or humans. The unknown is conveniently, conventionally, more virulent than the known, and it is exciting, which is why some people think about the future, since it might also, in addition to what life always is, be new, though I'm not very interested in what will come after me, but I can imagine becoming less inured to it just before I die, since I won't be able to have and see it, and the inability to know it will probably provoke a profound desire to live.

People who once ate in restaurants and drank at bars with smokers now refuse to or can't—they claim to be allergic to smoke and subject to pulmonary distress as well as skin irritations—when not long ago, few were allergic to cigarettes, although a rise in asthma and emphysema might have been the harbingers of this new allergy. My skin doctor told me that in the 1960s he treated three cases of a disease, purpura, which afflicted young women only, but he has never seen a case since. The phenomenon was that blood pooled at parts of their bodies, typically at their extremities, so that great purple swollen blotches formed at their lower forearms, and though the women were tested in every conceivable way, there was no organic basis found for the occurrence, and the disease crippled them when it commenced. Just before the onset of an episode, they would have a premonitory sensation, a tingling which always preceded, by five minutes, the appearance of the purple blotches. It was characteristic of this Autoerythrocyte Sensitization Syndrome, whose diagnostic feature was that if you spun down a sample of the sufferer's blood and injected the red blood cells, characteristic hemorrhagic or bleeding lesions developed. One young woman was hospitalized, and every test given, and after some of her symptoms were alleviated and upon being told she would be released, since they could do no more for her and she'd improved, marginally, at that very instant, she became paralyzed, as her mind and body were likely stymied by this turn of events and found another route to manifest her relentless distress, and for the first and only time in my dermatologist's career, he called in a hypnotist, who put the woman in a trance during which the hypnotist suggested that she could walk, that when she awoke from the trance, she would walk, and, that very day, when she awoke, she was no longer paralyzed and walked out of the hospital. My dermatologist has never heard of her again, and has not seen a case like it since the 1960s, so the disease or condition has disappeared, just as it appeared, suddenly, to represent some question or challenge, a neurosis, that a very few young women manifested in their bodies, since the mind is part of the body and changes frequently. I change my mind often, too many times to count, deciding I must walk to town, or read the history of the Empire State Building, listen restlessly to music, dance, doodle a design for a metal teapot, memorize some Zulu words, or sometimes I dwell on the faces of friends who have died or on conversations that were conclusive, ending friendships or sealing them, robbing me of certainty or teaching me trust, inconclusive and eternally titillating, the way romance is, especially an unfulfilled one, which may be why I can't concentrate as much as I want, to make headway, though the tarot card reader assured me I will overcome something that has been insurmountable, which I haven't yet recognized and that taunts me daily. When I'm in love, I am hard put to think about anything else, but I'm not in love now, in that way, though it can be said I have loved and may love again. Still, lunch is often a lonely affair, though generally I'm glad to eat it by myself, not pestered by the demanding man, whose great appetite for attention expands like a stomach, whether it's fed or empty, and if he could he'd gobble up and devour everyone's time in a banquet for himself.

If lunch includes a salad, romaine lettuce and tomato, shredded carrots and sliced cucumber, to stave off eating it, I toss the ingredients into an ugly, plastic bowl and make a dressing for it in a plain water glass, but often I don't have what's necessary for a good dressing, like mustard, and then I must decide if I want to walk to the main house, barge into the kitchen, bother the kitchen helpers, especially the young man who likes to glance slyly at me, the girl who transgressed the rules, or the cook or assistant cook, who may or may not be there, and ask for the missing ingredient. I will be considered bothersome, a pest, too picky, and difficult. But to be picky necessitates putting on shoes, a jacket and scarf, switching off all the lights, and making sure the fire is out, so often I can't decide, annoyed at myself for not having remembered what I would need from the kitchen while at breakfast, but then I'm not thinking about lunch when I rush away from the bustling, often tension-ridden dining room as quickly as possible, to avoid trouble.

Yesterday, after a midday meal of tunafish, pickles and low-fat vichyssoise, I walked to the library. Everyone here can use the library, which is a simple, four-story brick building, with four large, similar rooms, three of which have chairs, benches, and tables, and one, a piano, lutes, two acoustic guitars, and chess sets. There is an empty birdcage in each room, a golf set and tennis racquets in one, a few sweaters near the fireplaces in all four, where mementos from former residents dot the rooms, and in three of the rooms, dark wood shelves are crammed with forgotten novels and poetry, an abundance of manuals, especially on fly fishing, cookbooks, how-to books, outdated encyclopedias, and musty dictionaries. Some people from the nearby town are permitted, if they have been issued visitors' cards, to use the library, though most don't, and occasionally I have run into one when I have gone in search of a book that might help me. Yesterday, a disheveled, elderly woman emerged from the library's bathroom and inquired, brusquely, "Are you a teacher?" I told her I had taught American history and furniture and interior design occasionally, and then she asked, inserting herself into my day, "That's good, but do you have a man?" Quickly, I had to decide whether I'd answer her impertinent question, but then I wanted to, if only to see what might transpire, because I'm curious, lunch hadn't been exciting, pickles and tunafish are laughable, and I hope for novelty. I restrained myself from asking, Can you have a man? and instead answered:

—I did, recently.

—Dumb women don't have men.

—You really think that?

—Well, sometimes it's smart women who don't have men—

—How can you tell anyway?

—I'm not a mind reader.

—That's a relief.

—But I read. All my books burned in a fire, so I come here. I have good eyes. I can see what other people don't. Don't let that scare you.

Now the odd woman smiled, brushed off her tatty skirt and straightened her shoulders, all of which was appealing, because she had found a necessity to relate to me, another character, with some severity, and the encounter drew something from her, so she looked at me solemnly and announced:

—You have to use your time wisely, and then there's always chance.

—Yes, chance, you're right, there's always chance. And hope.

—Not hope, chance. People don't know when chance comes knocking. Mostly they're looking with blinders on . . .

She trailed off. When I said hope, I wasn't sure why, except that I wanted to hear what she'd say. The odd inquisitive woman scrutinized me again and rushed to the massive library door, opened it, the door yawning loudly, which it always does, no matter who opens it or how carefully, and turned:

—But what other subjects do you have than men?

With this question, she ran off, though I'm still pondering her and it, marrow in the bones, since how many subjects does a person have, she must know I have more, she reads, she seems worldly, but from a different world, and if you are a woman or a man, about which you have no choice, unless you elect surgery at a suitable age, but still you have to spend at least your adolescence and some of early adulthood in the sexed body into which you were born, you will undoubtedly spend some or much of your life absorbed in men or women, who are in a sense your subject, a singular and important one, no matter how general, no matter how you decide to dispense with it or them, if you feel you have a choice. There have been thousands of years of swamp-like argument about sex and the sexes, to which most succumb, since, for one thing, sex is often adventitious, taken on the run, and, to include it in the day, when it often isn't, some fold it between a bit of ordinary conversation during which the body is normally excluded, except for talk about illness, but then some experience sex as an illness or a rare occurrence like an acute disease, but anyway worthy to report about their day, or for some it's a healthy or perverse pleasure. Some here relish the flavors and smells of bodies, yet describe flesh with weak or pallid language, or dwell mostly on specific parts of bodies, breasts, penises, earlobes, necks, feet, toes; and I have conversed about sexual matters, about men and women, so, to be honest, the way a daughter of time must, I'd agree that men have been and remain a vast subject, which is also boring, especially when you have talked and listened for years, with an evermore rapid sense of the subject's inexhaustibility and futility, for everyone repeats the subject and their own behavior, too. Occasionally a person's sexual habits are unusual, such as Spike's, whose taste runs to much older men and has since she was twelve, when she attempted to seduce her sixty-year-old piano teacher, and, she says, wryly, she's the opposite of a pedophile, whose activity is illicit, while her disposition isn't, so she could work in an old-age home and prey upon the elderly. Instead, she, a math prodigy, born into a family of scientists, pursued mathematics, first, imaginary numbers and set theory, then the more abstract versions of the discipline, which include, she tells me, formulae elegant as drawings and so graceful the terms soar in the air before they disappear. She particularly follows the work of Frege and Abraham. Spike's affliction or desire, I must tell her, according to the Medical Sex Dictionary in the library, is gerontophilia. There is no equivalent for a deflowering mania, of a man or woman with hymen fever. Spike is not an arithomaniac, whose morbid obsession is to count constantly, she doesn't betray a hint of this, being, I suppose, well past real numbers. One day I will tell her I see numbers as colors and vice versa, she has already explained that sex is no substitute for mathematics, but mathematics does compensate during rare periods of celibacy, though sex is better for dinner talk, since few people understand abstract mathematics.

This morning, when I insensitively rushed past the two disconsolate young women, though they may not have noticed, since they were engrossed in their own lives and each other's happiness or misery, I noted that one of them, the skinnier of the two, was in her pajamas, which was unusual, and her image has now returned to me. People generally don't come to breakfast or dinner in pajamas. This signaled, in a small way, her distress, though it might also have indicated the lack of it and her contentment with herself, her indifference or even immunity to others' opinions. The other woman was dressed, and it looked as if they'd been talking all through the night, and immediately I wondered what they could have said to each other that would carry them from day to night to day. One of them has a selfish female lover, the other a narcissistic male lover who had recently returned home, and she has an eating disorder, as well as psoriasis, and now it is apparent that though in a long-term relationship with the man who recently left, she's enthralled by the tall balding man, who bends down farther each day, with bemusement, worry or despair, and it is his indefatigable anxiety and her anorexia and psoriasis that interest me, since she forces herself to move food around on her plate and take a few abject bites in his presence. The outbreak on her hands may have a subliminal effect upon him, but whether it will be one that marries him to her or causes a figurative divorce, time will tell, since time is abundant in certain ways, though it's always an elusive guide, which gets shorter, and characteristically leaves people wanting or short, too.

Psoriasis is a common, chronic, recurrent, inflammatory disease of the skin, causing the formation of dry, scaly patches of various sizes, mostly on the elbows, hands, scalp, nails, the surfaces of the limbs, like shins, and the sacral region, and the patches increase in size, and then stop, and become hard at the centers; old patches may be thickened, tough and very scaly, so that they resemble the outside of an oyster shell. Its course is inconstant, but it usually begins on the scalp or the elbows, and remains in those areas and doesn't spread for a long period of time, or it might disappear. Or it might begin at the sacrum, but I don't know if the young woman has ever had psoriasis there. There is even psoriasis of the penis. One of the disease's chief features is its tendency to return. The skin actually grows too fast. The young woman's hands and elbows were sometimes free of the tough, scaly flesh, which, when present, was in flagrant contrast to the pallor of her cheeks, though they became flushed when she drank wine, which wasn't often, since she feared gaining weight, though she was painfully thin. She couldn't stand to feed herself, she courted weakness, and when the psoriasis struck, she took pains to hide it, as she did her reluctance to nourish herself. If an outbreak occurred on the bottoms of her feet, she wouldn't have to hide it. Psoriasis may occur on the soles of feet, but its onset is usually in middle-aged adults who have no history of psoriasis or any other skin trouble. There may have been focal infections of the tonsils, teeth, or sinuses, and there may have been a causal relationship through an internal usage of antibiotics. But there is no resemblance to psoriasis histologically, only the presence of large, unilocular pustules deep in the epidermis and very little inflammation. I've had difficult, inflammatory friendships with women and men, some of whom have eating disorders, like anorexia nervosa and bulimia, slipped discs, bleeding ulcers, migraines, colitis, pernicious anemia, or who have a variety of other illnesses and complaints, and who have been subject, like myself, to fainting spells, nausea, pneumonia, tooth decay, yeast infections, colds, a nonorganic pressure on the heart, sciatica, nervous stomach, pulled muscles, disturbed bowels, strep throat, infected cuts, flu, or viral infections, and others who have been subject to chronic backaches, recurrent acne, vision loss, cataracts, shingles, herpes complex and simplex, seasonal and other allergies, asthma, arthritis, hypertension and stroke, heart attacks, cancer, digestive disorders, memory loss, auto immune diseases, including AIDS, or gum inflammation, gum loss, heroin, cocaine, nicotine, amphetamine and other dependencies or addictions. About psoriasis, one of its friendly sufferers here once remarked, "Please, always remember to mention the heartbreak of psoriasis."

Sometimes I have been unaware of what happens, colloquially, within some of my friends and that doesn't manifest itself in signs on their bodies, since people can worry themselves into high blood pressure, tension headaches, and heart disease. But few can accept that their bodies also take orders from their psyches, as well as their environment and genetic make-up, and generally a sick mind is more cursed and embarrassing than a sick body. But when symptoms of a disorder appear on the skin, it's fortunate, as they may only be skin deep, or if the body has a greater problem, a reader of skin has warning, a danger signal, since a change in the shape or color of a mole can mean a melanoma. When the skin is red and itchy, most people want relief. Other physical disorders—snoring, heartburn, insomnia—might be considered unimportant, but these can also alert a person to problems which are not necessarily organic, though snoring often indicates blocked nasal passages and, less frequently, sleep apnea, which can be fatal. One friend couldn't sleep without pills. In the mornings, for several hours until she sloughed off their side effects, she was a fury, a monster, she'd say, until two cups of black coffee and a cold shower made her what she called human. During this time if anything occurred, when she wasn't fully herself or adequately awake, something which she had to manage, she couldn't do it, since she could barely speak without a rising ferocity, and instead she quelled the violence that coursed through her, which was frightening to witness, and twice I did, regrettably, later worried she'd turn it against me, which she did more subtly, and she is a person who couldn't survive in a war or a world changed drastically, if her pills weren't available to bring sleep. They didn't console her, they subdued her, because her mother had died when she was six and afterward she couldn't rest, since in dreams, I believe, she twisted into the monster who killed her mother. She became a mother later and insisted it was to be what she hadn't had, she hadn't been mothered, and convinced herself that, even though she could barely awaken in the morning, she could meet a child's needs. It was about this time she left the father of the child, to raise the child alone, and I haven't seen her in a long time, since after she gave birth, she abandoned all of her friends, to enter into a bond with her daughter, like surrendering to a nunnery, while also trying to kick barbiturates.

After pouring the soup into the toilet, I was concerned that it might clog the old john, but I'd been at a loss to figure out what else to do with the soup, unless I put on my shoes and walked into the forest and spilled the unsightly red concoction onto the ground or on the small plants that grow at the edge of forests, which might invite unwanted animals, like skunks, near my room for solitude. I like animals, but I don't like some, especially when they inconvenience me. There was a raccoon who would sit at my door when I lived in the South for a time, so I couldn't enter the cottage until it moved, since it frightened me. I had no idea of how to relate to a raccoon, if it was rabid or friendly, and sometimes it ran across the roof in the night and terrified me, and then I wanted it killed. Usually, I don't want animals killed, but sometimes I do, like my insane cat after he stalked and attacked me. His sharp claws gouged flesh from my left calf, tissue oozed from the fresh wounds and blood flowed down my leg, and I grabbed the cat and tore him from my calf, while another tenant, where I normally live, who had stopped by for some unimportant reason, watched in horror. There are four indentations on my calf from the expulsion and permanent loss of tissue, which force me to remember my insane cat and to doubt my own behavior toward him during his lifetime, when I tried several methods to quell his ferocious, apparent hatred of me, but could not, and which culminated in my ending his life, for which there is no record except my own, and the man I lived with, who rarely mentioned it then, but he does probably blame me, since he and the cat were friends.

Yesterday, returning from the library after the intoxicating encounter with the inquisitive, disheveled woman, I saw six deer, and, when they noticed me, they became exceptionally still, looked at me or in my direction, so I whistled and waved, because I like deer and wanted them to see I was friendly and wasn't stealthily approaching to hurt them. These are protected deer and have grown up free from harassment, safe from being hunted and killed, a freedom everyone should have, but which many don't and have to fight for, though some never want to fight. Deer overrun parts of the country, because they are protected, and now many starve, so some want to kill them, to limit their number, so they won't starve, and others don't, though killing may be less cruel, still I wouldn't want to see them killed, and sometimes there is no solution to progress, except more of it. I stopped in my tracks also, advanced quietly and slowly, whistled, stopped, advanced, whistled, and only one deer bothered to continue to look at me, and I thought, maybe I'll make a friend while I am here, a deer who visits me, isolated or in glorious solitude, and well-cared for, and then I won't miss my young cat as much. Each time I see the deer, whether there are six or three—there is never one who is alone—I believe it is a fortuitous omen, but no one has ever said that sighting deer brings good luck.

The red tomato soup has coated the toilet bowl. It probably would have been better if I hadn't been lazy or cautious and had walked into the forest, but I didn't, and I was still hungry. To distract myself, I started a fire in the large, stone fireplace. Everyone here has a fireplace, and I started the fire by twisting single pages of old newspaper into rod-like forms and placing kindling on top of them, this time arranging the thin sticks of dry wood into a configuration I'd never tried before, but which I'd seen the older man here, Gardner, employ, effectively. He was, in his amused rendition of himself, and also became to me, a Count, adept at fire-building, and other things, and his wife had left him, he told me early on, or maybe he said she wasn't around anymore. On that first night at dinner with him, when all new arrivals appear like magic acts, wanted and unwanted, the Count befriended me and the tall balding man, who, after dinner, leaned over to talk with him and whispered, his mouth close to the older man's ear, as they sat near the fire that he, the Count, built for us, though I kept a distance from it, because it dried my skin. I wanted to know what passed between them, and, against my will, since I generally want little to do with others who might intrude upon my feelings and insinuate themselves into my thoughts, such as the two disconsolate young women, a curiosity about the Count festered, as I considered he might be the person who would change my life, a thought I'd wanted to renounce upon first hearing it from the cardreader, but which took hold, like my mother's tenacious tomato vines, which were rooted in the fertilized soil in the garden at home.

My mother loved tomatoes, when she didn't have trouble eating them, but now she requires the skin removed, and she once grew beefsteak tomatoes in her garden, the only vegetable, though a tomato is sometimes called a fruit, I remember her growing or that she had success with. Her tomatoes were tasty, large and firm, with real red, solid flesh, a glorious red deeper than skin burned under a Florida sun in April, southern Florida being near the equator, or a sirloin steak cooked over a charcoal fire to a perfect, rare purple, a deep bluish red. The beefsteaks were sweet and salty, warm if eaten fresh from the garden plot beside the house, and they smelled of rich, black earth beneath which lay sand, the swamp on which our house was built, and even the streams that ran and flowed to the ocean I loved. My mother's tomatoes set the standard against which I judge all tomatoes today, just as my father's steaks cooked over a charcoal fire set a standard, too. I watched my father charcoal broil while sitting on the grass or on the poured concrete steps that led from the blue and gray slate patio to the storm door to the back of the house, where my mother pushed her arm through the glass, and he was happy broiling steak over a fire, which he composed of briquettes and newspaper but never doused with fuel, which would, he explained, ignite it quickly but ruin its taste. My father loved the taste of good food, he took pleasure in eating, though he was never fat, sometimes plump, and he considered nutrition and diet and read serious books on the subject before the trends or fads, because he wanted to take care of himself and his body, and, when he became sick, his heart failing him, he always researched the latest medicines and procedures known for his condition. The texture of steak mattered to him, the texture of materials mattered, he held cloth in his sturdy hands and felt it with a tender knowledge, though he didn't think he was sensitive and didn't love animals. He liked our dog when she rode in the car with him, her sleek tan head resting on the back of his seat, her short body stretched as far as it could from the back seat to the front seat while he drove. He always liked to drive, he relaxed then, but he didn't really like animals.

The Count was rational, selective, and secretive, people who are secretive are often seductive and treacherous, though sometimes unattractive and without any real interest, but anyway they invite a field of controversy that can be deliberate and cover their inadequacies and lack of engagement in others. Some betray themselves, some betray others, I'm no stranger to these conditions, qualities, and circumstances. The Count collected extremely valuable antique timepieces and clocks, and I learned shortly after he arrived that he turned night and day around, arranging his life according to his own version of time, for when I awoke, he went to sleep, so his breakfast was dinner, and in this manner, he designated how he spent time. The mysterious Violet, or Contesa, wily and agile of mind, kept a close eye on him, since they'd been magnets to each other years ago, repelling and attracting each other, and it was when I realized the extent of their ill-fated, tempestuous past, I named her Contesa. In public I called her Violet, as did everyone, but during this period, when we were in seclusion together, sometimes, in her presence I'd mouth the secret name, especially when she wore shades at breakfast. I also toyed with the notion that she might be the person who could change my life, even as I renounced the idea, along with the tarot reader's charmed reading but not his charms. I didn't impose on Contesa, she didn't on me, I believe she understood the joys and limits of friendship, and her stories sometimes bore sharp points, though she wasn't a moralist, for which I was grateful, because they're dreary characters. A friendship grew between us as much by what passed unspoken and understood, though this can be misunderstood. When she says she's of a dying breed, I always think of the Shakers' unwitting resolve for extinction and their stiff-backed chairs.

One of the Count's unimportant secrets, divulged to tease me, I now think, was how best to start a fire. He taught me, as an uncle does a nephew or niece, on a moonless night after a lackluster dinner, the cook pleasing hardly anyone, in his studio where books on clocks and watches, mostly, but also of ancient history and poetry—Rumi, especially—tragedies and comedies, and mythologies lay stacked in the corners of his room and also lined two long shelves. Whenever he gave me the time, I asked him about his collection and interests, and his answers were brief, though responsible. Always, he looked at some clock, actual or imagined, while his lightly pocked skin never was anything but grayish-green, from lack of sunshine, and I could feel his horror of losing time, it slipping from him in perilous minutes and seconds, and yet I also knew how it augmented his daily drama by punctuating and compelling action and opinion. Day was night, night day, and this difference set him apart, as he was impelled to thwart time, which probably bore down on him with a unique force, pressuring his willowy, aging body, but he was someone, unlike the tall man and the disconsolate women, who didn't complain, and like Contesa, he refrained from ordinary disclosures and responses, having lived long enough to understand the futility of certain communications. I always believe I'll remember the best technique to start a fire, his method, but I don't. Today the fire caught easily, but I don't know why. Yesterday I placed the kindling in approximately the same way, and it didn't. There is a blazing fire now when yesterday the fire died out, because of the wetness of the wood or a slight difference in the configuration of the kindling or small logs with which I always begin, or because I became absorbed in other matters. Actually, I'd forgotten I'd started a fire, and because I didn't tend it the way the Polish woman tends me and remembers to return to the room where I sometimes lie with a heat lamp above my face, the fire died. If the Polish woman didn't remember, and I have at times worried that she wouldn't, when she speaks especially fast in

Polish to people who telephone her, probably some of the men she is or is not dating, because of her mother's objections, my dry skin might crack or be singed by the heat, or I might develop a rash or be burned and disfigured, and if the rash were chronic, full body atopic eczema or psoriasis, or if I had a type of recurrent dermatitis that was difficult to treat, I would probably visit her salon even more frequently, for other kinds of treatments, which might have no medical value, but which might help me, in some way. The salon offers a Glycolic Smoothing Treatment, an Intensive Lifting Treatment, a 100% Collagen and Elastin Mask, a Back Cleansing Treatment, and an Aromatherapy Treatment, which lasts one hour and twenty minutes and costs eighty dollars, and provides "deep hydration and proper nourishing of the skin, improves circulation and regeneration of supporting fibers in the deeper layers of the skin." A Collagen and Elastin Treatment requires the same amount of time and money and "helps to enrich the skin with Collagen and Elastin. It nourishes and relaxes, rejuvenates and exfoliates skin impurities. This treatment will create a younger-looking skin." Just reading these descriptions comforts me, since a word like "nourish" is soothing, because of its open vowels, a diphthong, since to pronounce the word, I must purse my lips, opening them as if I were about to kiss a lover, and though pursing my lips might etch lines around my mouth, I still like to say the word "nourish" aloud, but more I like to hear and read it. Also these descriptions, found in many catalogues or on salon wall signs, whether accurate or not, whether they actually produce what they proffer, are comforting, for I can immediately imagine a more pleasant future for myself when I read the delicious words.

In my Zulu language manual, it says that "the acquisition of a vocabulary is a primary and inescapable consideration in learning a language. Without words we are dumb." The magnitude of the second, simple five word sentence plagued me yesterday, and now today I learn the words for my father ubaba and my mother nnama, baba and mama . . . while eat and enjoy are the same word, dla. Chair is isihlalo, isifo is disease, umzimba the body, hleba to tell tales. The English/Zulu dictionary gives no word for skin, the largest organ of the body. People who suffer from eczema may have to be restrained from scratching off their perniciously itchy skin and some suffer a daily agony. It is impossible to feel another's agony the way the sufferer feels it, and nothing makes someone feel more alone than suffering, whether it is mental or physical, pain is unbearable but borne. I could have talked, this morning, to the woman with psoriasis, who needed attention, and given her the name of my dermatologist, and told her about treatments available that might soothe or temporarily remedy her skin, even if she and it were never cured. The young woman's psoriasis was in full bloom this morning, livid as the complexion of an ancient alcoholic, so that for her it appeared being in love assaulted her calm, the idea of love had attacked her peace of mind, as symptoms flourished on her cheeks, her elbows, and the backs of her hands. The tall balding man, it's rumored, has had many lovers, sometimes simultaneously, but when he is in love, Contesa generously explained, he is intense and engaged, so that the woman he directs himself toward in that moment feels she alone exists for him; and no matter that he has left many a woman brokenhearted, all of whom have felt the way the young woman might now, her hands blazing with discomfort, and reason demands that this will happen again, each woman thinks she will be the one to change him, as she does now.

I don't like tending a fire, since I'm easily distracted, I have many ideas, which are spread about the room and on the floor, and none I want to realize, but most I'd like to undo, if I could, like relationships and many experiences, and I don't like having to check on a fire to verify that it's burning well and not going out of control, the way the Polish woman tends to me and makes sure that, because my skin's sensitive, there's not too much heat coming from the chamomile concoction over which I lower my face, to absorb its cleansing and rejuvenating goodness, steaming open my pores, since too much heat is bad for such sensitive skin as mine, she tells me. Sometimes she won't permit me to place my face above this potion but instead positions me under a heat lamp, which is supposedly kinder to skin like mine. Then she leaves the room. I can hear her making phone calls, writing notes or opening nail-polish bottles, because she also gives manicures, though I have never had one from her, because during a manicure, you sit face to face, and I don't want to see her face that long. She speaks in Polish to those she calls or who call her, though not to clients like myself who don't know the language, but especially to the owner who phones often; I don't understand what she's saying, I don't seriously imagine she is talking about me, yet it's not impossible, since there are many things we don't say to each other. We talk about the same things again and again when I visit, rarely diverging from these by now familiar subjects, and I have no way of knowing what she is saying in her native language, her mother tongue, but she returns to the room within twenty-five minutes, to lift my head from the benevolent vapors of the chamomile potion and dote on me like a baby.

I once tried to imagine, to the extent I could, because I had scant knowledge of it, having a baby and caring for it. I didn't give it a sex, I wanted to see if I would ever want one, or if I could care for one, because I don't want one, yet women are supposed to want one, and if you've had the fate to be born a female, about which I had no choice, you have no choice about the most important things in life, it's expected and encouraged that you should want a child, that it's unnatural not to want a child, and that in some way you're selfish to have life without bringing more life into it, offspring who will be dependent for years. Human beings care for their young longer and longer, prolonging their infancy and effecting a mature infantilism in them, who will probably disdain those who raised them for a good part of that dependency and also later, tied to them with a hatred that's also love. My mother and my dead father live, in a significant way, with me, and lodge in an abstract section of me that I can't excise, mostly because I have no control over it, since I don't know where it's located or what its function is, unlike my relationship to other objects which I understand better and whose design, like a chair's, either pleases or displeases me, but unlike a chair I have no choice about its position.

When I first arrived, intent upon settling in, becoming as comfortable as I could, I spent several days finding a chair I could sit upon and look at, too, but there was only one, finally, that served, though I never really loved it, it was never comfortable enough, and it was certainly not beautiful to my eye, and also I had to get a cushion for it, so sitting on it was awkward, I had to keep adjusting the cushion. It was serviceable, so I accepted the chair and its limits, just as I learned not to hate my mother, to accept her more or less, or maybe even love her in the way an animal might, for warmth and comfort, which I never really received from her, she merely represents those qualities, but it doesn't matter anymore, since she's old, too old to fault, though my brother does, presumably, because he never contacts her, though our father is dead, my brother hated him more than he hated me, I think. My brother and father fought, I watched them, my mother took her husband's side, I was too young to know what the subject of their endless argument was. My brother hid, he slammed his door, locked it, I don't know what he was doing in his bedroom, he must have grown inward like a stubborn, short leg hair and become inflamed with pus, his furious objections never pierced and placated, and, as I record him now, his mouth is cast in a grimace. Scowling, he disappeared. I've known his kind of anger in others, I may seek it out, but I don't want to look for him.

An infant's tiny fingers and toes are terrifying, the least thing might damage them, and I don't want to look at photographs of their tiny toes and fingers, each toe is too little, the nails on their fingers like thin ice, and I hate to think of their nails being cut by scissors or clippers that are bigger than their feet and fingers. Their nails are dead skin, oddly, a newborn arrives with dead skin, hair, also, both shooting from delicate fingers or heads, the skulls of which are not yet closed at the crown, the crown covered by a membrane or slither of cells of alarming fragility. Their neurological systems are also not yet complete, so infants arrive unfinished and at risk. I once fell hard on the back of my head, by jumping backward down the poured concrete stairs leading to the patio of the house I loved, because I was curious if I could jump backward down stairs, but I never mentioned my fall to anyone, though my head hurt for months, because the act embarrassed me, and, after it I was less curious about feats that might incur physical injury. I believe my crown has never entirely closed. Adam and Eve acquired a knowledge of death for their human curiosity, the pair weren't innocent of sex but of mortality. Einstein said both human stupidity and the universe were infinite, but he was less sure about the universe's infinitude, and, as the very first humans couldn't have known about death, it still existed outside their experience of the future, it must have been an eternal punishment to suffer its awareness, which distinguishes people from other animals, except maybe elephants. Over a hunk of raw meat, which they tore with their hands and teeth before the invention of tools and fire, one of the cavedwellers—bush people were the first humans—clutched his heart and fell to the floor, lifeless. Or, Eve's death came first, maybe during a painful childbirth, though some people die in their sleep, and then it's intoned, "They just went." Death lives, but only for others, as Duchamp said, it's an impossible idea, the gravest in life, and every day I stare at pictures of my dead friends with wonder at their perpetual absence. But creatively, I believe, which is my will to bring into existence something I have not grasped before, both literally and figuratively, since even in undoing, there is a making, at least for me, I forge them into my life, and, also, looking at them, inert, I rehearse my end. I'd like to be prepared for it. Though change confounds fate, there it is, even death is a change, but also hope persists because there is change, but about hope and its virulent partner disappointment I am querulous.

I had rashes often when I was a child. In the winter, where I lived, near the ocean, which was a desolate gray-green, the cold wind whipped the sand in circles, and I was forced to wear heavy woolen pants and sweaters. My body felt on fire. I was uncomfortable and itchy, the inside of my thighs were hot and sticky, and unsightly rashes, little red bumps, would spread on my inner thighs, around my neck, and on my chest. In the winter, the harsh wool of sweaters and pants plagued me. Even the thought of a heavy wool sweater or a pair of pants stiff to the touch could bring discomfort, and I'd start to feel warm, my forehead would become hot, I'd sweat and turn beet red. Now I try never to wear clothes that cause me to itch or that irritate my skin. I can barely stand to touch materials that could torment my flesh, like a hair shirt, which was worn voluntarily, to cause discomfort, and instead I search for fabric that's gentle, one hundred percent cotton, or a silk or cashmere, and whenever I choose something to wear, or when I'm in a store surrounded by clothes hanging on racks or decorously displayed on shelves, surrounded also by women and men, or just women, who want something new to cover their bodies, to make them feel differently about themselves, even for a moment, one that evaporates so quickly they will soon need to visit a store again and buy something else to wear, first I notice colors, then I touch fabric, twisting the material between my fingers, to test its gentleness, and sometimes I press it to my face, to see if it is soft enough. I also breathe in the material, hoping to like its smell, and, in doing so, use a sense with no sense, though with consequences and blind motivations, since the senses have no insight, but a smell triggers the recurrence of a past moment or a scene which dissolves as fast as mercury slides, like the vainglorious past, and with it comes the realization of its loss, and these are called sense memories.

Material is rarely soft enough, it's rare to find good cotton. There are many kinds of cloth, material that is made of natural fibers, like the four basic, earliest fibers—cotton, wool, silk, and linen—and material from artificial or synthetic matter, like nylon and rayon, and later polyester. Rayon was the first synthetic material, the generic term for manufactured textile fibers or yarn produced chemically from cellulose or with a cellulose base, and for threads, strands or fabric made of it. Cellulose is a substance constituting the chief part of the solid framework of plants, of cotton, linen, rayon, paper. In its pure form, it's a white amorphous mass. The chemistry of cellulose is quite complicated. My father understood it and told me about yarns, synthetic and natural, when I was little. During World War II, my father and his younger brother innovated synthetics, nylon threads, because cotton was scarce and required for the war effort, but historically cotton is associated with enslaved African men and women toiling in cotton fields on Southern plantations, though I wear it usually without recalling that, and, even in the winter, a heavy cotton feels good close to the skin, because I don't like being too warm, and good cotton, of a higher denier, is usually comfortable.

There could easily be a mishap when clipping an infant's tiny toenails, with their uncountable and inherent vulnerabilities that immature or unfinished adults still feel, but I forgot that the fantasy baby I supposedly bore was in the room. I had become absorbed in what I was doing, I was busy, and when I realized I had forgotten the imaginary baby, it had already crawled to an electrical socket, stuck a tiny, pink finger into it, and was severely shocked, its toenails burned, or it was killed, for which I was to blame. Sometimes no one is to blame, terrible things happen, accidents and illnesses, and no one is to blame, yet I always want to bring something to account, or someone, often myself. I'd like to blame my father for the disappearance of my brother, or my brother for the death of my father, I'd like to blame one friend's sickness on another, I blame the ocean, which I love, for its riptides that pull hapless swimmers out to its depths and swallow them, I blame a mountain for a friend's accidental death, but with silly blame, there is added futility. I can't do anything about riptides and incessant desire, so I usually try to make lunch last, though there is a limited quantity, and today I fail again, yet I always hope to invent new ways to make it last, but rarely do, except to choose not to eat it or to eat it an hour later, which is an option people with food disorders select. If they don't eat now, when they are supposed to, they can eat later, which prolongs the possibility of a satisfaction that escapes them, just as the head cook escapes satisfying the residents here. If I like the soup that comes in the thermos, or even if I don't, I pour it into a white china mug and sit before the fire, stir it, and then take a spoonful, attempting everything in a leisurely way, as if I weren't hungry and had all the time in the world, which is what there is, nothing but time, and as languorously as I spoon the soup and stir the fire, as quickly does the fire wane and the mug empty. No matter how measured I am, how I alternate or retard my actions, eventually the lunch is eaten, finished, and the fire, if I don't throw a log on it, burns out. Here is the death of lunch, I think, bemused, but nonetheless a subsequent apathy arrives, the dreariness of uncertainty, and the dread about what to do with myself, since now there's nothing to do but face the afternoon and wait for dinner, though I'm not hungry, only perplexed and unsatisfied.

The residents often remark, at dinner, that they hope to make their lunch last, though there is a limited quantity of it, because it's a long time until dinner, and like me they need to find ways to make it last. Some do, but I never do. My brother played a game with me, one of the few we had, including Monopoly, though I wasn't good at it, when I was seven, he eighteen, called: Who can eat ice cream the slowest? No matter how slowly I licked the vanilla ice as it melted over the side of the snow cone, how I juggled the sugar cone and walked fast, because we always competed walking back to the house I loved, he won, he would never let me win, though I was many years younger, and then he was triumphant. We would reach the front door to the house that was sold over my protests, but my brother was already long gone from it and us then, and he would still be eating his ice cream and enjoying his victory, and, strangely enough, though I was frustrated and had lost again, since he was bigger, I believed it was his right to win.

After lunch, I sometimes take a walk, it's good to get exercise, but I dislike exercise for its own sake, and the fire is still burning. I'm reluctant to throw water on it, because later it might be harder to start another, when the ash is wet, the floor of the fireplace damp, but I'm reluctant to leave it burning, because it might consume the place where I make and unmake things or do nothing, which is mine for a short while and on whose walls I've affixed photographs, to remind me of my friends, as well as places I've never been and places I've been, where I may want to return. Some of my friends are smiling, some not, some will never be anywhere again but in photographs, and their weight burdens me. It is disagreeably stuck in me like undigested food, so I walk closer to their pictures, whose lack of animation might be undone or upset by my movement toward them, but they are always dead. Of a mountain's treacherousness, a bad heart, a brain tumor, a murder, AIDS, cancer, a car crash. On another wall are photographs of friends' well-fed, bright children, who are amply encouraged but who will anyway have problems and may one day turn against their parents, who can't help themselves, have tried their best and probably won't deserve their enmity, though people live with the consequences of their actions. No one can foretell the events that will have weight in a young child's life, which also incites anxious parents to more worry, but then most things in a child's life can't be accounted for, and they will remember almost nothing that happens before the age of three, four, even five. From the time I learned to count and read, when I read or heard a number, I saw a color, and when I heard or read the word for a color, or saw a color, I registered its numerical value and equivalent. Orange four, black ten, white one, red five, purple nine, blue eight, powder blue three, pink three, yellow two or three, depending upon how light, muted, or bold it was. The elements had weight, numerically, and shades and hues of color. Numbers and colors were figures in my imagination that fused into patterns about which I never spoke, though in some way it helped the world make sense, as things added up in my young mind. But the weight of death is heavier, there is no scale for it, and I shove it into a corner, where it lies, an insurmountable lump, threatening to spread its ugliness.

The Polish woman's salon is near where I normally live, an easy walk, and one I know so well I may no longer actually see where I'm going, but at least I'm unaware of exercising, unless I force myself to think about it, but then if I do, I also think about how little I actually exercise and that I'm hastening my end or allowing for a more difficult old age, though I'm reluctant to acknowledge I'm aging, that death's around a corner, while I also know that I'm dying and think about death daily, like a prayer I'm expected to repeat. Not taking exercise may hasten my end, or final rest, though it's not rest, just a nothing and something we can't know, but maybe thinking that is restful. Also I'm lazy, impatient, and dislike pain, though my dentist and a physical therapist have told me I have a high threshold for it, which also doesn't surprise me. I have watched people who are exercising, grimacing and grunting, especially when lifting weights or contorting themselves into peculiar shapes that are hard to achieve and hold, but many enjoy their effort, they may enjoy effort itself, as it makes them feel they're accomplishing a goal and also effort could make them feel alive. Many people don't feel alive.

The Polish woman is a great one for exercise, exuding a heartiness of appetite, which I feel is repulsive and attractive, when I'm lying on the chaise lounge, covered in a soft pink or fuzzy blue blanket of one hundred percent cotton, as she ministers to me in her attentive way, though it is sometimes perfunctory, because she doesn't really care about me or my skin, it is of no genuine concern to her, and she doesn't think about me or it when I am not with her. Her healthy face can look bored or vacant, the emptiness of which is intriguing and unpleasant, though her skin is unlined and, like a rough linen, straddles her broad Slavic cheekbones. She has a light red mole perched close to the corner of her lip, and it is that area of excess on her face to which my eyes often return. She has no facial scars, none I have noticed, while she, sometimes known as an aesthetician, has, I imagine, noticed every imperfection on mine. Once or twice she has given me a massage and seen or felt all or most of the skin on my body, where she perhaps noticed the scar above my knee, which is an inch long and a quarter-inch wide. It's ugly, but it is not on my face, whose placement might have inflected the course of my life, I might not have gone out in company much or been considered in any way a desirable partner, for sex or dinner or even talk, if several deep scars covered my cheek, chin or forehead, if my face had been slashed to ribbons with a razor or knife. If the cat I put to death because it attacked me had clawed my face and not my calf, if the cat had clung to my face with its sharp nails the way it clung to my left leg, I would now have four depressions on my cheek or forehead, which would make me a less suitable partner in many situations, and some sensitive people, such as myself, would have to ignore the imperfections or never engage with a character that scarred. But instead the scars were carved into my calf when so much tissue oozed from my leg that small craters formed, whose depressions could not ever again be replenished, so much tissue was disgorged, and my left calf will never be normal or beautiful again, but forever marked by the action of an insane cat, who will always be remembered for that, as well as for the mystery of its animus toward me and my inability to quench or limit its unrepentant hatred or protect its deformed life, and if it had attacked my face, my life would have been changed.

I like having a place to go toward, a direction consoles, and there are many places around here for escape. I could walk around the grounds and search for elusive deer or shy moles, I could stroll into town and have coffee in a café where local residents gather, or go at any time to the library where the odd inquisitive woman might await me, or wander around the local, historic cemetery, with its tombstones, graves or resting places, supposedly a sanctuary for the living, though for me this has never been true, as it is predicated—like some schemes and plots, whose repetitions advance an old story and make it appear inevitable—upon hoary untruths about eternity, since also life and death are repetitious, and if I know where I'm going, to town, to have a coffee or a tryst, to buy socks, and that I have a reason to go there, it doesn't feel like exercise. It's an adventure, even if the goal isn't exciting, but I become excited easily, like my father, when we drove to the Thanksgiving parade or returned to the fierce, gray-green ocean in winter, where he made me exercise, run along the sand to build up my calf muscles, one of which now has four indentations from the claws of my insane cat, but my father wasn't alive then. My everyday, unremarkable shoes are hidden from me, as I'd inadvertently located the spot most unlikely for them, but finally I discover them in the place I told myself I'd remember they'd be but didn't, slip them on and notice my all-cotton socks, which I like, because they were simple to buy. In the place where I grew up, girls and their mothers shopped relentlessly for clothes they didn't need but wanted, and I didn't ever want to join them, but sometimes went along, secretly dying because I was wasting time doing what I disliked, shopping and trying on clothes in too small rooms, where, awkwardly, women and girls undress and saleswomen ask them to come out and show them how the clothes look, or stand in larger rooms surrounded by other women and girls, strangers, who are undressed and then dressed, looking at themselves in mirrors, displaying expressions that betray avarice, despair, glee, and no one says anything except, Try this on, I don't like this, it's too big, small, tight, I like this, how much is it, and it's often better not to say anything at all. People have baker's dozens of yeasty, unspoken wants, they often especially want objects to make up for what they never had, and some ask for them, which makes them vulnerable, and those who never make demands may feel less vulnerable, but they are not, as they are hungry too, and unlikely to be fed, since they are afraid to ask for what they need. Sustained hunger must be worse than the discomfort of undigested food or the phantom pangs of unrequited love everyone suffers, but hardly anyone wants it known they do, since sometimes it's better not to say anything. Some people want to feel hungry, women, especially, who can afford to eat well but who deny themselves, some even want to feel faint with hunger, because they become alive then, eating themselves alive. Spiritual people also want to feel hungry, they renounce and deny the flesh, along with the rest of the material world, and when they fast for a week, they become lightheaded and feel closer to a higher power, which in high and hallucinatory moments they may be.

I buy one hundred percent cotton socks whenever I can, though often there's just a mix of eighty percent cotton and twenty percent nylon around, so I've mastered wearing this combination, adjusted to it, since it's healthy to be flexible, but many people aren't, and I, too, in my mind or especially my body, where habit and rigidity shape demands and inclinations, sometimes can't exhort myself to the plasticity or fluidity I know is good for my health, and often I think few would survive if war came and deprived them of what they thought was necessary. If they couldn't eat what they wanted here, many would be lost. Some fabric combinations are still better than others because better cotton is used, and the best thing about my father was how he touched material, how he let it drift through his adept fingers, while the expression on his face changed, his concentration attuning itself to the feel of the material, or when he looked through a small magnifying glass at a thread or weighed one on his golden machine, whose sharp needle could quickly pierce the skin on your finger. Socks can also scratch, but I have no worry about how they look or what they mean, though I accept they have some meaning, since nothing has no meaning, though some theologians think evil is nothing since a god wouldn't create it, but I dislike religion, since people are often promised a better life, a glorious afterlife, and worship deities who censor or condemn them to wretchedness on earth. Calvinism doesn't forgive its congregants, and most religions threaten those who don't subscribe to their beliefs, everyone suffers because of religion or from faith or the lack of faith. I don't know what to have faith in, except people, who are as irascible as the Bible's Jehovah, though not as omniscient.

I'll wander into a store and casually buy a pair or two of socks. Jerry Lewis throws away socks after he wears them once, and I'd like to do that, because it may be wrong and is certainly indulgent, and also because doing laundry is repetitive, and throwing away socks makes less laundry, though I dislike washing dishes and doing laundry less than I did when I was younger, when everything imposed on me was a big waste of time, but now I'm not certain what's a waste of time, or what's nothing, since I may find something when not looking, and because time is all we have, inexplicably. Almost lackadaisically, I toss a pitcher of water onto the blazing fire, dousing it while explaining to myself the reasons I shouldn't have, because I'll have to deal with the aftermath later, but I do anyway, as it's urgent that I leave this room, a temporary shelter or refuge, though some people here refuse to accept temporariness, although it's all there is. A woman chained herself to her bed, a man boarded his door against intruders, and they were removed, forcibly, returned to their respective homes, and I can understand not resigning yourself to the inevitable, but I wouldn't tie myself to my bed, I don't think. The woman who chained herself there also sucked men's toes, and, at night, uninvited, though some left their doors unlocked, she entered their bedrooms, they'd awaken with her at their feet, their toes in her mouth, she was sucking greedily, and some were annoyed, but some enjoyed it, though they never admitted it. Some may have a phobia about all types of sucking, and the library's sex manual cites many fears I'd not heard of or that may be out of fashion, like "Clavestitism, a morbid desire to put on the dresses one wore in childhood," or "Syphilomania, an inclination to attribute all illness to syphilis," though "Venerophobia, a morbid fear of sexual intercourse" persists, and one night at dinner, following a lackluster day, I recited some of the more remote sexual fears to the table, and Spike, with her enthusiasm, ready laugh, and brilliant, long hair, who always liked talking about sex, though rarely had an opening, joined in, charged especially by hearing about "voice fetishism," of which the dictionary said: "The voice is one of the strongest sexual fetishes, many men actually fall in love with a voice, even with a voice heard over the telephone, and cannot free themselves from its spell." I understand coming under a spell, though I didn't expect in my case it was a voice that seduced me, but I could imagine it, and I didn't mention my thralldoms to anyone at the table, and only Spike spoke uninhibitedly about men's voices she grooved on, she said, and phone sex that the dictionary anticipated but didn't define, in which she engaged with her necessarily absent lover, but the demanding man's skin flared and darkened, the disconsolate women's faces sunk, the psoriatic character shoved her food almost off her plate, while the tall balding man smiled, though not at her, since blatancy might shriek his mating call, and I thought: I won't do this again. Although, in some way, to be honest, the way the daughter of time must be, their active disdain also satisfied me. Not long after, a Turkish man appeared, a translator and poet in need of a long rest and quiet—his commercial interests allowed him to write what he wanted and to travel, he owned a paper and carton factory—and he muttered to me before dinner that there should be more sex here, everywhere, and that I in particular should have more sex in everything. He was passionate about his beliefs, especially about translation, sex and sexlessness, and he and I would discuss this more soon enough.

The town is two miles away, a reasonable distance for a walk, and it is also an oasis or a distraction, so I'm not trapped here, except with myself or by encounters with, for instance, the two young women, who have made my entering the main hall a problem; the staff, who subtly inquire if I'm making progress, did I enjoy the meeting, lecture, or session I attended, or the tall balding man, who, when he is alone might expound on his malaise, after he has run ten miles and smells rank, but is unaware of this, while his palms pool with sweat, the effect of primary palmar hyperhidrosis, which may be genetic, and causes its sufferers great anxiety. I don't want him to hold my hand, the way he likes, while employing his neurosis as efficiently and seductively as he can. But if I don't enter the main hall, I'm not deterred from my walk. Still, I'm often drawn there, as if a voice called me to it, and, like dousing a fire, when I tell myself I shouldn't and instead to think about the consequences, I do enter the spacious, dark wood room, whose corners are sometimes decorated with one or two residents gazing at photographs of lakes, deer, and birds, or the director and staff taking a break; but I'm eager for excitement or surprise, and there may await something unexpected, though usually here, and elsewhere, what is unexpected isn't. I know the Count is sleeping and Contesa rarely shows her face before dinner, needing all the solitude she can get after breakfast; Spike, with the ready laugh, is in her cabin, talking on her cell phone or studying and writing formulae; the inventor, whose restless innovations may be the result of prostalgia, is joining lengths of copper tubing together; the demanding man is sulking, though he might even be in the main hall, waiting for attention, and yesterday I attempted to avoid it but walked in, anyway, which I can't explain, even to myself, except that I'd scheduled a therapeutic massage later and had only time to kill, since that's all there is.

When I'm in the place I call home, where I have a young wild cat and an old, frail mother who may or may not miss me, I see a Japanese therapeutic masseuse, whose attitude toward the body is vastly different from the Polish cosmetician's, who twice has massaged me with gentle strength and kneaded my body respectfully, though she may not respect it or me. The Japanese masseuse acts against my body, she forces it to comply, as if trouncing a truculent enemy, and I can see her wringing her hands and canvassing my legs before moving toward them, to exact revenge. She prods my lower back with her sharp knees, jabs my taut shoulders with tight, rabbit punches, and thrusts hammer thumbs into tense, blood-deprived muscles. When she punishes my body sufficiently, after throttling it mercilessly, it might come around, resign itself, or relax. With her I am not a sensitive character, my body is physical matter, a noncompliant even unwilling agent, in which I, her client, am trapped or by which I am possessed. She hopes to free me with a method that produces majestic pain during a session, when I yell and grunt, but after a session, I experience some release. It's true that I have a body about which I had no choice, but with which I can choose to wrestle by volunteering for a painful massage, though I don't believe in absolute evil or the devil as a Frenchman here does and who claims he accepts and even courts its presence within him.

There are guest scholars, philosophers, scientists, spiritualists and mental health and community activists, who, on some days, both before and after dinner, speak on their subjects, since it is said to be a tonic which cleanses the mind, or that it helps the mind to encounter new ideas, or to fill ourselves with others than we have, and sometimes there are surprises. A resident can't avoid attending at least some talks, because the administration looks askance and concludes that you are not trying hard enough in your endeavor, whatever it is, and that you may not, through no fault of theirs and only yours, make progress. I skipped "Against Renaissance Perspective," "Spin Control Is Out of Control," "Live Food, Raw Food," "My Life in Accounting," "Beyond Repair or Damaged Forever," and "The Lures of Fly Fishing." On occasion the lecture committee brings in theater groups, whose plays and presentations are supposed to be thought-provoking but not so provocative as to disturb a resident's peace of mind. I heard a talk by a local member of the Audubon Society: "What is a voice to a bird?" as well as a carnival historian on "The Life of Frieda Pushnik, Armless and Legless Wonder," a forensic anthropologist on "The Natural

Fear of Death," and a local minister on "Banish Misfortune." Occasionally residents present, and the Count gratified me and some of the residents, including the tall balding man, Contesa, J and JJ, and their squarejawed midwestern sidekick, on an evening after dinner, which was his late morning. It lasted precisely ten minutes, the span of time he had decided was reasonable and appropriate, not to waste a minute of our lives, or his, every second was precious, and placed his gold pocketwatch on the table, noting its movement periodically.

"These are some offhand remarks," the Count started, characterizing them as his "Dead Hand" notes. "I will not be discussing my collection of clocks and timepieces, as you may have imagined. I will talk about other esoterica I have collected. Timepieces are my love and vocation. What follows are pieces from an avocational endeavor.

"Human beings were once covered with the same material our fingernails are made of, instead of skin. Adam and Eve were originally formed from this. When expelled from the Garden of Eden, their original covering shrank to the tips of their fingers and toes. For this reason we still resemble the gecko, whose nails twinkle like tiny crystals in the night.

"During the reign of King Ramses III, who lived from 1198 to 1167 BC, laborers went on strike for cosmetics." Hired hands in the Theban necropolis refused to work because the food was lousy, the Count put it, they had no ointment, and it was the first strike in history.

"Fourteen hundred years later Clement pronounced anathema against the cosmological theories of the Greek philosophers, labeling them astrology not astronomy."

Contesa snort-laughed, she followed her astrological chart, but the Count persevered, he knew his former lover's objections.

"Clement of Alexandria stated that cosmology spawned a swarm of bestialities. This he published during the childhood of Heliogabalus, but copies never reached Emesa. It was the Syrian desert city where Heliogabulus received the training that earned him the title 'King Catamite.' It also made him the greatest ruler the West has ever known. He ruled from age fourteen until assassinated at age nineteen in 219 AD.

Had Heliogabulus taken proper cognizance of the Christian Zombie boom, the course of history would have been reversed. His contempt for Christianity's potential for bad magic was his only serious political error. Like Pythagoras and Allah, 'he' was one of his many names. Emesa—then a sort of Syrian equivalent of Lhasa—no longer exists. It was swallowed up by the earth in the year 1219, exactly on the one thousandth anniversary of Heliogabulus's death."

The Count wished us a good evening and a peaceful rest.

"But I exhort you," he urged in an afterthought, "remember the ancient Egyptian proverb: 'Do not laugh at a blind man nor tease a dwarf nor injure the affairs of the lame.'"

He would take our questions now, he said.

There were none. Contesa arose, haughtily, and she alone would have words with the Count in private, but rumors flew that a devout Christian was upset by the Count's casual reference to Christianity and the Zombie boom. The Count didn't concern himself with sacred cows or interdiction, he cherished sacrilege, his rational mind insisted on it. I'd never heard of the boom and now thought about Zombies differently, but no one dared interrogate the Count or confront him, except Contesa, who knew him well, too well, she occasionally implied, since he was formidable, removed, and entirely in his own time. His unusual lecture, though short, I believe encouraged his former lover in respects and in a way that I couldn't have predicted, but which contained surprises for me and others and which arrived soon enough to be, in a sense, useful.

I am allowed to attend all of the lectures, which are held at 4 p.m. and 8:30 p.m., but I prefer those scheduled after dinner, when the day is over, and others may inject into it what they wish, with less damage to me. Massages are available but not facials, because massages, like hot baths, soothe the mind and tend the body, and a massage can have a salutary effect upon a tense body and fraught mind. Yesterday, after I saw the deer, I underwent a therapeutic massage during which tissue was manipulated, the resident therapist pressing on and into invisible fibers of my body, to release knots, and, as my tension released and fibers unknotted, I felt the painful pleasure I trust. There are some who can't bear being touched, even by a mate, to whom a massage would be torture, and it is said, though this may be apocryphal, that George Washington, a formal man, an American aristocrat, who wore a powdered wig, read little, according to his Vice President Adams, and kept hundreds of slaves, couldn't bear to be touched, even a hand briefly on his shoulder provoked his presidential ire, and in some this sensitiveness is extreme and extensive—most sounds, fabrics, voices, foods, and smells disturb them—and their new condition bears the name Sensory Defensiveness. The vexed head cook finds it almost impossible to feed them, since these characters are typically both sensation seeking and sensation avoiding. With the resident massage therapist, I may also talk, though not with the Japanese masseuse who greets my exclamations of pain with silence, but the resident masseuse encourages me to explain where my pain is, with what feeling or event it may be associated, to what other part of my body it may have fled, or where it may have come from, historically, then her fingers follow the line I draw with words to the spot, and invariably she locates the source of the trouble. Her skin is translucent, like alabaster, unclouded by worry lines, peerless and unscathed, and, with her, I feel attended to. Her hands are softer than the Polish woman's, though strong, too, and both of them tell me I have sensitive skin, but the resident massage therapist listens closely to every word I utter or every sound my body emits, while the Polish woman doesn't. She is invariably absorbed in her own life, which she relates indirectly in our many encounters, so that I experience or sense her increasing discontent in the place she works, because when she rushes for the ringing telephone and expels a sigh, it is more exhausted and bigger, like a diva's intake of breath before hitting the highest note in her range, and then I fear she may not return to me, in all senses, though I was never abandoned as a child, only forgotten or neglected in ordinary ways. On one visit, when the telephone rang, she set my head and face over the steaming chamomile brew and left, and I heard her speaking in Polish, but this time vociferously, and my regular twenty minutes of steam turned into forty-five, so my back hurt as I bent forward in an awkward position, wanting to lift my head but fearing I'd anger her and lose the benefits of the treatment, and when she returned, she said only, "That was my mother," and I surmised hastily, without having much reason, that the glowering man had no chance with her. She had been married once, she admitted during my next visit, which now came in three-week intervals, since it was winter, and my skin was perniciously dry, my hands chapped so badly that two fingers bled as if I had stigmata, and white flaky skin dusted my cheeks and forehead, so sometimes it was hard to smile, because my tight lips cracked and bled. She'd married when she was a teenager, she told me like closing a book, and I told her I'd been married, also, to encourage her further, but even so she didn't say more, and neither did I. Some women want nothing to do with men ever, some quit intercourse only after abysmal episodes with them, some say they can't be bothered anymore, or don't want to be what they become with men, some lose any desire. I've had one marriage, several serious involvements and lust-filled relationships, many light affairs of the heart, and other playful as well as potent nonaffairs, or romantic friendships, and sometimes it was I who withdrew, often I didn't know what I wanted or if I wanted anything, or what or who could make a difference. I wasn't sure about the Polish woman, suspecting that at the age of thirty-eight or forty, she had left them behind, though her studied appearance, even in a synthetic white cloth uniform, seemed staged for the advent of the right man. I admired her appearance, which could never be mine, because her eyebrows never had a stray hair that needed plucking, the eyebrow pencil she applied with a firm, sure hand created neat, thin lines that never went farther than they should, and drew two light-brown half-moons on her forehead, so her face had a look of expectation, when otherwise it might appear vacant, her full lips were painted with a lipstick that didn't smear or fade, her nails, shaped modestly, were never too long, otherwise she couldn't give facials or massages without clawing or gouging a client's skin, and her nail polish, blush pink, orange pearl, or sunny tangerine, never chipped. I once wore black nail polish to the cramped salon, and, though she said nothing, I could sense the Polish woman's disapproval, but I don't think it was on the day she abandoned me for more than forty-five minutes with my face over the steaming chamomile potion. The doorbell also rings from time to time, and she must answer it, since she's the only one there, except on weekends when her boss shows up, and they banter in Polish, but the ringing doorbell is a less frequent interruption than the telephone. I have learned a little about her former husband, her mother liked him and he was also Polish, but each time I visit I hope she'll divulge more, but then she never asks me anything much, except about my skin, which I don't moisturize enough, because I don't like cream on my skin at night, when it might suffocate it and me, and she asks perfunctorily about my various jobs, but since she's not interested in these various projects, I tell her enough to be polite. She never inquires about my friends or enemies, my cat, my aging mother, and her discretion sculpts our routine conversations, which are social but impersonal, though her work supplies a tenderness that most friendships don't.

In another place I lived for some months, in the South, near to former, thriving plantations on which cotton was picked by enslaved Africans, there was a florid-faced man who'd been a farmer, and in his late sixties, after retirement, decided to learn massage therapy, so he went to school and once a week offered his novice services free to everyone in the small town. I offered myself regularly to him. His farmer's hands were rough and big as hams, he read the Bible daily, he moved fastidiously, he kept the room very warm, and every time he worked on me, also very slowly, I melted into the professional table he brought with him, and under his rough-skinned, gentle hands and fresh sheets smelling of wildflowers his wife laundered, I let my mind wander as far as it could, since I mean always to untether it from its ordinary course, but habits were established early, in the neural routes of the brain, about which I had no choice. The apprentice masseur spent hours on me practicing his trade, and his efforts tired me, but also I had hardly a care in the world by the time he finished, and the big, tender man was also exhausted, when darkness had fallen in the place where wildflowers sprouted, bloomed in abundance, and the air smelled sweeter than the freshly laundered sheets, and no more was expected of either of us. I could return to my home, careful to avoid a man who, because I refused his seduction, would later take revenge, though I didn't know that then, when my fate was, in some way, enjoined to his unfulfilled, temporary desire. I remember the masseur's hulk, his benign face and large frame, I can assemble the sweet infinitude of those long nights in that overheated room where he practiced on me, where his tender concern and his religious convictions showed themselves, by acknowledging, in long, stroking motions and studious pummeling, his belief that the body was holy.

Today I'm determined to walk briskly and avoid the main house and to keep to the road. I wonder if facing the traffic, when it rounds the bend, or having my back to it, is safer, as I also watch for deer, birds, squirrels, and wild turkeys. If it is 3 p.m., the yellow schoolbus will wind around the road and drop off children, big and little, in a familiar scene that verges on a gluttonous, almost pornographic sentimentalism, so I hope to make my way to town before its nostalgic appearance. It is probably 2:00, not even, and there is hardly a car that passes and only a few trucks, and by the side of the road beer cans and used condoms are strewn, but not too many, and sometimes from the thick forest a hidden animal moans or a bird sings or screeches, or the trees and branches, some bare, shake from a sudden breeze, but it is mostly remarkably quiet. I can hear my heart beat and my second heart contract, and also hear my breathing, which I adjust to my steps, in, step; out, step; in, step; out, step, and while I try not to worry, only to breathe in and out, to think, what a day, since it is a beautiful day, but I do worry, also about how well I'm breathing. I keep up a pace but am passed by two women jogging who wave exuberantly; by the tall balding man running even faster, with his mouth hanging open, so he looks vulnerable and stupid, when he is neither; then the kitchen helper, who whizzes by on his bicycle, hits the brakes, turns to look at me, gets off, and stops to talk. Now I remember that I appear to be something.

—How you doing? he asks.

He kicks his bicycle tire.

—OK, I say.

—How was lunch?

—Spaghetti in cold tomato soup.

He laughs.

—What are you going to do in town? he asks.

—I need something, I needed a walk. Then I might have a coffee. Nothing much.

—Me too. Nothing. I'm going to hang out, then go home.

—Have fun.

—Yeah, you too. Bye.

—Bye. See you tomorrow.

I'm busy ignoring his long legs, I do want to buy something, and also I hunger for the taste of coffee and its pungent aroma, though I don't often drink coffee, and he rides off, jauntily, and I breathe again and march on, shaking my underexercised arms which hang from my sides uselessly, and realize the sun is strong for this time of day and season. The tall, old fir trees block its rays, and, when they don't, it casts a brilliant swath on the darkened road. Two chipmunks scurry across, darting forward then freezing in the middle of the two-lane blacktop road, but each scrambles to safety, and a bearded man drives up in an old pickup truck, rolls down his window to ask directions I can't give, but doesn't make small talk, and I go on. I pass the high school. Luckily the students are still inside, it may even be earlier than I thought, so I don't have to watch them flee its corridors, burst out of swinging doors, yelling and whooping, to escape into a transient liberation, or see mothers and a few fathers waiting for them, recalling a similar time in my life, which is present under my skin and which no massage releases. I don't need anything, but I'm at the perimeter of the town whose quaint buildings and shops appeal to locals as well as tourists, since it's old and celebrated for its early American history that the townsfolk superintend like a garden, the way Richard II didn't tend his, but I don't know why Richard II occurs again to me, when Richard III is more convenient, since this may be the winter of our discontent, or at least mine.

The battleship-gray cashmere scarf, wrapped around my neck, of fine soft wool from the undercoat of a cashmere goat, anomalously tickles the areas where yesterday the massage therapist pressed persistent knots and pummeled ropey fibers and, when she did, arcane images popped up, but I can't recall them. I stroll past a waterfall, though it's not the fastest route, since I'm trying to appreciate natural settings, but as I walk past, I forget the waterfall, since I'm easily distracted, and instead visualize the Count, who must be sleeping, and who, when he arrived, his dark-brown, thinning hair tousled, wore around his neck an antique timepiece that, I learned, was valuable and rare, and at which he looked with concern during the first dinner, sometimes the best meal of the day, but inconsistent. The regard he showed it was superior to his apparent feeling for anything or anyone else, but then he stopped wearing it, suddenly, and carried instead a pocketwatch that he took out gently, considering its face as I might a photograph of a dead friend. He was never rude. As I came to know him, he declared scant passion except for his timepieces, caring more about time in the abstract, its formation of daily life, and the watches and clocks by which regulation was set and followed, than anyone I have ever known or probably will know. The Count is a reticent polymath and keeps secrets the way a fine timepiece does time, quietly and in a subdued fashion, though about some he was profligate, like telling me early in our acquaintance that he was married, in a way, as he put it, but then never mentioned his wife and set a question in motion, maybe guilelessly, but perhaps there was something I just hadn't noticed. As I strolled past the waterfall that I also hadn't noticed, I reconsidered the words on a plaque near the entrance to the town: "The spirit of liberty spread where it was not intended."—John Adams

The kitchen helper's bicycle is thrown on the ground in front of the café I don't usually frequent, so he's there, and I could talk with him, learn what makes him tick, as my father liked to say, though that would be more literally true for the Count, and near this café is the town's sole antique and thrift store, which I enter instead, in hopes of finding something, if only a trinket or a dainty teacup. The shopkeeper glances up from behind a glass vitrine or cabinet, which houses an assortment of Americana and small, mostly brown or rusty objects, all of which seem dirty but may be relatively old, to note my appearance and bellows hello, because people are friendly here, though not as welcoming to guests as Greeks, whose love of strangers is the basis of their generous hospitality, or philoxenia, of which I have sometimes been the grateful object. I head for the shelves of used books, which I know well, since I walk to town about three times a week, and mostly they won't have changed, though a new one might have been inserted yesterday, or I could notice one I hadn't, the way I didn't notice the waterfall as I walked past, absorbed elsewhere, and today my eye lands on a book about the origins of the English language, in which I could learn about runic writing, for instance, but I first open to a chart, "The Organs of Speech," which diagrams the mouth, epiglottis, uvula, hard palate, parts of tongue, larynx and vocal cords, and so on, whose terms connect to places in me, and, also, to those of the demanding man, whose tongue is coated with nicotine slime, and suddenly my second heart is discomforted. The origin of the word "skin," like most beginning with "sk," is Scandinavian, skin is a loanword, and there are many such in English, and I wonder if when you borrow words, you return them in any sense. The kitchen helper has flawless skin. In adolescence, my dermatologist taught me, acne can deform the course of a young person's life so badly that its physical traces will be less severe even than its psychic scars, though its physical effects may be visible for years. Actors who play villains often have pockmarked skin. Acne vulgaris occurs primarily in the oily or seborrheic areas of the skin, and in severe cases, even the ears may be involved, with large comedones in the concha and cysts in the lobes; the comedo, commonly known as the blackhead, is the basic lesion in acne, produced by the faulty function of the sebaceous follicular orifice, when the plugging produced by the comedo dilates the mouth of the folicule and papules are formed by inflammation around the comedones. Atrophic acne is characterized by tiny residual atrophic pits and scars from deeply involved papular acne. My dermatologist insists acne is the single greatest cause of neurosis and distress in teenagers and young adults, but the kitchen helper's skin is free of depressions, pits, scars, and bloody wounds, and he clearly didn't and doesn't, the way some do, usually women, pick at his skin, a neurotic excoriation or self-induced illness, also known as dermatitis artefacta. The kitchen helper drinks beer, cokes, and eats chocolate, and is remarkably unmarred by what he ingests, as his genes have set his skin's design at least as much as his diet and environment, so he can guzzle all the Cokes he wants and never suffer unsightly pimples, though his teeth may be rotten.

I carry the language book to the postcard tray, where I shuffle through the frayed stack, and it too hasn't changed, the written messages are as repetitive and empty as they were some days ago. Yet I hope for surprise, more and more, though it's the twin of disappointment, and I want to disown its wanton seductions, but wherever I go, I wait for it, even when I don't know I am, but then I am trying to become more aware, with help, the arrival of which might also be a surprise. I had the surprise of a second mysterious postcard a while ago, when I needed it, like a good laugh. Its typed message was even more simple and blunt: Can't give up now. The signature again appeared to have been scratched onto the card, like a bird's sharp claw might make. On its front the word GREETINGS was covered in glitter, extolling the name of a town that could have been in IA or IN, but it wasn't clear, since the card was torn at the bottom, obscuring the state's identity, and the post office had enclosed the card in a plastic bag, on which they issued a formal printed apology for the poor handling and consequent damage their sorting machines had caused. Some people can't apologize, ever, those who should apologize rarely do, because in their minds they're always victims, like a woman I barely know, who was in residence briefly, a dour character who snubbed me for no reason I could ascertain, we barely made contact, but when I came near her, she showed her back to me in the main lounge, which disturbed my peace of mind. I have done this to others but with a valid reason, as when mutually recognized enemies appeared, their presence an assault, and I couldn't bear their contemptible faces, yet they understood my behavior, since they felt similarly, my presence disrupted their peace, too, but the dour woman's behavior also and paradoxically contented me like an ambiguous tale. She may believe I owe her an apology, which I might give if I understood her complaint, but her complaints are likely endless, for her longings go unfulfilled, she had many ambitions, to be in the foreign service as a diplomat, I heard her say to another, but her father and mother blocked her, and her older sister, too, and daily she grows more bilious, further from her goals. It's easy to perceive her injuries and disappointment when she throws her head to the side and peers with big, dull eyes at a group of people near her and displays, like an angry dog, her contempt. She quickly left the community, to seek another where she might not be as forlorn and receive better counsel, though it is unlikely. The post office regularly apologizes for its many mistakes, and as before when I received the first postcard, on the message side an illegible but familiar signature stood, and again, with the arrival of the second postcard, I recognized that a mysterious character had thought of me, benevolently, maybe a former lover or an amusing acquaintance, though that might not be so, since I do have enemies, like the two former, devious friends I avoided, as well as ones I'm not aware of, even the woman who suddenly snubbed me and disappeared may be an enemy, but I quickly determined not to prolong consideration of the message's meaning or its putative sender, pleasing myself with my sensible forbearance. It must have been six weeks ago that I hid the second elliptical and tantalizing card with the first in a drawer that smelled of pine and blanketed both under a one hundred percent cotton handkerchief, so that I wouldn't see them even accidentally, though I know they are there, the way I know that heavy, frequent snowfalls in the northern hemisphere offer temporary beauty by disguising, for one thing, the ugliness of slovenly and unimaginative architecture.

The shopkeeper wears an old-fashioned costume, because it is Founder's Day week, the town is two hundred seventy years old, and my interest in American history often brings me into proximity with characters such as the shopkeeper, who revere the past or want to simulate it in ways I don't. On this spot, she attests, and we both look down at the unswept floorboards, the town's founders decided there must be a library, and it is one of the towns in America that first had free, public schools and a free, public library, and in her shop, many yellow-paged books describe the town's illustrious past, along with outdated manuals and instruction leaflets, whose pages fall out when opened, on knitting and the other homely arts, as well as on languages, which contain a type of history, at least one of endeavor and of trial and error. The Polish woman might vacation in a picturesque town like this, with her mother or girlfriends, visit the abandoned mills, historic inns, or churches where Jonathan Edwards damned congregations, or go skiing, ski comes from the Scandinavian languages, also, and she might spend a long, active weekend exerting herself until a film of sweat dampened her skin, since, never liking to be idle, when the devil does his work, she's told me, she enjoys walking, volleyball, and most forms of exercise, especially going on outings and strenuous hikes. I don't go on outings or never call them that, though my trips to town might indeed be outings.

The owner of the store has hung photographs of her dog on the wall behind her, a large, black and brown mutt, a mixed breed, like most people, indistinguishable from many others, but I know, because of the way I feel about my animals, that for her there is no other dog like it. My slightly wild cat is black and unmarked, and, he would, if he were lost, be hard to trace, because, unless you loved him, as I do, you wouldn't notice his endearing characteristics, which make him unusual and appealing, since he is not just a black cat, though he is that, too, and only that to others who don't love him. The Polish woman has never mentioned cats or dogs, she might not like animals, or she might like them but not want them to ruin her furniture, a reservation I don't appreciate, because it betrays a respect or reverence for the material world or a materialism I don't admire, though I love chairs and textiles, and would not want either ruined by my cat, but people in this town revere their pets, people everywhere love their animals, and, on the picture-perfect streets here, hulking, aged Labradors creep after adoring masters, and in the town's two cafés and one diner, small dogs sleep on human laps, since dogs are allowed in the bookstore, antique store, drugstore, and health food store, and no one complains about allergies to dog or cat hair, though some people must be allergic to dander and own special vacuum cleaners to facilitate its elimination, in order not to have to expel their beloved animals. My dog was given away by my parents, who pretended to love her but must not have, or if they did, it's a mystery how they could have abandoned the beloved, innocent animal to a shelter and had it killed. Both the family cat and dog disappeared, taken by night or day, left somewhere or given away. The cat supposedly ran from the shelter, jumped out of its cage, and I have many times conjured the scene in the animal shelter, when the cage opened, and someone was about to feed her, and she, wily and desperate, took her opportunity and raced out, far away, kept running until she reached a highway, followed it, and tried to find her way back to the people who supposedly loved her, but then she was hit by a car and maybe killed, or she spent months on the road, wounded, and winter came and killed her, though she had been exceptionally sturdy and resourceful. When my family bought our comfortable house, which was built to my parents' and the architect's specifications, my mother decided that our cat, who was then very young, but very different from my cat now, should live near the house while it was under construction, and that we should visit her every week since we came anyway to see the house's progress. There were woods all around at that time, the area was forested and swampy, not a yawning suburb, which it would eventually become, and back then the cat was left there in the woods, to scavenge and hunt, and every weekend we visited the house and her. My mother, to whom the cat was devoted, because she delivered the cat's first litter, which included a breech birth, whistled sharply, two fingers tucked in the corners of her mouth, and from a distance we could all hear the excited scramble of a four-legged creature racing happily, even madly, through the leaves to her and us. The cat always came.

The shopkeeper's dress is wool cambray, coarse and brown, a simple design with no excess, no flounces or decoration, a studiously severe outfit like that which might have been worn by a Puritan prison guard, and she also wears a stiff bonnet tied under her chin with a gray grosgrain ribbon, whose serrated edges sink into her fleshy neck, reddening her olive skin at those points. In this town and the environs, the textile industry flourished from the beginning of the 19th century, when the region was home to many mills, as well as ball-bearing factories, and none of this is now evident except as historical lore on plaques. The town and state has many rivers and streams, great water power for running mills, and Eli Whitney may have passed through; his cotton gin is mentioned in the town's brochures, though it wasn't invented here. Rows of warping machines dwarfed child workers, whose fingers and hands must have bled from cuts, their soft skin hardened and scarred over time from the process of carting, spinning and sorting the rough raw materials, cotton and wool, into threads, yarns, and finally fabrics, while the multitude of spindles revolving in spinning rooms whirred and cranked noisily during the ten- to twelve-hour workdays. In 1860, not far from here, in Lowell, Massachusetts, there were more cotton spindles than in all the eleven states that combined would eventually make up the Confederacy, so the North had an industrial advantage, though both white Northerners and Southerners mostly disdained skins darker than theirs. In America the Industrial Revolution proceeded with strength only after the Civil War ended, and the first textile factory workers were like indentured servants. Max Weber theorized it was slavery that brought about the end of the Roman Empire, as Rome's troops were complemented by their slaves who needed to be fed and housed when they advanced, so they weren't productive labor, they didn't fight, but instead slowed the Roman army and cost it dearly, and slavery might have similarly ruined the American economy as it industrialized, since slavery was part of an agrarian society. In the postcard tray I search for something I might send the Polish woman, who wouldn't expect attention or remembrance from me, since she never thinks of me, and I sometimes believe she doesn't know my name, but because of that I'd like to mail her a pleasant card, since I do think of her. Choosing it prolongs my stay in the shop, and while I ramble about, the kitchen helper has probably left the café, as the shopkeeper tugs at her uncomfortable dress, looking at me with suppressed impatience, and at last I settle on a postcard with a pastoral scene that might be appropriate to the taste of the Polish aesthetician. The shopkeeper smiles now, relieved, and soon she'll ask me to return, which I will, but on a long-ago visit to a similar shop in the South near a similar town, where fate was summoned when I rejected a man's advances, I'd accompanied a widow whose husband had been a renowned scientist, who herself had written essays on science, popularizing the subject for the lay reader, as she put it, and after he died, she often spent time away from what had been their home, but then relief was not the outcome of our visit to this shop. The widow was ordinarily restrained, yet in the store marveled broadly and audibly about an object concocted by one of the town's craftspeople, of wood and paper, which, when she picked it up to see it better, crumbled in her hands and fell to the floor, ruined. The shopkeeper demanded she pay for it, and my friend, the widow, refused, at first calmly, since she had not misused it, she declared, or hurt it in any way, but then neither character relented, and when the irate shopkeeper reached for the telephone to call the police, the circumspect widow, who was then my friend, and I walked quickly to her car at whose door she wept from humiliation, collapsing in my arms, because standing up for herself had drained her of life. I never went back there, to the store or the town, though I think of it, because the woman was shattered by the experience, which reiterated earlier ones, and, shortly after our disastrous outing to the store, she returned to the place where she was lonely without her husband, who, she also confessed in her car, had drunk to insensibility most of his life, was cruel and violent, and where she once was the subject of an investigation, based on circumstantial evidence, when coincidentally she fled from her husband's drunkenness on the same night a robbery occurred in the town where she lived with him, relative newcomers, and she happened to be noticed in the middle of the night, wandering upset and aimlessly in the small town, and became a suspect, though she was merely in the wrong place at the wrong time, but circumstantial evidence stained her present with an enduring blot.

I pay for the English language book, along with a boy's story, *Adrift in New York*, by Horatio Alger, which begins auspiciously, "Uncle, you are not looking well tonight," as well as the pastoral postcard that I hope to mail but could also tack on my wall, and the shopkeeper nods her head under the stiff hat and mutters that her costume smells of mothballs, and, in a sweeping, balletic gesture, shucks off the stiff hat, revealing her flattened hair, which makes her seem childlike, hairless like a newborn, though some are born with full heads. I don't ever wear a hat, though I might if I'd been ordered, lost a bet, or was paid a million dollars. I look silly in them. My vanity is exhausting, it sits uselessly in me, since the body lies, certainly the eye does. Ruskin wrote, "All literature, art, and science are vain, and worse, if they do not enable you to be glad." Veins and vanity lie deep beneath our skins but can be more visible and on the surface in some of us. The pale blue veins on the backs of Contesa's creamy beige hands delineate her script, since she believes much of life is told in and by the body, with which, in a sense, I concur, but her mysticism isn't mine. She believes mostly in what can't be known or seen, which also can't be entirely dismissed, and in the numina which establish their spiritual, ghostly, or ethereal presence wherever she is, and this reality is confirmed and evinced by the fact that, when she found her Kafka, who died of tuberculosis, she contracted pneumonia, and her lungs inflamed in a physical emulation of her intimate tie to him. Now she has the beginnings of emphysema.

I haven't told her about the tarot card reader. His oracular statements echo and vibrate internally, just for me, and their truths or falsehoods are also mine, that is, I know I am also, I live as, in some sense, my arbitrary selection of his predictions. The tarot card reader's blemishes weren't distracting, they were not even notable, it was mostly his hands and lopsided mouth I watched when he announced, portentously, Ah, let's see what happens. He contemplated the three rows of cards and explained that there was the past, present, and future. The high cards were in the middle, the past on top, and there were the qualifiers, the details, he said, which he explained but which I didn't catch even as he spoke. A woman sat in the middle, he said, that's you, but he didn't look at me then, for which I was glad. He told me that fives were not bad, since they were in the middle range, and I had two fives on either side of the present or the past, but I remember he said: Coins dot the table, you have more of those than anything else; and logically, I thought, he started at the past, where, he said, lifting up a card, there was the last judgment. Look, the angel is blowing his horn into the skies and the dead are rising out of their coffins.

Even now this harrowing image sits inside many others, but maybe it won't come to pass too soon.

It was the recent past that the cards showed, which was behind what lay before us, like a settling of accounts after which you could clear the table. I liked this idea of clearing the table of the past. I also like tables, but not as much as chairs. This suggests, he continued—he looked me in the eye—some epoch has closed. I thought of many things, including the man who no longer lived with me whose presence was a comfort and a bother, or comfort itself was a bother, as I fear complacency, and so I threw out the baby with the bathwater, when I should have, I'd heard, kept the bathwater. The reader now said, You may be starting something new—it is not a break, a rupture, but in the sense we use the word now, a closure or resolution, and so the thing has been completed and makes some ground from which to proceed. These characters are resurrecting into a new life in heaven. They're not just finished. But this period is done for you.

His sensible hands appeared to have done manual labor, each finger had calluses, though only his index and third fingers on his left hand were stained from nicotine. They fluttered and danced over the cards to draw more prophesy. His lopsided mouth was probably his best feature, and I waited to hear my fate from it. He said, alarming me, that the exception proves the rule—these two in the present—coins, worry, and this heart, disappointment, and my handmaidens—heartbreak and worry in the world—they're fives, in the middle—two fives—well balanced—they're probably true for you anyway most of the time—the heart card equals a crush—it could be your work or a person—but it's mastered in the outcome—the queen is a master, so she can handle it, and improve the situation immeasurably—you might not have the problem again—it could be financial disappointment—but you lose something, and get to keep the rest—they follow exactly—you do hard work and some goes to waste—premature excitement of the heart and there's a letdown—just like real life—this is a monkey holding a mirror up to this girl who's doing her toilette—it's a very old image—it may have to do with the mockery of vanity, an opposition to vanity.

My vanity isn't merely useless when it makes me glad, though it does gladly waste my days. The circumspect widow's vanity mostly didn't make her glad, since it allowed her to marry a man who humiliated her and about which she said nothing, so she also cohabited with heartbreak and worry, believing that it's better not to say anything. Leslie Van Houten vainly insisted during the penalty phase of her trial that LSD did not make her follow Manson's orders to murder, to helter skelter, to stab Mrs. LaBianca, or to wipe off her own fingerprints, which, if she hadn't done, might have earned her a lighter sentence, because destroying any evidence, erasing traces of venal acts, though Mrs. LaBianca might have already been dead when she stabbed her, indicated Leslie knew what she was doing was wrong, and that alone distinguishes a person who is legally sane from one who is not. It wasn't LSD, Leslie avowed, "it was the war in Vietnam and TV." Leslie Van Houten's history includes mine, the town's is also mine, since I'm an American, and outside, the kitchen helper's bicycle lies on the ground in front of the café, so I could discover what makes him tick, young, gawky, full of piss, longing, and very pretty, and he might be interesting no matter what he says, but I never used to think that everyone young was pretty, but lately I do, and so was I, once. After JFK was assassinated, hippies appeared, and young myself, I observed them, startled, since they came out of nowhere, kids on the street, runaways, they'd left newly broken homes, colleges, jobs, the girls with long, straggling hair, flowers in it, who wore long, cotton dresses, boys with thin, wavy hair, in blue jeans and sprouting ragged tufts of beard, everyone like rag dolls, and I was so very young and pretty then, too, unaware and untouched, bewildered and removed. The girls let hair grow on their legs and carried flowers some days, daffodils, the boys appeared stretched to their limits, so long and skinny, new to sex and redfaced under their uncertain facial hair, awkward, they all were, dumb and eager about life, and everyone was pretty in an insipid, unmenacing way, the way the kitchen helper is now, as youth seems now, when years ago, at that age, I would have noticed their imperfections, and mine, the way I still do. But their flaws don't matter, because like kittens and puppies, the young are adorable, which can protect them from predators, though children and their predators is a vast subject, and also it's debatable what a child is. Kennedy's was the common death of the common father, and after it, the cortege snaking its way home to a national graveyard, the children went wild, loose and suddenly orphaned, wandered around the streets, talking about peace and love, or, in squalid, urban tenements that their parents had fled years before, they stirred tasteless, watery soup in communal pots, and everyone young was for rock music and sex, against war, straining for pleasure, wanting a bit of strange. Everywhere was disarray. I dreamed JFK was my father, my father was an anxious man, he especially feared rats and heights, and years later I still remember the dream vividly, along with my shock at discovering I was JFK's daughter, but now I think I was in some way. Memory is motivated, while the uncontrollable stories people tell themselves during REM sleep reveal unbidden messages experienced with scant awareness of their warnings. Awake, sense memories, like some friendships and all snowflakes, dissolve.

In my version of history in which all are renegade children, I confound memory and dream, or nightmare, the minute with the monumental, private and public. I heard about Malcolm X's murder on the radio. I heard a TV newsman announce that Martin Luther King had been shot. I ran to the set and kneeled in front of it. I watched TV reruns of Robert

Kennedy's murder. I wasn't involved in demonstrations or protest marches, I was engaged in a singular battle with the world, and the world kept intruding and winning. I witnessed events and was often sleepwalking, but anyway I opened the door wide, and many singular, deranged people entered, and I thought they were angels. Manson told Leslie he was God, a stranger named Mel told me he was, but I didn't fall under his spell, while others flew into his godlike arms, like my childhood friend Johnny and a girlfriend called Buckle, whose mother had painted abstractions in the suburbs, who was different from other mothers and whose daughter was haughty and knowing, but anyway Buckle fell to Mel and disappeared, while Leslie succumbed to Manson, not totally or not as much as the other girls, who were older, but even though less submissive to him, she has been imprisoned for life. Three years after Buckle and Johnny's god died, possibly murdered by a distraught follower, his band dispersed throughout the land, and I don't know what happened to them, though I wonder, since Johnny and I went to grade school, when everyone was pretty, and he was one of my little boyfriends, with thick, black hair, clear, pink skin that turned scarlet in blushes, and a timorousness about life I could see even when we were twelve. I remember him, small and already wary, hiding behind a tree, but I didn't foresee he'd search for a messiah. I walked out of his life and Buckle's, my brother walked out of mine, and when something I suspected might annihilate me rose to the surface like scum, I vanished or disappeared inside myself, since I thought I knew what could destroy me and, actually, I'd mandated myself to protect my mind, but I didn't know what to do with my body, didn't want to obey its laws, blood, curves, holes, and I didn't care about it, was profligate with it, and still nothing of it could be forgotten, nothing.

The café is steamy, its brown wood walls suffocatingly close and similar to most establishments' here, except when their walls are painted glossy white to cover wear and rot. There was hardly any light when I opened the squeaky door with a bell whose annoying tinkle announces all newcomers, but I quickly spotted the kitchen helper and his two buddies and instantly regretted my decision to enter. Yet I enter, having chosen this adventure or outing, and he calls out, embarrassed, "Want to join us?" and I do that also. The TV is radiating like a fire in one corner of the room, the café owner, also dressed in 18th century costume with a wide leather belt and clunky, metal buckle pressing comically into his round belly, is in the other, but his traditional vest, adorned with several contemporary metal buttons, announces his green and other tastes. Residents of the eclectic community of strangers I represent, even fleetingly, amuse the local townspeople, who view us as special, obnoxious, or queer, and some desire our business or conversation, which might be why the kitchen helper has beckoned me to his table, to meet his friends, and where, surprisingly, I'm confronted by a comparatively small, light-wood chair, with an oak frame, a seat and back of birch veneer designed by Jean Prouvé in 1945. It's a chair I love, since it looks and feels right, and I concur with Peter Smithson that "it could be said that when we design a chair we make a society and city in miniature." It's a cozy proposition I also nestle into when I sit on this chair, akin to a school chair, and I'm with schoolboys. Its molded back holds mine, the way the Eames chairs at home did, so I settle into it with familiarity and smile expectantly at the café owner in his historical gear, order an American coffee, and ready myself to listen to the kitchen helper and his two friends, who are, like him, awkward, but one is fat, the other skinny, and their thighs and asses are lost in vast stretches of heavy cotton or denim that swim around their worried bodies. Each drums his foot on the floor. The skinny one's pockmarked face is lean and pointed, arresting in its intensity, while the fat one's is a fiery red presumably from a heat treatment or way too much B_6, or niacin, and they're talking about papers and tests, a local band called Killer Crank, and a buddy busted for weed. I watch the pearly face of the kitchen helper whose eyes fasten on mine, half-smiles shyly but inquisitively, but then I withdraw my eyes to gaze upon the warm screen in the corner, since TV is a friendly face, though many frown upon it. Every resident could watch it in a small lounge, off the third floor, in the library, if they desired, though most didn't, or, alone, they could listen to the radio, if the speakers' broadcast-worthy voices didn't become cloying to them as they do me, but everywhere TV can make life more bearable, since it's always the same, and when conditions are not of your making, and there may not even be the appearance of choice, though TV doesn't offer abundant choices, especially if you receive only network programs, a sad or silly problem on the box lets an evening pass in relative tranquility. When I was a child, looking at TV, even as my parents argued about which programs I should watch, I felt invincible, because I threw myself into my mind as if it were a place of protection, and believed it didn't matter what TV programs I watched, and also felt I could visit other bodies or be many people, like those in books, movies, or on TV, mostly female, sometimes male, though from that pretense I was dissuaded by the shadowy presence of my brother, as well as others who encouraged and discouraged me. When my brother vanished, there was nothing to say, I suppose my parents whispered interpretations in their bedroom, where my father's dresser stood on one wall, his coins and cigar humidor on it, taller than my mother's, which spread across another wall of the spacious room, her sewing machine near my father's dresser, there were white cotton and linen shades on the four windows, white fustian, or cotton and linen, curtains, also, but I was too young to understand my brother, they said, and they didn't, either, but this old story of irrationality underwrites any tale of love or hate, since men and women are great, illegible subjects for each other, along with their families, cats and dogs, all of which reach an end, anyway.

Unfinished as these boys beside me are, they are sufficient, just like the boys I knew as a girl, though in the present we're divided by period or time or generation and age, but it also doesn't matter what has separated us when I listen to them and watch the TV in its cozy, habitual corner, and yet don't hear much, either. I'm seriously considering inquiring of the café owner if I can buy the chair I'm sitting on, a precious, valuable misfit in this bizarre room, with its chaotic accumulation of chairs, more like a scattering of mismatched shoes, where everything is helter skelter. The boys' sincere discussion of their college friends in trouble with the law, or some dropouts like them, or kids broken by excoriating love, instigates blurred snapshots of fast cars on stoned streets, greasy-haired girls and bearded, hunky guys, and I say, "When she was young, Leslie Van Houten supposedly beat her adopted younger sister with a shoe," and the kitchen helper asks who Leslie Van Houten is, and I realize, or acknowledge, that I have reached the age when I have to tell everything I know.

There was still less light in the room, and the mild darkness incited the past to recur as a sequence of sepia-tinted slides on the room's brown walls, and the faces of the boys melted into those warm walls. I warmed to my subject, my skin rosy with passion and heat, and explained: "Some Americans think it was Manson who ended the 1960s, along with a rock concert at Altamont, where the Rolling Stones sang and the Hell's Angels acted as cops, and they stabbed to death a black man right in front of the stage. Everyone who hated the protests against the war"—"which war," the skinny boy asks; "Vietnam," I say—"and civil rights, women's rights, sexual liberation"—at this they all leaned toward me—"just lots of people think Manson's gang and those murders, their murder spree, sum it up, that's what the Sixties were. So because of that, Leslie Van Houten will probably never get out of jail. Even though people who murder, and she was just an accomplice, usually get out in seven years. She looks like a secretary now, she's had a lot of sun. She's in jail in California, and you can tell from her skin, she doesn't protect it, not that I would either, probably, in jail for life, except for a fear of skin cancer. She's been up for parole at least fourteen times. Most recently the judge tried to help her, but she'll never be forgiven."

It's not just history to me the way it is to them, but they listen with some curiosity, their bodies ever restless, shifting with nowhere to go, but now my coffee cup is empty, and I might also be finished, while the kitchen helper's presence has turned as insubstantial as a leaf fallen on the ground. I believe I'll soon leave his long, strong legs and beguiling vulnerability, since even desire can't keep me, though I'd like it to, because what then keeps me anywhere, except duty or obligation, though I'm not sure to what, but when I watch him, I don't feel the lust I want, and instead rise to ask the café owner about the Prouvé chair. Bemused, he says he'll think about it, that I should return, but I bet he won't let me buy it because he's cunning and knows it's worth a lot. The kitchen helper looks at me, confused and muted with abstract longing, and I could rent a room in an historic inn, where I might stumble upon the Polish aesthetician and her friends, and invite him into it, to disappear with me for a time, and he might, he would, and now I think it's either the chair or him, since both could provide comfort or be a distraction from what I believe I must accomplish. Near the bar, where the café owner looms over the cozy, light-deprived room, in his 18th century gear, a frail woman with red ridges on her thin face, which mark it like rings on a tree trunk, remarks adamantly to her balefully attentive female companion, "If I had the money, I'd have my entire face planed." Her skin shouts of that rough adolescence my dermatologist explicated, her teenaged years spent buying pimple concealers to cover unsightly red bumps and holes, picked at with furious hands and nails raking the skin, and her sobbing in a bedroom in a modest two-story house near here.

Opening the café door brought me to near-collision with the odd inquisitive woman from the residents' library, who was, like the kitchen helper, on a bicycle, but hers was rickety, as she herself might be described, and when she was forced to slow down and jump off it, rolled her bike near to me, and I became aware of the blotchiness of her skin against the dove-gray sky. She, flustered from her sudden stop, declared:

—Some people are full of hate. Have you thought about it?

—I think about hate, I say.

—What do you think?

—I don't know, I don't know you. Or, are you also still talking about men?

—You're waiting for what kind of other information about people?

—There are other subjects than men, but the way you put it the other day, men are important. Some people are filled with hate. I've known some.

—Yes, they are. Listen, you don't know what's what. I can see that right off. Look at the sky!

A motorcycle roared by, I looked up, I wasn't sure what she pointed to, the sky high up was a pale blue, so pale it was thin, a few cumulus clouds, and her words were garbled by the sound of the engine. But I heard her say, "The people you believe are your friends aren't . . ." Then I couldn't hear her, as the bike roared again. Next I heard: "But you have to stop thinking there's more to life than what's right here before you. Look, you're at a crossroads." She pointed at the ground beneath us and smiled at herself, me, her words, I don't know, and then it was, "Goodbye, I'll see you again soon enough."

The odd inquisitive woman clamped her lips together, climbed onto her bike, and rode off, which was when I noticed she was wearing jeans from The Limited, baggy ones, incongruous on her as a tuxedo, and I wondered if they might have been a son's or nephew's; whether she bought all her clothes at secondhand stores or church sales, or if she stole. I looked around, to see what's what, and discovered that she and I were at what might be considered a crossroads in this small, quaint, early American town, where the main road shot off in two directions, which struck me as funny, also what she pronounced about me, and even if it was presumptuous, I couldn't entirely dismiss it, since I'd been stung by the card reader's prediction and because I like to hear advice and warning, and have often asked people to tell me something I don't know, tell me what to do, or, more urgently I ask, what would you do in my place, though I may not do it, but tell me anyway, because I'm curious. Occasionally people declare this eccentric or think I'm lazy and unimaginative, but I appreciate arbitrary direction, since mostly I have no choice, not about where I was born or to whom, into what skin or sex or town, and another person's vision presents an alternative to which I could say no, or it might be an option entirely unusual for me, one I'd never think of. Some of my friends might not be my friends, this has happened, but is that an obstacle, unless the friend is an enemy, who actively works against me, to thwart my progress or freedom to advance in life, to the extent anyone can, as a rejected suitor did by blocking me from tenure in our department, with his lies to the chair, but it is history, and I have left the field. Another friend manipulated me, wanted things from me, and, when she had them, she worked against me. She is most likely a pathological liar, whose cover was to complain that everyone else lied about her. Some people steal and lie all the time. The skin doesn't lie, my dermatologist says, and chronic and acute pain also don't, though they may have no organic basis. Acne comes and goes in a sufferer's life, though it sometimes can be cured, but still its depressions, pits, and holes leave traces and last, and like an eerie memento can remind others of what the person endured during adolescence. My dermatologist insisted twice, rare for him, because he's economical, that acne was the single greatest cause of neurosis in teenagers, but I haven't inquired if that's in comparison with having been beaten or molested, or demeaned habitually, but now I look at the pitted and scarred faces of adults with keen interest, consider their teenaged years, and picture them withering from the shitty glances of snotty kids in the popular or fast crowds. Their acne humiliates them as they skulk from class to class in the hollow halls of high school, anxious corridors in most Americans' histories. My dermatologist, whose skin is unblemished and who is also an oncologist, can tell at a glance, having looked for years at many varieties of skin problems, though he's particularly sensitive to a young person's outbreaks, if a mole is cancerous, and I have wondered how he feels when he spots a mark that could be fatal, or how he would proceed if at gatherings where people who aren't his patients come into view, he notices, without thinking, an abnormal mole on a neck or cheek, and, if he or any doctor, like an off-duty cop, would be required ethically or as professionals to act. I like my dermatologist and have a good relationship with him. I am not sure what a good relationship with a doctor means, except that people want to be taken care of and be cared for, and that it can occur with a professional, with a modicum of good will, even with a cosmetologist, like the Polish woman who has given me facials for years, but whom my dermatologist doesn't know, though they both care for my skin, but I trust him not to damage me, so that might make a good relationship. It was he who years ago cautioned me about the deadly effects of the sun, prescribing sun blocks and offering me samples of protective lotions, and told me never to go out in the sun without protecting my skin, to wear lotion or a hat, preferably both. I rarely wear hats, because I look silly or bad in them and, even if wearing a hat meant saving my life, I might not, in company especially, because I'm vain, just as I don't go into the ocean, though I love the beach and the ocean more than many sights, places, and people I go to regularly, because I would have to expose too much of my body, not just to the virulent rays of the sun, though that is always a danger, but also to society's gaze which is immediately worse, though I am not apanthropic, since my attachment to solitude is divided, and have an erratic aversion to human society, whose opinion matters less the longer I am here and the older I become, so that, when I approach death, it might be a matter of indifference whom I leave behind, since I won't care about living or dying, though my mother's longevity indicates I might be here longer than I can stand. My dermatologist is cautious; he does not want to scar my skin when he performs a procedure. It is possible he has noticed the cherry birthmark on the back of my thigh, but he's never mentioned it. If I had one on my face, if it covered half of my face as I've seen on other people, my dermatologist and I would talk about it frequently and doubtless he would suggest methods and means, if they were available, to handle or ameliorate its effects.

The brand of jeans that the odd inquisitive woman wears could have meaning, since everything means something, even if it is not anything much, negligible, or hardly worth mentioning, and, even though interpretations change and often meanings are temporary, especially those about a brand, her jeans still affect my relationship to her, since much harbors in trivialities, though not as much as in profound words and acts, whose significance can also be debated and more likely is. It was the second time I had seen her, a stranger, and both times she'd been presumptuous and provocative, calling attention to her ability to see through me. She had given advice and asked questions, and she had made warnings of a sort, like a sibyl, so I would remember her words, even if I didn't want to. Yet little of what I want may be remembered, and what is, is memorialized, since each of us builds an altar to our memory with tokens and objects set on it, since memory distinguishes humans from animals, though some animals appear to remember, and my favorite stories are about cats and dogs who have lost their way or been abandoned and who have traveled hundreds of miles to find their way home, even when they weren't wanted, though sometimes they were, and, without a map or a way of asking questions, they have returned.

It was when my dog found her way after having been lost in the woods that my father's resistance to her, since at first he didn't like her, because he didn't like dogs and she was pregnant, transformed into something approximating love, and I too have had the same experience about a cat I didn't like that was, nonetheless, mine. The idea that the cat might fall out of a window and would not be, as he usually was, hiding behind the refrigerator, pricked me, since I'd left my window wide open, I realized later at the library, and the diffidence I felt toward the difficult, troubled cat turned into affection, at least for a time, when I found him safe, concealed behind the refrigerator. Later, he went mad and attacked me, leaving four indentations on my left calf. When my father began to love my new dog, it was Christmastime. We were on vacation, my brother had already left us, the dog might have been a substitute for my brother, a present or companion, life offers a plethora of substitutions, since I was an only child now or their substitute son, but still I didn't go into my father's business. It had been snowing for days and days, and a magical terrain lay before my happily startled eyes. The dog and my father marched into the woods once we were settled into our rustic cottage in the mountains, snow everywhere and more of it falling, and, while walking, the short-legged, long-tailed tawny dog was swallowed by winter's heavy coat, and soon my father lost her, but to his credit, though he doesn't deserve much in regard to the dog, he looked for her for an hour. Not finding her and having become cold, he returned to his room, where the dog sat at the door, so glad to see my father, her tail whipped in gleeful circles, and my father now loved the dog he decided was smart as well as loyal. But this love was disastrously short-lived. Everyone has a tale about an animal's devotion that exceeds reason, the loyalty demonstrated by it and its heroic acts. People love their animals because their animals love them, they say, in ways no one else would, without carping judgments, and animals help the sick and elderly, they know not to hurt small children, except my deranged cat who couldn't make distinctions, and after a while, no one could enter the house for fear of the cat's attack, but in many ways I didn't mind, since I don't want people to come to my house, to see what I have on my shelves or my walls, to make judgments, which are necessarily inadequate, since what I think I am, unlike an animal's love and undying loyalty, is impossible to display. But then this is a notion, disposition, habit of mind, or humor I'm working to disinhabit or more completely inhabit, an understanding of which I'd like to accomplish here, to discover its validity or lack, and in the room that is not for sleeping, where I light fires and watch them, my ideas or objects lie strewn over the floor, and I mean to do something with them in this regard.

If I can imagine it, I often ask myself, does it need to happen or be accomplished, and, do I need to realize it, since fantasies impress upon the senses as much if not more than actualities. I'm in a room in the clapboard hotel near the edge of town, an airy old building, where it's cold inside, and the kitchen helper has sneaked up the stairs, though the reception area is cheerfully free of guards, and in the bedroom, with its inviting white comforter, he and I undress. His skin pleases me, since it didn't yet show the stress and weight of life, except in a few patches where he'd bruised or scratched himself, with a scar or two, the one beneath his chin endemic to kids who ride bikes, but caressing his skin is touching a new velvet, he's almost hairless, like a newt, even more naked in the frigid room, since nakedness never is familiar entirely, not to me, anyway, because the body has its own legislation, yet it's also legislated by individuals, families, governments, and religions who spend a lot of time conspiring to restrict and limit its disorderliness, which attests to nothing being natural in the way human beings use the term, because what could be more natural than a body's excretions, secretions, farts, noises, and hungers that are restrained and suppressed most everywhere. Though many women, like a few in residence, starve themselves and pretend, especially the psoriatic one, to the point of fainting, that they are not hungry, when they are more hungry and have greater appetite than many others, even those who eat and eat and are still not satisfied. Anorexics look hungry, have poor complexions, and are cloying dinner partners, since they refuse to admit their condition as they inflict it upon others in sly, petulant doses, and sitting next to the disconsolate woman at dinner as she haughtily denied herself, cherishing how little she ate and how much everyone else had, is inhibitory. Inhibition is contagious, especially in its righteous versions. Anorexics spend most of their time hiding, especially their bodies, most curiously wearing layer upon layer of clothes to appear heavier than they are, when they want to be perceived as thin, since they know that exposure reveals their fleshless, skeletal bodies, and so they conceal them. Also they are as cold as corpses.

His erection might have been for anyone, democratically hot and hard, and I felt a palpable reversal of positions, for when I was his age I sometimes lay with men many years older, who were supposed to teach me something, as if we were in France, and mostly I wasn't taught—the most unappetizing sex I ever had was with a Frenchman—and the older men were meant to be gentle, but most weren't, only one or two, and, since I was free, supposedly, and strong, even if just a girl in school, who supposedly knew what she wanted, who spoke well and read seriously, it was assumed I could do what I wanted and be what I hoped for, so then I could and should pursue pleasure, part of my birthright, though as Alexis de Tocqueville wrote of American women in the 19th century, it was that lone, unique freedom which damned them to unhappy marriages. The American social order, he theorized, was different from the European model, where a society that arranged marriages, which performed the social and economic work they were contracted to do, permitted and expected infidelities, and because they were not manufactured by love, these sensible, loveless marriages granted the partners ex-officio pleasures. But a free American woman, at liberty to choose a love match, paid the highest price. I have made choices, I have loved freely in some way, as I did little Johnny and others, and I have recollections of my lovers, or have retained knowledge of their smell and some unimportant habits. I have left men and been left by them, I have been cruel and made promises lightly, said I would return and didn't, and this is insignificant now except for inevitable remorse. In seclusion, when I honestly compare myself or try to distinguish myself from animals whose love is assumed to be indiscriminate, I apprehend my capacity to love both differently and similarly, since after its demise, I often don't remember the lover, can't comprehend why I had desired the object of my temporary affection, and can't recognize myself in the match. Also memory revamps itself. The temporary is contemporary, flowing in the veins, though humans behave as if permanence beat steadily in every transaction and feeling, in imaginary edifices of lifelong connection, inspired and conceived to deny their limited lifespans. Some love lasts, though. My mother and father were tethered to each other, my mother loved my father more than anyone, my father adored his brother, he didn't give my mother the kind of love she wanted, as her mother and father, whom she never mentions, didn't, so she couldn't know how to love, but then she may have received from her husband what she wanted, since love is perverse and enjoys its opposite, to which it reverts most conveniently. I never understood my father, his sadness and rages, I saw his joy and hope, and his humiliation, too, and when my brother vanished and his brother died, something left my father never to return. My brother might have broken my father's heart and contributed to his death. I should have taken over the business, yet when I was young, I didn't want to, but there is no business now, and also my father taught me too little about it, it wouldn't be the same, anyway, though I can imagine starting over in the American way. One morning, when I was caring for my mother, while she was eating a breakfast of loosely scrambled eggs and a lightly toasted English muffin, which she liked if it was soft enough, though her appetite was erratic, she was lucid.

Looking at me, my mother said, "Your father was a very good lover." Stunned, I kept silent, and then my mother peered across the table at the windows to an unimpeded view of the city that included my favorite monument, the Empire State Building, which was constructed in sixteen months during the Great Depression that my mother and father lived through.

The kitchen helper may be unique to my experience, which recently I have understood as what I have had and own but also don't have and can't own, except that somehow it may add up to what I am. With him, in the sense I was, I pulsed with amorousness and stealth, but an experience is fleet footed and is always something in passing, whether it's profound or not, and still, I had categories of feeling for and comprehension about the event and because of that I could set it and him within these temporalities, while I hovered sensually and mentally over, in, and out of myself. In this and other passing moments, I looked for lessons in everything and everywhere. I had always learned lessons fast if not commandingly, I itched to know it all, when it seemed easy to learn, when nothing was barred from entry, and, later, implanted ideas threatened to oppose alternatives, which is when, if a deliberate excavation doesn't begin, the mind clamps down and shuts. As a child, I wanted to run along, not be bothered by anyone, feared quitting or failing, and also people I perceived as static, who carried immobility in them. I wanted to move, had to keep moving, or I'd die. Without realizing it, I was an American, I didn't know the specifics then, only embodying and enacting them, while I ran along the track of my formal and informal lessons, skipping over cracks, and I didn't see what I didn't want and shed ideas like a snake does dead skin. While I craved attention, I believed that my machinations—and I—were profoundly invisible, and often I sat in the corner of a schoolroom holding firm the theory that I was unseen because what I thought was invisible. Experience and neurosis are temporal and local, as it was for those young female patients of my dermatologist who had suffered from purpura, a skin disease that is no longer a current medical problem but whose causes might return in other forms and with other symptoms. Some Chinese develop pa-feng, a fear of wind and cold; in Malaysia and Indonesia, there is latah, a psychosis that leads to an uncontrollable mimicking of other people. The kitchen helper may also not be unique but an imitation, or derivative, but my pondering of unforeseeable consequences, questionable acts and chaotic decisions, with remorse and regret accompanying them, is not good for my progress, though I don't really believe in progress, only change, which is also rare.

In the beginning, when just being alive was magical, with sleights of whimsy I could ward off the evil eye and recede into what I told myself was true. I winged like a hummingbird at a feeder, nurtured by assuming singular flighty poses, and it was easy to please people, especially by dissembling. I pleased little Johnny by paying attention to how he stood, distressed, behind an oak tree, and I could please myself and the kitchen helper, I could buy the Prouvé chair, too, but being pleasing isn't always pleasant, and sex sometimes isn't, which is what I discussed later with the Turkish resident, since he was interested in having more sex in everything, as he insisted daily, though I wasn't sure why, since I wanted not to be wanting, though I couldn't divorce myself from lust and its sensorium of treacheries.

The kitchen helper's grandmother had worked in a mill nearby and his great-great-grandfather carved roughhewn furniture and lost an arm to a lathe. His grandfather was a foreman in a cotton mill, so I told him cotton textiles was the key industry early in the Industrial Revolution, that John Kay's flying shuttle in 1733, James Hargreaves spinning jenny, patented in 1770, Richard Arkwright's spinning frame, in 1769, Samuel Crompton's mule in 1779, and Edmund Cartwright's power loom, patented in 1783, facilitated an incredible increase in production. Then I told him I wanted the Prouvé chair from the café, which made him laugh, he'd never even noticed it, and I went on about the early 19th century, before the Industrial Revolution was in full gear in America, explaining it was then that the first attempts had been made to shift the chair from a crafted good to a designed product. We were in the health food store, he talked about organic chocolate, I had imitated my first American history teacher, JJ Tucker, for him right in front of the jumbo Medjool dates. When I taught American history, I modeled myself after Mr. Tucker, I explained. Dates, fat and sweet, "those dates, they are like sex," the Turkish poet teased later, "and, you see, dear, they're called sweetmeats for something."

Walking back, following the same route with the plain exception that I avoided the waterfall, which almost disappears when it is past dusk, as it is now, a plaintive time, though if you were to walk beside the water, you could hear the falls' pulsating roars—not like a lion's—I wish I'd brought a flashlight, to light up the rushing waters. Even the woods have receded into an exquisitely quiet evening, while the blacktop road is illuminated only when a car appears, spotlighting the white line running down the middle of it. I was afraid, yet there was nothing to fear except freak accidents. The large, friendly dog who sits in front of its master's white, shingled house ran toward me to say hello the way he always does when he sees me or anyone, he's bigger than my dog, who was killed by my parents and whose life I should have saved. I walked in the dark and hummed, I tossed about internally, I stretched my legs, I swung my arms, and I thought and didn't think. No one was around. I crossed a tricky intersection and, worse, rounded a dangerous bend where a drunken driver could careen off the road and kill me but didn't, and by then I was approaching the compound, with its several beaming lampposts, and relaxed, since now I didn't expect an accident. I could enter the main house and check in with the attendant, but I might meet someone whose presence might ruffle my fur or serve up an obstacle as sticky as a jelly apple, or who, upon closer acquaintance, might become a friend or an enemy. Mostly I have been able to avoid the intimacy and wrath of the residents by maintaining a distant or cordial restraint in conversation, but each day my posture loses its rigor, so my pose is dropping, since I am off guard more often than I know, and surely I will be challenged, since people come and go, not long ago, the partners, Henry, who's supposedly white like me, when actually my skin has a yellow cast, because of Mongolian ancestors, and Arthur, who's supposedly black but nothing like the night-time forest when I walked past it. The pair arrived with their secret plans, spend time freely even lavishly, especially with the Turkish poet, and they might challenge me. More newcomers will have arrived today, to become our dinner companions, clustering expectantly beforehand in the lounge or social zone, where everyone gathers to discuss their day and the news, and where each of us habitually asserts similarity or difference from the others, so I forestall this commonplace adventure and walk on, because I might yet get something done. There might be time to have a bath, too.

Some embers are still glowing in the flagstone fireplace when I return, but it is no miracle, one log smolders, ash white or red like a rare charcoal broiled steak, heat and smoke rising from it, so then I feed it again, as if giving my wild cat a treat, and watch it for a while, to decipher a rhythm to its movements, like a song's on the radio, but there is none. I poke it twice more and remember the Count who might now be awakening for his breakfast, and recollecting him provides a peaceful sensation, after so much restlessness, thrill, and agitation, and then I turn on the radio to hear an actual song, but I don't like anything, since the beat isn't mine. The Count is the bohemian scion of an early Virginia family whose money came from a land grant, they had grown cotton, the cash crop of the South, on their vast holding, a plantation, dependent on the labor of enslaved African men and women, and later during Reconstruction and still later in Jim Crow times, they'd invested well and opened first one, then another bank, which was in turn absorbed in bigger corporations, from which the Count still benefits. By now his inheritance had a history he couldn't deny but wanted to, and, when it was known, he was chagrined by it, so he rarely mentioned his family, except he must have to Contesa, in Paris, since she had inherited the South, also, and I sometimes marveled that some of her ancestors might have worked his ancestors' land before their emancipation. His family never spoke of him, when, after a Princeton education, the Ivy League university best suited for a Southern gentleman, where he excelled, he'd escaped to

Paris, where he also excelled in idleness and dabbled in available and some esoteric vices, until his body rebelled and, like Samuel Beckett, whom he also knew, boils formed between his penis and his rectum, violent headaches threw him onto his bed for days, so he took one drug after another to quell the pain. Then, one day walking along the Seine, he was stopped dead by a beautiful clock, small, with a blue enamel face, and it was then that he discovered time's equipment and wanted to live if only to collect it, and his pain left him. The majority of his collection of precious and unique clocks and watches, timepieces so fine museums vied for them, were kept secure, locked in his bedroom, lined with fire-resistant materials, far from here, and those specimens were never seen, not even by his closest friends. Even when absent, with the assistance of his employees, the Count assured their excellent care. Close or far, he was enthralled by their mechanics, age, fragility, the fact that they went on, as he did, would go on and on, if preserved well, as he wouldn't, and once he showed me his pocketwatch that to an untrained eye such as mine didn't appear special but was. This, the Count avidly informed me, was designed by Abraham-Louis Breguet in 1795, in Paris, and signed "Breguet et fils." It was gold with a mechanism invented by Breguet to adjust for a pocketwatch's generally not keeping good time, as it is constantly being moved and held in different positions. With great cleverness, Breguet mounted the escapement; I asked the Count to define escapement: a device in a timepiece which controls the motion of the train of wheelwork and through which the energy of the power source is delivered to the pendulum. Breguet mounted it to balance on a small carriage that averaged out the errors by rotating at regular intervals, "just a marvel," the Count remarked with delight, studying its simple gold face, its delicate roman numerals, its secondary dial for counting seconds and which, like a small moon, was positioned at noon or midnight. Because of its revolving motion, the device is called a tourbillon, a whirlwind. "This is Breguet's invention," the Count repeated to underscore with awe the Frenchman's achievement. Breguet was unrivaled during his time and patronized by Louis XVI and Napoleon.

—Its face looks modern, I said.

—It's a classic, I shouldn't wear it, it's wrong, but I can't resist. It's my one vice.

—Really?

—Did you notice that its hands are midnight blue? he asked evasively

In his way, the Count, who loved timepieces, and whose addiction to them obliterated his pain, turned night into day, designing an existence that also escaped regular time's exigencies. Time itself was a fox—his progenitors had hunted fox—an agony for him, but like a wily mistress, he paid for and kept it, knowing he couldn't subdue it, but punctuality was essential, and he accumulated its objects, and so, in a sense, he collected time, it was a sweet illusion, though he was no fool, less foolish than I was during this time in my life, when I was brought together with him and others, residing with them, when it was expected—I expected it on the prognosis of the card reader—that a great obstacle would be confronted and a magnificent change effected in me. There is usually interference or an obstacle, small or large, as there was even during the card reading, when a headache pulsed above my eye, so I found it difficult to concentrate, the stiff deck was nearly impossible to shuffle, but once I split it in half, as the prognosticator or reader dictated, while dogs barked outside and my young cat followed the shadows he made when he arranged the cards, it was primarily his hands and lopsided mouth I watched.

After that, I no longer was permitted to touch the cards, and about them he repeated several times, They're in the past. Some think that the page represents a female, but we don't know, and this—he exclaimed—is like a love letter, the page is carrying a love letter, he or she is a student or messenger of some kind, this is the page of hearts; he's carrying a cup, but it's generally thought to be a love letter. With another card beside it, since context is important, it could mean a pregnancy, he explained. When the king of the suit wants to get something done, he sends the knight. One of my cards was the knight of coins, the tarot reader said, he's a hard worker, he's stable, dependable—like a Ulysses S. Grant, he won the war, gets the job done but he's not long on style—the page has style, but not the knight.

It's an emotional card. The card of the hearts—and you've got a work card, it's a good balance of work and love. The middle row is the present and the middle card tends to represent you, and this is, he said, happily, a great card, it's literally the whole world, the world is your oyster, the world is good, it's not the political world, and, look, here's the sun, it's beneficence and good fortune. Nothing can go wrong here—this is the brain. You have the Queen of Coins, the highest female figure, very capable. Coins are money, money is a token, you move money around and your world moves, coins became pentacles, but they're money, worldly capability, and she's the Queen Bee. You have hearts and coins, there's only one of the swords, and mostly they're bad because they're tricky, but you have only one of them, a good one at that, but if you had two, it could turn the whole table and the reading.

He grimaced at the cards.

There was also a page and a knight, I recall now, they were in the past or maybe the present. The reader was staring at the cards the way my dermatologist does my skin. In the present and the future, you have hearts and coins, he explained, money and love, and one of the swords, you've got the best one, because they're more mental. Mostly they're bad because they're tricky, since the brain turns into anxiety or viciousness, treacherous in the extreme, but you have a very good one at that.

He tapped my head twice. But if you had two, it could turn the whole table and the reading. I liked having my head tapped. Then he saw an obstacle and commented, reassuringly, that because I had the best mental card, I would know when to stop. But then he stopped the card reading. I am not sure I know when to stop, but that may be the most important thing to know: When to stop sleeping, when to stop eating, when to stop exercising, when to stop crying, when to stop talking, when to stop a friendship, a romance, when to stop trying, when to stop having hope, when to stop waiting, when to stop.

All my life, I've been stealing fire, it is a persistent image, and, as the fire before me raises its red head, a welter of phantasmal shapes leap and roll, dance like the tarot card reader's hands, and with them the words Stealing

Fire—in blue script—flicker overhead. The kitchen helper is figuratively inside me. It is impossible to steal fire, but I hope to steal what can't be robbed, like love, devotion, purpose, because then I wouldn't have to return it. Isaac was Abraham's son, and his throat was almost cut, with a fire nearby, until God relented and allowed Abraham to sacrifice a sheep instead, in honor of which sheep are slaughtered in Morocco every year, commemorating God's compassion. If Abraham had murdered his son, he would have obeyed arbitrary commands, as Job did, to confirm his faith in God, but Job isn't celebrated, though his churlish arguments with God nag at faith and free will, and he was the Bible's antihero. I suppose my father might have sacrificed his son to his business, or that's what my brother feared and ran from, it's an interpretation. I became a son by default, a mimicry that probably failed, and studied American history to make sense of the past, any past that wasn't entirely mine or of my own design, I believe it was my remedy or rationale, though it's not what I thought then. Now history assures me no longer of sense and reason but of the human effort to document and legitimize its humanity, its triumphs, laws, flaws, to make legible what is incoherent, to remember a past that might help people in the present—a persistent belief that is rarely ever justified. I know the difference between right and wrong, yet I am always stealing fire, and now my outstretched left hand scoops the air above the wanton, undulating flames, as they leap out of reach, impossible to catch and control, like a body that recoils from constriction. And like a human being, a fire dies, especially when it's not tended, but it could do the opposite and spread rapaciously about the room, but then certainly I'd notice it, because the heat would be overpowering, and I'd sense it. If I didn't, I couldn't escape, I could be badly burned or suffer grotesque disfiguration, then require costly and repeated surgeries to return my face to normal, though normality is relative, but undoubtedly never again to be pretty or even attractive. I don't want to be scarred or grossly disfigured, but I feel a compulsion to look at the fire-scarred faces of strangers in the street, whose skin is stretched tautly across their faces, covering it like enemy territory.

I have walked, at home, near a transvestite whose facial skin is like mottled rubber, and I have often witnessed her chatting with neighborhood people who by now don't appear to notice how she looks, but I couldn't forget the distress her face connotes, like a memoir written by a survivor, even if we were friends for many years, which would be impossible. I couldn't be friends with her, since I could never forget how badly scarred her face was, how her uneven eye make-up dripped down her face in garish streaks and marked her rubbery cheeks, or how her lips drooped and her lipstick smeared onto her pocked chin. Sometimes her hair, amplified or enhanced with a wig of peculiar material, is pulled up and piled in a bun near the front of her head, matted and about to topple over onto her forehead, and, as she thrusts her rippled chin forward in apparent defiance, crossing the street, her massive bun moves, too, and threatens to fall onto her rouged cheeks. Rouge streaks her nose and chin also, and if there is deliberateness, which there appears to be, the effect she has in mind and has designed is inaccessible to me, though Adolf Loos believed the origin of fine art was "the urge to decorate one's face," so in her haphazard application of rouge may lie artfulness. The Zulu say, Ngiyakubona kalukhuni, which means, I see you with difficulty. In the city where I walk past her and in which we reside together separately, my lunch is not carried to me in a paper bag and I do not dump it, like tomato soup with cold spaghetti, into the toilet bowl. I once threw grapefruit peels into a city toilet, which immediately overflowed, and I suppressed a scream as the water poured over the seat onto the floor of the place I was renting, but I never threw any other food into a toilet in the city. The Count, to whom I cautiously mentioned my fear of overflowing toilets, when we were in the main house before dinner discussing the creative impulse, was wry and elegant, with an exceptional horse face, eyes like black jet, and tiny pits dotting his face, remnants of adolescent acne, especially on his high cheekbones that were like flying buttresses I thought, his winged victory. He was a handsome man or stately, and, during this period, when I was far from people I knew well whom I could trust even moderately, I sometimes felt I had all the time in the world, that time was abundant, another sweet illusion, but his presence, whenever I was near him, established its passage. Of all who were in residence during this sojourn, when something might occur that could change my life, though I also doubted it, it was to him I expected to speak about chairs, my aging mother, American and other history, my dead father, my sensitive skin, friends and enemies, maybe even the Polish woman, how she cared for me, how I depended upon her being alien and close, too, as in most intimate encounters with strangers like her. Immediately he had struck me as a person who could listen. His wife, whom he mentioned the first night, but never again, flourished as a fantasy, and she might have been Polish, like the beautician, off with a lover, or had abandoned the Count because of his devotion to clocks over which she had no power or control, and he had none, either. To distract himself, or as an amusement, he was learning Sanskrit, during, I supposed, the long nights that were his days, while I was, I said to him, unmaking stuff, sketching chairs, and haphazardly studying Zulu, but I was no good at picking up foreign tongues. In the town antique store and book outlet, I had acquired a Zulu manual for beginners, with exercises, published in 1960, and toyed with mastering a language no one I knew could speak, not as yet anyway, though mastery is a residual, even fugitive idea, and Zulu I believe may be more complex than other languages to which my native language is related, because it likes to join words together; still, no one I knew could test me on it. It might have been then that the Count, my timekeeper, decided to befriend me, while simultaneously embracing the tall balding man, who was increasingly suspicious of me, since he knew I observed him and the disconsolate woman flirt, as she pushed her food around on her plate and eyed him with limpid hunger. It also may have been shortly afterward, when I recited to the Count, in beginner's Zulu, "The lion slept in the east," ibubesi (lion) impumalanga (east), an image I found beautiful and had no reason ever to say in English, that he taught me the best way to start a fire. "It is lucky," he remarked in his droll way, "that you don't suffer from pyrophobia, because this would be the wrong community for you." Later, as we watched a fire he had built, he told me that the poet Rumi started the whirling dervishes, the real ones, and that he saw them dance in southern Turkey, but that was a long time ago.

In Zulu the word for time is isikhathi, and many nouns, generally those indicating time, or periods of time, may be used adverbially, without change or inflection. The noun is the master of the Zulu sentence, and the verbs, adjectives, relatives and possessives in the same sentence must be in concordance with it. The Zulu verb with all its inflected forms and manners and implications and tenses and moods is a very intricate and elaborate instrument of thought, capable of conveying many shades and refinements of meaning. I don't know that I could say this about English verbs. The words and simple sentences the manual requires me to learn first must be of signal importance to its users, so I started a list of commensurate phrases and words I would set forth first in English. My name is. . . . Your name is? Name isn't in the Zulu manual, and that's a pleasant surprise, since everywhere I go, people learn each others' names, though here only first names, because it's considered an imposition to know a fellow resident's last name, as it might reveal more than the person wants, since society, the one I now inhabit especially but all of it that I know too, sometimes needs anonymity and protection. When a newcomer arrives and comes across a resident, the newcomer is instantly transformed into a fellow resident and asked his or her name, it's automatic and expected that you provide it, but were you to answer, "I prefer not to," as Bartleby did, your stay might be thorny, since resistance to protocol disturbs the peace of mind of others, so that, at breakfast, it would be remarked that you hadn't given your name, along with speculation and comment about the head cook, the assistant cook, the freshly baked muffins that were served to unanimous acclaim, or the sorry meal at last evening's dinner. The staff would also object to a resident's not being agreeable, since agreeability is a necessary trait allowing the community to persist, since all residents are allowed a high degree of freedom, even though many carry pasts that could, in other situations, engender or call forth a more rigorous guidance or surveillance, but all have been placed on their honor, which is also at stake, and asked to rely on their consciences, a murky business, and must demonstrate regard not only for themselves, but also for the others, as well as for the staff who serve the community for a price, which many residents don't pay in sufficient amounts. A man here called JD, whose wife ten years before was murdered and whose murderer hasn't been apprehended, can't pay his fees, but a fund exists for such residents to provide them relief, especially when they're able, as JD is, to trade or contribute skills. JD sweeps the leaves from the grounds during the fall, washes windows and scrubs floors, fixes the plumbing, acts as a handy man, and, with help from a generous donor, whom no has met but who has come forward anonymously to several of us over the years—the Green Lady, she's called—he is permitted to come and go frequently, to attend lectures, eat all meals, and to further his investigation into bees, whose hives he knows how to care for and about which he has spawned several theories and projects, especially about honey, which is no better nutritionally than white sugar, but which he believes has healing powers. He smears honey on his body, shapes objects from it, and always smells of it. His dominant smell in no way deflects me from seeing him always as the man whose wife was murdered. Honey is the dominant ingredient in the wax the Polish woman uses on my legs.

After she finishes working on me, I religiously wonder if the tip I hand the Polish aesthetician is sufficient, but I can't figure out precisely the right gratuity, not being privy to her salary, and how much I'm meant to augment it, I may give her too much or too little, and I'm also not sure whether to offer her the same amount each time. On my second visit, I felt I had given her too little, when I had little cash with me, and the next day I returned, ringing the doorbell, which she had to answer, as she's alone in the cramped salon most of the time, and when she came to the door, her skin flushed from her exertions over another client, I couldn't discern whether my unannounced appearance was an annoyance or simply one more neutral incident in her workday. She unlocked and opened the heavy, glass door, I slipped my hand into hers, with a five dollar bill in it, and said, "I believe I didn't give you enough yesterday," but nothing registered on her vacant face, so I can't record a reaction, since the vacant expression that usually is hers didn't change, not even infinitesimally. I have no idea if she appreciated my returning, disliked it, or if making the effort to bring her a larger tip might have in some way humiliated her, since people are quickly humiliated. Humiliation colors the skin, floods it, actually, with blood, or unwanted feeling, and few escape its ravishments.

The English built a society around and against embarrassment, since they fear it, no one of them wants to be embarrassed or to embarrass others, but it's more than not wanting, it's a potent, silent anxiety, so subtlety condemns them to understatement, but when at parties they drink heavily, rage, make false or true accusations, or behave licentiously, they forget embarrassment, and their bad acts are usually forgotten the next day when no one mentions the other's objectionable behavior, since they aren't Puritans. Persecuted Puritans fled England for America, where they thrived, and in America conversations and news about crimes, sinful nights, or a sinner's bad acts are received with a thrill, since the wickedness of others invigorates Puritans, and many go West, young men and others, to be lawless, since outlaws are Puritan Antichrists. As a consequence of their sins, sinners—Methodists believe everyone is a sinner—who bring shame to themselves and their families will just work harder, supposedly, to overcome their weaknesses. The English upper classes especially don't want to appear to work hard or to be called intellectuals, and they despise Puritans. Here, in this place for serenity and repose, not a day goes by when I'm not privy to some small shameful or shameless episode, loose talk, or am established even briefly as a subject of conversation, of which I am mostly unaware, happily. One resident or guest, who prefers "guest" as she insists she makes her own decisions, complains incessantly about her closest friends, who are not here, and I am glad not to be one of them, and in her complaints, like most sensitive people, she is blameless. But I am a Puritan who also has ignoble and disgraced thoughts. Separatists chose to be Congregationalists rather than Presbyterians whose church had a hierarchy; the Separatists formed individual congregations with as few as four members, on the basis that sainthood could be divined from those who desired to be members, a tautological wish. The Separatists wanted a holy kingdom, and probably most English people thought theirs was holy enough and felt bothered, since another's righteousness is a nuisance and insulting. In the New World, the Puritans strove for salvation, unimpeded by Parliament, the king, and venerable and rigid traditions, though they knew sin was inevitable, that no matter how hard they worked, they would never have certainty of God's love or if they were good, which was anyway preordained. Still, they had to prove their virtue in this life to achieve a place in heaven, and so they praised rectitude and accumulated, and the more they had, the more they decided God had demonstrated his love to them. They saved and prayed they were saved and followed their God's law, and, far away from the landed gentry they once feared or honored, they took possession and claimed the land, directing a furious violence against its brown- and red-skinned possessors, the earlier claimants, whom they smote with the vindictiveness and passion they felt toward the English and other Europeans who'd persecuted them. The Puritans slaughtered without compunction, because they would not be stopped in the creation of their heaven on earth. Manifest Destiny is also a Puritan's idea, and the history of civilization is dominated by the missions of righteous conquerors.

Acceptance is American love, shunning is a Puritan's punishment, animals do it regularly, mother cats shun their three-month-old kittens from one day to the next—I have witnessed this ordinary cruelty—turning away from or hissing at them, but human mothers shouldn't, though some do in other ways, and mammals such as humans are both obvious and subtle, like people at parties who turn toward and away abruptly, who search crowds for a partner, for sex, friendship, advancement, or to wile away time, and there is an imposingly tall woman here, the acerbic one who now leads the women's table, occasionally there is one, who peers intently over the tops of people's heads, seeking a better connection, since love and acceptance, like fame, are also pursued in this secluded place where residents hope to make themselves into something, or to escape something or themselves, or to realize themselves in a novel guise, and where some seek renown, goodness, or worthiness, while others seek calm, peace, and quiet. The Count may just want peace, he's had the other. His Calvinist relatives speak ill of him, or don't speak to him, his wife may have abandoned him, his Parisian gang deserted him, all of which is etched in deep creases on his skin, in the deep lines on his high forehead, around his mouth, and on his chin, but time is his constant friend, even if it passes and is ambivalent.

Puritanism successfully infiltrated America, nowhere else so completely, and in this country fame is a visible proof of God's love, it sits beside material wealth, intangible but a form of temporary approval, and may be gained and lost, possibly the devil's work, whose business easily fools sinners, and so the famous, whose celebrity rests on the effervescent fascination and mood of non-famous others, must maintain that goodwill through incessant appearance and reappearance, to fix their stars in a worldly firmament and also in limited imaginations. The famous become paranoid. Celebrity is coruscating and fleeting, since its value isn't attached to anything, there is no logic to fame and no use to it, except for exciting suffocated imaginations that consume hope. Dante's paradise became tiresome, blandly beautiful, because in it there was nothing left to hope for, while hell was vivid and detailed. I'm an American Calvinist who rebukes herself, also with other lives, a desperate convict on death row or an escaped slave, Harriet Jacobs, caged for years in an attic hardly bigger than her body, whose authorship was disputed because she was black, but I still can't discount all lesser anguish, and I also don't believe I should, though others' pain overwhelms or even shames mine, but relativity is also historical, so my ethical compass wobbles. It must be why a dark night is endless, when I often remind myself that I must unmake everything, but the best I can achieve is a temporary, furtive indifference to myself, the others around me, and my projects on the floor.

The transvestite frequently sat on the stoop of her tenement building with two of her friends, a woman who might be a dwarf, another in mismatched clothes, with no teeth, and I've watched them from across the street, never joining their conversations, but drawn, in a ghoulish way, to their irregular animations. The imperfections I notice and remember include skin tags, achrochordons, the excess skin or flaps that form on the human body in response to the skin's irritation in areas of friction, heat, and moisture, where a bra strap or a waistband might rub the flesh. I notice moles at the corners of lips, bristly hair shooting from them, or large, flat hairy moles that patch upper arms and backs of necks, which can be removed, but when they aren't, invariably catch my eye. There are some discolorations that can't be removed, some moles or sebaceous cysts also that, if removed, would leave small craters in legs and arms, since they run beneath the epidermis like underground rivers and more than what was apparent and visible on the skin would require removal. A cyst on the upper arm that is nearly flat on the surface of skin may have deep roots beneath and connect to another cyst farther down the arm that may be larger, and it would be a mistake, my dermatologist told me, to have it removed, because the excision's scar would be more unsightly than the cyst or mole. But I don't like moles. Also I notice stooped shoulders, wandering eyes, palsies of every sort, harelips, limps, because, for one thing, I am interested in defective bodies that function anyway. Over the years, my dermatologist has treated me for a variety of nevus, or nevi, birthmarks or moles, which he excised; seborrheic dermatitis; dilated blood vessels or telangiciectasias; benign growths, or seborrheic keratoses; solarkerotses, or sun damage; skin tags; acne rosacea; xeroderma, or dry skin; tinea, or a fungal infection of the feet or skin pads; and nummular eczema, or coin-shaped, blistery and encrusted skin, and none of these was life threatening. I didn't ever mention the pressure or weight on my heart, since he wasn't a cardiologist, and since my internist insisted, after she ordered an EKG and echocardiogram, that there was no physical cause for the pressure, that it might be stress-related, which should have been reassuring but wasn't. Each mark, redness, or patch has its characteristics, which my dermatologist recognized immediately, and when he did, he said aloud the name of the malformation or minor disease with an intellectual's satisfaction, and I always asked him to repeat and spell it, so I could see its design and remember it. Every imperfection and unsightliness of my flesh, since failures and mishaps are worth recording, he noted, and I watched him write up, in his neat script, each defect, chronic or acute skin condition, dutifully, even lovingly, in his increasingly thick file on me.

After the removal of a nevus, my dermatologist presses cotton soaked in an antiseptic lotion or salve on the fresh wound, then he asks me to continue to press the ointment-soaked cotton against it until the blood stops flowing, and, without looking, only feeling the slight burn of medication against the skin, I do so, even though I easily become nauseated at the sight of blood and on occasion have fainted. I regret fainting at the sight of blood, a revulsion I can't control which begins as revolutions in my stomach, the second heart, and I have often envied my dermatologist's job, which involves blood spurting, but affords him the right to stare with childlike attention, professional concentration and intense pleasure at the deformities and growths, ugly moles, with hairs shooting from them, on the bodies and faces of his patients, numbering into the thousands, and then his expertise in knowing how to burn or cut them off complements his desire to rid the body, or the world, of its abnormalities and threats. When he performs a procedure, I look, if I can, without dizziness, or follow the procedure's reflection on his glasses, though sometimes he takes them off, as the blood rises to the surface of the skin and spills onto the cotton square he holds in one hand, when he appears to trust his naked eye only, and with the knowledge that he has removed some imperfection, some excess that has, in some way, gracelessly defined me, one of his patients, he confidently sprays antiseptic on the wound and covers it with a Band-Aid.

Scars form on areas where people have been badly cut or burned about which everyone has some memory, whose presence never lets you forget the event, which may have been dramatic or even traumatic. I have sometimes touched a trail of dead skin on other bodies and felt its inexpressibility, since other people's scars are different from the ones I have but not in abundance, though mine are more internal, I like to believe, but there's one that's visible, right above my left knee. My dermatologist may have marked it in his file on me. It was caused by my walking, absentmindedly, lost in the promise of a delicious, troublesome boy, angry at my mother or father, sad about my brother, or worried about a best friend, past a car with a broken fender, while I was in summer camp. By that time I longed to go to camp, to escape the place where I lived among people who had more than enough money to be content, though they were not, because money doesn't bring happiness, just its possibility, which is usually squandered, and to escape my parents and neighborhood. The jagged fender tore into my flesh. Blood streamed from a deep cut, or gash, I felt faint, collapsed, and the worried owner of the camp quickly carried me in his arms to his car, to have the cut looked at, cleaned up and stitched by a local doctor. He did a poor job, even though the cut required only six stitches, and sometimes I touch the ugly scar just above my left knee, but I can't remember all that it covers. It is the same leg on which my insane cat tore my flesh, leaving four indentations, the left leg that is controlled by the right side of my brain, which has some significance, especially to people who research and rely on such ideas. The wound was bandaged for a week or two, the raw wound and its secretions hidden, while it healed into an unsightly scar. It hid something terrible, though wounds are not supposed to be obscene.

In the place where I was raised, there was much ordinary obscenity, many girls disliked their faces, especially their noses, and had their noses broken and surgically fixed when they were teenagers. They were bandaged for weeks. I was invited to visit a friend whose nose had been surgically broken and fixed, who had just come out of the hospital and was lying in bed, having a party for her new self and newly straightened nose. It was attended by her friends, of which I was one, though I was much closer to her cousin, who died not long before in a car accident, a traumatic event that changed my life, though there is no visible scar covering it. This girl lay in bed, bandaged and bruised, and happy, though her eyes were bloodshot, black and blue, and her face was swollen, and her skin a fabric of purple blotches. I sat at the edge of her bed, which was covered with a fluffy white comforter, surrounded by her other friends, and looked at this girl's swollen face and bloodstreaked, black and blue eyes. I turned green, I was informed later, in a disparaging way, and fled the room, raced down the stairs, to the front lawn, which was covered in a fresh, light snow, and fell upon it and fainted. For a while, I rested in the snow, cold, relieved, dizzily unattended by my friends, not caring then that they may have thought I'd been insensitive to the girl with the purple, swollen face. But I was never again invited to such an event in a place where girls regularly had their noses broken, straightened and thinned, because they saw their noses and themselves as imperfect and ugly, inadequate, in part because of the religion into which they were born, whose clannishness produced certain facial characteristics, which they wanted to abolish while remaining tribal, though they wanted also to be accepted into the larger society by looking more like it.

An accumulation of newspaper and magazine clippings, photos of chairs, boxes of loose papers, objects, postcards and letters, yellow pads with doodles, notes toward serious projects, such as my essay on the futility of strict constructionist readings of the Constitution, various sketches and designs, lists for lifetime affairs, favorite quotations, my archive of forgotten and failed ideas, and a number of small paper and wood constructions, which lacked necessity or conclusiveness, clutter my room. I often move in my chair, restless on the seat, most chairs don't satisfy, chairs send messages about attitudes and values, their designer's character, too. A chair is an idea. I shift and squirm, because my skin itches on another's idea, since ideas can be uncomfortable. Shakespeare's line, "a Barber's chaire that fits all buttocks," amuses me, and I conjure an image of a bawdy chair, which I haven't ever seen, and a lap, to suit Samuel Johnson's "Mistaking a lady's lap for my own chair." I might sit upon a lap of carnal disaster, or I have, or I might be that lap for another. I can leave a chair but not the past, I like chairs, I like history, not my past particularly, because I'm wedded to it, there is never a respite. I can fly away from a chair, while my mother can barely rise from hers, what I take for granted takes every ounce of her will, concentration, and energy, but it's nothing for me to rise from a chair, I can rise over and over, and at her age and in her condition, she can't. I also can forget and even dismiss what I look like, because I don't really want to live in my body or in the past, even if I do, which is against my will or without my knowledge or approval, since about most things I don't have a choice. I'm compelled to trust in imagination, it may offer, when it presents itself, something like choice, even though Shelley wrote, the Count says, "we have lost our ability to imagine." But ingenious chair design disproves the poet and also the Count, unless he wouldn't consider design imaginative, and many don't because of its attachment to function, but then imagination itself as well as creativity may be attached to the human function, and they have been discredited, since overvalued and extravagantly praised, they fell from grace, and also because they spring from what can't be known, reasoned with, or controlled, the unconscious, a force of nature like that the 18th century named "genius." Of the Moderns, the Count preferred the Romantic poets, though he also liked William Burroughs and Jean Genet, but not nearly as much as the Sumerians and Greeks, and once reminisced about his memorable warrior summer of '68, recalling it with Wordsworth's phrase: the "perishable hours of life." Chairs don't perish in that sense, design doesn't either, history may, I think it may, I worry that it does, I'm not sure what happens when we forget to remember. Languages carry a history, which is often forgotten, but which also communicates itself in every word.

The Zulu alphabet contains the same letters as the English, and in English the word "Zulu" is mostly deployed descriptively and with prejudice. A Zulu is a member of the Bantu people mainly inhabiting Zululand and Natal in South Africa. The Zulus, since the 19th century, have been noted for their fiercely patriarchal social organization and aggressive defense of territory, first against the Boers in 1838 and subsequently against the British in the Zulu Wars of 1879-1897. The Zulu noun a-ba-ntu means men or people, but in the Zulu language there are few short words, while there are many in English. My first introduction to Zulu was: "Don't behave like a Zulu," which was said to me by a teacher when I was seven, so I asked my mother what Zulu was, and she told me to look it up in the dictionary, where I learned it was a derogatory term for a black person in the U.S. At that time the only black people I knew were the women who worked in our house, the boy I roller-skated with sometimes, and Junior, who worked for my father and my uncle. A Zulu hat is a kind of straw hat with a wide brim, which I might wear under a hot sun, if I were alone, and astronomers often keep track of events according to standard solar time that corresponds to the Greenwich time zone. This is called G.M.T. (Greenwich Mean Time), U.T. (Universal Time), or Z (which is colloquially called Zulu Time). I want to ask the Count about Z Time.

I drag two cardboard boxes close to the fire, stare at the ordinary clock on the mantelpiece, and think: There is time, I can burn some of it, my clutter, and still have a bath. The fire is very excited, jumping and waving, and its heat arouses the wrath of my sensitive skin, so slowly I turn in the direction of the boxes and lift a yellowed news clipping, a veterinarian's obituary notice, she'd devoted her life to capturing and sheltering abandoned and feral cats, a life I also should lead, and feed it to the wood fire, which solicits more flame and heat. My mother adopted our exceptional family cat when I was three years old, the kitten was six weeks old, and soon, with no knowledge of the ways of cats, I taught her to beg, crawl, and roll over. The cat agreed to learn the tricks to humor me, she never scratched me, she complied, uncatlike. She also hunted mice in the woods and brought them regularly to my mother; she let herself out of the house by pushing against the screen door or leaping up to the handle and turning it with her body, and she followed my mother on her visits to friends' and neighbors' houses, where she waited outside until my mother emerged, or the cat walked into town behind my mother, accompanying her like a dog. She was devoted to my mother, who later gave her away and had her killed, but my mother remembers only the story she wrote about the cat's endearing traits and marvelous antics and how the cat played with me, her baby, and how much I loved the cat, and she always mentions the cat's devotion to her.

Mechanically, without reading the next yellowed clipping, feeling impetuous, since who knows what will be lost, I toss it into the fire's greedy mouth. A sheet of newspaper immolates what might have been meaningful at a certain time in my life and which I'd wanted to keep for research, some scrap of information I might need for the future, whose coming I wasn't interested in unless it was close, unless there was a freak event that stopped me from engaging with it, is destroyed. I feel about its disposal as I do many things, including friendships and ideas I'd once held dear but was later able to shunt off or metaphorically incinerate, and this capacity casts suspicion on what I currently regard as important. But I don't destroy photographs. Burning sheets of paper, drawings, clippings, the detrita stored to spark consciousness, relieves me, since I am unburdening myself of the past, which includes more than I can remember, but some of it I try consciously to leave behind, though I fear discarding anything, since I'm not sure finally what will be significant, and, in this way I lose history.

In one year, three people inimical to me died, so my patch of territory opened up, I breathed more fully when I walked around in it, knowing I couldn't meet them, and though I didn't wish death on them and hadn't ever considered it, since I never thought of them except when they screeched into view like two cars crashing, my three putative enemies uncannily died in the same year within months of each other. Ever since, this fact, for it is, has held a perverse satisfaction and terror for me, and I have recalled my unimportant enemies more than I did when they were alive, since death keeps its own accounts including those labeled coincident fates. They might have been or become obstacles to me, though I don't believe their interests or fates were sufficiently entwined in mine to have made them the obstacles the tarot reader addressed. In an obituary notice, one was cited for his charitable work. Another, before her untimely demise at forty-three, was caught redhanded embezzling from her mother who was under her care, though she had previously married a damaged, aggressive man who assaulted her and so she was pitied. The third was distinguished by his not being particularly bad or good, yet each, at a certain time and in a specific manner, had disturbed my peace of mind.

A cardboard angel drops out of a notebook, a memento from a scholarly Irishwoman who befriended me in London, when I was there for two months, and who told me, one chilly afternoon, of her boredom with life. I was too young, without experience, I didn't understand her meaning, but now I think I do. Her mind instantly mandated the establishment of a foreign country, which I wanted to visit, she studied angels, but I refrained from asking too many questions and imposing on her time, and anyway I might not have been able to understand her or her belief in angels. Here, this morning, a blond-haired girl from Oklahoma rushed past me, brushing against my body nervously, even aggressively, as I walked toward the dining room, and this has happened especially when she has noticed that I have mail, and she doesn't. She has been here longer than I, we have never spoken, she is usually at the women's table, an informal congregation that takes shape from time to time, as does a men's table. Occasionally I decide I will inquire about her, delve into a relationship, but as she brushes past me, in the manner she did this morning before I entered the dining room, when I then rushed past the disconsolate women to the kitchen, I am confirmed in my decision not to engage her. I know only that she has a number of allergies to unlikely foods and has caused the head cook consternation. If I had lived in the scholar's Ireland, in the early part of the 20th century, I would have a troubled relationship to God, with sin, not to poetry but to politics, and, I imagine, irritated nipples rubbed raw from the starched white sheets on beds in cold bedrooms. In her Ireland, I sit on a stiff, horsehair-covered chair near the fire, watching her long wavy blond hair as it drops onto the back of a chair, where, with scissors shaped like angel's wings, she clips pictures of angels and cherubs from one book and pastes them into another. On those chilly days, by artificial fires or electric heaters in London, she told me about chilblains and, because my skin is sensitive, I was prone to them, or vulnerable, and usually I sat near the fire with my hands and arms over my forelegs to shield them. Then my hands became chapped and red like hers and many English people's.

Many English people, with whose country America has a lasting and broken kinship, once had red, chapped hands from sitting in front of electric fires, many still resist central heating, and believe a cold room is good for them, though mostly they aren't Puritans. I like watching a fire, not an electric fire, which doesn't change, and I like watching TV, which changes and doesn't change, like a fire changes and stays the same, a recognizable blur of blue, purple, yellow, orange, and red flames, to my mind also numbers, leaping about, borrowing evanescent shapes, and with just a sheet of newspaper tossed casually onto it, roars approval and grows bigger and bigger. It can also become boring and dull, the way anything can, especially when you get older, mature and still dependent on the people you love and hate, and increasingly on novelty and surprise. So I like to make the fire grow, to make it huge and magnificent, to have it consume everything, and feed it like a child, nourishing it until I lose interest, which I shouldn't if it were a child, but my fear is that the fire will get out of hand and take over, overwhelm me, which is probably also what I want, an insane desire. A magnificent erection shown to me and for me in its first glory is moving and overwhelming, an obvious sign of pleasure, one that cannot be missed or obscured, though its source can be misunderstood, like imagining its hardness is for you alone when in fact it could be for anyone. A fire is always the same and yet different and could become uncontrollable, like the kitchen helper, were I to fan his flame and our nascent fantasy, since he is of scant reality to me, even though he is a daily piece in it. I like burning things, I like undoing and unmaking things, nowadays I take apart what I put together, pull one sticky side from the other, then scatter the bits on a table or the floor to see its fractured entirety. It's innocent behavior, no one gets hurt, there was a whole object and then there's an object ripped apart.

It is at these moments especially that I miss my cat. He might be uncontrollable, wild or just independent, he may always be frightened of people, but he is my cat, and if I imagine him dead or lost, I become distressed, even griefstricken. We are not allowed to have animals here, it is strictly forbidden, and many people miss their animals, figure out elaborate ways of visiting them, or have them lodged, though I know a man, he called himself an inventor, who kept his dog in a disused barn on the bounded property, and did not get into trouble, even when he was found out finally, since later he was allowed to return and took the same room and barn for himself. I remember him vividly because one night he stood on the balcony in the main hall and dropped his jeans and jockey shorts and exposed his well-shaped, rosy ass to everyone—the guy's callipygous, someone shouted. His ass was pink, startling, its flesh sublime against the dark wood of the old large room, and its shape, like two halves of a ripe peach, and though having this image was an embarrassment then, it maintains itself. A spark of sexual interest ignited, the way a dog's might in sniffing another dog's ass, but it passed, yet, like his ass, the interest was also surprising, but sublime, carrying beauty and horror. The inventor always returns with his dog, though I have not seen him again. Time has passed, all we have is time, prosaically, and there's nothing that is not in some way affected by time's passage, so anything anyone makes, does, doesn't do, or thinks is in debt to time, and all must pay their debt.

The tall balding man owes a debt to the disconsolate, psoriatic woman, I can tell he has promised her something, so their union does compromise her time and his, he's engaged himself to her in his cryptic way, and it is usually better not to become intimate with another while in this community, because complications arise that must be faced at breakfast and dinner, though lunch is taken alone and then everything and everyone may be avoided, but seclusion comes to an end, always, with a generally unsatisfactory meal, and the person or persons whom you've contracted to yourself for a short or long while, in subtle, unspoken, muted, or direct ways, steps forward and wants something, everyone wants something. I do, often. Limitlessly I want, since I don't know when to stop. The tall balding man runs daily, for hours and hours, he runs up mountains, ablaze, hoping to better his speed to the peak, and he might have a case of anorexia athletica, which must bind him, sympathetically, to the psoriatic one, whose eating habits parallel his excessive exercising. He can't stop racing, his head high as he runs along the road, his lanky, muscular legs moving like a machine's under him, his chest thrusting against a brisk wind, and always he is sweating, shunting off fluids, his palms especially, the effect of primary palmar hyperhidrosis, and also he glows, but his skin is taut, his cheeks sunken. He is considered healthy since he achieves much physically, but his will to stay in shape unnerves me, though the Contesa insists he is a great success with women, and she supposes it's because he runs.

Now I can burn nothing more, have lost the heart to do it, and the fire is dying. I shut the lights, gather my things, put on my coat, grab the keys, close the door behind me, test the lock, walk energetically past the field outside the window, and hope to notice it better, so I open my eyes wide, but the light is weak, and I don't see anything differently from before. It could be that I haven't noticed a changed effect, so I scour the land fitfully, failing again to witness new beauty or defect, and soon reach the quaint building where I sleep, opening the door gingerly so as not to make a commotion, since I don't want to announce my arrival to the others—the disconsolate young women, the tall balding man, if he's about, a dour man and fretful woman, who may or may not be sharing a bed, neither has ever sat at my table or I at theirs, by design or chance—one of their beds squeaks and cries in the night when I walk to the toilet. This hotel is too full, I think. I tiptoe across creaking floorboards to my room, whose bed is pristine since I didn't lie in it yet and ruffle its smooth facade. The bathroom is empty, my towels hang untouched, and I turn on the hot water, rinse the tub, though no ring's around it, no trace of other bodies that have lain in it, I can become repulsed imagining strangers lying there, especially the demanding man, but I quickly shake my head and open the faucets, watch the water stream into the porcelain tub, and, after cleaning it cursorily, turn the water off, let the bath drain, and begin again, now liberally pouring in scented bath oils, whose dubious promise I gratefully accept. Then I walk briskly, not landing heavily on the balls of my feet, to get my portable radio. My father insisted I step lightly at all times, veer to and guide myself along an imaginary straight line, and, even today when I walk, I visualize a line on a road or dividing a room, the invisible pretense of which frequently unbalances me, since by concentrating on what isn't there, I almost forget how to walk. Actors' bodies are their instruments, they learn how to walk, J and JJ say, and to hold their bodies, for to embody their characters, they must have carriage and control. They frequently discuss their craft and have cited techniques for standing and walking, and some might scoff and sometimes do at the table, especially in the morning, if the actors are holding court, which they occasionally do, with spirit. I never scoff, because I often forget how to walk and wish I'd been taught properly, so that my back would never hurt. Still, there are many ways to walk, the variety astonishes if you analyze individuals navigating their way along a street, arms swing high or don't, heads jut forward or shake, short strides are taken or loping ones, some move with fluidity while others awkwardly assert one foot after another, and there are those who take strong positions on approaches and techniques, as well as for teaching, walking, and standing. My father was a firm believer in standing up straight. Many believe standing and walking are activities, hardwired like language into the brain, that wouldn't require training, but since some walk better, speak better, some know the grammar of bodies and sentences better than others, and many walk and stand poorly, though genetically transmitted, these inherent and humanly possible activities are at least educable. It's a pity to see stooped adolescents, whose parents don't know how to model them as birds do their little ones, to teach them by example how to fly and find food, yet even some baby birds fall to the ground and then they are finished, but I know a man who saves fallen baby birds. He is not here now, but he was for a while, and observing him tend birds and feed them worms was particularly heartwarming, though I can scold myself for caring more about their feeding than I do humans other than myself, but then I don't understand the complaints of birds and can't decipher their whining from their singing, so they aren't annoying. Birdman was nourishing three fallen baby sparrows, with tiny white worms whose fate didn't matter to me, that he bought in a pet store, caring for their mother, too, feeding three stray cats and two dogs, while managing, by cell phone and fax, a tourist company with his diabetic partner. I wondered what possessed him, how his mercy had developed, if he were ruthless in some aspects of his life, very cruel in love or business. We talked intimately one night for a very long time, and I've heard Birdman may return soon, and, if so, I'll feed worms to birds with him, in order to find out.

Usually the natural world doesn't attract me, but I have urged myself to pay it attention. There is a meadow beyond my bedroom, the one I recently walked past, where deer occasionally gather, especially in the early morning, and other animals, chipmunks, mice too small to see at a distance, or tiny creatures who can't be seen even close, and there are grasses, weeds, trees, bushes, boulders, stones, and pebbles, and these I can also see from my window, creating an overall impression, usually indistinguishable in my mind from other landscapes, and often I try to recall those, especially if the ocean figures in the scene, but my impression of the ocean doesn't vary much, though the image of the Mediterranean is bluer, calmer, than the Atlantic, which is greener, choppier, than the Penobscot Bay, which is imperturbable and pellucid, but these descriptions lack sufficient detail and prove what a beggar my memory is. I also easily forget what I have just seen in the distance out of my window, a constant view for months, even on this morning, since it's not imprinted the way exacting events, histories, faces, and stories often are, and the landscape around me, encircling me, the so-called outside world which I hope to understand but often can't recall, is mostly a vague picture, as general as most terms denoting it. I look at a tree and exhort myself to remember a specific leaf whose odd shape and burnished colors appear unique, because I'll never see that leaf again, I tell myself, but then I forget it, remembering just the admonition not to forget it.

I place the radio on a white shelf close to the bathtub and find a suitable station. I will rest in the tub as long as possible, but I can rarely lie in hot, oily, even salutary water more than ten minutes, because I quickly become restless when nothing happens, and nothing happens in a bathtub, though something might crash to the floor, or I might be jarred by a scream outside the bathroom which would excite my curiosity, but inside the small, white room, it's quiet. I worry that I can't relax, as my skin is vexatiously hot and my forehead burns. The voices on the radio are melodious, mellifluous chants, but also they drone on, irritants, their human interest stories inevitable and inevitably self-serving, since human beings invented their humanity. Some speak piously, some humbly, famous ones blather about their movie, book, music, and the voices communicate one message or another, occasionally slipping into rants, and I am rendered mute by the demand to be heard. Everyone wants to be heard, most don't want to listen. Under the oily bathwater my body lightens and floats, defies gravity, and is only a shadowy impression of its form. I scoop up handfuls of bathwater the way I did when I was a child, while my dog sat by the side of the pink porcelain tub, ever watchful. My fingers open wide, the water cascades down my body the way it always has, and I lie there as long as I can, minutes pass, I don't know how many, but then I can't stand it and leap from the bathwater as if scalded, grab my towel, click off the radio, let the water run down the drain, wrap the towel around me, wash the tub, because the bath oil, which rose to the top of the hot water like fat, has left a ring of scum around the sides of the white porcelain tub, epidermis, and maybe some dermis, with its enriching collagen that dissipates daily, and, scrubbing the porcelain, I feel annoyed by the tasks, things I mustn't neglect, which are expected of me here and elsewhere, and which clutter my mind when I mean to free it, since the weight of the world is a burden. I am here to shuck it off, almost required to do it, otherwise I won't feel well, do better, achieve a goal, and I must accomplish what I'm meant to do in life, there must be something. I carry everything back to my room, with a sigh of regret, because it was pleasant but also an ordeal, a lot of bother for fifteen minutes. Still, I'm cleaner, even if my skin is slightly greasy, but in some way I'm refreshed, my flesh is pinker, hot to the touch. I'm not soothed in my mind, though my body has been hammered by heat, not the sun's, which can be deadly, though I prefer my pores to be opened by steam, steam baths and saunas are preferable to ordinary baths, especially after swimming in the ocean.

In the hot summers, where I grew up, near the ocean, though I couldn't hear its roar unless my father or someone else drove me close to it, on some of those sultry, long nights, even at some distance, I believed I smelled its green, roiling, salty odor. The sun and heat were fierce, the humidity terrible, and when I wasn't in camp, settled in the mountains' coolness, when I was instead at home, my skin erupted into prickly rashes on the insides of my thighs and on my chest. Also I was bitten and eaten by mosquitoes that, after I'd killed them, if I was able to kill them, would leave blotches of my own warm, salty blood on my arm, neck, or thigh, but my own blood sickened me, though sometimes I licked the blood off my fingers, the way I drink tomato juice, to taste it. I wish they wouldn't serve so much tomato juice and soup, because warm tomato juice especially tastes like blood. During the summers, our family cat, who was later given away and killed, because my brother and I were too attached to her, my mother explained, though it was no explanation, and she never said it again, because by then I couldn't discuss the miserable fates of our cat and my dog, would have her litters of kittens, usually three and sometimes four. The first dead thing I ever saw was one of her kittens, the fourth, whom she couldn't feed, or which didn't get fed because of its innate failure to thrive, its incapacity for life, an idea that has stayed with me ever since. The dead kitten was wrapped in a piece of plain black woolen cloth, my father's fabric, and lay near its mother's body, the mother who didn't want to or couldn't feed it. It was a black kitten, so tiny it could have fit into my six-year-old's palm, whose dead body I didn't pick up and hold, but instead from which I recoiled, frightened of the inert black bulge near the mother and her living kittens. They nursed at her succulent, sustaining nipples, unaware of or indifferent to their dead sister or brother, and the mother cat was also indifferent or unaware, but in nature such cruelty goes on every day, because the will to live governs, and survival depends on certain cruelties, which most consider necessary for the various species, although animals sometimes act, like human beings, against mere survival, to protect their young. A mother elephant and her one-year-old daughter stayed with an infant son and brother, who, after its birth, couldn't stand, while the pack strode away, and even though an elephant's survival depends upon staying with the pack, the two wouldn't leave the infant who struggled to get up. Born prematurely, the baby couldn't stand because the skin on its legs didn't stretch as much as was required for it to stand up, and, when finally it could, the baby rose on its legs and took its first unsteady steps, and the three elephants marched off to join the pack. The dead kitten has stayed with me, its perfect or imperfect mother by its side, because imperfection and failure are intriguing and devastating, and often I recall entering the garage where I had hoped to raise a Shetland pony and where the mother cat and her newborn kittens lay, protected from the outside world, which might hurt them, especially dogs and tomcats, and I was thrilled by the kittens, soft as balls of angora yarn, and by new life. They were blind, the mother sleeping, and then I noticed a piece of black cloth wrapped around a bulge lying in the corner of the box. Black is for mourning, white can be, also, though that may not have been why the cloth was chosen, my father may simply have had some black fabric nearby, a remnant stored in the garage, and while life progressed and vibrated alongside the dead kitten, its mother wholly absorbed in the three healthy kittens who suckled her, I stayed in the garage, entranced by the horror of death, with its egregious untimeliness that soon came again to shock, when I was very young, but which I never accept, no matter how often it strikes.

The transvestite's badly scarred face, her naugahyde-like skin pulled over lumpy bones, when I have seen it in passing, entranced me. She is not a female, I sometimes think, but a male in out-of-fashion women's clothes and make-up, a contemporary antique, who has many friends in the neighborhood. Sometimes I think she's not male but female, a girl who may have been burned in a fire at an early age, whose entire existence has been tendered strange by disfigurement. An ordinary sunburn is a first degree burn. Both first and second degree burns will have complete recoveries, without scars forming or other blemishes. But if the heat is extreme, underlying skin tissue can be destroyed, which happens with third and fourth degree burns, when in the third there is an actual loss of tissue of the full thickness of the skin and even some of the subcutaneous tissues. The skin appendages are also destroyed so that there is no epithelium available for regeneration of the skin. An ulcerating wound—skin ulcers are rounded or irregularly shaped excavations that result from a lack of substance due to gradual necrosis—is produced and in healing leaves a scar. A fourth-degree burn is the destruction of the entire skin with all of the subcutaneous fat and the underlying tendons, and this may have happened to the transvestite, she or he. The pain would have been unimaginable. Both third and fourth degree burns require grafting for closure and are followed by constitutional symptoms of varied gravity, their severity depending upon the size of the surface, the depth of the burn, and, particularly, of its location. The more vascular the involved area, the more blood vessels affected, the worse it is, and the greater the symptoms: Shock, toxemia caused by the absorption of destroyed tissue on the surface of the wound, and symptoms from wound infection. The prognosis is poor for any patient, my dermatologist told me, as I reported to him on the so-called transvestite, while he listened thoughtfully, perhaps wondering at my interest, checking my bare back for irregularly shaped nevi or moles, and especially poor, he went on, if the majority of the body surface is involved. But I haven't seen her naked and don't know if just her face was subject to extreme heat, though I figure more was, that she ran from an engulfing fire, her hair ablaze, the skin on her face, her limbs, and her clothes on fire. I expect she'd been asleep and was in flannel pajamas. I nurture this fantasy each time I see her, and it is how I fit her or him into my categories of experience, which is what I have and that are also historical, specific to my time and place and its antecedents. I can't fail to notice her skin deformities and surface imperfections and not just them, but also how she marches past people, as if they were not there, head high, bun toppling and falling forward, to spare herself the embarrassment of others' brazenly curious gazes. People who glance or stare at her or him never believe they're being noticed, a contradictory condition for self-conscious beings; it may in some way be necessary, this blindness or sightlessness, but I know I do stare, I catch myself, vigilant, but I can't stop myself.

My father, his brother, who was his partner, or Junior, the stockboy, would unroll a bolt of their cloth on a long table, the fabric's unfurling like an exhalation of breath, accompanied by a whooshing sound, and then one of them would search for minute imperfections, bumps or lumps in the weave, discolorations, since so much could be wrong. Briskly, my father would have taken out his magnifying glass, a golden instrument, shiny and compact, and carefully scrolled it down the length and width of the cloth, the fabric of his and his brother's design, to ascertain the cloth's status, its condition for selling. Watching him read the cloth, I saw that his face was calm, in repose, when mostly he wasn't, but his concentration assured me of its possibility, and one day I wanted to be absorbed, too. I have a bolt of his fabric, and, in small boxes and cartons here, swatches of fabric and some yards of cloth I've saved and that I won't sew into clothes or curtains, because I don't know how. I possess them because I like the material and the touch of them reminds me of places and times I can't visit. My mother sewed, as well as knitted, but after several procedures on her brain, she forgot how, but then was retrained by the patient ministrations of an instructor, though now she's forgetting again, her brain is tired, but having the swatches and cloth remind me of the bolts in my father's stockroom, the intimacy and care with which he looked at material, as well as the stockboy, Junior, his forthright helpfulness to my father who fired him later because business was bad, so usually I don't want to remember Junior or consider his fate.

Textiles didn't seem to matter to the Polish woman, though while I spoke of them and my father's work, when I searched for topics she might like and that we could discuss, she managed a decorous smile, and a look of interest flittered on her attractive, broad face, which was also distinguished by its vacancy, but whether that was because she worked at a job she disliked, endured daily annoyance and boredom, which cemented her face in a placid mask, her serving face, or because she was dull, I don't know. When she urged me to have a massage from her, after two years of my having facials, though she wasn't especially expert in its practice, she expressed the determination that I relax, she didn't talk about my sensitive skin, she kneaded my skin like dough, and she might have noticed the cherry on the back of my upper thigh, but about it she has never remarked.

The inventor loved his dog, who was always with him, except at mealtimes when he entered the big house, where his disregard of the community's pet prohibition would be noticed by the authorities, and where he also met and fell in love with a woman who seemed to appreciate him, but then she stopped, or she never did like him; his friend, another resident, told me she was too classy for the inventor. He confided his suspicion after the inventor had dropped his jeans and exposed his rosy ass from the dark wood balcony, so I wondered if the woman had been disillusioned by an act of cheap bravado and considered him vulgar. She left before I could ascertain if she was a classy character; anyway, class is meant to be shunned, and here anonymity fosters and superintends the myth of American classlessness, an aspect of American Exceptionalism that also claims the nation as an entirely new world, unlike its parent Europe, especially England, so it can't have an empire and doesn't have a hierarchical social order. Still, I'd be surprised if she had lost interest in him for that, because while it might be considered an outrageous act in our motley, possibly disreputable community, his well-turned ass was beautiful. I was surprised that it affected me, that I perceived his skin as a riotous invitation, tempting, and often I wish I were a dermatologist. Mine advised me to stay out of the sun years before others acknowledged the terrible damage it can do to skin, but people still lie under a blazing sun, without sun block, and imagine they are soaking up its beneficial, natural rays, when, in fact, they are harming their skin, aging it, and making themselves sick.

People with sunburns look clown-like under their coat of sick skin, though when I was a child I was often tan and hoped to get as dark as I could, though when I was two or three, I saw a dark brown or black infant, dressed in blue, in its carriage on the street and loudly asked my mother why the mother didn't wash him. At this time our family had a maid who was black who came to the house three times a week, and she had a son, whose name I don't remember, with whom I played. We roller skated, there's a photograph of us with our roller skates on, I'm looking at him, he's smiling at the camera, I usually didn't look at the camera. It was an awkward moment on the wide sidewalk, the two embarrassed or humiliated mothers, who were strangers, with their innocuous children, one older than the other and talking, and my white mother, who's not sensitive, must have been stunned by her child's impertinent, revelatory question, because she apologized, and the black mother graciously or uneasily accepted her apology. Then my mother apologized again, grabbed my hand, and yanked me away. It is my earliest memory of skin, though it's possible that when my father first remarked on the cherry on my upper thigh, I was the same age, and that could have been the first reference to skin I heard. When my friend and I walked around Vienna, and it snowed, he joked about how it was telling us something. My friend explained he was at greater risk than I, because he was a young, black man prey to other men's aggressive impulses, if he read on the subway, he might be challenged to a fight, and generally men die before women, and I do have more dead male friends than female, they must take more risks, be less concerned with their health, less observant of danger, or in some sense court death more. He lost his life on a mountain, where it was snatched from him, so he will never return. The cherry may still be there, fading on the back of my upper right thigh.

In my sleeping room, lying on the bed, with a white, bath-size, damp Egyptian all-cotton towel over my overheated body, and only the night-table lamp lit, I miss my wild cat and envy the inventor's idiopathic behavior. It is, of course, what makes him, and I'm not him, yet I would like to expose my ass and act brazenly or indecently, though some here may believe I already have. Every day, my cat matures without me, housed by my mother, though fed by her paid companion, and my mother says she loves cats, especially hers, who now sleeps on her bed every night, but she had the family cat and my dog killed, which she doesn't remember, so my own cat may not recognize me when I return. It's a wonder that I have left my young cat with my mother, though I don't really expect she'll kill him, but, on many days and nights, I'm troubled by my abandonment of him, or exasperated by it, but I couldn't help myself, they don't permit animals here, they're a nuisance or a bother to the staff, are considered unsanitary, and the staff might fear undulant fever, a bacteria that causes disease in both domestic animals and people, producing pain in the joints as well as great weakness, and which can be contracted in humans from infected animals or from consumption of their products. I'm not like the inventor, even if I'd prefer to be, I am primarily incapable of disregarding a rule that might put me on probation, take away my privileges, or summarily send me home, so I resist making trouble, though I am trouble to some, I have caused distress to some, I believe it's inescapable, since human beings can be obstacles to each other's peace. Yet I don't want to be sent home in disgrace or, worse, to jail.

Leslie Van Houten spends her days writing letters, reading, doing chores, working, hoping for release, teaching new inmates what she has learned being inside, and she washes her face and brushes her teeth, eats breakfast, lunch, and dinner, wants snacks, exercises and stays fit, and she goes nowhere in the large cage to which she has adjusted. Most human beings can adjust to almost anything, except severe physical and mental torture, though some have a higher threshold for pain than others, and our elasticity is a comfort, though I find change difficult and am resistant or reluctant to face or in a sense pardon the new for dispensing with the old, like the shoes I loved that the manufacturer stopped making, which may be why American history appeals to me, when it does, once almost exclusively, but less so every day, and design increasingly more each day because, though design has a history, within its history is a will to disown the past, too, or at least to sidle away from it, all the while looking back reflexively. I can configure or conceive from my mind and with my hand, but I must accept the hand history deals, since about most things I have little or no choice. For instance, I might be forced to leave this community before I am ready. Because of her actions, Leslie Van Houten was forced to live in jail and has accommodated herself to a highly regulated and restricted existence, she has matured there, received an education, made and lost friends, she may die there, though I believe they'll let her out when she's very old, as another kind of punishment, to experience completely what she has missed. I haven't experienced her restrictions, I can't know hers in my skin, just as I don't know being imprisoned in my body with all my limbs paralyzed, or suffering the insane discomfort of full-body atopic eczema, or to have been a slave and borne the lash of a whip. When in the millennial year 2000, Van Houten was up for parole, she wore her partially gray hair in a bun, and instead of a dress that made her look like an executive secretary she wore a long-sleeved cotton T-shirt, mostly white with red sleeves, an aging cheerleader's get-up, for she was a cheerleader in her own defense, but to deaf ears, even though, in 1982, the chair of her hearing had told her she was "much closer than she might realize" to going home. But she isn't home and still can't leave her cell when lights are off and the block is in lockdown. But something could transpire, she could be paroled, and she's asked, we're all asked, to have hope. I don't expect I'll be sent to jail, but I might not return home, even to my young wild cat, and, to be honest, as the daughter of time must be, I regularly wish for an event such as was prophesied by the tarot card reader, a bright, definitive occurrence that transforms me or casts the next day into something I haven't known, though I don't wish for more catastrophe.

My skin itches, the hard bathwater has dried it, I slather on enriched cream, and stir greasily on my bed. I hadn't thought about mail, but it's an inducement and might be waiting in the mailroom in the main house, which hastens my dressing for drinks and then dinner. Everyday I wear the same thing, I buy several copies of the same shirt and trousers in different colors and shades, shoes, too, since, as much as possible, I don't like to consider what I wear or look like. I bathe frequently and shower daily, I do my laundry weekly, with Ivory Snow, for sensitive skin, all residents are expected to do their own washes, one of the conditions for staying here, as it's considered beneficial to perform sensible or practical duties and care for ourselves. One resident did her wash daily, because it made her feel worthwhile. My clothes are simple and free of ornamentation, though I like a cable stitch on heavy, all-cotton hand-knit sweaters, and I like stripes, solid bright and dark colors, small dots on cardigan sweaters and loose pants I can put on and pull off quickly. My mother and father urged me to do things fast, it was important to them, and even now that my mother is very old, she grows impatient when I or she can't accomplish a goal quickly, and one day I asked her, "Why is speed so important?" Without glancing at me, continuing to knit a yellow sweater for her internist's granddaughter, not missing a stitch, though her hands tremble, my mother said: "Speed's the thing." Then I realized that modernity had a room in her old body. She also likes buttons, not as much as I do, I'd like to design buttons and might some day, I have a button collection which I occasionally spread on the floor, marveling at their intricate designs and details, God is in the details, also the devil, and innocuousness. Buttons are undone all the time, they're supposed to be done and undone, one of the first things a child learns is to button a jacket and tie shoes, though zippers are fine, and, like flight, fast; still, I prefer buttons, a well-designed and perfectly suited button cheers me up, and though buttoning a cardigan sweater can slow my getting dressed for dinner, if the button slides through its buttonhole easily, I'm not very inconvenienced, since a bit of beauty is worth it to me.

Beauty is disputed, its relevance to society, whose values are temporary, beauty rises and falls like stock on Wall Street, since its fate is tied to the changing shape of history, crafted by good and bad times and events, and it's either an impediment or an incitement, since it's always arguable how beauty behaves and functions, for what reasons, yet it instills itself, with reasonable and unreasonable demands, holds sway or merely creates an insistent pressure. I have renounced its claims and been possessed and dispossessed by it, or I have embraced it as a renegade, disruptive hero. Once I carved the word beauty into a large bar of Ivory soap and floated the soap in a bath of hot water to efface the letters, it was beautiful. Once I wrote the word beauty a thousand times on a greenboard, but the word didn't become nonsense. Once, late at night, I shouted the word beauty over and over, it never sounded ugly to me, and oddly I could repeat it again and again without its becoming nonsense; it's only a word I said to myself, but I couldn't negate what had happened, because I can't pretend something didn't happen. I told myself it was because the concept joins to something beyond me or so much a part of me I couldn't recognize it, maybe an obstacle to my peace of mind. I like beautiful faces, though what kinds I think beautiful may not be anyone else's, yet often they are, so a perplexing consensus on beauty, when its value is regularly disputed, begets trouble. History is not beautiful, not elegant, the way design and formulae can be. I prefer a beautiful chair and beautiful skin and beautiful fabric. In a corner of my sleeping room, like a soldier, stands a bolt of beautiful fabric, which my father and his beloved brother designed and manufactured. Golden threads are woven through it, a silk and nylon material, Junior may once have carried it in his sturdy arms, and the fabric shimmers when sunlight hits it or when at night I shine my lamp on it. I call it the "Fabric Monolith," at attention and on duty near my bed where I sleep, sometimes fitfully, an object never done but complete in itself, and, in a sense, finished. I have thought of designing and commissioning a shirt from it, but then I would have to undo the bolt, worse, cut into it with big scissors, in the process ruining the integrity of the Fabric Monolith, which may never have been unrolled, except in the presence of my father, his brother, their salesmen, and Junior. Now I long to unfurl it across a long, wide, wooden worktable and hear the whooshing noise it emits when it breathes, but I don't. I satisfy myself by imagining it, I can always imagine it without ever ruining it.

I propel my body off the bed, Where does this will come from? castigating myself for malingering when the promise of mail, drinks, and dinner awaits. Like breakfast, dinner is a complicated affair but, unlike breakfast, the meals are inconsistent, the quality varies widely, they are rarely good, though not regularly as poor or inadequate as lunch consistently is. At dinner, a hot meal is expected, and the head cook is even more constrained by everyone's diets, allergies, and preferences, which are both frivolous and serious, for a diet lacking in Vitamin D will cause rickets or defective bone growth in children, insufficient B_1, or thiamin, appetite loss, beri beri, and nervousness, a deficiency in Vitamin E causes sterility in rats and possible sterility in humans, but here many take vitamins, though I imagine the bulimics among us disgorge any nutritional benefits after eating. Of the three meals, dinner most challenges the head cook's capacity to meet, with flavorful, variegated dishes, the residents' diverse tastes, needs, and desires, but a rumor persists that she is leaving, since she has been working a long time, she is past retirement age and pleasing fewer and fewer residents, whom, over time, she views as disagreeable. During dinner, in the same room where breakfast is served, but with a different atmosphere, the lights are lower, because I lower them, disliking the harsh glare of electricity and also publicity, people talk about their day or don't, but most tell stories. Residents are more expansive at dinner than breakfast, and I listen attentively for the eruption of the unanticipated, an exceptional reminiscence, attitude, or behavior that enlivens and affects me, even with consequence. Though this hardly happens, it has, and, at the time, the moment appeared not to have contained a direct consequence, so I was unaware of its potential for harm, as when I spurned the callow advances of a man, who'd sent me a lurid seduction note that accomplished its opposite, but he made sure I'd suffer for my lack of interest, which mission he accomplished stealthily, so our dinner talk and my subsequent rejection had consequence. He is now an enemy, but he behaved dramatically, and a man who would seek revenge and hurt a woman who wouldn't consent to have sex with him is oddly impressive. Revenge is a great motive and regularly indispensable for drama, and, if I ever see him again, especially here, it will be uncomfortable, but I'll pretend I don't know what he has accomplished and be kinder to him than he has reason to expect and for which he might feel unworthy and have sleepless nights. Health professionals, medical doctors, and laypeople have long recognized the importance of restful sleep. John D. Rockefeller, Sr., quoted in *How To Sleep and Rest Better*, lived by this single rule: "I do not permit myself to look at a timepiece after retiring at night," and I remembered the Count, who surrounded himself with timepieces and looked at them for consolation, but then he didn't retire at night, he arose. Going to bed should never be used as a punishment, the manual says, yet I trust the vengeful man's sleep will be shattered by punitive dreams in which he is rejected constantly, and though cognizant that such a vicious hope might rebound in my own sleep and distress it, I can't stop myself. "Go confidently in the directions of your dreams. Live the life you have imagined," Henry David Thoreau extolled, and I would prefer to be an exalted American dreamer. My mother's sleep is poor, in the middle of the night she awakens not knowing night from day, in thrall to devastating dreams in which she is again with her husband, he's alive, he's waiting for her in the car someplace she can't find, her sister is alive, her brothers, she's with her mother, no one is dead, her dream life is indistinguishable in her damaged brain from a waking reality that includes death, so she is often fearful and confused, and no one can help her when she awakens at 3 a.m. believing that she's not in her own bedroom, that she is a prisoner, and in a way she is, but not imprisoned by anyone, though she can't leave. Unlike Leslie Van Houten my mother has never been in jail, but she can imagine and fear it, the way Kafka did but not Genet.

Rattled, though wanting to live a life I might imagine, but haven't yet, and to escape myself, in seconds I throw on my thick, all-cotton black trousers and a real red cashmere cardigan sweater, and, with what I believe to be a determined air, quit the sleeping room to engage society again until I may return to this room and sleep unimpinged by its demands. There are loose ends, my mother loses a stitch and picks it up, I lose the will to resolve a problem, then pick it up the next day. Before dinner, when a productive or nonproductive day is nearly done, I can have a drink, often a Campari and soda, for my nervous stomach, my second heart, and read the newspaper, since I remain attached to the world and remote events, which may or may not have significance or consequence to me, like the relationship of the tall balding man and the disconsolate woman, anorectic and psoriatic, and others I notice, who should have no real interest for me, and, still, because I'm discontent or in need of distraction from worse contemplations, I pay a subversive's attention. There is a half hour before dinner, and the main room or lounge is almost empty of people, few residents have arrived, they include the dour man and fretful woman, with whom I have no relationship, or enmity, and to whom I nod and walk past, addressing myself only to the mail room at the side of the main hall. It is larger than a spacious walk-in closet, and once inside this simple enclosure, I have minutes alone to experience hope or disappointment, since mail or no mail is a daily fate. In the wooden slot, with "Helen" marked on it, there is a square, kelly green envelope and a postcard. I open the envelope, invariably it's envelopes first, the envelope's pale green letter contains a one-line question: "Where Were You When It Happened?" The alarming words were printed by a person with sloppy penmanship, which is common, since a neat hand no longer matters and few write by hand, as I don't. My mother learned a perfect script, but now when she writes, her hand trembles and her words are written by a spider. My father crossed out or wrote over individual letters, to make them clearer, rendering them less readable, but drawing and making graphic the insecurity he felt, and I have often felt, when my mother's handwriting never showed doubt, that it should have, because she killed the cat who loved her more than anyone, to protect me, she explained when I was nine, because the cat had killed my parakeet. I didn't care about my parakeet, and it was soon after my brother left home, before my dog was given to me for Christmas, who was also killed by my parents but for whose sad demise I accept blame. "Where Were You When It Happened?" I read again, and in the closet-like space that smells of pine trees and Murphy's Oil, my skin clamors, my cheeks redden, my nose grows cold, and, quickly, I turn to the second piece of mail for relief from the first, and, as if I'd willed it, which occasionally happens, something

I hope for turns up, so I can believe I've caused its appearance, people conjure anything to believe they are in control of their fates, there is a third postcard, this time of a church in Italy, its stamp Italian and franked ten days ago. Typed on its message side, three elliptical sentences: "We are thinking of buying a church. Would you come visit me? I promise you nothing, and everything, too." The familiar, indecipherable, birdlike signature at the bottom, the same as on the other two, might represent two people, or the royal we, so once more I am enmeshed in a serial drama, its welcome embrace, and, instantly, I decide not to think further about its significance but rather to nurse its inscrutable promise. With this third postcard, the series' provocative messages intimated possibility, I could anticipate more treasure as well as cherish the postcards already received from the sender or senders, and, with the third, since good things come in three, though I don't totally subscribe to this, I do usually think it, I may hope for a satisfactory coda.

Tonight, before dinner, I sit on the plump pillows of a two-seater brocade couch, on impact they make a whooshing sound like the couch in the living room in my family house that was sold against my protests, but I don't have to plump these pillows beneath me now. I reach for the newspaper, scan the headlines of the first section, read all the small items, a man has been indicted for the murder of his female lover, whom he met at a convention for devotees of the 1960s TV show *Dark Shadows*, then turn to the obituary notices and stock market prices, but in mind I tenderly carry and weigh the image of the scholarly Irishwoman, so when the tall balding man and the disconsolate woman enter, separately but close in time, their intimacy flies around the room with an angel's fragile wings. Now they stand by the fire, not far from me, close to each other, speaking in low tones, as the Count and Contesa emerge through separate, noisy doors. The Count will sit beside me soon enough, and the Turkish poet, who is often late to dinner, which disturbs the staff, especially the head cook, and also Contesa. Though I should resign myself to or accept change, since it's inevitable, and flexibility signifies health in body and mind, though someone who changes too easily is perceived as weak, I dread the arrival of new residents, who may present fresh obstacles, as well as some of the older residents, like the demanding man, who arrives with a sigh and a wave of his hand, so that all will notice him, though most don't. At dinner, he will inevitably grab a chair at any table that has one free. I avoid his company, but it is sometimes thrust on me like a cold. Meanwhile, I discreetly study the fragile couple and new residents who arrived in the afternoon, while I was walking into town, visiting the shop, buying a postcard for the Polish cosmetician, or seeing the kitchen helper and his two buddies, and my dry skin tingles. I sense beet red rouging my cheeks, it could be the heat of the fire, and many here are aware of how sensitive my skin is.

Without removing her dark glasses and floor-length black fur coat, worn to protect her from the cold, as she is old-school and confirmed in her habits, and, I believe, to annoy the environmentalists and vegetarians, Contesa crooks her index finger and points to a corner of the room, where photographs of local and national birds hang, entreating me into a conspiracy, and, hesitantly I rise, not just because I'm uncertain whether I can manage another conspiracy. I will instantly forfeit my comfortable seat to the dour man and the fretful woman, both shadow my movements and echo them, mimicking me in some way, and, as soon as I rise, with alacrity, they do replace me on the brocade couch. Mentally, I denounce them.

Contesa has planned an event for the evening, she tells me, ever mischievous, which will happen in the lecture hour after dinner, upstairs in the Rotunda Room above the main hall that has a small stage or raised platform, a reading of her first one-act play on whose creation she has labored in silence, since she wanted to surprise us, the Count and me especially. It's true I desire surprise, but my second heart rebels, my intestines twist slightly, and I blush again, for the play might reveal something I don't want to know or watch. Contesa has enlisted some of the residents, but she won't say whom, as well as others, to play the parts or read them. "You'll have it before your eyes soon enough," she teases, impishly lifting her dark glasses onto the top of her forehead, and her words echo someone else's, but I can't remember whose. We walk to the leather couches where we sit beside each other, while the new arrivals, a sallow, bearded man, who, I learn, is an obituary writer and professional magician, a gregarious, pretty woman, with smooth skin the color of eggplant, a poet and activist, named Rita, or "the saint of lost causes," she explains ironically, and a stout, florid man with a network of broken veins on his bulbous nose, a wine writer and art collector, make conversation with each other. They dot the area of the room near the big fire. Listening to their conversation with my eyes on the floor, I finish my Campari and soda, while Contesa draws out her gin and tonic. The magician has them engrossed in a story about a girl whose mother suddenly disappeared. The police listed the woman as a missing person, and after two years the case was closed. But every night the daughter dreamed her mother was locked up in a place and couldn't move. The nightmare was always the same, and the daughter began to suspect that her mother wasn't missing. One day she remembered that the freezer in the basement was locked, but it hadn't been before her mother's death. So she and her younger sister pried it open, found their mother's body, and went to the police station. Their father confessed to the murder. He had kept her body in the freezer for three years, he explained, because he didn't want to part with her. "Morbid," says Rita, the saint of lost causes. "I'm claustrophobic," says the Wineman. "But you know it gives me faith in people's dreams," says the Magician.

It is now just past 7:30, and the kitchen helper has entered to announce dinner, he catches my eye slyly, as the Count waits at the doorway of the dining room, staring sympathetically at his gold pocketwatch, and now my skin burns fiercely as if at noon I had stretched out under an August sun. With the announcement, Contesa entwines her arm in mine, and we head toward the dining room. The new residents stroll slowly toward the dining room, and, like most new fellows, two of them hang back, observing the flow and custom of the older residents, and only the stout, florid Wineman or connoisseur has broken away from them to join the other disconsolate woman, they already know each other, since he walks forward with assurance, hovering close to her, and plies her, I believe, with anxious, gratuitous questions, though he might be bringing her news from the outside or spewing his recent biography. When we have entered the dining room, whose lights I discreetly lower, they take seats at a small table near one of the windows, which is close to where I sit, alone for a moment, while the Count and Contesa confer in a corner.

—Is this table OK? the stout Wineman asks.

He looks about, so does she, she sees me and nods.

—Great, she answers.

I nod to her. The Wineman's fleshy nose is a map of purplish spider veins.

—I had a stroke last May, he says, loudly. I nearly died.

—I'm sorry, that's scary.

With this, he tucks her into her chair.

—I'm recovered. I just need rest. Want a glass of wine?

He sits down.

—I brought a case of Mouton Rothschild, he says.

—I'd love it, thanks.

—My son's turned eighteen, lives with my ex-wife in Des Moines, usually. He's the one who found me on the floor, unconscious. I had a seizure.

—That's terrible, but he found you in time. You're lucky.

—I'm alive.

Brusquely, in the manner, it seems, he performs everything, he uncorks the bottle, smells the cork, rolls it in his stubby fingers, pours a splash into his wine glass, swirls the glass, inhales the wine, and drinks, first rolling the wine on his tongue and in his mouth.

—Excellent. Needs to breathe. I think the food here is great compared with other camps I've been—everything but lunch. So, I was in the hospital for three weeks, and they discovered noncancerous polyps.

—You've had your share, she says, drinking greedily. I have asthma.

—I've had three colonoscopies, two angiograms.

—Bodies. I hate bodies, mine especially.

—But I'm good now, I have a clean bill of health. So, what do you think? Like the wine? It's vintage.

—It's great. To health.

She toasts and smiles, shows her red pulpy gums, I'd never seen this solemn twenty-eight-year-old smile broadly, her teeth are uneven and milky gray, as if she hadn't had enough calcium as a child, and, when she smiles, closes her eyes, like an ecstatic or someone who can be happy only when the world is absent. Her lower teeth are especially set back, recessed, which caused her weak chin, I suppose, she couldn't have had braces, orthodontics, as a child, what did her parents think, did they have no money, or didn't believe in straightening teeth, did they think it was just cosmetic, but the face grows with the body, sometimes ahead of it, my nose was suddenly long when I was short, then I shot up, my face filled out, while I lost my puppy fat. Orthodontics might have saved her from this unfortunate structural fault that makes her appear sadder than she may be, because now she hardly smiles, and when she does, displays sickening gums, and I feel an uncomfortable wave of nausea.

My mother often becomes dizzy, but not nauseated, she can barely stand without some dizziness, and when my mother had a seizure, after the first operation on her brain, she sat up in her hospital bed, her head pushed forward, her back bent forward, also, and sewed an invisible cloth, her fingers stitched neatly and never quit moving, in precisely the same way, again and again, seemingly inexhaustible, and she was unseeing, unaware of herself and me, the doctors, she said nothing for hours. Now, when she stands up too quickly, the room whirls pitilessly, her legs weaken under her, she holds her forehead dispiritedly and moans, so I tell her to breathe slowly in and out, count, one, two, three, four, and she does, imitating me like a child, but I have no idea if this actually helps her. In the days before my father died, when his heart failed and he lay in a coma for a day, brain-dead, he recognized trouble, and, ever vigilant about his body and medical condition, in a weak hand he had noted, with few crossings out, his symptoms: 1) I have no appetite, nauseous, 2) some stomach pain (little), 3) sleepy, and, at the top, he wrote: I do not w . . .

He halted then. My father had many fears, of playing the stock market, of heights, of his mother, of incapacitation, of death, as I do, though I believe death is nothing, but then nothing can be frightening when it swallows your days and you don't know where time has gone, which may be why he didn't finish writing the sentence: "I do not w . . ." I'll never know. On the other side of the note, just a slip of paper, he wrote "wheeze-phlegm-sleeping" and recorded his meds, amiodaroni, lasix, coumadin, lanoxin. My father recognized he was dying, in his last night of consciousness, and he must have been disappointed with himself, afraid and failing again. He admired Winston Churchill, inordinately, for his bravery, and Churchill's final words were, "No more." Before my father fell into a coma from which he never returned, he smiled at his doctor, he was happy to see him, his doctor told me later, maybe he thought he'd beat death, but when my father died, he said nothing.

I notice the Count speaking to one of the new residents, the professional magician and obituary writer, and now he is steering him over. I shift in my chair and arrange the pillow under me, but comfort is not forthcoming, as they are wooden chairs with hard, wooden slats at the backs and woven cane seats that squeak, designed, built, and carved by JD, and I don't dare complain about them, ever. The Turkish poet has arrived, Henry and Arthur, who enter with him, Spike, and Contesa, too, and suddenly the table is complete. The anorectic disconsolate woman and the tall balding man seat themselves far from her friend and the stout Wineman, when actors J and JJ, and their sidekick, the guilt-ridden, silent lyricist and the demanding man slide into chairs near them. All the others are settling in at various tables, the young married man next to the new resident, Rita, or the saint of lost causes, and beside them the dour man and fretful woman, whose addition surprises me since they generally keep to themselves. My second heart grinds with nameless worry, and ungracious doubt rumbles in my intestines, so I fear gas. JD chooses his seat, his boots muddy, his overalls sticky, he smells of pungent raw honey, I sense when he's around, and he sits next to some nondescript characters, who will stay for a week or maybe two, whose first names I don't know, and who often don't come to breakfast but eat instant oatmeal or peanut butter and jelly sandwiches in their rooms.

The head cook has created an order and routine to her dinner menus, which, after many, many years, she has honed into a three-week pattern, so that a resident or guest who has been here for a while, as I have, and the Count and Contesa, will have several times eaten her array of dishes and know her preparations, the ingredients of, and dressings for, salads, the sauces for meat, usually leg of lamb or pork chops, fowl, chicken, roast or fried, and roast turkey or turkey loaf, and fish, mostly cod with capers and broiled or poached salmon, the side dishes, rice and beans, broiled mushrooms, always available for vegetarians and vegans, creamed broccoli, fresh, steamed asparagus with a lemon sauce, potatoes gratin, boiled red potatoes served with chives, wild rice, and her range of desserts, chocolate or vanilla ice cream, bread pudding, tapioca and chocolate pudding, cherry, peach, and apple pies, and chocolate, banana, and vanilla cream cakes, there is always a serving of fruit, so dinner is rarely a surprise, except for the night she presented us with bowtie pasta swimming in melted caraway cheese, which caused us all consternation except the young married man, who, though regularly grumpy, likes every meal. The wretched dish reeked of the head cook's despair. Sunday night, when both the head and assistant cooks have the day off, and a substitute cook arrives, it is vegetable risotto and pizza, and all diets are attended to with meatless, cheeseless pizzas, vegetable pizzas with and without cheese, pizza with cheese and pepperoni, pizza with cheese and tomato, pizza with no cheese and no tomatoes, and so on, they are labeled, and there is a generous bowl of green salad, without tomatoes and peppers, but with several dressings, on the side, a term much used here. Sometimes a resident's first name is written on a card that is set on a table, and then you must take that chair, the chairs are serviceable, poorly designed and lacking in any quality, such as charm, and the card's placement indicates you have specific dietary requirements, which have to be accommodated by a special meal, and then you feel singled out, not necessarily in a good way, but a few like any attention, though it's not auspicious to demonstrate certain types of need. It augurs well that the Magician is beside me now, since as soon as I heard him tell Saint Rita that he performs magic for a living, a striking conceit, I hoped to learn about his ancient, perplexing profession.

Dinner is three courses, the most elaborate of the day's meals, often poor, and its longest, but at breakfast everyone can find something to eat, unless they are late, though there is usually bread, milk, and cold cereal available, which is not the case at dinner. At dinner, there is an appetizer, tonight it's crudités, then there's the entree or main course, and a dessert. There are warm, packaged rolls, which one resident steals and hides in his backpack for the next day, as he is already anxious about the next day's meager lunch. Another regularly pilfers fruit and raw vegetables and is known to arrange carrots in rows on the top of his worktable, where he does computations, to watch them dry and curl up. Salad is served with the main course, and the few Europeans among us have it after, while the Americans have it with the entree, and then there is dessert, and, with it, coffee, decaffeinated or espresso, tea, black, herbal, or black without caffeine, cream, whole milk, skim, and soy milk, and everyone can find something to eat, special diets are accommodated, in moderation, though most residents are dissatisfied, because lunch is invariably poor and at dinner most are hungry, except the anorexics, who are starving but will not eat and who hide their disease until they are almost dead, and thirty percent of them die of this kind of contemporary wasting.

Looking at Contesa, whose dark glasses are perched on the bridge of her small, sharp nose, obliterating her gray eyes, I imagine that her play will be inhabited by her spirit, which I must count on, as I do, one day sliding into and negating the next, though irregularly in the Count's upside-down schedule, so her mind will be present onstage, which could inspire me. Nervous doubt unclasps my stomach and it quiets, and, with that, commences an appetite. The demanding man is also gazing in Contesa's direction, his large brown eyes morose as a moaning cow's, but she ignores him once again and nibbles a stalk of celery. The night the inventor exposed his rosy ass was exciting, since it was beautiful and the event out of the ordinary, this morning the psoriatic woman and the tall balding man revealed their intimacy, there was nothing indecent about it, but it held some content and provoked memory, and in the moment, again the demanding man seeks Contesa's aid for what her interest enlivens in him, and I await or have hope for an entertaining evening fomented by the Magician's novelty and Contesa's liveliness or spirit.

—Poached salmon again, laments the Count.

—But it's her most flavorful dish, says the Turkish poet, with good cheer.

—I can't bear it, Contesa says, mournfully.

—But salmon's good for brains and sex, urges the Turkish poet.

Almost in unison, Henry and Arthur intone, "it could be worse," which is an uncommon observation here, but they're relatively new residents and often ironic. The Magician watches us like rabbits. He shoves the cooked tomatoes on his plate to the side, and they fall off next to Spike's dinner plate. The Magician is allergic to tomatoes, which is sad, because tomatoes that have grown during a hot summer, without too much rain, so they don't get mealy, are magical, ripened under a brilliant sun, as they were in my mother's garden, then sliced and served on a plate, succulent beefsteaks warm from the rich soil and hot sun, but now my mother doesn't remember her tomato garden and doesn't like to eat tomatoes because of their skin which she can't chew or digest. "An old hell," she said once, cavalierly. The Magician is also allergic to bee stings, bees produce their sting by the ovipositor of the female abdomen, and when stung, a poison—apitoxin—containing formic acid and a neurotoxin is introduced into the skin. I was stung by bees twice. Once I was practicing the piano in camp, when I thought a stabbing pain in my stiff fingers was caused by a lack of daily, rigorous practice and that my piano teacher was punishing me for my dereliction, but it was a bee. The ovipositor of the honeybee breaks off and remains in the skin after stinging. The bumblebee is able to retract its stinger, but the reaction to stings may vary from a mild, local edema and pain, to severe anaphylactic shock and even death, which occurs more frequently in the case of multiple stings unless prompt therapy is undertaken. The imbedded ovipositor containing the poison sac should be scraped away with a sharp knife, but I don't believe that was done when I was in camp. I took an antihistamine the second time I was stung, yet the area around the sting swelled and throbbed painfully, but unless the Magician carries a kit containing a syringe, epinephrine and antihistamines, when stung, he could go into shock and die.

My dermatologist has treated many cases of infected bee and wasp stings and encountered serious cases of maggots, when, for instance, the Wohlfahrtia vigil gravid fly lays its eggs on the skin, then the hatched larvae migrate to the folds of skin into which they burrow. An inflammatory reaction, first as a papule, then as a lesion, is produced, and maggots may be seen in this lesion, where it seems to pulsate. The female of the human botfly, or D. hominis, glues its eggs to the body of a mosquito, stablefly, or tick, and when the unwitting insect punctures the skin by its bite, the larvae emerge from the egg and enter the skin through the wound. He has seen innumerable cases of crabs, or pediculosis pubis, contracted chiefly by adults as the result of sexual intercourse, not infrequently from bedding, railway berths, and toilet seats, as well as human flea bites. Fleas exist universally among people and animals, and the three most common in America are the human flea, Pulex irritans, the cat flea, Ctenocephalides felis, and the dog flea, Ctenocephalides canis. Fleas are small, brown, wingless insects about one-sixteenth of an inch long, and are very flat from side to side, with long hind legs. They jump actively when disturbed and are known to be extraordinary jumpers, helping them travel from host to host. They extract their food from the superficial capillaries, causing hemorrhagic puncta surrounded by an erythematous and urticarial patch, characterized by intensely itchy welts. The irritation is produced by the injection into the skin of a fluid secreted by the salivary glands of the parasite, and some people have an apparent hypersensitivity to this secretion. Fleas carry disease, endemic typhus, and plague, which is transmitted to people by the rat flea, Xenopsylla cheopsis and other species. Parasitical fleas sucked the lifeblood from my cat's kittens in Amsterdam, where most summers they infest the city and suck their food from humans and animals, and about their fatal effect on young cats especially I had no knowledge and no warning, so all the tiny kittens except one died, for which I am to blame.

Table talk segues to mercury in fish, solid white meat tuna versus flaky tuna, both in cans, the fate of the poor salmon, to America's polluted rivers and streams, during which the Count adds that fish and other creatures are consuming medicines and vitamins humans beings pass through their urine into toilets that flush into streams and rivers where fish feed.

—Imagine what hormones do to fish, says Contesa, tapping the flesh of her salmon.

—Some have already become androgynous, says the Count.

—Everything mutates or dies, says the Magician.

—I'd love to learn magic tricks, I say to him.

—I can't tell you how, I can't show you tricks. Magicians can talk to other magicians about their tricks. That's it. We're a closed shop.

—Are you allowed to discuss your interest in magic?

—I belong to the International Brotherhood of Magicians, and there are rules. We have secrets, it's our trade. But let's say it sprang from my interest in mathematics and numbers. I'm what's called a close-up magician.

—What's that? Spike asks.

—I work small groups at tables or standing up in front of small audiences. I do card tricks, coins, hand/eye magic, and patter is very important.

—Patter? Henry asks.

—Everyone has patter, says Spike, intimately.

—I've got a routine, I talk my talk. Patter's very important, it's part of the art of misdirection. I can't say more, but I can say there's lots of rehearsal, a lot of work goes into my act. But I really can't say more.

The Count and Contesa pay close attention, and she even removes her dark glasses. The table is staring at the Magician, who accepts this matter-of-factly, but then he's used to small audiences and even absorbs our interest with magnanimity, while Contesa leans toward him from across the round table, her palms up, as if to show him her past and future, and her canny eyes resemble crystal balls.

—Do you contact spirits? she asks.

—I don't do séances. I've done a few, but I don't like to. I can. They're too emotional, I can't sleep afterward. I don't do stage illusions. I don't do escapism. I'm not an escape artist.

—Houdini was, she counters.

—Houdini did it for the money, the Magician carefully explains, he was a close-up magician, but he couldn't support his family. That's why I have a day job. There's big money in staged illusions. But I wouldn't do one of those for a million dollars a trick.

—I collect antique timepieces, the Count interjects.

—The spirit world isn't just illusion, Contesa goes on. Houdini and his wife made a pact, they developed some code or other. She did a séance to contact him.

—Actually, she tried to contact him ten times, the Magician says. Houdini was a skeptic, but skeptics need convincing. They're insecure.

—Sex is real, big magic, says the Turkish poet. You think it's so, Helen?

I blushed.

Like the Magician, I wouldn't be buried alive, chained and bound in a coffin, and dropped into the ocean for money or any other reason, but its appeal probably is sexual, since there's the lust to be smothered under mounds of flesh, all senses buried, the brain pressed to do its commanding submerged below layers of skin and fat. Right now I could insert a forgotten word "amaxophobia," the morbid fear of riding in a car or carriage, which is cited in the library's sex manual, but Spike jumps in, relishing his challenge, and, for the delectation of our table, though possibly not to the Magician's taste, she reveals an episode at a sex club, where she discovered her wholesome, strapping massage therapist in the middle of a large, noisy room being whipped, her nipples in steel clips, her ample flesh quivering in pain-filled excitement. Spike hoped that she hadn't been seen watching her, but she may have been, nothing was said, and now during massages, Spike's fantasies are flatter but less humiliating.

—This is no sex to me, the Turkish poet says, almost stricken. It hurts my heart to hear.

—Like bad poetry, says Arthur.

The Turkish poet claps his hands.

—Yes, yes, bad poetry hurts the heart.

—And bad sex, says Spike.

—They're episodes of stupidity, stupidity has no sense or sensation, says Contesa. Sex can be dumb.

—Einstein said, and I quote, "The imagination is more important than knowledge," says the Count.

Contesa glows.

The Count plucks his pocketwatch from his jacket pocket and looks at it with affection, while I'm considering saying I miss my cat or another remark that might establish a point of departure or even misdirection. Last night some of us engaged in an intense discussion about domestic and wild animals who'd performed extraordinary feats, a skunk who unzipped tents and stole food, a cat who turned doorknobs, a wild bird who bathed in a kitchen washbasin, a pet mouse who frowned and smiled, a cat who mothered a parrot, a large dog who lay on its owner and saved her from hypothermia, and I told the story of our family cat who, in addition to her other miraculous feats, was once left alone in our house, whose den had the six Eames chairs and table I loved, which were sold over my protests with the house I also loved, and when she couldn't go out, instead of fouling the floor, she defecated on the drain of my parents' bathtub, after which she tore sheets of toilet paper from the roll and placed them in a mound on top of her unsightly mess, and all of this was especially pleasing to my mother, who nonetheless killed her later. Usually no one is wrong or mistaken about animals to whom an unqualified love is due.

A jarring crash and shrieks disrupt us, erupting from the kitchen, and I jump up, as do several other residents, we run in and discover the kitchen helper on the floor surrounded by broken glasses and crockery, plates, cups, saucers, and near him the head cook is screaming, but when we enter, she claps both hands over her mouth, because the residents are meant to live in peace and quiet here, and no one but we can demonstrate distress, and the head cook must restrain herself on our account. The kitchen helper's hand is cut, his unblemished skin torn, there is a gash, blood on his pants leg, his long legs, and I feel as weak as a kitten drained by fleas. Wobbly, I walk out of the kitchen, bump into someone, experience additional pressure or a tighter grip around my heart, then collapse in a faint on the dining-room floor. I never know where I am when I faint, when the blood rushes from my head, flees, my brain empties, I can feel it until I feel nothing but a lightheaded coolness, and I can only hope my end is similar to fainting, since to die like this would be nearly pleasant. Then, as I awaken on the floor, the coolness leaves, I open my eyes and sense the Count kneeling beside me, with his pocketwatch near his face, he drifts around in soft focus, and I hear him say, "Helen, you lost consciousness for forty or fifty seconds. Are you well enough to sit up? Your friend will be fine, it's not deep, he'll be all right. Tea and cognac will fix you right up."

After I faint or swoon, I must always rush to a sink and splash cold water on the pressure points, wrists, at the pulse, on the neck, the jugular vein specifically, then all over my face, where the skin appears drained and blanched, and, when color returns, with blood to my brain, so do I. I return to the dining room, where, by now, my table, relieved to see me up and conscious, or almost conscious, is all sympathy for a bit, but also showing restraint because they are loath to interfere with me, to my detriment, and also they're ready for dessert, which tonight is chocolate pudding with chocolate chips and fresh whipped cream. I drink black tea and swallow a shot of cognac. This anaglyphic scene reforms and becomes again one room with just four walls and just three dimensions, the chairs and table return to their regular shapes, and the residents' disparate triple noses, eyes, lips, and brows congeal into single features and recognizable faces, my lightheadedness dissipates, a process I'm used to, and then Contesa rises from the table, and, in her spirited manner, announces to the room, first ringing a bell, that she has written a short play or spectacle, and hopes all assembled will attend a dramatic reading of it, but that is our decision, and she will understand our need for solitude, especially after what's happened, looking at me and toward the kitchen, which could be embarrassing but somehow isn't. It is tonight at nine in the Rotunda Room, she declares and sits down again. The tall balding man and disconsolate woman immediately leave, which the demanding man notes, sullenly, as the Turkish poet searches my face for explanation, so it is a moment to appear enigmatic.

"Wait, I'll do a trick for you," the Magician says sharply. He's looking at me. "You wanted to learn about tricks, I'll show you one, and it'll get your mind off it." It, I ask myself, what is it?

The Magician displays a quarter and sets it on the table near me. I look and then hear him say something and it's gone. The quarter's gone. "It's under the plate. Move it," the Count demands. The Magician pushes the plate slightly and says, "No, see, it's not." Then the Magician produces three more quarters and moves them around on the table, he slides them effortlessly, one after another, like baby silver mice, through his fingers, he holds them up to show the table, while he asserts: "I'm not good at doing magic acts, I'm really bad at it, but I belong to the International Brotherhood of Magicians, I don't know how they let me in, and the American Society of Magicians, and to the Magic Castle in L.A., it's been there in Los Angeles since 1906. But I'll make mistakes, so watch me very closely, I'll make a mistake, but do you know anything about physics, because there's a theory about the third dimension that . . ." As he talks, boldly and fast, he walks around the table, stopping at each chair, to demonstrate to each of us that the coins are real, he has us touch them and look at them, he bites all of them, after which most at the table wipe their hands and mouths, and, when he sits down again, having performed his patter without a lapse, he pulls out, from his sleeve or pocket, I can't tell, several items.

—Anyone missing anything? the Magician asks.

Each of us pats our pockets, even if we don't have any, looks down and up, looks at him, and then at each other. He sets on the table the Count's Breguet pocketwatch, Spike's hemp purse, the Turkish poet's slim purple notebook, Contesa's dark glasses, Arthur's and Henry's 1960s designer wristwatches, and my silver Bauhaus button I carry in my pants pocket. Everyone gasps, but the Count looks as if he might faint, too.

—What about the coins? Spike asks.

—I can do that another time.

—I hate being manipulated, numbers never do that, Spike says.

—I applaud it, the Turkish poet says.

—Jean Cocteau would choose the thief over the cops, says Arthur.

—I'm not stealing, ladies and gentlemen, I'm just showing you that the hand is faster than the eye.

—It's amazing, I say.

—You distracted me, says the Count.

—I practice the art of misdirection, I told you that, the Magician reiterates.

The Magician remains calm, but the Count fidgets in an active state of confusion that I'd never witnessed in him, he could jump out of his skin, but Contesa addresses him, talks softly, and strokes his arm. He pulls himself together and asks the Magician to hand over his treasured Breguet, and, with its return, his demeanor rejigs, but he must now experience the Magician as an enemy or an obstacle to his peace of mind, which was just shattered, while Contesa, though not delighted by the Magician's attitude toward spirits, asks to speak with him privately, later, and gracefully excuses herself from the table and leaves the room. The head cook, who rarely steps into the dining room, she keeps to her domain, except for special occasions or holidays, when she takes our applause for an elaborate meal, which she cooked for us when she wished to be home with her husband and grown children, if they're still on speaking terms, is now among us. She claims the room's attention by clanging a small triangle. Her long apron wears stains of recent meals, including splatters of the kitchen helper's blood, so I have to avert my eyes, otherwise I'll become lightheaded again. Finally, when everyone stops speaking, except the stout Wineman who is mostly audible throughout, she says she's very, very sorry for the commotion, that the kitchen helper is fine and probably won't need stitches, and we should just pretend it never happened. "Please pretend it never happened," she repeats, and her hands flutter absentmindedly. My tablemates shrug, their shoulders shunting off the immediate past, but I've never been able to pretend something never happened.

The Magician touches my shoulder, "Watch this, Helen," he demands, and sets a playing card in front of me. He moves it around on the table, lifts both his hands, and, in that instant, the card disappears. His sleeves are up, they're well above his bony elbows, often an unattractive part of the body, often plastered with elephant skin, psoriasis is frequently found there, and the card has vanished.

—Thanks, that's terrific, just what I needed, I say.

He looks into my eyes, nakedly taking my measure, and it's a little weird, as if he has imperceptible sightlines into me, but it's not creepy, because his eyes are warm, like the friendly dog's up the street.

—I'm glad, Helen, because the truth is, I'm not going to be here long, it's a pit stop, so to speak.

The Magician continues to look at me but in an especially kindly way and appears to have reached a decision.

—You know, I have a feeling about you, I'd like to get to know you better, as a friend, he explains, with some urgency.

While this is unnerving, it is also pleasant and a surprise, since he has seen something in me that I don't see in myself, I'm sure, but instantly I hope he isn't going to compromise me in some way or make my time here more complicated than it already is, become too demanding, or like a rejected suitor be disappointed and want to harm me. We all saunter into the main lounge for after-dinner talk and drinks, offered by the staff, who serve us with a casual propriety, and then the Turkish poet bundles my arm in his, whisks me away, and asks, "You are truly all right?" because he's nervous for me, since people don't faint "hugely in these times," and, while patting my back solicitously, observes, "You are 19th century woman in trousers." It's a funny idea, he's wrong, I feel no kinship to the 19th century, except that it preceded and fomented reaction in the 20th, whose difficult progeny I am, but then I remember my Polish cosmetician, who wouldn't say that, and instead would repeat in her thudding English, "Your skin is very sensitive," then she'd slather cream on my face and tell me to close my eyes, while moving her fingertips lightly across my cheeks, forehead, and chin, never touching the thin skin beneath my eyes, which is too fragile even for her trained touch. "A sexual act is perforce and perchance a fainting," the Turkish poet stage-whispers dramatically, as we are joined by Spike and the Count who sit close to us. The fire rages. The Count hears the Turkish poet's commentary, and, from his store of knowledge, pulls out, like a rabbit, the word faineant, an adjective, which means given to doing nothing, of which I am frequently guilty, but it's also close to feigning, faignant, from the French for idler, he explains, and faindre, to feign. "It's the word closest to fainting in most good dictionaries," the Count says, after which Spike adds that John Cage became an expert in mushrooms, since it was the word in the dictionary closest to music, so Cage kept seeing it, became intrigued and maintained an interest for life. Spike, too, may often look at the M's because she is a mathematician. The Count strolled along the Seine and saw an antique blue watch, fell in love with it, and still loves and collects timepieces, Contesa read Kafka's *Amerika* and, because he hadn't visited it, she fell in love with his writing and mind, next with his brilliant cat-and-mouse letters to Felice, who may be Contesa's *Amerika*, because she couldn't visit her even in letters, whose symmetry she might enjoy, but I don't remain faithful long to my person, others, and my interests, except I have habits, but I resent them.

The present into which I've landed from my swoon might be a fine one, I feel this maybe illogically, having just returned from the oneiric empire and been released here, so I can listen to other voices, while the fire throws heat on my sensitive skin, it prickles, but I want more, sensation of any kind. I don't actually mind fainting, except for the feeling of added pressure or weight on my heart, fainting is a habit about which I have no choice, when I lose consciousness, which relieves me in the moment from worse sensations or in short consciousness. But the Count takes out his Breguet and announces, "It's time." Even where our days and nights are relatively unstructured, it's always time for something, with too much or too little of it, everyone complains, then asserts, it may be my time, or I had my time, but what would that have been, yet it's said people live beyond their time, which seems on the face of it a worthless idea, I don't know what it serves, like a cheap design. A neurotic often realizes it is better to live in time, and some of the residents cajole each other, Be present to your experience, get over it, get past it, or just move on, metaphorical phrases that proselytize a physical approach to static mental conditions, practical if mostly useless. The staff encourages the residents similarly with ambiguous regulations and rules that rest on flexibility, except no one knows when that relaxation will occur: for instance, the inventor was allowed to be with his dog when I couldn't bring my young wild cat, and they probably know he dropped his jeans and exposed his rosy ass, and nothing happened, but if the demanding man did it, his act might incur a negative reaction from the administration. Certain fellows' complaints are handled by the staff but others they expect the residents to sort out among themselves, but none of us knows exactly why, since their reasons and rationales are their own, and while we are encouraged also to be ourselves and to be inquisitive, there are some things we must accept, because that is the way things are, it is life. If I could cleanse myself of memory, I would, if I could abandon the sensible or rational world, I would, I'd like to, I think I'd like to. I'd also like to be unafraid and full of faith, like Samantha, who was here two years ago, who followed various teachers to the ends of the earth and never again returned to our ordinary one. Instead she wanders, untethered from any single person or place, in a day-to-day existence of happenstance. If I could, I might be able to pretend that our cat and my dog had found good homes, that beloved dead friends hover like guardian angels or are alive, which happens in dreams, and that I'm not alone and without purpose, subject to forces bigger than myself, about which I have no choice. At my mother's grand age, with her damaged brain, whose irascibility none can predict, her memory's extraction occurs daily, but she forgets and remembers the same things, so even loss has a pattern. She never forgets her husband, my father, only that he is dead and not waiting for her in his car, she forgets she killed our cat and my dog, she forgets my brother or remembers him as a child, she remembers her mother, whom she believes was perfect, and when she awakens from a dream, she's believes she's in prison, trapped in an apartment that is not hers, and nothing reassures her.

Longing to be sure but without the cunning for certain kinds of pretending, which allow for ecstatic drifting or dour certainty, I can imagine and fantasize, I can even will myself toward something like hope when I'm doing and undoing things, which is why Contesa appeals to me, also the Count, both of whom dwell in made-up elsewheres, my dinner partners, also, with their resilience, will, or fortitude, like the Magician, who, though a new resident, responded so graciously to a stranger, me. My incapacities and limits must be internal truths, which is why I do what I do and don't do. I can't unring the bell, I can remove the clangor, I will take apart a bell tomorrow, I can see it, the clangor lying on its side, useless, but if I set many clangors on their sides, and have many, many bowls on a table or on the floor, the patterns could achieve something. A staggering number strewn on the floor, so many inert, disentangled, disconnected objects might become something, or only things on a floor taking up space, but that is what everything does, take up space, all things need room, so I might try the experiment, since nothing succeeds without failure, failure has many charms, a mistake might bear a thrilling offspring. I want sensation, even though I don't know what I'm looking for, while scientists, whom I admire, know what they seek, so their experiments are conducted with an aim, an order, a logic, purpose, as they are interested in outcomes and in proofs. I am mostly interested in ways to the end, processes closer to living, whose outcome is always the same, a reliable fact of life, so there's reason to be curious only about when it comes, and for most there will be no proof of anything, another reason to follow, yet also question, science, with its assurance of repeatable outcomes. History repeats itself, but differently, people repeat themselves, there is a compulsion to repeat, which is not chosen, and few actually appreciate conscious repetition, except psychoanalysts, scientists, salespeople, and shopkeepers, who depend on regular customers, and artists, who might find elegance or beauty in it. Many repetitions are numbing, some might be propitious mistakes, or just useless error, though eating the same meal for breakfast, lunch, and dinner has a certain beauty or intelligence because you could have more time for other thoughts, though they may be plaintive and less sensual than deliberating about food, when, and only if, it is plentiful. The abundance of recipes and menus can be a bounty or a burden, but it can be stupid to hold the same position toward things, because you have always held it, or as a principle. I ruefully acknowledge mistakes, as well as episodes of stupidity, as Contesa called them, which aren't only sexual, but some have been and continue to be, and wrongness lumbers on in a range from pathetic, poorly conceived, or subtly incorrect acts or thoughts, to indifferent, crude, and manipulative ones, sometimes similar to cruelty, whose sting is worse than being struck dumb, or being incapable of knowing what to do or why. The sprites who forgive and forget taunt me, and some obsessive thinking is disheartening, while most is a mistake.

There was a time when I wanted people to like me, but now I want to like people, once I believed them capable of what they espoused, I suppose I wanted to believe them, now I like them if I do, despite what they espouse, and, as I look around me, I marvel at the characters here, yet still long to be in my room, lying on my bed, drawing a chair, reading or musing, listening to the radio, or taking apart a tape recorder, scattering its tiny innards in the air and seeing where they fall, as if they might be an omen, but it's probably good to be with people, not to avoid them, which I mostly want to do, because I'm not sure what they hold in store, yet when the Count recounts how, in the 4th century AD, it was Clement, Ignatius, and Tertullian who determined the twelve books of the New Testament, after years of dispute, or Spike expands on her riotous, ingénue's repertoire, or the Turkish poet sighs about sex and life's recondite treacheries, I am also at home. I can believe that I am supposed to be here, a curious feeling, one that has been growing in me, maybe since I've been here, that it's right that I'm here, or I'm right to be here, that I shouldn't be anywhere else, a sense I don't often have, though I am usually aware of being in or being a body, because I'm encased in dry, sensitive skin, and during the winter, especially, it cracks and bleeds, but anytime a detergent touches my hands, my skin will immediately react to its poisons and for many days afterward the affected fingers, usually the middle and index fingers and thumb, will be inflamed, the skin flaky and tough, tearing and bleeding, and very painful until it heals in the requisite four days. The disconsolate woman with psoriasis opines that her problem is solely environmental, a word I abjure, though my dermatologist told me that most doctors think psoriasis and many other skin diseases have a genetic and psychic origin, because their outbreaks can be triggered by trauma, for instance, shingles, or the chicken pox virus, or herpes complex might live but lie dormant in the spine for many years and break out when a person is under extreme duress. The disconsolate woman has her ups and downs, mood swings, which are marked by patches and flares of red and lakes of pus on her arms and hands, and the world is increasingly poisonous, or toxic, as she'd say, but psoriasis has been around longer than laundry detergents and emissions that have destroyed the ozone layer, though its cause is still unknown. Hippocrates described the disease in the 4th century BC, but it wasn't named until much later. Heredity appears to be significant, and it appears equally in both sexes, but it's uncommon in black people, and I've read that the American Indian and native Fijians don't have psoriasis, and, I guess, must, with assimilation, change, unless they have resistant genes, and then they should be studied. I know my body is in a place, either when it hurts or has pleasure, otherwise I may forget it. The other disconsolate woman, who has asthma, hates her body or hates bodies, a common phenomenon here and in the place I call home. The word for body in Zulu is um-zimba, and if some Zulus hate their bodies, their reasons may be different from those of us in America, where women were historically free to choose their husbands and damned for it, and for whom men, whatever a woman's sexual desire, are an important subject.

On each chair in the Rotunda Room, Contesa has provided a typescript of her one-acter or spectacle, I have it in my hands when she announces that the performance will soon start, explains that she has never done this, that her way is not necessarily ours, though she hopes it will entertain and enlighten us, and she rebukes only herself for what disagrees with us. "You may not like my cuisine," she says pointedly. The head cook may be here, and I watch Contesa's mouth, it sets decisively. The Rotunda Room, which dates from 1838, is painted rustic gold, or sienna, features a high-domed ceiling, and oval windows that are inset around its perimeter, there's some echo in the wood and plaster room, but its black wooden chairs have sensibly curved backs, so that, like a chair by the Eameses, they respond to the lower back, providing lumbar support. Their flat, svelte cushions are covered in thick, tufted dark-green velvet, a gift, no doubt, of the Green Lady, who is known to appreciate theater. The seats are comfortable. During the late 1860s, after the Civil War, a local history book records, séances and sessions of spirit photography occurred in this room, and back then William Lloyd Garrison and Horace Greeley, both abolitionists, attended séances, as did William Cullen Bryant and James Fenimore Cooper, and some might have been in the Rotunda Room. Spirit photography's early practitioners were often women, who were usually mediums and who manufactured miracles in which dead people shimmered as palimpsests pressed onto glossy surfaces, chemical ghosts invaded the present, all of which people want, against reason, and probably Contesa elected this space for its redolent, spirit-laden past with which she may feel connected or in which she feels she can better contact the numinous world.

The room is full, its thirty chairs with our bodies on them absorb oxygen and noise, and also we make sounds, I hear inharmonious wheezing, coughing, and some shortness of breath. Contesa leaves the podium, the lights dim, and, to my shock, from the wings, the odd inquisitive woman wanders onstage, looking about in all directions as if lost, replacing Contesa behind the podium. The odd inquisitive woman holds herself erect in her tatty skirt, a black pullover sweater, while her unruly hair is tucked under a brown suede beret. She would see me soon enough, she said to me in town, I remember that now. She stares at the audience and projects a strength and purpose that is impressive; there is something almost magnificent about her bearing. I cast my eyes quickly over the cover sheet of the typescript: Four Players—The Narrator, Franz Kafka, Felice Bauer, Max Brod—written by Violet.

The Narrator: This is a work in collaboration with the letters of Franz Kafka and the spirit of Felice Bauer. Her letters are lost. So I will take liberties. The Saints preserve pariahs like me. Please touch the hand of the persons beside you, please touch their hands.

The Count and Spike are beside me, and there is an awkward touch from the Count, who once embraced me, but nothing more, and I hold his hand for a second, and, from Spike a rhythmic pat or two, she is usually affectionate, and behind me I sniff the sodden odor of the demanding man, but can't know if he's touching anyone or being touched.

The Narrator: Kafka wrote to Felice, "He who belongs to you keeps wandering about in the distance." In the present, Kafka's and Felice's souls, they will mingle. Here comes Kafka.

The inquisitive woman, the narrator, points stage right, and, augmenting my surprise, the tall balding man walks on, his shoulders a pair of parentheses around his body, which is stiff as an exclamation mark, and

I wonder what J and JJ will think of his truculent carriage. He's wearing a black suit and black derby, like an undertaker. He removes the hat and takes a chair, he is himself and not himself, and I recall that he played Kafka in my dream some time ago, and, now his secret lover, the disconsolate woman, enters, stage left, and I feel my stomach contract, while the demanding man groans, Spike chortles with muted pleasure, and the Count sinks into his chair. The tall balding man, or Kafka, waves to her, his Felice, feebly. She nods, and the disconsolate woman, or Felice, faces the audience. She's staring above our heads, toward the rear of the Rotunda Room.

Kafka: "There are times when impossibility swamps possbility like a wave."
Felice: He whips himself for us.
Kafka: Never. I'm no Christ, but I am a Jew.

Kafka looks aghast, then sad, then he breaks up at his own preposterousness, and I contain my laughter, but some suffocated or constricted noises come out. The tall balding man is so expressive onstage, he exaggeratedly throws back his arms, demonstrative in a way he never is, so watching him act, I'm nervous. His flesh confronts me, he even appears to have an aura or charisma, and, spotlighted, he becomes an object whose every deficiency is on exhibition, people exhibiting themselves can produce some embarrassment. I anticipate that, even shame, but not guilt, thankfully. The other bodies around me stretch their legs, their asses shift on the tufted dark-green velvet cushions, their mouths smack, and noses snort, a being-human chorus.

Kafka: "But how could my writing to you, however firm my hand, achieve everything I want to achieve: To convince you that my two requests are equally serious: 'Go on loving me' and 'Hate me!"
Felice: My heart, I have no answer.

Felice seems to speak from her heart, since she has no technique for walking, standing, or acting, and whatever merit there is in her acting comes from her inability to conceal herself, so she is herself, or an exaggeration of herself, and I'm following, with distractions, people I've had breakfast, dinner, and drinks with, if they are allowed to drink, as they transform into characters like or unlike themselves. I can spy unguardedly. The disconsolate woman, Felice, sits down and pretends to write, but then she looks again at the audience, now directing herself to the Count, I think, it's hard to say, it could be to the demanding man, whose odor penetrates. The inquisitive woman shuffles to the lectern, once again as if she's lost, it's deliberate then, and she's wearing purple lipstick, I'd missed that before.

The Narrator: Kafka wrote that in 1913. He started it all, Franz began writing Felice in 1912. They were engaged twice and Kafka broke it off permanently in 1917. By then Kafka coughed blood. But from the beginning, he created her. Kafka enchanted her, and she was his enchantment.

Kafka strides to the side of the stage and looks longingly at Felice.

Kafka: "I'm afraid that soon I shall no longer be able to write you, for to be able to write to someone (I must give you all sorts of names, so for once you must be called 'someone') one has to have an idea of the face one is addressing . . ."

Felice plucks a hand mirror from behind or under her chair and looks at herself, the disconsolate woman's psoriasis has flared, reddened slightly, she's not my image of Felice, though it's sly of Contesa to have cast her, but she must have wanted the role. I appreciate Contesa's discretion, how she kept this a secret, I appreciate this and also some forms of deviousness, but the disclosure of secrets can alarm and be destructive, especially if they expose a long-kept masquerade with intricate roots, whose undoing rips foundations, because change has unknowable effects. I know several people whose fathers had second families they kept hidden, who performed as double husbands and fathers, in elaborate hoaxes, for years and years, making the task seem easier to perform than it is, or it is people's necessary gullibility, their desire not to see what might hurt them, that permits such inestimable deception. I have a friend a part of whose life may be secret, but by now I don't want him to reveal it, because there are things I don't want to know and whose exposure might destroy our relationship. He may or may not have a married lover, whose husband is ill, I've often considered he does, and that when he departs on a journey, for he often travels, he's not going anywhere but to his furtive mistress, and for some reason he wants even his closest friends to think he has, as he says, no one to love, and this possibility fascinates me, so I'd be disappointed if it weren't the case, but also I don't want to know absolutely it is, because then it would change our relationship.

The Narrator: Max Brod, Kafka's best friend, interpreted Kafka for Felice. First Felice wrote to him. Brod wrote back to her. Later, he disobeyed Kafka's will. He didn't destroy Kafka's unpublished work, his letters or diaries. Kafka trusted Brod, but he also had invoked chance. Or, did he know what Brod would do?

Arthur saunters onstage, the fourth player, he is Max Brod, a jaunty figure, and his partner, Henry, sits in the first row beaming, looking around, human beings want approval, even their approval approved. Arthur's thick, long hair is tied in a chunky ponytail, and he too is in a black suit, but no hat, and sports a cravat and monocle, and, because of the style, I sense another time, as style marks periods, even years, with its date stamp, or maybe it's because I know too little yet about Arthur, since he communicates mostly to his partner, and this allows me to enter the period better, though Max Brod was Jewish, like Kafka, and Caucasian, but there are also black or African Jews.

Kafka: "I have always looked upon my parents as persecutors."

Brod (to Felice): Franz was furious when his mother read your letter to him. But "Franz, thank God, is gratifyingly stubborn and sticks precisely to what is good for him. His parents just will not see that an exceptional man like Franz needs exceptional conditions to prevent his sensitive spirit from withering . . ."

Brod walks downstage and sits on the edge of the stage, while around me the dour man snorts, the Count squirms, Spike restlessly taps her foot, but I don't see the Turkish poet, though he must be here, exultant with these confabulations before us. My beloved father was a persecutor and a pleaser. One night he took me out to dinner, and, after he paid the bill, he looked sad, I asked him why, and he said it wasn't good enough, he'd wanted to take me for a very good meal, he was sorry it wasn't better, he repeated downcast, as if everything had depended upon this dinner, which I remember now, but don't know why.

Felice: I love my garden. I want to grow roses for you. Roses are ancient. They are Aphrodite's tears and Adonis's blood. I want you to be happy. I will sit beside you, nurse you. But each letter upsets me, each of your thoughts undoes the previous one. My mother grows increasingly upset, too. When will we marry, she asks. I am weary sometimes. I don't want to be a burden.

Kafka: "You know, there are wonderful sanitoria in this wide world."

The Narrator: Do not laugh at a blind man nor tease a dwarf nor injure the affairs of the lame, Kafka.

Kafka: I? Never. Aren't I afflicted, too?

Brod points his index finger at the narrator, scolding her, then she puts her script aside, and, with mirth, points her index fingers at the audience. Saint Rita harumphs loudly to the Frenchman beside her who courts and esteems evil and smiles with glee, then Rita's mouth screws shut in a universal sign of disgust, while next to the Frenchman, the Magician appears rapt. Where is Contesa sitting or hidden, I wonder, she's quoted the Count about the lame, from his "Dead Hand Notes" lecture. My skin seethes with vermiculations, which promiscuously derange my body, and now the Count encloses my warm hand inside his icy one, and I jump at the surprise.

The Narrator: To Kafka, a bourgeois marriage was a strangulation. According to his friends, he was humorous. He was full of fun, a barrel of laughs. But for him marriage wasn't funny, and he feared he'd become a fat bourgeois.

Kafka: (walking quickly from side to side onstage) There was a very religious man who never doubted God's existence. One day a flood came, and he went to the top of his house and sat on the roof. People passed by in a boat and offered to row him to safety. No, he said, I'm waiting for God to stop the flood and deliver me. A second boat came by, filled with people, and then a third. Each time the religious man said he was waiting for God's deliverance. Finally, his house collapsed, and he drowned. The man went to heaven where he beseeched God: Why did you fail me? God said: I sent three boats.

Kafka holds his sides and laughs demonically, Felice isn't laughing, standing at the edge of the stage, and will she jump off in a symbolic suicide? Just now she reminds me of my sleeping-pill-addicted friend, whose infuriated neediness could only be quieted with barbiturates, and maybe she enters because it was in a theater when I last spotted this former friend, but because she'd had plastic surgery and looked similar to herself at the age when we met, I couldn't tell if it was really her or someone who looked like her, but younger, and I didn't say hello, because it's often better not to say anything. The person I thought she was could have been her daughter, or it simply may not have been her, but whoever it was was crying.

> Brod: She hoped that the mordant man, who abhorred violence, would be the right one for her. A good husband. He explained to her he couldn't be. But Felice was a slave to her love.

The Frenchman applauds inappropriately, I don't know precisely why, though he may cherish enslavement, and Saint Rita moves farther from him. Is there a way to avoid such metaphors? I can take apart a chair, even a beloved chair, because it can be taken apart and is only a chair, and slavery is also slavery. I'm tense, preparing for a decisive event, or wishing for it, because, without a complement of elements cresting conclusively, I may not feel satisfied, fulfilled, or able to rest. Where will things go? Where will these images and words go when we've left here? I like to place objects where they should be, in the right containers, to avoid mess and spills, and, at the end of the day, dirty dishes in the sink are sometimes maddening. Yet the trivial, broken, and incomplete are dearer to me, more precious, since what can't be spliced together, cleaned up, and unanimously credited propels novelty, as an antic irrelevance may also parent art and science. I want contentment and satisfaction, things falling into place, not apart, which is incongruent with my impulse to take apart and leave things in pieces on the floor. But, generally, I would prefer to be indifferent to every outcome.

Felice: I might soar if I were not stuck to the ground by his exceptions and rebukes. His strange writing! I am lost to it. I never see him, he never visits, he breaks our appointments. He writes me every day, twice a day. I should leave him. But his words are life to me now, and he loves me. He needs me.

The Narrator: Woman, beware your needs!

Brod: Ach, ach . . .

Kafka: "The first evening we met . . . what a lot has happened between that evening and now, and since to blush is to admit, your blushes on that occasion . . . implied the following: 'Yes, he loves me, but for me it is a great misfortune. For he thinks that because he loves me, he is free to torment me . . . He always talks in riddles.' Dearest Speaker: I would give my life for you, but I cannot give up tormenting you."

Felice's and Kafka's torment is that his love is a torment, so agitated when I'm supposed to be calm, I turn from the picture onstage to the picture window that frames the dark forest beyond the Rotunda Room, whose jumpy spirits may be quivering, fornicating with abandon, or sleeping, though they don't need to rest. Beyond the window lies the beauty of the world, I tell myself, not believing in spirits or the world's beauty, yet the ideas aid me, pull me off Kafka's words, and soothe me like a subtle emollient on the skin or a lovely description of a facial, and I wantonly reckon the possibility of there existing a magic that has the power to console, and, if so, how it might trick me, if it hasn't already.

Some believe cats are magical creatures, I don't, but I have a limited idea of magic, I like illusion, and don't need to believe it, but cats have the power to console. An affectionate cat lying on your chest, as it purrs, is a consolation for the horrors of the world, though its being in no way alters the plight of the world, apart from fostering your sense of well-being in a reclusive, evanescent moment. A cat can sense when you're unhappy, even my wild cat once lay on my back when I cried, he didn't lie on it for long, but since it was the only time he did, and I was crying, I believe he knew I was unhappy and he was trying to help me. He may be purring now, keeping my mother company, if her old cat permits, as she and her brain age, I know of a dog who lies on the beds of dying people in hospitals, he always knows when a person will die, he senses death coming, and he's always right, or my cat could be in a corner, lonely for me, which I doubt, but in some way I'd like him to miss me though not be miserable. Actually, I want to be surrounded by many cats, hundreds, if I didn't have to take care of them all the time and be responsible for cleaning their litter boxes, because when looking at them, at their sleek coats, their serene indifference, their implacable calm, unless they've gone mad like my cat who stalked and attacked me, the world's horror leaves temporarily.

The disconsolate woman and tall balding man come to the center of the stage, hold hands, and stare into each other's eyes. They embrace and slide back and forth across the stage, wordlessly, and, with each movement, Kafka tightens his grip, so her anorectic body disappears inside his embrace, she is affixed to his body like a stamp, then he pushes her away from him, and this happens again and again. At last, Felice shakes her head and disengages, wrests her painfully thin person from him, while she covers her face with her hands and then, in or out of character, weeps softly.

The Narrator: If Felice could fly. If she had wings! They'd be clipped by her Kafka. He created her for himself. He didn't talk about her to his friends. In fact he didn't talk about her ever. When her name came up in conversation, he pretended he didn't know her. He hoped a visiting friend would bring news of her, unaware.

Then Felice, or the disconsolate young woman, heaves and sobs, she weaves in place, circles the stage, and stops short, then she collapses, still weeping convulsively. Her breath comes in fast bursts, she can't rise.

"She's hyperventilating," shouts the stout Wineman, the stage. Her wailing can't have been scored in Contesa is spectacular and would be a feat if the disconsolate woma but now an anxious staff member rises from his chair and t as well as the Count rush forward to help, I move forward everyone is clustering around her downcast, skinny shape on th The Wineman turns her over deftly, strokes her forehead, breathe her mouth, counting one two three four, then breathes into her mo again, until her breathing regulates itself, and she settles down, her bod released. The residents spread out and give her more room to breathe and orient herself, as well as themselves, while the tall balding man caps his hand over his bald spot, rubbing it in circles, and the Count and I stand by, not knowing what to do, or if anything more is required of us. Usually, I believe, a paper bag is slapped over a hyperventilator's mouth.

Silence sounds like a clap of thunder.

At last, Contesa calls out that her play is over, even if it's not finished, and please everyone return to the lounge or your rooms, have a drink or a tea, and then she declares that our Felice will be fine. Each of the emerald green tufted-velvet chairs is empty, except for the Frenchman's, who remains and glares in her direction, also the site of the unplanned spectacle. He doesn't seem to be at a loss the way the rest of us are, he appears miffed or outraged, as if he might be a sophomaniac, which, according to the Medical Sex Dictionary in the library, is a form of insanity characterized by a belief in one's own supreme wisdom. He approaches the stage area with a saturnine visage and confronts the Count and me, asserting, in a still-charming French accent, that when Galileo was tried during the Inquisition, as he rose from his knees after he swore the earth was the center of the universe, not to be a liar, he muttered, "E pur si muove." With force, the Count repeats in English, "Nevertheless it does move." "He was a fool to die for this idea, it would be found true, anyway," the Frenchman spits out, and takes off, looking back at me, daring me to rebuke or despise him, a look that might have sexual connotations. The Count remarks, casually, "I've met others like him."

I have also, and in the past I might have wanted to have sex with him, bitterly provocative man, whose active disdain for common things and love of evil might have carried the day and myself to his bed, briefly. But I don't like his skin, which is rough with large pores and a few blackheads around his nostrils, his tidy moustache, which hyphenates his lower from his upper face, and his height, he's too short for me. Imagining myself with him feels athletic and tiring, as if we'd played sex against each other in the Olympics. I once regularly used to carry a torch, but I no longer want to die for love, I might for an idea, but maybe that's also a romance, because I'd like to die for something and not nothing, which is probably my fate, and I'm here, with time off and on my hands, as well as the ambiguous luxury to consider such questions.

On July 3, 1826, Thomas Jefferson was in a coma and awoke long enough to ask, "Is it the fourth?" They were supposedly his last words, he died on July 4, 1826, at 12:20 p.m., and John Adams fell ill and died later the same day, at 6 p.m. His last words were: "Thomas Jefferson survives." At my finale, I'd like to have inspiring words like those on my dry, feverish lips, and someone to hear them and care enough to write them down, the way my dermatologist writes about my skin in his file that grows bigger and bigger. The Frenchman also has a regrettable brown mole on his cheek, its border is regular, if it were irregular, especially a new brown lesion, I might be compelled, though I wouldn't want to interfere or importune, to advise him to see a dermatologist, but I believe it is benign, even if he's marred in my eyes by an indefinable unsightliness and by his stupid beliefs. I can't understand why he, and many others with ugly growths on the face, especially when there is more than one, doesn't have it removed.

The residents amble, reluctantly or moodily, toward the thick, wooden double doors, where the Turkish poet looks distressed, so I wave at him wanly, he returns the wave, then disappears with Henry and Arthur to discuss this local and other more exotic scandals over cognac. But I feel suspended or caught and don't leave, or can't, so time passes, and, like much of time, I can't remember its passage, where it went, what occurred to me, only that for a while my legs were wooden and dense as a chair by Wright, and I stared into the room, not seeing, and, as in a dream when a monster appears, I couldn't budge, but I didn't faint or even come close to swooning. A former enemy once turned her back on me, and I couldn't move, but then she died, one of the three enemies to die, extraordinarily, within the same year, which left a vacuum or more space, and then I could travel safely in territories where once they might also have been, inhibiting my movements and spurious sense of freedom.

The disconsolate young woman's heaving sobs bother me. Her rebellious body intimidated and stunned us with its bursting, explicit urgency, exceeding the bounds by which we residents are circumscribed, and, while Kafka and Felice were subject to exquisite conflicts, the disconsolate woman's, involuntarily revealed, disconcerts me more in the moment. Curiously, her self-exposure awakens the balcony scene in which the inventor was displaying his peachy ass, though the two events had different causes, motives, and held very different excitements. I become aware of myself alone in the Rotunda Room, surrounded by empty, plush green velvet cushions on black wood chairs, and, in a sense, its many ghost stories, as well as Kafka's and Felice's, so when a loud crash at a window startles me, though probably just a stiff wind, the sudden sound jars me, and I shoot out of the room through the rustic, dark and heavy double doors downstairs to the main room, where some residents linger, JJ, the demanding man, one of the disconsolate women, not our Felice, and others. They are also confounded by her naked collapse and talk about it among themselves, but I require quiet and need to be in my room quickly, to undo the unforeseen, unsettling events, though I know that's impossible, so I turn toward the external door, stepping lightly and keeping to an imaginary line on the wooden floor, hoping to be invisible, to leave without further contact, since there's been enough socializing and vivacious or rigorous content to last for days. Perhaps I should round up Contesa for a heart-to-heart, but she must be with her actors, and the Count and she, more than anyone, will understand my need for flight, as she regularly flees, and, with that, I escape with relief, but outside on a pathway leading either to the library or one of the guest or resident houses, I notice the Magician, who is scowling or concentrating hard, with an incandescent light from a lamppost illuminating him. He crooks an index finger at me. I walk over without thinking about why he beckons me; actually I don't think at all, I walk over, drawn too easily.

—Helen, like I said, I have this feeling about you, you were the only one who didn't freak out when I did my trick. Did you see their faces? They wuz robbed.

He contorts his face to mime comic displeasure, then waits a second for me to speak, but I don't, so he goes on.

—Anyway, here's the proposition, it came to me in the room, with Violet's stuff going on and all, the play or whatever it was. Would you like me to conduct a séance?

I say nothing.

—I'm serious. Violet would, I mean, the room's perfect. If I'm ever going to do it again, it'd be right for me to do it here. The room has that history. I'm ready to give it a shot. What do you say?

—A séance?

—I told you I'm not staying here long, so now's the time.

—But I don't believe in spirits or séances.

—I'm a skeptic, too. Big deal. Why not give it a shot? How about a genuine experience? Isn't that why you're here?

An excellent question, I tell myself, not the Magician, and it also doesn't matter what I think, since I also believe it's good to change my mind or open it, and I'm not willing to doubt everything all the time, because then doubt isn't doubt, but a form of certainty. What I may need is greater than my capacity for doubt or knowledge, for instance, about the workings of the universe, about which scientists can't rest, driven day and night to fit its entire machinations inside a total theory. I might try a séance, since the most improbable experiment could beget auspicious progeny, and, even though I don't believe in the dead returning and speaking, the idea draws me to it. I like surprises, and I can't stop myself.

—I have reservations, I admit.

—Me, too, for dinner. Lighten up, Helen. I have to find Moira before she leaves.

—Who's Moira?

—Moira was the narrator in Violet's thing, I met her in town the last time I was here.

Lighten up. One easy reservation is that I question his sanity, my sanity, and my need to question sanity, a concept I hold in abeyance, then I question his reason, as sanity and reason are often synonymous, which can make for deadly dull days and nights. I wonder who else will join us, apart from Contesa and Moira, that odd inquisitive woman, whose appearance in my life has been accidental, but this encounter will be deliberate, a séance with Moira and unnamed others, but I don't ask the Magician to reveal them, because he might name the demanding man or someone else about whom I'm uneasy.

He wants to meet in the Rotunda Room at midnight, which is in less than two hours, and he'll gather other sitters—a sitting, he informs me, is a séance—and exhorts me not to worry, because he'll make sure they're sympathetic people, and, it's an adventure, he insists.

—Why are you doing this? It's strange. We just met.

—Violet started something in my head, she started me thinking.

He repeats vigorously, his jowls shaking, that he has a sense about me, he explains that he acts on his impulses, because he writes obituaries for a living, and death is in his face every day, and the fact is you never know when you're going to buy it, unless you kill yourself, you never know. He's adamant.

—If the spirit moves me, I just do it. Life is short. Hell, there's no time to lose.

He rushes off to find Moira.

I wish he hadn't said that, No time to lose. I'm in his sights, his excited behavior disallows time's unfolding casually, to be crafted carelessly or by pondering and reflection, but now his impulse crashes into me, so I may have to let things drop or get out of control, I may let myself go or not go but I can't stop, it's hard to stop when something has been set irresistibly in motion. I may want a genuine experience, whatever that is, as everything is in some sense experiential, and also there could be an obstacle I might overcome, I'm mindful of that, and in a curious way a séance, which appears nonsensical, might make sense. Wittgenstein said, "If no one ever did anything silly, nothing intelligent would ever be done." Plainly, it is an accident, a cosmic joke, whatever that means, that I'm in the Magician's path, since our conjunction is unplanned, which idea instantly delights me, its novelty supplants others that raise caution, and my impatience festers, while anxiety blooms. But time drags before the adventure, time to kill, that's all there is, I hate killing it, but I'm not averse to killing other things. I heard about a woman here last year who refused to kill a living creature, who'd taken a vow in a ceremony at the peak of a local, snow-capped mountain, and then allowed cockroaches to thrive and encouraged mice to breed in her room, until there was an infestation of cockroaches and hundreds of mice, since a breeding pair can produce fifty thousand in a year, and the stench and filth required the town authorities and residential staff to remove her forcibly. She is a purist and would not, rumor had it, listen to reason and kill the creatures mercifully, but her ethical position, logical if not reasonable when taken to an extreme, also distinguishes saints, activists, and visionaries. I protect some animals and not others, I eat some and not others, some vegetarians eat fish, most wear leather, to be stylish or warm, most are indifferent to some types of killing, particularly the kind that inconveniences them, and, when a cat I owned turned vicious and stalked me, after employing various tactics to subdue its fury, behavior modification training, exotic music, unearthly sounds, and tranquilizers, I had it killed. If I participate in this séance, it will not be as a purist, but a temporary renegade from categories of reason. I'm free not to submit to the experiment or experience, but experience is what I want, or it is the only thing I have, I'm its sum, a vaporous being, since, like time, it disappears and leaves only memory, which is unreliable and about which I have no choice, and, when I pile up more experiences, I'll have more history that I will forget or inaccurately render, so I'll also be the sum of more regrets and mistakes. It could be the reason not to do anything, which I also do, nothing. I incline toward the new and also bend back toward the old, to an appreciation of history, though in recent years I prefer the study of design, but neither is escapable, and I would like to imagine communication with the dead, my dead friend explaining how he died on a mountain, my father advising me to tell my mother he still loves her, that he didn't want to leave her alone, or that he applauds my quitting history for the study of design and to make or unmake objects. I don't believe or expect any of this, but I'm susceptible to what I don't know or believe, too, since after my father died, on the same night he was taken without saying a last word, a mist of steam or vapor rose and hovered over my mother's body, I watched the little cloud from a chair, because I couldn't sleep, and I thought it was him, bidding us farewell, his spirit having departed his body, leaving just a mistiness, which I don't believe, so then I locked myself in the bathroom, read the *Farmer's Almanac* for 1994, and scrawled lines about dying that in the morning were illegible or made no sense, but uncannily also made sense, since death takes everything, every sense, apart and renders everything indecipherable. If my father visits, I might voice what I couldn't or never did before, but I scarcely can let myself think of the impossible and also don't visit cemeteries, sit on graves and talk to my friends' tombstones, as if they could hear me, though I'd like to believe they do and that if I spoke to them and they heard, it would reassure them of their not being forgotten, that somehow they live in death. But I refuse to talk to a tombstone, I reject its efficacy, reject the fantasy, although paradoxically I acknowledge the truth of the fantastic, since imagination is also knowledge, before it knows itself as useful.

On a serviceable, dark-brown wooden bureau or dresser against one of the walls in my bedroom is an array of creams and potions, to reduce or lessen wrinkles, to smooth, lubricate, or moisturize, to coddle the body and face, and I might relax that way. I watch them, inanimate containers of soothing, energizing hope. New anti-aging creams claim to do as much as medical procedures, these contain pentapeptides, small groups of long-chain amino acids that function as medical messengers throughout the body, initially developed to help in the healing of wounds. As part of the body's natural response to helping skin heal, peptides were found instrumental in increasing cells to generate more collagen, and collagen is critical to how the skin ages. My Polish cosmetician sometimes applies a collagen mask to my face, during which I lie under a pink or blue fluffy blanket for at least twenty minutes while it nourishes my skin, and she talks on the telephone in Polish, so that I don't know what she's saying, which is a blessing probably, but because my skin is sensitive, she avoids dramatic changes, oils and creams, treatments that might cause a rash or, worse, hives, or urticaria, but a collagen mask isn't an irritant. It is supposed to supplant or augment the natural collagen I've lost as I've grown older, it's supposed to replenish it and plump up the cheeks, and for some hours after the mask, I believe my cheeks are plumper. She says so, she insists on the beneficial effects of her work, as everyone does, few want to believe that what they are doing is insufficient, ineffective, or actually damaging, parents slap their children in the child's interest, surgeons perform unnecessary hysterectomies, people abandon dependent pets in parks and on streets, because they've become a nuisance, pets bring out the best and worst human behavior, and the Polish beautician believes in her work and in herself, and I do also, since much well-being is facilitated and benefited by a placebo effect. On a rare occasion, when she was nearly garrulous, she told me that she took care of her elderly mother, who wanted her to live with her, which didn't surprise me, that she cooks meals in advance for her, places each one wrapped in aluminum foil in a freezer, when she goes on an outing with her friends, and that every Sunday the two attend church together. She sighed and then patted my forehead with a potion that smelled of honeysuckle. Occasionally I desire an orderly life such as the one the Polish cosmetician narrates, designed with weekly appointments with her mother, by a religious faith and a God who watches her mostly with love and sometimes disapprobation to whom she can confess and by whom be forgiven, by an adherence to discipline, by strenuous outings with like-minded, robust friends, and a regular job during which every day but Sunday and Monday she waxes legs and moustaches, cleans, shapes and cuts nails, polishes them with a full range of brilliant hues and colors, applies soothing masks and salubrious if worthless creams to women's faces, but I can also imagine she dislikes her boss, who is rarely there and who calls from home and gives her orders, who is married and has children, and that my cosmetician also seethes at her mother's strict regulation of her, a woman of thirty-eight, who doesn't want to marry again or have glum men visiting her unasked in her place of work, or who may want their sexual advances, but whose deepest interests or dissatisfactions lie in areas she'd never express to me. Or, she may have none. Next to the creams on the plain, wooden dresser, a crystal ball, a gift from a dead friend, insinuates itself now as an omen.

I may walk to the library, since there's none of my clutter there, and much to distract me, I could read manuals and encyclopedias, or listen to music and dance, but other residents may be there with their chatter and clutter, and I must clear my mind of its current static. The study of history once offered me a blanket of security, and I miss its reticence about what it can claim, what proofs it needs, its methodical labors, so, rather than my destiny, should I have one, which I don't accept, yet in some way can't entirely reject and which may anyway await me, I roust Manifest Destiny, whose self-serving assumptions have, since I was a teenager, fascinated me, though I was never able, when I taught teenagers, to transmit my wonder. "We shall be as a City upon a Hill," John Winthrop wrote, and on they trekked and settled their new Israel, which the Louisiana Purchase doubled in 1803, and "Westward Ho," without qualm, where settlers annihilated natives who obstructed their mission, since it was sanctified by God, these revolutionists who'd swapped beliefs, from God's having blessed monarchs with a divine right of succession, to having blessed them with a bountiful land, theirs at any cost. The Puritans were hardworking, unforgiving, and practical people, though Winthrop's letters to his wife were tender, immoderately affectionate, and even lustful. I felt so sad about America, suddenly, I had left it, or it had left me.

Homer believed that the gods spin ruin to men in order that there might be song and remembrance, and, in *The Iliad*, Helen thought Zeus brought evil to her and Paris "so that in days to come we shall be a song for men yet to be." Some write songs about ruinous beliefs and philosophies of the past, which at the time appeared undeniably true, but more revel in a placid pool of amnesia and swim with forgetfulness, since remembering can be an encumbrance, delaying rapid movement. I don't want to cherish or memorialize memory, create and keep it in its own image, call its loss a sacrilege, confuse it with nostalgia, since I forget more than I remember, though I can recall facts, dates, what I've read, and conversations easily, but I'm not sure what obligation I have to memory's cause, uncertain what remembering signifies, or why it necessarily makes human beings better than animals, since memories are two-faced, they avoid trouble or lead to it, as revenge is a motive for drama and war that might die out if not for the resilience of memory, though some think revenge lies waiting in DNA, which is a problem. Everything is a problem, I can't think of anything significant that isn't a problem from the past for the future, and though I erect temporary altars to what I remember, some of which feels permanent, as I remember scenes exactly the same way for years until I don't, I'm wary of its drastic claims on the present, especially for sensitive people.

If the Puritans hadn't been persecuted and left England, if scientists hadn't wondered if the world were round, if adventurers hadn't despised ordinary limits and sought vistas beyond their eyes, since people have wants and can't stop themselves, if there hadn't been a slave trade, then if Manifest Destiny hadn't been theorized, there wouldn't have been an expansion of the territories or the extermination of Indian nations, if righteousness didn't prevail, there wouldn't have been a Bloody Kansas, there wouldn't have been a Civil War, except states' rights were from the start a singularly important, pernicious issue for our new nation, and without slavery there wouldn't have been a war, the Emancipation Proclamation, and Abraham Lincoln wouldn't have been shot by John Wilkes Booth. Mary Todd Lincoln attended séances after her sons died, but if her husband hadn't been assassinated, she might not have attended more of them, certainly not for him, or have gone mad, but she was rumored to have been mad also when Lincoln was alive, and I might be

Austrian, never born or already dead. None of this supports a cessation of sensation, or a sensible quiet in the present. I can't undo it, thinking doesn't, I can better take apart a chair in another corner of my room, one that is wrapped in white muslin cloth around its back and seat, damaged and in need of repair, but I may keep it as is, imperfect, a material journal of wounds. I want a perfect chair, like the Minola armchair, by Carlo Mollino, designed during World War II, in Turin, when quality materials were scarce but skilled craftspeople were still available, with an ebonized wood frame, covered in velvet. I have sat in it twice and considered buying it, but I might one day want to take it apart, and no chair held me or my back better or felt more right for my frame, nothing held me better except the arms of a certain man. Wrapped in a Minola armchair, I could dream and speculate, also about my history shadowed by a bigger one, I might have done other than what I did, about some things I had some choice, though about most I didn't, and, in the middle of my life, I can look back and be content or restive. I may pursue my interests, I have time, it's what I have, proverbially I could walk other paths, or invent new versions of the past to believe, there are songs of ruin worth mentioning, and some of us live with the threat of mortification.

Across from my bed, the dark wooden bureau is off center and a framed print above it, not of my choosing, of a bearded doctor, the founder of this institution, is also askew. His impervious, dark eyes, even aslant, peer at me. The housekeeper must have, when making the bed, moved the bureau and picture to clean both more thoroughly and then she must have forgotten to return them to their original places. I feel an intense heat in the room, often the furnace goes berserk or one of the residents adjusts the thermostat to suit him or her better, which inconveniences others, who often return it to a lower or higher temperature, and this can go on all night or morning, surreptitiously, except that everyone may experience the change of heat. My skin actively dries, shrinks, and is fiendishly itchy, augmented by my condition, dermatographia, and I get off the bed and walk to the dresser, first, employing my weight to align it against the wall, to center it as well as the generic portrait of the founder, and then I discard my clothes, which scratch me like a hairshirt, choose a thick cream that promises Immediate Relief and slap it on my arms, and hands, rub it gingerly on my chest, breasts, stomach, and shoulders, and select another for my face, Revitalizing Richness, which I carefully apply, patting the skin and moving my fingers in circles, while making sure to keep off the soft tissue under my eyes. For a moment, I forget my legs, at the bottom of one is a scab or a circle of scaly skin, pinkish, the size of a dime, and it could be psoriasis, I will telephone my dermatologist, he might diagnose it over the phone, even though he doesn't like to, though in my case he makes exceptions, because I have been his patient a long time, he believes I can report my condition in detail, and we have a good relationship, whatever that means. Now I wrap a queen-size all-cotton white towel around me. Outside, the wind gusts, shaking the trees, it blows frantically and whines, I'm protected in this room, relatively safe or merely sheltered, which is a privilege, too, so I think about Lincoln's Second Inaugural Address in which, with the Civil War just ended, Lincoln said that each side claimed the same Bible for different ends, "each invoked His aid against the other." He called for "malice toward none." My father and I watched JFK's inaugural on TV, in our spacious den, with the blond Eames chairs and table in the back of its two open, connected rooms, with its walls of sliding glass windows. JFK proclaimed "we dare not forget today that we are heirs of that first revolution," a heritage I claimed, and, later, with his hat, the new president shielded Robert Frost's old eyes from a noon sun that glared and obliterated the words on a bright, white sheet of paper, from which he attempted to read an occasional poem, "Kitty Hawk," and failed; then from memory Frost recited "The Gift Outright," whose lines also suited the occasion, as if penned by a recidivist Puritan: "The land was ours before we were the land's. . . ." My father leaned in toward the television, and the venerated poet, aged and stooped, his brilliant white hair like a halo, leaned against the handsome, young president, who was not healthy, but very few knew that then, who would soon be assassinated, but no one could know that then except a seer, and everything was helter skelter.

By now Leslie Van Houten has finished eating her institutional dinner and may lie on a cot in her cell in the women's prison at Frontera, California, planning for her next parole hearing, expecting the worst, since her crime was heinous, and she might never be released or pardoned. I veer toward an unshakable admiration for the rule of law and, in the American way, with undeniable fascination toward those who break it, and to those who, failing to find truth, mete out justice, or for those who, professing any and all law restrictive, violate it, especially a criminal who applies a unique standard that appears just or more human, though I don't support violent crimes against persons. Leslie Van Houten was the least culpable of the girls in the Manson Family, she's now sustained by hope and religion, she's been born again, and even if she's released when she's old, her youth long gone, she knows in her heart she's been rehabilitated, she knows it, she's not that girl who stuck a knife into Rosemary LaBianca's back nineteen times. Still, Leslie relives her absurd and terrible crime, her lawless association with Manson and the Family, her devoted love of him, and does penance, but it can never be enough, she can't explain herself, the girl she was then, she doesn't know why she did what she did. It doesn't make sense, it doesn't matter that she'd never do it again. This too doesn't make sense, and she can't recognize that person, but it doesn't matter.

For me, only a séance lies ahead, with its bizarre seductions, and I focus on it, conjuring the Rotunda Room and several faces and bodies convened around a dark wood round table. I'm wondering how the Magician will conduct it, if it has specific rules and rites, like a religious ceremony, when I hear my name shouted several times by what sounds like several voices, an unusual occurrence, since there's an unwritten law, part of the honor code, that we residents shouldn't raise our voices and interrupt another's peace. They shout my name again, more insistently. I put on my robe and go to the window, there are some residents waving, "Come outside," they mouth, so I gesture my willingness, but I don't want to join them. They appear anxious, even stricken—JJ, the demanding man, the dour man, the fretful woman, the disconsolate young woman with asthma, and her friend, the Wineman, an unfortunate group, but at least there is no one of the staff, for which I am grateful, I fear bureaucracy and its devotees, and this must be spontaneous and ex-officio. Reluctantly, I pull on the clothes I recently discarded that lie in a mound on the floor, so the pants are wrinkled, and grab my one hundred percent virgin wool black coat, battleship-gray cashmere scarf, and furtively pat the crystal ball on the way out.

Now, what happens is strange and unbelievable, and, even as it happens, I can't believe it or countenance it, even in this peculiar, portmanteau community, it is also unique in my experience, and their fervor, a group who acts like a mob, immediately offends my sensibilities, since generally I don't appreciate outrage or moralisms of any sort from a group, and especially in a setting where we residents are encouraged to be ourselves, although that they are being themselves is a likely, unhappy fact. The demanding man speaks first. News has come to them about the séance of which they heartily disapprove and in which they want no part, they believe it's wrong for our place to have such a thing happen "under its roof." He repeats this phrase three times. I wonder if the Magician asked them to attend, though I doubt it, but some of them were in the main room when I left it, and someone must have stirred their communal bowl by dropping in the word "séance," an unpredictable seasoning. The dour man objects to séances as voodoo, the fretful woman is offended by the idea that the dead might be raised and disturbed by the living, a more arcane objection, so, with deliberateness, I explain that they don't have to be and aren't involved, the séance is harmless, since it will be ineffective, and I don't expect miracles, but the Wineman complains sourly that this kind of silliness brings bad karma, while JJ invokes the townspeople who will know we're crazy as loons, absolutely crazy. The demanding man insists our reputations must be upheld, and, if word gets out, if the townspeople and administration hear about this, it'll bring disgrace. "There'll be trouble," the disconsolate woman reiterates, holding her stomach. I notice I have placed, in a cross, my hands over my heart, where a pressure or burden lives. Everyone has an opinion and speaks it, and, in this way, a democracy works, which is admirable, but in our democracy the rights of the minority must be protected, I think of Jefferson's First Inaugural Address, "the minority possess their equal rights, which equal law must protect and to violate would be oppression," but don't mention it. Instead, I inquire why they care so much about what others think, a solemn question, but to it the disconsolate woman, whose asthma the cold, wet night air might bother, mutters, "You obviously don't care about what people think, because otherwise how could you. . . ." There she halts, tantalizingly, biting her lip, her face darkening or maybe reddening, but it's nighttime and I can't be sure. Unable to hold her tongue, though, she actually sputters:

—You monopolize Gardner at dinner. He's never shown me his Breguet.

—But Helen, the dour man exclaims, it's not that we don't like. . . .

—I don't like you, the demanding man vehemently interrupts.

—That's not the point, JJ objects.

—What is the point? Is this any business of yours really? I ask.

The disconsolate woman's cheeks look pinched, JJ and the Wineman are uncomfortable, shifting in place, and my skin is burning even in the cold.

—It's for the good of us all, JJ finally exhorts, not to engage in hocus pocus. It's ridiculous.

We stand there, in the cold night, the wind whipping us, they in a semicircle, I'm the isolate across from the group, but in at least two minds, one, I must assuage them, the other, I must ignore, pummel, or maybe vanquish them, though this seems extreme, so first I attempt the former with an appeal to history, specifically to the psychic or parapsychological history of the Rotunda Room, where spirit photography sessions took place, where séances were held, which celebrated poets attended, and this pleases the disconsolate young woman, whose grasp of history is likely meager and who, I have just been forced to acknowledge, is inflamed with jealousy about my relationship with the Count, which now threatens my peace of mind. I believe JJ is somewhat mollified.

—Think of it as theater, I say directly to JJ, courting her.

The demanding man is immune to my discourse or infuriated and scolds that the room's history makes no difference, it was shameful doings then, it still is, and this silliness will bring disgrace, and even haunts us now.

—It is silly and evil, he sums up.

—How can something silly be evil? I ask him.

He repeats his denunciation: the past infects us, haunts us in very bad ways. I again appeal to history, a recourse that's generally a cheap trick, but I started it and can exploit it, with interest accruing from his old chestnut, since if the past haunts the present, I can press for its validity, for if a notion holds, if it remains resilient from one century to the next and impresses us still, then there must be something to it. With this, which isn't necessarily true, the fretful woman looks as if she will explode with fury at me, the dispute, and her colleagues, she is certainly not the ringleader, and, unable to bear one more second of it, she shouts:

—All right, all right, we've said it, let's go, for God's sake.

They stride away in three different directions.

I'm left alone in front of my residence, gazing at the peerless, black sky with its uncountable stars, or dead planets, not thinking about stars in ways that interest me, until I can drag myself from my arrested position. I return to my bedroom, first carefully opening the door and then impetuously slamming it shut, where on the bureau my crystal ball and potions greet me silently, like my young wild cat who stands by the door when I come home, in the place I call home, and sometimes runs out, either to escape his fate or to play. Impulsively, I upturn the ball and watch the fake snow whirl and occlude the scene. I should prepare mentally for the séance, but I'm much less composed than before, after their hyperbolic and anxious warnings, readying me for tragedy or a flaunting of fate that might bring ruin, but I'm more intent upon it, not just because I'm obstinate and know my rights, or because it may be foolish or disreputable, all of those things, and, now in addition, by attending, I will solicit chance, which written history excludes regularly, but which art, science, and design count on, since mistakes or accidents pry open spaces for imaginative endeavors and uncover clues or keys, good and bad, for, as my design teacher insisted, "There are never stupid mistakes, only mistakes whose potential isn't recognized." I'm grabbing an opportunity or the ring of chance, exposing myself to risk, of what nature I'm not sure, nevertheless I visualize the righteous assembly again, the demanding man fulminating about evil, their stern faces, and, as I do, undress and dress again fast, pulling on the slightly wrinkled but soft trousers, with my lucky Bauhaus button in the pocket, change my sweater to a purplish black, gentle lambswool and cashmere pullover, no buttons, no hooks, nothing to catch, and, looking down, I slip on and tie my patent leather and suede oxfords, while admiring their sleek lines. Even here, where I'm to rest and move on with my life in any way I see fit, I can't take a step that isn't blocked or threatened by others' opinions or irrational responses, by characters who never admit their failings or the deficiencies in their behavior, that their children are cruel, that their feelings can be dumb, that their experiences and emotions don't trounce everyone else's and can't be recounted as gospel, that their dogs are vicious, like the ones who attacked a cat and whose owner thought domestic cats should fend for themselves rather than her leashing her aggressive, territorial dogs, that people mostly don't listen, that they lie easily and fart, that they cover up and connive and will do anything to survive, rationalizing every sorry action, and those who don't are martyrs and fanatics, and, regrettably, I have my lapses, remorse flagellates me, it's my melancholic whip, because I can't stop, but the fault can lie outside me in human and other obstacles, though the tarot card reader said I would meet an obstacle or person who would change my life soon, or maybe, I believe, I will overcome an obstacle, which could be embodied in a person. Still, I might be impeded by powerful or petty ambitions not my own, and, by the stars, I suppose, whose description is frequently prosaic and certainly inadequate, whose capacity for prediction or prophesy is beyond my comprehension and which I don't accept. There are rumors, they abound, but few songs of ruin worth mentioning or remembering.

It's close to midnight on a dark and stormy night, and with this oddly reassuring allusion, I slip into my warm, virgin-wool black coat, down to my ankles, wrap my battleship-gray cashmere scarf around my neck twice, and march outside, hoping to suspend disbelief, since I don't hold it in abeyance for other performances, unless they are awful, but I want mindlessness and mindfulness, too. I'm less worried about which residents will attend, as some of the worst have announced their disdain, so I can expect a congenial crew who have fewer prejudices, less fear, or more curiosity and recondite wishes. No one is in the main room, all the lights but one are out, I can't see any of the photographs and paintings on the wall, there are some embers burning in the grand fireplace, and without hesitating I start toward the stairway to the Rotunda Room. I'm excited and scared, the way I was entering kindergarten, but then I walked beside my mother who left me at the door and didn't accompany me into the classroom to meet the new teacher, the way the other mothers did, I had to push open the heavy door and present myself alone, but my mother doesn't remember this incident, along with mostly everything about me, except that I did things fast, and now she has little short-term memory through no fault of her own, but my mother remembers her name, my name, that her husband left her alone, and also our family cat, but not that she, without mercy, put the cat and my dog to death.

Birdman crouches, in shadow, at the bottom of the stairs, he's just driven in from the airport, returned from Italy, and smiles beatifically, showing his gold-capped front tooth, reminding me that he is mostly a happy man, seemingly not oppressed by severe complexes, except that he must care for any sick bird he finds, that he is driven, day and night, by worry for animals, sometimes he has become ill, his intestines in a twist for weeks, bordering on colitis, about the fate of a wounded baby sparrow or precious falcon hawk, and he buys worms or whatever food they eat and nurses them as if he'd birthed them. Birdman, or Desmond, lean, blond, and tall, his oval face set off by large navy-blue eyes, with dark lashes, his fingers long and graceful, has a good complexion, though somewhat sallow, but his skin is leathery from exposure to the elements, he probably doesn't moisturize his skin as many men do. He asks why the lights upstairs are on, and I explain what's happening, concerned about his response, since he might take exception, too, but he appears not to care.

—I don't tempt fate, he says.

—Some of the residents are angry about a séance happening here.

—Judge not lest you be judged, Birdman says.

—Really? I ask.

—Did you get my postcards? I sent four.

It was Birdman, I realize with shock. Birdman.

—I got three, one today, I say.

—Just today? I mailed you four.

—Just you?

—Me and my shadow.

No wonder his scratchy signature was familiar, residents sign in and out on a register and see each other's first names daily, so I ponder Birdman, with brand new eyes, that's what my mother would say, brand new eyes, consider his mailing me cryptic, thoughtful notes as he traveled far away from here, venturing in distant lands. The night we sat on a couch in the library, he told me he grew up in Bloomington, Indiana, radiated charm and helplessness, which allied with his determination and grit, and I liked him, then didn't and did. His father was taciturn, kept secret his beliefs, since in his thirties Birdman's father joined a white supremacist group, which offered his father's flaccid white rage terrifying, subversive expression. Birdman was furious with his father, his mother, who was silent, then an impervious world that anyway engulfed their alienated patch. He wandered back in time, his eyes rolled to the left, reliving the war with his father, when any pity for the man turned into a violent hatred, as they watched, in the 1960s, the riots on television, Watts and Newark, because his father laughed and laughed, so Birdman stiffened into rebellion, did every drug he could get his hands on, fled at sixteen, traveled to Los Angeles, New York, then Austin, was a short-order cook, wrote plays, though he'd not seen one until he was twenty, and gave that up, also, when he rescued and cared for his first bird. Every gentle bone in him responded to that bitty mess of feathers, he said, he didn't know himself, he was one with a baby sparrow, with its wounded wing, a tiny being who couldn't fly, who needed him, but he needed the bird more, it was a white-throated sparrow, he soon learned, and, almost as a lark, he started a tourist company, with a partner, so he could travel and support himself and his avian causes, Birdman reveres even the relatively common raven, in some parts, he's told me, it's considered the prophet of birds, and, curiously, at least to me, he and the young married man, an ornithologist, have nothing to do with each other. Birdman no longer hates his father, who has Alzheimer's disease and doesn't know his son. He urged me, his sallow skin pinkening, to give up anything and everything, to leave it all behind, to follow my instincts, but I told him I wasn't sure what they were. That night, he and I were stationary on the couch, intimate and sedentary, so long, we might have triggered a relationship of some kind, slow or fast, but it's not wise or healthy to be involved in this community, it's discouraged by the staff, and I've been in love, its terrain isn't novel or untrodden. More, I hoped to sunder myself from, not adhere to, objects and people, to break things down into elements even senselessly, since I might discern something about an object's integrity or necessity in the process or by its result, and now I might rather die for an idea, since there's a liberty that chooses death.

Birdman and I keep company at the bottom of the stairs, when a prolonged silence settles into a profound ambiguousness, so I stare at the floor, embarrassed the way an English person might be, recalling each of his three postcards and my not having a clue it was he who wrote them, I hadn't once thought of him, and the mounting minutes cement our impossibility, so I swear off any further intimacy. With this, the spell breaks, some potential is buried, I can feel it diminish in breadth, collapse, and the loss of its potential and energy debilitates me. "I'd better go upstairs," I tell Birdman, "since they're probably waiting for me." He nods, exhausted from the rapid rise and fall of intensity, and also because he suffers from severe anemia, in which the hemoglobin count in the red blood cells is very low, often dangerously so, hemoglobin is composed mostly of iron, which accounts for his sallow complexion. He and I would have been a mistake, this relationship another blot, most start as mistakes, with promise, they might have possibility, but they begin as accidents, any relationship in the universe is, some can't be avoided, some are embellished, raided for treasure by a lover's piratical need, drained and dropped, or taken up for life, people balance good and bad on a human scale usually weighted against the other, since they demand love, wanting more, rarely getting enough, wanting everything, and they can't stop themselves. I've teetered on the verge and gone over, when an imperious love, overwhelming and magnificent, raised me from despair to a blind ecstasy. But an intimacy's death in infancy, like mine with Birdman, is irrevocable in my experience, which is, in a way, all I have, or nothing much at all.

The Rotunda Room is lit with an assortment of strategically placed and motley, unimportant small lamps, as well as tall, white, tapered candles in brass candleholders, but the large room and its objects are mostly dark or in shadow, especially since the green damask curtains are drawn nearly to the bottom of the windows. On the stage, there are two artisanal metal candelabras from Mexico and in front of the stage, a large, round walnut table that could be Mission furniture or a good copy. The sitters: the Magician, the Count, Contesa, Arthur and Henry, the Turkish poet, Spike, the young married man, the disconsolate young woman, our Felice, anorectic and psoriatic, the tall balding man, our Kafka, whose posture saddens me, and Moira, the odd inquisitive woman. The presence of the young married man and our Felice is a small surprise, which I appreciate. Without pomp, the Magician motions to a chair, one of the Green Lady's, and, first moving its pillow into a better position, I sit down between the tall balding man and Spike, and everyone says hello in a manner unique to each, I remember the Turkish poet's gold ringed hand touching his heart and Contesa's fateful double wink. Then we, eleven of us, await instruction.

The Magician explains that we are supposed to center and open ourselves to what is out there, way out there, and also in us.

—Death is the master of transformation, he says in his mellow, nasal voice. Some believe there is no death, and the spirit or soul continues after death. We learn from physics that matter doesn't die. You could say we survive death, because human beings are matter. In the 17th century, the scientist Emanuel Swedenborg believed that when a person dies, they're welcomed by angels. In the hereafter, they live the style they did on earth.

—The same lifestyle? Is this patter? Spike asks.

—Please don't interrupt him, Contesa urges, gently.

—I get your skepticism, the Magician says, but what I'm trying to do with you here—actually I'm not sure what it is. I'm not above entertainment, that's true. But, for what it's worth, I recently lost my mother.

—I recently lost my best friend, the young married man says.

—I lost my older sister, Contesa says.

—I lost my wife, the Count says.

Is the Count's wife dead, I wonder again, lost, literally lost, or is it figurative, she's lost to him?

—My dog died two weeks before I got here, the disconsolate woman says.

—I don't know anyone, no one I love, anyway, who's dead, says Spike, her unmarked face an embarrassment of riches.

—I can see that, Moira adds gravely, lowering her eyes.

The Turkish poet exhales operatically, straightens up in his chair, and begs the Magician to get on with it.

—Please. I am inspired by you, my blessed, extravagant companions.

The Turkish poet's hands are outstretched, palms peacefully up.

—And by whatever spirits come, even if they don't. I've lost . . . I am not so brave anymore to admit, maybe like you.

—Everyone, please, close your eyes, and let's be quiet now, the Magician says.

I shut my eyes reluctantly and reflect on the history of spiritualism that lives in this room, which we twelve now occupy, in a building not far from where witches burned at the stake in the 17th century. I consider that if there's death in life, that is, we recognize death will come and live with it, there might be life in death. In Zulu the verb fa means to die, the noun fa means inheritance, which encourages solace, since when someone dies, there's something you inherit, death leaves a gift.

A blast of Arctic air sets me shivering.

—Everyone here, the Magician goes on, except for Moira, Violet, and me are nonbelievers. In the 19th century, mediums didn't allow nonbelievers into a séance, because of their negative energy.

—Everyone wishes to speak to the dead, Moira announces, definitively. It is a universal wish.

—Good, the Magician pronounces.

The Magician says you have to want to believe, and then, to my surprise, the Count admits that against reason he hopes for belief, at least now, since belief might soothe him in time, though it's time that might heal, but he can't let go of reason.

—What's so great about reason? our Felice demands.

This leaves Arthur, Henry, the young married man, our Kafka, Spike, and me.

—What are we supposed to do? Spike asks. Believe or not not believe?

The young married man cracks up.

—We're not supposed to do anything, Contesa says.

—Double negatives, Arthur intones dolefully. We're here, right. Is our belief really essential?

Arthur speaks, at once serious and ironic, on both sides of the issue, then he and Henry, in unison, look with a passive or benign contentment at the Magician.

The Magician rises slowly, not to alarm us, and walks around the table, demonstrating that there is nothing attached to him, and, as he does, he explains that in the 19th century it was revealed that many mediums were hoaxes, the séances rigged, that the medium had helpers, which he doesn't have, that the medium might have a signal or two for the helper, and that the notorious ectoplasm, a luminous substance believed to ooze from a spiritualistic medium's mouth, was sometimes regurgitated surgical gauze, that mediums who suddenly levitated were discovered, when the lights were switched on by nonbelievers, to be standing on a chair, but he had no tricks up his sleeve or under him, no assistants whose voices doubled for him or our loved ones. Some probably still fear that the Magician will pickpocket them again—I notice the Count clutch his Breguet in his right fist—but soon the Magician extinguishes the candles on the table and has the tall balding man turn off the various lamps in the Rotunda Room. In the semi-darkness, there's easy and labored breathing through the nose and mouth, bodies shifting and settling in their chairs, shoes tapping and shuffling on the hardwood floor, legs shaking in place, and rocking, and I feel uneasy, everyone must feel uneasy except Moira, the Magician, and Contesa, who have experience with spiritualism and its manifestations, but apart from a narrow beam of light coming through the windows from the moon, the lantern on the lamppost outside, or an occasional car's headlights, the near-dark cloaks us, and, separate from each other, we are shapes, shadows, or shades of our corporeal selves.

—Be still, everyone, be still, the Magician commands. We must keep still. Empty your minds, release yourselves, open yourselves up, stop thinking, and breathe. Don't move around. That's important. Remember everything you can about the loved one you want to contact. Feel their presence beside you. Will it. I will act as your conduit, your medium, to the great beyond.

There's a single guffaw, probably Spike's, a few more minutes of freighted silence, during which, my eyes shut, I hazard believing or not disbelieving, because when I adumbrate my various zeals, that chairs communicate ideas, emotions, and values, that democracy is conflict, that justice and truth are often opposed, or that a subtle design could one day cause a revolution, though subtlety is usually derogated, I see myself avow one idea, drop another, see that I change my mind, but not easily. In the here and now, I could momentarily embrace spiritualism, as I could, in the abstract, a poorly designed or uncomfortable chair.

Contesa's head drops or falls onto her chest, she may be asleep, but then her head flops from side to side, and, adjusting to the darkness, my eyes fasten on her, as she begins to mutter phrases just beyond decipherability. Her voice is a strangled or undulating moan. The Magician whispers that Violet is in a trance state and we are to continue our reveries and investigations, to let her be wherever she is, to follow our memories to our loved ones and feel their presence beside us, to let go of the now and reach out to a world with no past or future.

The odd inquisitive woman, Moira, erupts into the stillness in a voice that sounds drugged, hers is a thick, slurred speech, which may signal her submission to or immersion in the other world, or this may be the otherworld's speaking voice, since if the dead speak, their speech must undergo transformation, too.

—Your aura, Ataturk, I see it.

With her eyes shut, she delicately indicates the Turkish poet.

—It is blue, sky blue. The color of hope, yes, there is hope in you and for others.

The Turkish poet acknowledges her murky address with a rich sigh.

—I am no Ataturk, he says mournfully. I wish for him.

—Everyone wishes to speak to the dead, Moira asserts again.

Silence. Breathing.

Then Moira, agitated, shouts: "Get off me, leave me. Go to her! To her!"

Contesa awakens or, rather, lifts her head, and she also speaks slowly, as if drugged, dragging her words and placing many breathy pauses between them: "What, what? You've come, my sister, you're back. I did NOT steal Mother's ring. She gave it to me. You're the selfish one. Your husband is terrible. He . . . No. Yes. Stop it, that's not true. No, I didn't turn my back on my people. Never, no. But don't go. Can't we . . . ? Please stay."

A defiant quiet surrounds us, it or solitude penetrates me severely. I don't know where to set Contesa's admissions and entreaties, since I heard what I should never have heard and can't accept, I did hear her, and, for this reason alone, I should run away. But I don't, I can't, my legs are leaden, my head and skin throb, and I'm stunned and humbled by seeing and hearing what I don't believe.

The Magician waves his hands in the air, directs his gaze at the table with an aspect both friendly and stern, but he makes me nervous and tired. I close my eyes, I open my eyes, Contesa's eyes are closed, she doesn't stir, I close my eyes. The unique quiet mutes my incredulity, its constant eeriness has substance. The roof becomes alive, a giant animal, my chair arouses me, the round walnut table creaks with suspense, the brash wind hurls itself against the antique windows. The room is agitated by the racket and rustling, by hawks nesting on the roof, where Birdman must have crawled to rescue a wounded tree sparrow, where nocturnal cats chase each other.

The Magician performs another ceremonial incantation and requests us once more to unburden ourselves.

—Speak as you wish, freely, at will. If the spirits want to, they will show up. You will feel their presence. Stay as still as you can and absorb the darkness. Open yourselves and unburden your heart.

I cringe and feel glad, too. I see something like a cloud or smoke issue from his mouth.

The Turkish poet chants drowsily in Turkish, his sounds pleasing and harmonious, until he switches to a halting English, and, with his head wrapped in his hands and his eyes shut, makes a confession: "I want to be in serenity, because once a long time ago, I did very wrong thing to a friend. Now that friend he is dead, and I would give him my true feeling, if he would come now to me. I am sorry, more sorry each day I live. I can say this. I admit. When I look to the sky, I am seeing your face. I tell you this, I took your friend for me, your final lover, with lust, I did sex, and I told him what I knew bad about you, and it was not true. He came to me, we lay, but you never knew it. I am in shame. If you come to me, I plead your forgiveness. I want to speak to you."

He yawns, and his face relaxes.

My brain-damaged mother often talks in her sleep to her dead husband in complete sentences, holding a conversation in which she asks him questions and responds to answers that only she hears, while her voice remains steady and low, and, though unsated, fatigued in sleepless sleep, she awaits answers that may imperil her contentment.

The Turkish poet drops his head, like a supplicant or penitent, and there's muttering in the tremulous semi-dark. "But even so," he protests, in a low, guttural monotone, "I can believe truly for more sex in everything." With his head down, he slaps the table. "More sex in everything" raised, apparently, for my benefit, since he's inexplicably insisted on this point to me before, but not in such a strange context. The young married man's voice comes in a cry from across the room, he must be far from me or the table: "You're all crazy, this is nuts, but Arthur's right, I'm here, and I'm sitting in this crazy room with you. But so's the devil, he's in this room, you know, he must be. He's in me, I'm evil, and that's my perverted wisdom." I hear a bizarre, intermittent cackling and chortling from him, but others say he ranted about ravishing infidelities and an insatiable hunger for stray women, even on his marriage day, when he had sex with his best man's girlfriend behind a boathouse. Two years later, his best man died in a boating accident, in a motorboat stored in the adulterous boathouse, and it is to him he addresses himself, begging him to return so he can ask forgiveness. Between the scratchy noises or static, I believe I hear him calling a name over and over, until the young married man sobs, I hear him, I do, I know it's not me. Contesa and Moira awaken or sleepwalk over to him, to wherever he's gone, to comfort him.

—The devil's here? Come on.

That's Spike.

—No one said this would be easy, a voice says.

That's Henry, I'm pretty sure.

—That's right.

Arthur is agreeing with him.

I press my eyes closed more tightly and assure myself it's not bizarre, just uncanny, when raging fires and words written in scarlet ink cross my eyes, the Reverend Samuel Willard's account of Elizabeth Knapp, a Salem girl possessed by the devil: The devil has oftentimes appeared to her, presenting the treaty of a covenant, that he urged upon her constant temptations to murder her parents, her neighbors, our children, especially the youngest, tempting her to throw it in the fire.

I might have recited this to everyone, I'm not sure if I'm speaking or when I'm speaking what I'm saying. In my head, I'm awake, aware of everything, the way I am when I'm breathing nitrous oxide, inhaling its sweet sickness, on the chair of my earnest periodontist, who keeps the radio tuned to public stations, whose programs become confused with my thoughts, so I may be speaking aloud to the host and his guests, but then I don't care, because waves of pleasure slap inside my body, during which my periodontist often asks me to open my mouth wider, but I believe my mouth is open wide.

—My skin is so dry, you can write on it. I need to shed it.

—Like a snake.

That's Spike speaking, after me. Maybe I told her human beings shed their skin completely every twenty-eight days. No one Spike loves is dead, and she doesn't know what she's doing here, except hanging out, so she proposes in a singsong voice to implore Einstein to return, which strikes her, a young mathematician, as ridiculously comic and tragic, so she can barely sit still, jumps away from the table, and races out of the room through the wooden, double doors, only to return, because she doesn't know where she is otherwise or what to do, and she may anyway be asleep. I don't know how much time has passed, when the Count rouses himself. I'm sure my eyes are open, I see him as plain as day tuck his Breguet into his coat pocket, satisfied it won't be pickpocketed again, then watch him as he gathers himself together to address the Magician, Contesa, or his lost wife, sometime before I rouse myself and say whatever they tell me I did, about which I have intermittent and vague recollections. The Magician hasn't talked yet with his mother, though she's the dead person he wanted to contact, the motive for the séance—which is no longer a séance to me; I don't know what it is, except an extension of so-called reality into so-called hyperreality or unreality, though in my head nothing is unreal, I don't know what unreal is. Dizzily, I try to catch hold of it, it slides away, splitting into pieces.

The Count murmurs and rises, even more angular than I recall, in shadow he's a portrait by El Greco, and he flings and jiggles his arms, maybe pushing off something, a spirit, but that's unlikely, since it wouldn't have mass. The Count's voice sounds dreamy, even though he appears to be lecturing someone, partly because he's standing at attention as if behind a lectern, but his eyes are shut and there are many pauses between his words: My rare horological artifacts. French and English, I bow to their artistry. Serviceable clocks, to be blunt, ugh, grandfathers, grandmothers, wall units. Comme il faut. American Blind Watch, yes, ingenious. Big numbers for the vision impaired. Ingenious.

He swings his arms again and yawns.

—Let me say this about the devil: He exists. Made his acquaintance, many years ago in the South. My family, in my town. I ran as far as I could. RUN. I told you to run. You. Not to leave me. Run from me, and now you're . . . A barn door face. You said it. I don't know where. No answer is an answer . . . My darling, when I leave this world and join you, to be with you again, wherever you are, would you . . . Oh, please, let me leave this necropolis.

Perfectly still, not shuffling and shifting, we're waiting for the end or hanging on to dear life, expecting to hear another outburst about what the dead have in store for us.

The Count drops to his seat, breathless, as if he had been running, and his head also drops, like Contesa's, and rests on the table, where soon he falls asleep or slides into elsewhere. I'm witness and participant, spilling from one to the other, I can't tell inside from outside, I mean, I can't control my utterances or guide my thoughts.

—Helen, Helen. Listen to me, you're safe here.

It's the Magician's mellow voice.

—No, I'm not.

—Helen, it's your turn.

—No, it's not. It's . . .

I point to our Felice and our Kafka, but they are fast asleep or dead to the practical world.

—This is not what I believe at all. What's happening is unacceptable to me.

—Be yourself, the Magician says. Use your intuition.

—I hate that stuff. I think I'm dead.

—Maybe you are.

—That's all right then.

—Stop fighting.

I'm always fighting, I shake myself, I may not be dead, but I don't want to withdraw from this ghost theater in which I'm a spectacle to myself and where I must shuck off disbelief to reap any benefit, though benefit is unlikely. I will disbelief, and this is when the events occur for which I was definitely present and also not. I let my body slacken, knowing my father preferred me to sit up straight, while mentally urging him near me and invoking his spirit, thinking my posture shouldn't matter anymore to him.

—I want to . . . I'd like my father to talk to me. And my dead friends, I really want to hear their voices again.

I announce this abruptly.

—But I know it can't happen.

I need to concentrate on one dead person, my father, instead other faces crystallize with wispy features and deathly poor complexions, they zoom in and out, stagger by, now my dead friends' faces, their deaths cavorting in a murderers' row, where arbitrary mortality judges and sickens me. I open my eyes and with horror notice the other sitters' critical expressions, so I might be on a jury, I'm litigious, American, I like to watch vicious trials, I'm probably a judge. My breathing quickens, then slows, quickens, then regulates itself, so I forget it, but my sweater scratches me like crazy, I could suffocate inside my skin, I need air, melancholiacs are helped by a change in air. I command myself to smash the decayed faces thrust in front of mine.

—Dad, visit me, come on, it's my wish, tell me about being dead. Come close, I will it. I can't do this. Dad, visit me, stand beside me. I can't . . . this is stupid.

Green, moldy bodies in morgues, inflamed, bloated, white faces, mutilated corpses, half-blown-away bodies, maggot-ridden, in blue uniform, Gettysburg, lynched black bodies hanging from a despicable tree. Terrible death, I fear you, I have to get out of here, it's sane fear, I answer it, I'm a coward, I should stay, I want to hear them again. My head splits in two.

Did I speak this aloud or is it internal?

I don't think I'm talking in my darkness. I can't halt these alien sensations. I place my hands over my eyes and press hard, scrunching my eyes closed again, so that their veins radiate bloody patterns, garishly colored shapes, pale ashes, the papers I burned this afternoon maybe, everything recognizable is ablaze, like my family's Eames chairs. I can't hold onto an image, so I tell myself, in a stately manner, Mark this now, fire burns complacent things, and in a flash it occurs to me why I take things apart, and I want to remember the reason but can't. Another gust of arctic air makes me shiver, there's nothing to think about, I open my eyes, it's all gone, I shut them again.

I hear my name, "Helen, Helen," so I turn toward the Magician, who stares at me and directs me, "Follow my hands," which I do, I can see his hands waving in front of his face, but suddenly his head belongs to my friend who disappeared. I can hardly breathe. Then the Magician's head enlarges, his eyes expand, enormous like universes, much larger than my mad cat's just before he gouged my left calf, and I follow his agile hands, how they weave in the air, like weavers' hands at looms, my head drops onto my chest and rolls around, or from side to side, oddly enough I recall this because while my head feels detached and airy, I'm still holding on, so a question about consciousness wings by, about how markedly it can differ from self-consciousness, when it emerges from a consciousness aligned to a self, then questions disappear. I'm not concerned about fainting, I worry I'm dying, even if my skin still itches, my arms, chest, legs, and maybe my dead friends or their ghosts leave messages on my back.

Against my will—I have no will—while the Magician mumbles something, my skull empties, and the inside of my head becomes dense. I enter a deeper trance, or I might still be in a hypnogogic state, but I do believe the Magician may have hypnotized or entranced me, because from now on what I am certain of is negligible, what I remember is beyond description in ordinary terms.

I'm near the ocean, because I hear waves, I ask someone, my father, or my friend taken by AIDS, the question I'd asked my mother as a child: Is life worth it, even though you die? She said then, Yes, because you have happiness when you're alive, you have a lot of good times before you die. I didn't accept what she said then. I don't get an answer now. I breathe in the green ocean, fall headlong into a whitecapped wave, let it consume me, I'd been hungry for its endlessness, the hot sand, the summer wind's raw perfume, the innocent exhaustion after swimming. I take off my itchy sweater and walk unsteadily toward the windows, calling desperately for a birdman, and then Moira, who is apparently clearheaded, throws my sweater over my head, puts my arms through the sleeves, and leads me back to my chair. Moira whispers in my ear, "Did you know my name 'Moira' means destiny?"

Hearing the word from her mouth shocks me, and I jump back, exclaiming, "No, I had no idea, I didn't know." Moira's face transforms, it contorts grievously, and, if that is destiny, it's an ogre, so I slap her. I suppose I never really liked Moira, though her oddness and inquisitiveness attracted me from the first. Moira smiles and transforms into my young wild cat, but I'm in a chair, looking down on myself from above, an out-of-body experience, and in it I feel estranged from the world, but long for it, wanting to return and to live forever. In scarlet ink, fluttering on my eyelids, "Live the life you have imagined," but soon I perceive the closeness of the ogre, destiny, snarling like my mad, dead cat, but destiny can't be put to sleep, the way he was, it doesn't go away, and, worse, death wouldn't. Death stops everything. It's unfair, but not unjust, since everyone suffers its democratic tyranny. Things flow along, whole and disintegrated, I have at least two minds, so I exhort one, maybe aloud, "Don't stop, don't stop. I wish . . . I wish . . ."

Then my father appeared, I think he did and I also think he didn't, and my best friend killed in a car crash showed up, with her young, toothy grin, "You haven't changed," I exclaimed, and there my brother stood, dead the way I thought. "Everyone wishes to speak to the dead." I heard that again. My father wore his dark brown trunks, I saw him swimming behind the breakers, far from shore, swimming farther and farther away, until he disappeared.

The Count produced fearsome yowls, I reclaimed my body and wondered if he were possessed by the devil, but didn't accept that could make sense. The Count enunciated disconnected words and phrases—"tiny second hand, poison ivy, Descartes, lacquer and jade, the antichrist"—with many long pauses, as if completing his sentences in an interior monologue. I waited for more revelation, but if it came, I missed it. The Magician hushed him and snapped his fingers, and the Count's seizure, if it was, halted miraculously, and then the Magician sang or chanted, I don't remember the lyrics, though I usually have extremely good recall of conversations and dialogue, but none of his words stayed with me. Yet with them, we woke up from our sleep or trances, conscious of leaving one peculiar world for another. And so, the sitting reached its end, the way everything does, and, slowly, one after another in an orderly single file, we walked from the Rotunda Room, all but the Count, who, after his outburst or seizure, vanished. No one said a word. It was a few minutes past 1 a.m., so only an hour had passed, but it seemed, as they say, an eternity.

The storm had also passed, and remote, brilliant stars littered the sky. In my room, I stripped, my skin was exceptionally dry, the largest organ of the body stretched to its limit, I slathered on creams and worried about the scaly spot on my leg. Not surprisingly death, or mortality, hung about after the séance, especially when the pressure around my heart turned into sharper pain, heartburn, or an event, as cardiologists call an undetermined episode, and, since my father died of heart disease, I worried, but the pain left in no time, and anyway I'm not prone to hypochondria.

I slept fitfully, awoke twice, walked to the bathroom, hardly concerned about waking the two disconsolate women, since they might occupy other beds, and the third time I awoke, I gazed at the Fabric Monolith, at its hidden potential, its unleashed energy, and imagined I'd unfurl it one day, but only in my imagination. If my bed were covered in Egyptian 600 denier all-cotton sheets, I'd sleep better, but the séance, whatever it is or was, carried novelty's unruliness and disturbed my rest; the sleep of orphan children, the sleep manual reports, is "made more restless when they leave the institution to see a motion picture in the evening," so it exhorts readers to "make their mind as blank as that of a wartime flapper," the Great War, that is, the manual came out in America in 1937, when rationalization, bureaucratization, the New Deal were the rage, like liquor, hard-boiled novels, Communism. With age, it's said you need less sleep, though my mother, who's very old, needs her sleep and often drops off in a serviceable reclining chair, covered in light brown naugahyde, in her living room, watching a movie on TV, but not when she is reading, which she does with near-perfect eyesight and in a state of total concentration, her head craned to the book on her lap, its covers lovingly cradled in her small, white hands. She has a little arthritis, but it's not disfiguring and doesn't keep her from knitting, though as her neurological condition deteriorates, her once-skilled fingers lose their way and trip, she drops a stitch, a line, then complains that it's the fault of the wool—too thin, she says—but it's not. Soon, knitting wearies her, but her skin glows, translucent and smooth, free of wrinkles, though not as plump and lush as her older sister's, who used Jergen's Lotion only, and whom she envied and outlived, but my mother's greatest rival was her husband's mother, whose ancestors emigrated from Egypt, whose green oval eyes and beauty captured him, and whose impetuous, incessant demands he always met. Now my mother envies only youth and worries that her brain will fail her completely and she will not know herself.

Egypt is the world's largest producer of high grade, long staple cotton, most grown near the Nile Delta, and maintaining the quality of its higher grades has been troublesome; the U.S. imports considerable amounts of it for making thread, lace, and tire cord. Foreign imports, from China, India, and the Far East, have vastly changed the U.S. textile industry, and now mill workers in North Carolina can't find work. Imports drastically affected my father and uncle's business, which was why it wasn't an option for me when I finished college, even though my brother hadn't taken his place in it, but business was bad, it wasn't encouraging, and I hadn't wanted to design fabrics and sell them then, which I regret.

I looked again at the Fabric Monolith, with its plenty of secrets.

The following morning, I didn't go to breakfast, I didn't want conversation, contentious or pacific, I didn't want to leave my bed, I wasn't very hungry, I ate a navel orange and banana, and knew there'd be lunch, usually the poorest meal of the day, but edible and eaten in private. The radio voices complained and joked, anonymous company, harbingers or bearers of bad news, prejudice, and expert advice or ignorance. I didn't attend breakfast all week after the séance and, like some of the former residents, entered the dining room when no one was likely to be around, no residents or staff, in order to forage food, so that I wouldn't go hungry until lunch. Dinnertime during that week, the third in the cook's cycle, was subdued, even though the Turkish poet, Contesa, Spike, Henry, and Arthur were in residence, and though there was the usual banter, benign grumbling about the lunches, especially from the demanding man, and the appearance of a few new residents, who blended into the walls, whose acquaintance I didn't want to make, though they appeared to be lively under their skins. After dinner, I hastened to the sanctity of my bedroom, which isn't mine forever. Life, and everything in it, is temporary, and this oppressive, venerable fact I reckon with and contest daily, if subliminally, and, in a modest, morose manner, attack, which doesn't afford peace.

When I'm at home, I may hold my young wild cat, if he allows it, and, especially when he lies near or on my face and I inhale his familiar musty male feline smell, I feel calm, content and also able to recall the family cat, with her kittens, but not the one who died at birth who lay near her and her other healthy kittens, wrapped in a small piece of black wool. I rub my face against my cat's coal black fur, soft as cashmere, and if loose fur doesn't enter my nostrils and cause me to sneeze, after which he cries—my sneezing upsets him—the cat is a temporary consolation, and when I tuck him even closer in my arms, he objects, usually quickly, and leaps off the bed. When the family cat was given away and killed, because it ate my parakeet, a creature I didn't care about, though it had once jumped into my soft-boiled egg in a small, white bowl, endearingly, I was allowed to adopt a homeless, six-month old pregnant mixed-breed dog, around the time my brother disappeared. I had my dog for nine years, but I've never had another dog, because there can be no other dog but her, or I don't deserve another, since, if I had protected my dog, if I'd been aware, not lost in myself, my parents wouldn't have been able to give her away and kill her, for which I take the blame. I feel sorry for people who treasure their furniture more than animals or for people who are allergic to them, since people live longer who have an animal to pet and love, to be in sympathy with, but some people don't want the bother, have never liked animals, or care more about material possessions and how they appear to others and to themselves than longevity. Allergies are different from intolerances, real food allergies are rare, but here many believe they are allergic to various foods, including milk, which is extremely rare, though some have trouble digesting it; if there is an allergy, an allergic reaction, mild or severe, proceeds, because the immune system is involved, while it's not involved if a person is intolerant of, or just sensitive to, a food group. Intolerance to foods or food idiosyncrasies, as health professionals lately designate food sensitivities, are reactions and discomforts but not allergies, since allergens are not involved, and many believe they are sensitive, women especially like to think they're sensitive. I don't care who sees my black, second-hand, two-seat modernist couch, which my young wild cat recognized as his scratching post and whose raised one hundred percent wool upholstery he ripped, fabric I selected in ecstasy at a warehouse of sumptuous textiles, many of which I touched and smelled, I won't let any people enter my apartment, since my young wild cat might claw them badly and then they might insist I have him put down, or they might imagine they understand me or can defend themselves from me, by what I have on my walls, shelves, and with which furniture I surround myself.

The next week, I returned to my usual schedule, needing regularity in most things, and it was on this day that, after breakfast, which the head cook prepared, because the assistant cook was ill again, so the head cook was annoyed to be on duty, though she would, we residents now knew with certainty, retire soon, the Magician left. He said he had been doing a flyby, and moments before he left I urged him again to tell me what he'd done, especially to me but also to the Count, during the séance, but he persisted in saying everything that happened I'd wanted to happen, with no coaxing from him, and I don't believe him, so, even if my father appeared, which I question, though it was my wish, he was dead, nothing had changed, but that wasn't the Magician's fault. The Magician shook his head ruefully and told me I didn't understand. The Count was no longer in residence and couldn't argue. The young married man, who didn't appear as content again, but who still liked everything the kitchen presented, left a week and a day after the séance, that is, last night, a Sunday night, Sunday can be the worst day here, and Sunday dinners are often the worst of the dinners.

This morning, when I rushed into the breakfast room, past the two disconsolate young women, who were both in their pajamas, apparently in distress, I didn't hesitate to ignore them, not engage in their business, especially because they sat near new residents who might be stuck in time or who believed themselves ahead of it, since time was and always is of the essence, time's in everything, it provokes currents and forms in design, it resides in art and history, but I was hungry, nearly late, and feared that the head cook wouldn't allow me breakfast, because she doesn't like me or any of us. After I rushed into the kitchen and printed my order, smiling at the cook, so that I might not earn any more of her wrath, but barely looking at the kitchen helper, though he looked at me, the Magician waved me over to his table, and it was then he told me he was leaving, his work here was done, but since he's an obituary writer, I couldn't imagine what work he'd accomplished, except maybe the séance, which I discounted, and it was at that moment I received his disappointing answer. When he arose, the Magician rang a bell and announced to all assembled that he was about to make himself disappear, which he accomplished by walking out of the dining room. I felt the need to accomplish something, having spent the previous week indifferently or unremarkably, though deliberately so. For instance, empty headed, I rocked and swung in a decent copy of an American swinging porch chair, the original dates from the 1920s, while the snow melted incrementally from the main house's roof and icicles cracked and dropped, and also I reclined on a 1940s leather couch in the library, but didn't read or listen to music, and watched other residents, surreptitiously. I slept at all hours, day and night, in my room, exhausted, as if recovering from major surgery, an amputation of some sort. In the evenings, before dinner, I telephoned my mother's companion and listened most carefully to every complaint, to the nuances and shadings in her voice to detect a reason sufficient for her to abandon my mother, because it can be exhausting to tend a person who asks the same question over and over, or believes she's lost a ten dollar bill, when she hasn't and yet searches, agitated, all day for it, or, worse, a necklace she never owned, and the whole day frets about where it might have gone, since it must be found, and then she wakes up with it on her mind, and if you say it's a fantasy or a dream, she is insulted and furious. These problems might require my return to the place I call home, and, against my will and desire, to bear the weight of my mother's care, relinquishing some of my liberty. People move in with their ailing, aging parents, some sacrifice their lives, in a sense, but I'm incapable of it, though in another society with other customs I might, as I might also have eaten human flesh in a ritual ceremony or walked ten paces behind my husband, but in America, where I'm at liberty to make my own mistakes in marriage, which I have, a woman's walking behind men has never been required, probably because of the need for their labor from the start, while, in the Donner Pass, westward-bound settlers who followed a little-used route to California, trapped by snow, cold, starving, and near-mad, ate human flesh. After the Magician, I also left the breakfast room, stopping to make an appointment with the Turkish poet and Spike for drinks after dinner, but Contesa said, reticently, that she was already engaged. "A sweet date?" the Turkish poet asked, teasing her and me, "is it a sweet Medjool date?" Contesa paid no attention to his insinuation, but it awakened something in me, and, later, when no one was around, I walked to the kitchen.

I like to make any fresh start on Monday mornings, and a few weeks later, on a Monday, I decided on a strenuous, long walk, since usually I don't walk after breakfast, but instead return to the room where I sleep or to the room where I take apart objects and place them in different configurations on the floor, burn old notes and useless designs, or study Zulu and read about chairs, or dwell on some event in or theory about American history, which lies in wait of contemporary interest and whose avid pursuit was once mine. Against myself, another freedom, after changing into suitable hiking boots, appropriate jacket, heavier all-cotton pants and sweater, risking disdain by approaching the head cook to request my lunch in advance, a cheese or turkey sandwich on dry whole-wheat bread and an apple, which she reluctantly dispensed, never looking at me, I walked into a woods in which I'd never ventured and followed a trail I'd never taken with a destination I didn't know. Spring was finally coming, the ground and snow melting lazily, the cloudless sky a poignant, pale blue, while the morning sun burnished the ground, so that I had to shield my eyes from the glare of the last snows which cloaked some of the treetops and still lay on the fields and had forced most creatures into their hiding places, though there was the occasional chipmunk to whom I spoke that as usual scurried away. The sun's rays flared and warmed me, spring warmed me, and I hoped to be alert to my surroundings, part of my renewal strategy on this Monday. A medium-size black bird alighted on a branch and two gray ones, mourning doves, I hoped, streaked across the pale sky, Birdman would have easily recognized the birds, and the farther I walked the less I knew where I was because soon the main house wasn't in sight. In the distance, three deer leaped across my path, a family, sudden and surprising, they stood still for a while, but when I began to approach, they fled, their forelegs kicking in the air like merry-go-round horses. I meant to walk swiftly, until my heart pounded, my leg muscles stretched and loosened, and I tired. Aerobic exercise raises endorphin levels, I've occasionally experienced its benefits, while the tall balding man who runs twenty miles a day and sweats profusely experiences it daily, though it doesn't seem to make him sanguine, unless lust or appetite signals optimism, even when his numerous loves disappoint, which he may desire, as it frees and confirms him, so I walked quickly, then slowed down to pay attention to the vegetation and growth, so my desires were split, I couldn't have them simultaneously. I walked on the path, not fully aware of my surroundings, since I was distracted and didn't know how to be what I wasn't. Tree branches and pine cones littered the way, encrusted in some packed-down snow, melting less because the tall trees hid the sun, and sometimes I slid or slipped. Deer might have leaped across the field, or a pair of mourning doves, who mate for life, might have sailed above me, patterns of brown and gray against a pale blue sky, but I was concentrating on the ground under my feet. Then, before me, about twenty feet ahead, I saw a large clearing and the dregs of a campfire, with some fire or red embers, and knew a person or two must be around, so I turned and looked in all directions, and saw no one, but at the campsite, near the fire, I noticed its almost-burnt configuration, resembling the Count's firebuilding method, since four of its ash-white logs were stacked just as he would have done, at least it appeared to me.

The Count hadn't disappeared, he'd fled and found residence in a woodland setting, and, since it was daytime, he would be asleep in a cave or under shrubbery, ferns, and his own blankets or in a sleeping bag. The Count's unexplained departure left unresolved more than is usual, usually almost everything is left unresolved, but thinking the Count was asleep nearby placated and also aroused my imagination, though imagination is hampered by its imaginer's limits. The Count's seizure or paroxysm may have been fantastic, crotchety, a delirium, or poetic inspiration—furor poeticus—and, if so, it might approach genius, according to Kant; however, superstition may be compared, he says, with insanity. Kant's Classification of Mental Disorders was on a library shelf and now lies under my bed, unless the housekeepers have moved it, and I don't subscribe to all his categories, superstition, for one thing, can't be insanity, since too many people are; I won't walk under ladders, open an umbrella indoors, or toss a hat on a bed, all of which I heard about and with no reason adopted for myself, so perhaps this is insane, or maybe "normal" comprises a wider range than he thought, since to him "brooding over a spouse's death is utter madness." My mother has brooded over my father's death for many years, with cessations, but grief thrives in her days and nights, and she is not mad, but lonely without her husband and suffering from brain damage, whose cause is organic and unknown, like most of the workings of the brain, while I also brood over dead friends, and I'm not insane, or, if I am, according to Kant's precepts, it doesn't matter to me.

Across from the near-dead campfire, I sat upon on a large, flat, gray boulder, or natural chair, shaped like an ellipse, at whose center was an indentation appropriate for a human bottom. I gazed into the vast woods, the rotund fir trees, other trees whose branches looked forlorn though some buds and new leaves were evident, while I listened for the woods' sneaky inhabitants, and also looked out for hungry wolves in packs and prowling black bears, since even mountain lions are known in these parts. The brisk wind rustled and shook the trees and solid chunks of old snow fell randomly, black and brown birds shrieked into the sky, then settled elsewhere, chipmunks scampered from one hiding place to another, the forest's floor was alive but ninety-five percent was invisible to me, and soon the fire's embers were dead. It must have been around noon, the sun was directly above, its rays filtered and thwarted by the tall trees, but in my fleece-lined hiking jacket, with its stiff collar that sometimes irritated my skin and my battleship-gray cashmere scarf wrapped about my head and neck, where most warmth leaves the body, I wasn't cold. My thick-soled, ankle-high, waterproof hiking boots, lined with flannel and sheepswool, are functional, occasionally itchy and even too hot, but not on this hike. The Count sleeps all day, so it was senseless to wait for him, and he'd fled to the vast woods, because he didn't want to see people, which I respected, since often I don't want to see people, like at breakfast, so then I lie in bed, though seeing the Count now would be different. I ate the lackluster turkey sandwich and listened to the silence, the wind, the birds whose names I didn't know, and saved the shiny Macoun apple for later.

The woods stretched ahead, like the universe, with no time and no horizon line to sever sky from earth, only irregular treetops that pointed to the atmosphere which turned lighter and lighter, until there was no color, or white, an absence, or just endlessness. I walked to my own rhythm with an old ditty circling in mind: White is zero, black ten, all the colors, red five, orange four, and pale blue three, paler blue two. Number one? Off-white, a creamy white, there are many whites, or absences, many shades of black, when the entire spectrum is present, so that two whites look strange against each other, two blacks, also. White is zero, black is ten, pink three, yellow three also, and shocking pink slides into number four territory, ordinarily claimed by orange and some shades of green, though green is usually a six, lime green may be five. Real red like my mother's lipstick is five. Pink is three, orange four, and I repeated numbers and colors as I walked farther into the woods with no fear or sense of mission and time. Occasionally, I hoped something, even I, might give the walk substance and shape, the way a designer constructs a chair to communicate an idea, like a chair by the Eameses, though a designed object also refers to its maker, marks its author, but if I were a Transcendentalist, any walk, a walk itself, in nature might have meaning. I didn't feel this, I was a solitary walker on a path whose direction I followed because it was there, and I wasn't prepared to machete under- and overgrowth, chop down fir trees and shrubs, which is probably illegal in this region and will bring trouble, to forge a new trail, so I was aimlessly treading a well-worn path in the woods, a picture of anonymity or an unrecognizable object, and, if photographed from high above, just a splotch or blot on the forest floor, if that. Discovering the Count in hiding near the community could give me purpose, depending upon what I make of it, what interpretation I pursue or how I bring the news to the community, particularly Contesa, if I do tell her, but I'll mark it, as I do him, so this walk differs from others. If his comedy and tragedy genuinely engages mine, though lately I want to sunder relationships and take things apart, then leave them in desuetude, a true connection has asserted itself. Aqua can be four and sometimes three, a light shade of brown is seven, darker eight, and a brown-black will be nine, while navy blue is always nine, royal blue eight, and if I'd gone into my father's business, I'd have concentrated on the spectrum of colors and sinuous threads, I'd have spent hours handling cloth and smelling it, counting warps and weaves, as I designed and manufactured textiles, since people need clothes, the way they need food and shelter, though what kinds, what styles, and consumed for what intentions, aren't simple, so people budget, steal, or spend inordinate amounts of time and money, expending furies of anxiety and plenty of hope on their selections, though everything is temporary and inconclusive. Clearly, the Count must have run from the séance into the woods, after gathering his necessities, right after the paranormal event, which I'd mostly forgotten, but now it assumed a funny but confusing face—Moira's. I beheld that odd inquisitive woman, destiny, and heard her vivacious, rolling voice: "We all wish to speak to the dead. It's a universal wish." I cringed or started, and looked everywhere around me, but Moira wasn't there. Often I see faces, the dead and living who aren't present, I conjure them, but this is normal, since normal vision fuses incoming sensation with internally generated sensation, when the brain fills in what it's used to seeing or expects to see, which encouraged a vision scientist to conclude, "In a sense, we are all hallucinating all the time," and this explains the haplessness of police line-ups and eyewitness accounts, their innate tendency to inaccuracy, but Leslie Van Houten's complicity was never in doubt, just the measure of her guilt. I've never before had an auditory hallucination, if hearing Moira's voice was one, though it seemed to come from outside me, raising several kinds of doubt, but I hadn't willed it, unless I had, since it's hard discerning a thought from a desire. I might have been thinking aloud, I must have been. It was about 2 or 3 p.m., the sun hung closer to the west, still bright. Wishing on a star is a childish impulse, but I gave in to that wish and, reluctantly, might again, because of a slim hope unknowable forces might help me, there's nothing lost in doing it, except the future of hope's credibility; still, my impulses and desires have left ruinous monuments in their wake. Attending the séance qualified as an impulse, and, even if the séance was unsettling at the time, it was an experience I must have wanted, though I'd never wished for it, didn't ratify it, and, anyway, haven't thought much about it, because there's no place to store it, since a mental apparatus I don't choose—about most things I have no choice—decides its fate, along with other stark, improbable events I can't categorize and remember. Before the séance started, I recalled the tarot card reader's prophesy, which I discount and yet can't forget, hope against hope, to overcome an obstacle or encounter a person who will change my life. Now, "Everyone wishes to speak to the dead" had lodged itself, and so, the odd inquisitive Moira, whom I didn't like, resided in me.

Things seem plain, and they aren't, but there's no going back, everything's in motion, matter doesn't die, and some human matters, especially, persist, because they're irresolvable and irremediable, people accumulate consequences. I kept walking, staring at the sky as it imperceptibly changed color, then down at the trail and the snow beneath my feet, while listening for the songs of birds, their elaborated calls, which I didn't understand, and often halted in my tracks to watch them, whose identity I didn't know, except for finches, mourning doves, crows, seagulls, and sparrows. For about ten minutes, a strong wind blew the trees and shook old snow, so that it fell and lightly dusted my coat, scarf, hair, and trail, but it stopped quickly, and I didn't feel worried or cold; instead, while the light snow swirled, I imagined that the crystal ball my dead friend bought me as a joke souvenir accompanied me, a good luck piece, and even owned the power to transform the woods into venerable, ugly, and beautiful Vienna, whose early 20th century architecture and design I revered, so the tallest trees became monuments or memorials. The snow must be telling us something, he kept repeating, impishly, and he may have been right, it uncannily foreshadowed the unidentifiable future, since snow blankets on a mountain hid insidious crevices through which he probably fell and disappeared. In my room, I can easily lift the crystal ball, turn it upside down, shake it with vigor, and the fake snowflakes occlude its scene, nothing else happens, but now the city of Vienna vanished, and I chided myself for wishing, since it was only the woods, vast, natural, weird, and when a fine lace crested on my hair, scarf, and shoulders and touched my face, I wondered if it was moisturizing or drying it and also remembered other snowfalls, which smelled the same as this one did now. I took several breaths, sucked in the fresh mixture of spring and winter air, and filled my healthy lungs. I was so alive, but it's strange to be alive, it is very strange to live. There's imagination and knowledge, I'm free to wander toward no end or for no discernible reason, but also I often duel with purpose and rarely beat it. The light snowfall ended quickly.

I stood in place, suspended by a thought or a desire, I couldn't tell, when I heard rustling and noises I was sure weren't mine, and again, I looked around, everywhere, maybe Moira had followed me, since she'd popped up before, unexpectedly, and now hovered in mind, but I didn't see her. I heard louder noises, closer, and hoped it wasn't a bear, but if it was I wouldn't move, and if it approached and was about to attack, I might bravely strike it hard on the middle of its chest, because bears have poor balance and fall backward if struck hard at the center of their chest, and, when that happened, I'd run fast, I'm a fast runner. A small bird screamed excitedly and three nearby flapped into the air, agitated by noisy company, when, to my surprise, through a gnarly thicket, the Count and Contesa emerged, shaking leaves and snow off them. So, Contesa knew all along where the Count was—or maybe he was staying with her—which was the reason she hadn't been noticeably upset after his disappearance, instead she appeared supremely introspective and somewhat removed. I had questions for the two, especially the Count—was it his fire? was it a seizure? were they looking for me?—but I decided not to ask, just to listen closely, they might have something to tell me.

—I hope we didn't give you a bad start, the Count said.

—Happy to see us, right, Helen?

I was, especially now that it was growing colder and darker, it's always darker in the middle of the woods, not yet dusk, and it was harder to see, but anyway we walked farther into the woods or farther from the main house, miles by now I figured, sometimes the Count veering one way, Contesa another, he to the east or, in my vernacular, left, she west or right, where the sun was setting. After they compromised on a direction, I followed contentedly, having no idea where we were headed, though the Count assured me they knew, and also I didn't mind, like a passenger along for a joyride. I even hoped the hike would never end and that I'd remain in the dark, because I like surprises, and, if I knew the destination, I might be disappointed, also I liked to imagine there was no destination, nothing teleological or driven, but all things come to an end, like breakfast or dinner or an evening's entertainment, when I can return to my room, take off my clothes, placate my skin with rich emollients, and read into the night, then when the house is still, reading is like listening, and I like to listen. If I listen well, I might gather why the Count and Contesa scrupled to find me, trace my steps in the woods, since they must have been looking for me for a reason, although they might not and just came upon me, but I didn't want to know, when usually I do.

Out of nowhere, at least to me, as we march along, while I'm walking behind Contesa, she calls to the Count, "One thing ends, another begins."

—The Roman Empire, the Count retorts.

—The British Empire.

—Or, World War I.

—You're a cynic, Gardner.

—A skeptic. When you die, you die. You're never yourself again, Violet.

—I'll be something else, she said.

I dug inside my pocket for the apple I'd saved, then inquired of them if they were hungry, but they'd eaten not long ago. The red and green Macoun was crisp and tart, the way I like, not mealy and slimy, its skin crunchy, and my appetite abated, as the sky darkened, though the sun, while it dropped, left behind radiant streaks of pink, orange, and blue, two number threes, because of their pale hue, one four, and soon the Count decided he'd make a fire and we'd rest for a while. I had begun to worry about hiking when the sun had set, but the Count was not only a good fire builder, he could survive in the woods, which soothed my doubt, though I also wished it would never end. Contesa's capacious, mohair shawl served as a blanket, and she and I sat upon it, while the Count expertly built his fire, and I, filled with questions but wanting to listen, checked my tongue. Contesa offered up a remark about the beguiling sky, while the Count hunted for tinder and logs and I reminded myself that Contesa and I both disliked small talk. She was intense, a Kafka of the spirits, who might now be communing with Felice or other numina, though if it were so, I'd be uncomfortable. I'd never been alone with just the Count and Contesa, the pair had a history, wholly outside my experience, and with it an apparent rightness or ease in being. When I looked toward the fire, even it seemed new, and I was surfeited with nameless expectation, I guess that's what it was, about what might occur among us or between them, since being with them provoked me, and though our temporary arrangement was a comely shape or configuration, which I liked, something out of order might develop and instigate a calamitous denouement. We three might suddenly be enmeshed in intrigue or poised upon an invisible but unfathomable foundation, sink into menace, a daunting sub-layer that could undo our symmetry, since people are flawed and arbitrary, and, unlike a worthy design whose decisions aren't arbitrary, when a subtle mistake might even augment an object, peoples' flaws rarely enhance them, though people learn to love, usually temporarily, their friends' and lovers' mistakes. I determined to stare into the fire, not think into a future I might never know, and kindle reverie, but stick figures emanated from the wisps of flames, the way they usually do, my skin dried and itched, my face burned, and, restless, I shifted about on Contesa's shawl.

—So, we're around a campfire. We could tell stories, Contesa said, drolly.

—Which kind? the Count asked.

—Any kind.

I had no stories of any kind to tell, I felt as empty and flat as my stomach.

—May I ask for one?

I was hedging.

—That depends, Contesa said.

—I'd like to know, if you don't mind, Gardner, when you began to change night into day.

—It's not a proper story, he said.

He poked the fire, bothered, laid on another bunch of thick sticks, turned from it, and sat upon the ground in front of us, tucking his calf-length, leather, fur-lined coat under him, and, as dusk neared, his horse face was almost frighteningly enigmatic or unreadable, with its high cheekbones pulling his skin taut, crafting craters or vaults beneath them.

—In Paris, I found a timepiece along the Seine. I fell in love, you know. Rather, I decided to live. I returned to America. I had already inherited a great deal of money, with my father's death. And when my mother died, I had even more. Too much, no doubt.

I wondered how he felt about his parents' deaths, but he didn't say, and it was his story.

—But I wasn't idle. I studied. Languages, especially, and ancient history, the classics. I collected many museum-worthy pieces. Word got 'round. I was plagued by, let's say, enthusiastic acquaintances. It's not easy for me to send people away. One day a man showed up on my doorstep. He said he'd known Violet in Paris.

Contesa's face turned gloomy, impassive, or stricken.

—He importuned me. I gave him money for a scheme. It went badly. He was a con man. He had come to my house at midday. I'm a rational man. And I knew two things. One, time is of human origin, and, two, since it is, I could use time as I wanted.

He etched a circle on the ground with a pointed stick.

—If I slept all day and rose and lived in the night, no one could bother me at lunchtime or during business hours. I hired a secretary to do what needed to be done in daytime hours—banking and so forth. I saw only a few close friends. That's why I turned day into night. You see, it's not a story.

It was not what I expected or imagined, not at all, his story was simultaneously simple and complex, of a bizarre practicality that surpasses reason. Without response, Contesa and I absorbed his tale, the Count too, but unlike the silence between Birdman and me, it was full and comforting, and I felt less empty, though my stomach gurgled softly. While each of us rested, or not, in our own minds, I realized I'd missed an opportunity to inquire about his paroxysm. But the Count rose to fix and fuss with the fire again—I imagined he'd once been a heavy smoker—when Contesa nestled against me, like the beloved family cat my parents had killed a long time ago.

—What would you like to hear? she asked.

—What's the story about your friend who conned Gardner? I asked.

—Not that. Ask me another.

—Unfair, the Count said.

—It's OK, I said.

—I have a story, Contesa said. In the late 1950s, early 1960s, I was friends with a famous fashion model. This was in Paris. She was very beautiful, everyone knew her face. I knew her lover, actually he was my friend first. We were friends from back when. He was smart, great, but a dog. I adored him. I lived with them, in fact they took me in.

The Count's head had dropped. I couldn't see his face, his eyes.

—I was at loose ends. I'd been designing clothes, but it wasn't working. So I took up social work, but that's another story. I was twenty-nine. At loose ends. The model had a spectacular house in the 7th arrondisement. One Wednesday morning, she invited me to join her, that very afternoon, to fly to Rome. She was doing the shows. She wanted me to accompany her, she said. My friend would stay home and work—he was a soul brother, as we said then or maybe later. He wrote scripts. God, they're a desperate breed. He made some money reviewing films, his French was flawless. I went to Rome, as her companion. Why not? She worked, and I walked around. I visited all of the museums and churches. I lit candles in every church. It was spring, I think. We ate fantastic dinners, on elegant patios overlooking the seven hills, way into the night. Always surrounded by her celebrity friends. There was a darling photographer . . . another story, another time. Rome lives at night. I drank too much.

Now the Count followed Contesa's every gesture, she was becoming a little Roman, her hands, patterns in the air, and he hung on her every word, just as I did.

—Then Sunday came. I was about to go to Mass. As a pagan. But the model took me aside. She said, "I've changed your plane ticket." I expected to fly back with her on Monday morning. She wanted me to go back to Paris, that very night. She said, I remember this exactly, she said, "I'd like you to make sure the house is in order." That's all she said. I was put on a late flight. Everything had been arranged neatly. The Paris-Rome flight is fairly quick. But on it I felt uneasy. I didn't know why. It was about three in the morning when I arrived at her house. I unlocked the door and entered. I heard moving around upstairs. There was a commotion, hushed voices, I just stood there. A woman, Lord, her lipstick was smeared, and her mascara, maybe she'd been crying, she came running down the stairs. She didn't look at me, just ran past me, and went straight out the door. Then, my friend came down the stairs. He was like a sheepdog. It was almost funny. I helped him clean up—scads of empty wine bottles, ashtrays with red-lipsticked cigarettes, dirty glasses and dishes everywhere. It took hours. In the morning, the model arrived. Her house was in perfect order. I'd done my job, I'd done a great job. All was well on the homefront. The next day, I left. She and I said nothing to each other. Nothing. I never saw her again.

The finality of the story and her response alarmed me, I didn't know what to make of it, why she had told it now, to us, but it must have been after that episode she returned to America, around the same time, I reckoned, as the Count.

—You never saw her again? I asked.

—Never, she repeated.

—Tell us your story, Helen, the Count said.

—Let me think. I need a little time.

In their accounts, they'd been betrayed, they'd changed the directions of their lives and returned to America, but their stories also had different kinds of content. I could tell one in which I was good, bad, indifferent, young, cruel, sensitive, a helper, a hindrance, a victim, a victimizer, hero, bystander, or, like them, betrayed, by a colleague in the American History department, a best friend, a lover. Or one in which I'd betrayed someone, though I'm a sensitive person, and sensitive people need to believe they wouldn't, so they often don't recognize when they hurt others, but the worst kinds of sensitive people are those who believe themselves to be victims, so they victimize others righteously and viciously. I could tell them about my brother's dramatic disappearance, but I knew too little about it and him, since my parents hardly ever mentioned it, then my father died soon after, but then the two might ask why I hadn't searched for him, and I didn't know myself. I hadn't known him, that was an explanation, he was so much older, my birth was planned, or a mistake, but I didn't want to tell that story. I could talk about how I became an atheist, an historian, why I left the field and how I feel sad about America, or how I became a designer of objects, but now I want to undo things.

—You're taking a long time, Contesa said.

—It doesn't have to be a big deal, the Count said. You don't have to, you know.

—I've got a story, I said, impulsively. It's funny. My mother had open heart surgery about ten years ago, to correct a valve. They were going to give her a pig's valve. I waited in the hospital while she had the operation. It's a long operation, and she was seventy-eight, but pretty strong. She was old but healthy. Except for that valve. The anesthesia was almost the biggest issue, really. I waited in a very ugly reception area. Really awful. I became focused on the other people there, mostly families. I suppose that's how I distracted myself. Some were already grieving, preparing themselves for the worst, the end . . .

—Is this really a funny story? Contesa asked.

—I think so. Everyone was so anxious, they barely knew anyone else was in the room. Some of them ate all the time. A lot of Chinese food. Everyone talked a lot, some were very loud. Some were quiet, and they looked totally blank. People constantly used the phone booths outside. They repeated everything they'd said in the waiting room. It drove me crazy. Hospitals look horrible. This waiting area was disgusting, and all the chairs had grease stains. Finally, the doctor came out and said I could go into the ICU and see her. I remember thinking when I walked there—major operations are life-changing. Some people never recover from the operation. People age overnight. I was thinking all this, when I got to the ICU. You had to push a steel square to open these big doors, and they swung open, at you. And then I was facing the bed where my father died, the same bed. I was really thrown by that. But I found an ICU nurse and asked if I could see my mother. She asked her name and I told her, and she said, without hesitation, Bed Ten. I walked past the other beds to get to Bed Ten, it was almost the last bed. So I looked at all the people lying there, with gray faces and tubes everywhere. I kept telling myself that my mother might not be recognizable anymore. I prepared myself not to recognize her. I got to Bed Ten and went to my mother. I looked at her face. Her face was very different. Her nose was much wider. Her face was wide, it was very swollen, so I thought, OK. But her skin tone was entirely different, she was a different color—then I figured that came from the anesthesia. She's sensitive to meds. Anyway I really didn't recognize her. I stood there for a while, taking this in. But she looked so unlike herself, it was crazy. So, I went back to the nurses' station. I said to the same nurse, "I'm sorry, but that woman doesn't look like my mother." Then the nurse glanced at her clipboard and said, "Sorry, your mother's in Bed Twelve."

The Count laughed, Contesa did, also, a little after him, as if against her will. I'd recounted the story easily, all set in my memory, so I knew I'd never forget it, until I did, when I no longer needed it or couldn't retain it.

—There's your darkness, Contesa said.

—A gallows humorist, the Count said.

I lay my head on Contesa's lap, the Count fed the fire some more, and it leaped up energetically, exhausting me further with its dizzying patterns, so I shut my eyes.

The Turkish poet was in the room, I was having sex, with him, "Why do you wear a bar?" he asked. "Don't you mean bra?" I asked. "No," he said. I was nineteen, his name was Adam, his long hair hung in waves, and in the room, there was a perfect chair, it was beautiful, but was it mine? I wanted one, and what would it mean about my life if I didn't have one. I could design it, so I searched for materials in a desert, but where was I looking, there's nothing to use. "Why do you need a perfect chair?" someone asked, maybe Contesa. "That's a tall order," someone said, not me, I'm tall, but not tall enough, and I climbed a high chair. Many cats played underneath, all of them black with white paws, but I had to care for an abandoned dog, when my father appeared and said, "Don't look . . ."

—Helen. Helen. Wake up.

I heard my name.

After I had rested my head on Contesa's lap, I instantly dropped off, briefly but completely, and I wanted to keep on sleeping, but the Count said I had to wake up, we had to go, it was getting dark, soon it'd be dinnertime in the residence, and I remembered I'd made an appointment for drinks with Spike and the Turkish poet. The Count and Contesa had flashlights, there was nothing to worry about, nothing at all, and I brushed myself off and traipsed after them sleepily.

—We're nearly there, just a few more minutes, Helen, Contesa said.

—Where are we?

—Near the main house, the Count said.

—What do you mean?

—We walked in a very wide circle, then smaller ones, behind, around the community. Actually, more like an ellipse.

I have no sense of direction, and, when the main house came into sight, the Count was beside me, he was returning, after all, if he was, but when we were leaving each other, to prepare for dinner—I thought I might check the mail first—I wished I'd told a story about the family cat instead of the one I did, I wasn't sure what I had told them, really, but I wished it'd been something else. I'd rarely thought of wishes before, now I was thinking about them often, Moira's dictum lodged in me, not so much about a wish to speak to the dead, but about the wish itself, and I realized that, if you have wishes against all reason, immune to reality, if you have wishes no matter what, then the wish trumps everything, always, and so in a sense, nothing else matters as much. There it was, the triumph of the wish. This notion satisfied me, though if valid or true, it wouldn't permit satisfaction, because most wishes don't come true and instead ache like unanswered lust. Still, wishes foment relationships, history, design, there are so many wishes, unacknowledged longings for the impossible precede every endeavor, and consequently, there are so many failures, but then there are significant exceptions, history often tells the story of exceptions. I might wish to make my skin immaterial and stop itching.

To mark the day with the Count and Contesa, as well as to humor myself, I called it Triumph of the Wish and imagined that very soon I'd design and build a chair that deserved that title, so that I might sit upon a wish. I might also unfurl the Fabric Monolith, not now, but someday, because it was a wish. I contemplated doing it, spreading out the cloth, or unrolling the material past itself, and, as I entered the main house, I avoided the gaze of certain residents, especially the demanding man, signed in, and walked along an imaginary straight line to the small, woodsy, cedar mailroom, to see what news awaited me.

I can live with, among, and in almost anything anywhere for a while, most arrangements satisfy for a day, a week, six months or more, occasionally not at all or never, not even for an hour, if, for instance, you're being suffocated, starved, or tortured, but mostly free of restraints, I want to start over and try something else, because I'm dissatisfied, restless, form an opinion about the possibilities available, and reach the end of my rope. Not long after Triumph of the Wish, I awoke to the clock radio, listened to the mellifluous, empty radio voices, turned them on and off with increasing agitation, avoided breakfast until I couldn't stand the idea of not eating until lunch, which is usually poor, and also chose, maybe arbitrarily, choice often is, if you have a choice, which is deceptively uncommon, but nevertheless I decided, as I dressed quickly in lightweight one hundred percent cotton black slacks and a gray and black striped, long-sleeved cotton boatneck jersey, to leave the community. Its residential flux no longer compelled me, instead, it grated, the view outside of my window as I worked or contemplated palled, a silly story, which involved Henry, Arthur, the kitchen helper, and myself, exasperated me, but it implicated me, in a sense, in more of the same, an expected occurrence in a small community, indicating also it was probably time to leave. Spike, whose wit and humor I relied upon, whose ramrod straight posture my father would've liked, had turned peevish and severe as a Shaker chair, while the Turkish poet rarely left his room, the disconsolate women fought at dinner, and the tall balding man shifted his desire to a new resident, a prematurely gray-haired and attractive vegan, whose occupation I couldn't figure out. I considered mentioning to the tall balding man, more than once, the new moisture-management fabrics, such as Coolmax and Moistex, that quickly absorb and dry sweat, knitted from polyester fibers, an aid to sufferers of primary palmar hyperhidrosis, but when he clasped my hand in his wet palms, with a sincerity I didn't know he felt, I didn't tell him, because usually it's better not to say anything. Even the demanding man felt familiar and bearable, so in opposition to what I might also become, especially to myself, I knew it was time to go, though it's impossible ever to grasp time's truth, if it has any, which is dubious, or discover with absolute surety the right idea, but the staff encouraged me. Soon I prepared for my return to the place I call home by spending a good week deliberating about and sorting my clutter, a day or two burning what was no longer necessary, which entailed building many fires by the Count's method and making more decisions than I wanted to make, and often I tossed small cardboard objects, bits of paper, doodles for designs, notes, quotations I collected (Curt Flood, "I am pleased God gave me black skin. I wish he'd made it thicker;" Oscar Levant, "I can stand anything except failure;" Sigmund Freud, "Consideration for the dead, who, after all, no longer need it, is more important to us than truth, and, certainly, for most of us, than consideration for the living;" Hannah Arendt, "Appearing beings living in a world of appearances have an urge to show themselves;" Ralph Waldo Emerson to Oliver Wendell Holmes, "When you strike at a king, you must kill him") into cardboard boxes labeled "Miscellaneous." I instituted a novel system to allow for contingency by which I filed shapeless or promising concepts into colorful folders, whose colors corresponded to my color/number system, at last employing that idea usefully, and washed my clothes in one hundred percent Ivory Snow for sensitive skin, my lamb's wool, angora, and cashmere sweaters in Woolite, and packed them, actually rolled them to avoid wrinkles, in two sturdy, black nylon suitcases with wheels.

I returned all of the books under my bed or by my worktable to the library, where Moira appeared, which was and wasn't a surprise. She wore her Limited jeans, a white wool, loose-knit sweater, no hat, a lightweight orange polyester jacket, it may have been deer-hunting season, and we said hello in a friendly way, but nothing more. Moira watched me place books on shelves, write my first name and the book's title in a log on a line next to the day's date, indicating that I'd returned each and when. I must have been there an hour or so shelving and collecting my thoughts, some of which were about the Dewey Decimal System, when Moira said:

—You're leaving?

—It's time, I think.

—You're not sure?

—It's time.

—Have a good life. Life's fascinating. Just let go every once in a while.

—Thank you, and you, too.

—Violet's play boosted me way up. I'm thinking of becoming an actor. It's never too late.

—That's great, I said. I wish you success.

It's never too late, I considered, good-humoredly, unless it is, I also thought, as I left the library, when, on the path to my residence, I realized that I'd never see the odd inquisitive woman again, that this person whose characteristic impertinence annoyed me would disappear from my life, as I would hers, that we had met, sniffed each others' asses more than once, or labored in an army of ants building anthills, and even though I didn't especially like her, I'd probably remember her for a while, until I never thought of her again, and might even miss her, though I might not know what it was that was missed. The head cook was also leaving, that had been made public weeks ago, and there was a party planned to be held in the main house, to which all of the residents were invited, and most decided to attend, even though her cooking in her last weeks had become more than lackadaisical, and, if I hadn't had to eat it, I might have called whimsical. Some residents stayed in their rooms during dinner, preferring to starve, as they put it, but I never did, I needed dinner, which marked the end of a day during which I had or hadn't accomplished anything, along with the others, and also a bad dinner was preferable to none. I'm not sure about the head cook, but I left the morning after her farewell party, and, as I waited for the taxicab to take me to the train, the Turkish poet showed up unexpectedly, carrying a gallon bottle of water. My luggage was placed, or thrown, into the trunk by the overweight driver, whose clothes smelled of cigarette smoke, and the Turkish poet kissed me good-bye on my forehead. I took my place on a backseat, strapped myself in, hoped my driver wouldn't speed or brake sharply, causing me to become nauseated, and worried if the trunk had been shut properly. When the car started to pull away, the Turkish poet ran up to my door and exclaimed, "This brings good luck. Remember me, you." Then, trotting behind the car, he sprinkled water onto the path, the water cascading from the gallon bottle until it was gone.

I arrived in the place I call home late that night, it appeared to be the start of a hot summer, and, early the next morning, because the air would be cooler than later in the day, and cleaner, the streets quieter, I walked to my mother's house to retrieve my young wild cat from her indifferent care, but when I arrived and opened the door using my key, because her companion was in the shower, she was fast asleep in her own world. Her unconsciousness gave me the chance to study her unabashedly without her asking questions, which I often have to answer many times, unless it's a day when she's lucid, which also happens, fortunately. My mother had aged, the skin on her neck was looser and fleshier, her nose thicker, since, at her age, the ageing process gallops to the finish line, but still no wrinkles creased her cheeks, no fine lines radiated from her shut eyes. My mother's mouth twitched from time to time. Yet sleeping offered her a serenity she lacked even at her advanced age, when age is meant to carry with it at least that compensation, because when awake, she insisted adamantly she was half her age. Her skin, normally glossy and pink, had maintained its usual high color, and I thought, she's not dead yet, maybe she can live forever.

Coincidentally, just after I had these thoughts, my mother tossed, unsettled by my attention or, more likely, rocked in the arms of a dream lover who caressed her, who stirred her the way she wanted to be stirred again, since she missed sex, she'd told me, but she didn't speak aloud to her husband, my father. When she rolled over and faced the wall, I left her bedroom to talk with her companion, who brewed coffee in the kitchen where I asked how she was doing, what her troubles were, if any, how my mother's doctors' visits had gone, what new bills needed payment, what my mother's complaints were, and, most important, how they were getting along, if any immediate issues required my daughterly attention. For months, I'd been spared most of this. All the while, my young wild cat, technically no longer a kitten, stared at his cat carrier, which my mother's companion had removed from a shelf in the hallway closet and set on the floor by the door, so he knew something was up, or he was going home. I grabbed him when he turned away from us and, before he knew it, my cat was in the carrier he hated, so he cried pitifully, and, not saying hello or goodbye to my mother, who still slept, I rushed out of the door to the elevator, to the street, where I hailed a taxi. Soon we arrived at my apartment house, and, quickly, in my apartment, I released him. He jumped out, walked the length of my place, and settled on a yellowish-white naugahyde Thonet chair, where he remained for the day, keeping his distance from me, even when I dished out his favorite food. My young wild cat didn't know me, though I knew and loved him, but also, in a sense, I didn't know him, because he'd changed in his manner to me, yet that also would change, an experienced cat lover explained, and you must give it time, she cautioned. Several days later, I awakened with my bottom lip split and telephoned the beauty salon to set up an appointment for a facial. It was a Saturday, so the pleasant boss answered my call, and I arranged an appointment for a facial on Tuesday at 11 a.m.

Tuesday comes, and my cat is somewhat more responsive, though he still behaves as if he doesn't know me, which may be an act, indifference, annoyance, or an actuality, he may not know me. I dress in lightweight, loose all-cotton gray clothes, and take a route I know like the back of my hand, but also don't really see, to the beauty salon for my regular treatment, since my skin is perniciously dry, I need treatment, a collagen mask is advisable, but, ominously, the salon owner greets me at the door, and it's no longer the weekend. She tells me, her eyes darting quickly away from mine, that my Polish cosmetician has left, that she is no longer working for her, she has taken another job for more money, and then the salon owner's eyes leave mine again, as she explains that there is a new cosmetician, a Polish woman, also, who is excellent, better than mine was, much better, and who will care for me very well. The salon owner graciously draws open a curtain to one of the two small rooms, and, uneasy, my skin itching, I enter the cramped space, which is, in all other ways, the way it was when

I last visited, and then the new cosmetician enters, tells me her name and to undress, please, that she will be right back, and leaves the room. I hang my all cotton, lightweight clothes on a hook and change into a long-sleeved, plain blue wrapper, a twenty percent polyester, eighty percent cotton blend that feels slightly rough against my skin, but it's durable and serviceable, and then I lie down upon the chaise lounge and cover myself with a soft, nubby pink blanket, and soon the new Polish woman enters again, but I hardly see her, since she turns the light low for my greater relaxation, and, when she walks toward me, her face is hidden in shadow. She takes her place behind me and, tenderly, ties a ribbon around my head at the hairline to keep loose strands off my forehead and temples, impeding her work, and lightly and gently she pats my cheeks twice. Speaking in a calm, accented voice, she says, "Pardon me," as my former Polish facialist would have, comes forward, switches a harsh light on, to examine my skin closely, and bends close, to study it with concern, screwing up her face, which produces creases or wrinkles on her forehead and at the bridge of her nose, and only after this, she touches my face again. With the help of a mild, hypoallergenic cream on a cotton pad, she moves her dancing fingers in an upward fashion, careful not to create new creases on my skin but to smooth and lessen old ones and remove surface impurities, inaugurating the facial. Soon the Polish woman says with professional certainty, "You have very sensitive skin," and I close my eyes, and she goes on.

Acknowledgements

I thank Dr. George Lipkin for his skin genius and giving me an informal education in dermatology; Dakis Iannou, for lending me a house to write in, and Katerina Gregos, for facilitating it; Lydia Davis, for helping me get me started on this book; Geoffrey Cruickshank Hagenbuckle, for his understanding of the tarot; and Robert Gober, for the perfect cover image. David Rattray, who hovers always in memory, is the novel's touchstone, and Carol Mahoney, recently gone, is, even if such things can't happen, its guardian angel.

Portrait of Lynne Tillman by Stephen Ellis

Lynne Tillman is a novelist, short story writer, and critic. *American Genius, A Comedy* is her fifth novel. Her previous novel, *No Lease on Life*, was a finalist for the National Book Critics Circle Award in fiction (1998) and a *New York Times* Notable Book of the Year. Her stories have appeared in anthologies and journals, such as *Bomb*, *The New Gothic*, *New York Writes After September 11*, *Conjunctions*, *Black Clock*, *The Literary Review*, *McSweeney's* and *Cabinet*. Her art and literary criticism has been published in *Art in America*, *Artforum*, *Frieze*, *Aperture*, *Bookforum*, *Nest*, *The Village Voice*, and *The New York Times Book Review*. Her most recent book, *This Is Not It* (2002), is a collection of stories and novellas that responds to the work of twenty-two contemporary artists. She is Professor/Writer-in-Residence at the University at Albany, and in 2006 was awarded a Guggenheim Fellowship. She lives in Manhattan with bass player David Hofstra. Lately, she collects succulents.